PRAISE FOR *MOTHER*

"What a remarkable book. Totally different to most anything. Perhaps the Philip Pullman *Northern Lights* is as close as I can get but even that is not the same. Would I recommend it? Definitely; a real book group choice."

> —Sue Lawton MBE, global expert on women and enterprise

"In writing the *Mother of Floods*, Madeleine White has marshaled her vivid imagination to challenge our thinking about life as we know it versus life as it might be in the future. She weaves a tale of a new type of digital being who aids seemingly ordinary women in finding their innate wisdom and internal strength, while also developing their deep connection to each other. By doing so, they work together to pull out of the ashes of disconnection and discord a transformed world that is bountiful and loving. As a reader, be prepared for twists and turns that will take you through many countries and cultures and across time, in a tale that will stick with you long after the last page is read. In the end, the reader is left with the reminder that people all want the same thing, regardless of where they live or their station in life—love and personal connection with others. I would recommend *Mother of Floods* for anyone who wants to enjoy a great story with real impact!"

> —Linda Denny, President Emeritus, Women's Business Enterprise National Council

"I was transfixed by *Mother of Floods* and quite simply couldn't put it down. Madeleine White's ability to bring her characters to life in ways where we lose ourselves in them and their stories is exceptional. She is a wonderful and gifted story teller. I can't believe the resonance and the synchronicity of messages that this book brings during these unprecedented times. The supposed end of the world as we know it, the opportunity to come together and reset, and the ripple effect when people and dimensions come collide, merge and transform what has always been. This book is powerful, touching and incredibly thought provoking. I was left wondering what could be if we had the courage and the possibilities were endless. An internet with a soul, just imagine!"

> —Rabia Siddique, best-selling author of *Equal Justice:*
> *My Journey As A Woman, A Soldier And A Muslim*

"The storyline of *Mother of Floods* is not something that I would usually have pulled off the shelves as my preferred reading material is usually more thriller or based on scientific fact. However, I was thankfully seduced by the mix of the hard reality of our physical world, the comfort of our spiritual world and the challenges we face with our digital world. I really loved the book and found it an absorbing, thought-provoking and most enjoyable read. "

> —Nicki Hattingh, Film Producer & Dog's Best Friend!

MOTHER OF FLOODS

MOTHER OF FLOODS

MADELEINE F. WHITE

CROWSNEST BOOKS

Crowsnest Books

www.crowsnestbooks.com

Distributed by the University of Toronto Press

Edited by Allister Thompson

Proofreader: Britanie Wilson

Cataloguing data available from Library and Archives Canada

ISBN 9780921332664 (paperback)

ISBN 9780921332671 (ebook)

Contents

Acknowledgements

Despite a lifetime of writing and storytelling, *Mother of Floods* is my first novel. I couldn't have done it without the help of a number of people and organisations and would like to take a little space here to say thank you.

So many stories contained in *Mother of Floods* are based on the wonderful women in my family and those I have met in my work; women's whose bravery, resilience and determination to do the best they can, with whatever life has given them has humbled me. I very much hope that I have done them justice. Many will recognise their names in these stories, although to protect identities, they are not in context.

There are a couple I can name though. Emmy wouldn't not been born without Emily Jackson's bravery, both in overcoming anorexia and then sharing her story with me. The white rabbit analogy is directly based on a story she Emailed me and is extracted in *Mother of Floods* with Emily's permission.

Indira Abidin, my birthday sister, and Chief Happiness Officer (her own term for CEO of the Fortune PR corporation in Jakarta), sadly lost her battle against cancer last year. However, her enthusiasm for her country and Anjani's story was critical in bringing the Indonesian narrative to life and I thank her for it.

I would like to thank my early readers, starting with Eden Jessiman. Without her help I'm not sure I would have had the courage to push past the initial chapters. But unflagging enthusiasm for the story and the characters, along with her insightful editorial comments, was key to bringing this story out of my imagination and onto the page. The many positive comments from Marianne Schoening, Linda Denny and Sue Lawton MBE also kept me going through the many rejections. Pen to Print, an organisation that supports emerging writers and connects diverse voices in print and online, had an important part to play as well. Being placed in their national poetry competition helped me believe in myself again when I felt all hope was lost. Similarly, Thanet Writers provided an outlet and forum which kept me writing.

Expert help has come from IT specialist Andy Green, economist

Callum White and leading technical strategist Tom Pelc, whose wife Jenny also supplied Emmy's drawing of Dennis. The Crowsnest team, with particular thanks to publisher Alex Wall and editor Alistair Thompson, have helped slough off what was not needed to reveal the novel I wanted to write, but didn't quite know how to.

The Rain Song cited by Khalid, was taken from Iraqi poet's Badr Shakir al Sayyab's formidable body of work and indeed, the beauty of Arabic poetry, albeit in translation, has inspired some of the wider songs contained in *Mother of Floods*.

I do hope my Canadian family will forgive me, for drawing inspiration from my First Nation roots and indeed my quest for identity around them. Joe Friday was a real person and was indeed the twin brother of Charlotte Friday. I have however, taken significant license with Charlotte's character. Her presence in *Mother of Floods*, therefore owes far more to my imagination than who she was in real life. However, Friday Memories, by June Friday MacInnis provided some fascinating family background.

I have spent my life cobbling together my identity through safe spaces that have presented themselves, and have indeed created many of my own, through websites and print publications. I believe that we are all storytellers, with stories of worth and value contained within each of us. I therefore invite others to join me on this journey of connection, using vehicles such as Write On! magazine at pentoprint.org and maketrade.se. You will be welcomed! I'd also love to hear what you think, so please do leave reviews and comments where you can or get in touch on social media – I'm @madeleinefwhite on both Twitter and Instagram.

Finally, a huge thank you to my long-suffering husband Evan and children Callum, Lucy and Erin. Without your faith in me, *Mother of Floods* would never have been conceived, let alone created.

Mother of Floods is dedicated to my family, past and present across the UK, Germany and Canada

*"My ancestors' wisdom drums through bones
That hold me upright as I run towards the future
While cupping the delicate flame of now in my hands."*

Foreword: A note in the wake of COVID-19

Mother of Floods was written two years ago, around the Age of the Downfall I perceived as reality at the time. Climate and social disasters drove me to use my words to present a world pushed to its limits. As inspiration, I looked forward and back. To new possibilities of social and spiritual life, imagined through exhaustive research around our digital age, as well as ancient myths and legends that have formed our social foundations for millennia.

In our COVID-19 ravaged now though, these topics have assumed a powerful reality.

Our challenge is not just to emerge unscathed, but to be wiser and stronger, more connected to ourselves and a planet we need to sustain us and future generations. Therefore, instead of focusing on how bad it is in the traditional dystopian fashion, I used the voices of six women, spread across multiple geographies and cultures, to weave the urgent call to action our world has presented us with into the narrative, creating a workable blueprint for positive change. They show by example, how coming together and playing small roles individually, translates into much bigger roles collectively.

Mother of Floods challenges us to open our minds and imagine something new, a place where the world unseen collides with what we perceive. If we take heart, this too shall pass. And when it does, I hope this book will help signpost a way for us to look beyond the looking glass, put there by others telling us what to see, into what truly is.

Follow the breath of the earth - It will help you breathe
Follow what you know to be true - It will help you believe
Follow what is good - Not what you think you should
Follow what is beautiful - Just because it is.

Yours in love and hope,

Madeleine

Prologue

Baba John sat in his one room, wrapped in the orange and saffron robes of his calling. Despite his long white beard and mane of hair, he had a strong, healthy physique that belied the many decades he had spent in Gangotri. When he had moved into his guru's hut nearly seventy years ago, it had been virtually inaccessible. Not any more, though. These days, it seemed as if everyone wanted to come here, and corresponding numbers of roads and houses had been built. India's Tiger Economy had consumed most of the subcontinent's untouched places, including this, the source of the Ganges.

The Western journalist was typical of those who came to see him now; paper people, blown here and there by a desire to be whole and yet missing the point entirely. Did they not realise that pilgrimage started within? One just needed to "be." Barely registering the woman's proclamation of how her journey would start here, at the birthplace of the Goddess Ganga, he cast his mind back to the splendid wilderness as it had been. To the time before the number of those seeking to connect with something beyond themselves had smothered it all.

Feeling compelled to pursue those memories, he used the ubiquitous "Shanti" to cut off his visitor. Watching her departing form, his eyes found relief in the black-and-white photographs of the once verdant flora and fauna that had covered this region. The next set of images, though, depicting all the hotels and houses that had sprung up in the wake of the receding glacier, caused him to feel physical pain. With each decade it had got worse, and the farther down *Gaṅgā*'s length one travelled, the more despoiled her healing waters became. By the time she swept out into the Bay of Bengal, this goddess of wholeness and purity, whose wild advent on earth had once needed Lord Shiva's hair to bind her, had become the embodiment of death and decay.

There was, however, always hope. He should know. Many years ago, his truth had been broken into pieces, and it was that hope he'd come in search of.

Once he'd been Amresh, a bright, middle-class Indian boy and typical product of the British Raj. Thanks to a number of unfathomable coincidences, the eighteen-year-old had been given a chance to study in the UK. Seduced into being part of a culture that was not his, he had grabbed the razor-sharp spires of 1930s Oxford with both hands. At the time, he hadn't realised that he was cutting away his name and colour in the process.

It was only twelve years later, when the self-styled John had found his hollowly echoing soul too much to bear, that he turned clay feet back to this remote part of northern India. As his squeaky-new climbing boots made their way up the Gangotri glacier, the empty shell of his carefully cultivated identity fell away, leaving a bleeding, childlike soul to stand bare before Gaumukh. Released by his scream of brokenness, water seeped from the fissures in the bedrock, lacerated vocal chords heralding a new existence.

Having heard his call, a shrunken figure reclaimed him and led him back down to safety. Baba John remembered deep, welcoming eyes of kindness. He had come as Seeker but was told, when the time came, that he was to become the next Watcher. As his damaged voice recovered, so did his soul, and like raven's wings, a sense of purpose brushed his consciousness. He must wait. Another would come. There would be other screams, more pain, but no longer his.

By the time he was back on his feet again, his rescuer had taken to the pallet John had so recently vacated. From his deathbed, hoarse whispers set his successor's task.

"The time is coming when the balance will be lost. The world of spirit and our physical world will be consumed by one that is yet unseen. This emerging dimension will take the earth's energy, causing Ganga to fail, but in her death throes the next Seeker will be birthed."

A weak hand clawed at his sleeve, the inexorable will of a dying man shaping the rest of Baba John's life.

"Watch for the signs. You must help the next Seeker shape this destruction. Only so can resurrection be found."

Casting his mind back, the nonagenarian remembered the billowing, acrid smoke from the perfumed fire as if it were yesterday. He'd still breathed it in, though, along with his predecessor's prophecy:

"When I die, you will be the last Watcher, the very last of our lineage. You will watch for the failure of the Ganges and the Seeker able to harness the energy of the death of one source to birth of another. You will find her, but she will not know you. She will, though, recognise your will. It will cause her to blaze out, calling others also. They will release the spirit realm along the ancient paths it once owned in the physical world to pass into a new one."

He died shortly afterwards, and, as with countless generations of Watchers before, the passing of one transferred visions and signs into the consciousness of another. The succession of impressions that flooded through the new Watcher bore no relation to anything meditation had allowed him to access previously. It came at him much faster than he was able to process, and he had felt himself drowning in information. The reality of it was unbearable. Then it stopped. In his mind's eye, the fissures of Gaumukh closed up and Ganga's waters ceased. There was a moment of blessed silence.

From that emerged a throbbing. Like a heartbeat at the centre of the earth, it made him feel he was not alone, made him believe that the Seekers' voices would eventually come to him. But when he thought he heard the screams of new voices through the reassuring regularity of the thrum, his momentary calm turned once again to an anxious urgency. It took him back to the beginning of his journey, when he'd chosen to be known by the Western name that had caused his own primal scream — prefixed with the Baba that bound him to his Sadhu vow. It was a reminder of what was needed.

Reluctantly, the old man dragged himself back to the task at hand. Seeking the reassurance of the familiar, his eyes swept over the pictures one more time. In the end, all his meticulous records had proven unnecessary. Having come back from an arduous trek to Ganga's Source only yesterday, her death had been clear for all to see. All that remained of the bubbling, crystal waters was a red-tinged pool. It confirmed what he had suspected weeks ago: the Age of the Downfall was upon them. In order to be reborn, creation would have to be consumed, and if anything was to be salvaged, he must hear the call of the next Seeker.

He pulled the curtain across. Trying to settle into a meditative state, Baba John found that a grey cloud of fear was stopping his spirit from soaring. Despite scouring his memories for other reassuring moments, the gathering gloom became increasingly suffocating. His guru had been mistaken. He wasn't up to it. The last Seeker was too elusive. He wouldn't be able to find her, let alone help her shape what was to come.

To still his ragged breathing, he started humming. And then it came. *Thump, thump.* A steady drumming that reminded him of that first heartbeat. The same need that had once forced a scream of rebirth, propelled him beyond the smothering darkness to the place the physical and spiritual planes met: the Source. Here he must wait. This was where the calls of those who were broken would echo. Among them would be the Seeker, the one who would bind the new energy as Shiva had once bound Ganga. Only so would the coming flood be managed.

But even as he assimilated this newfound knowledge, he recognised there was something missing and returned from the elsewhere that kept on eluding him. He reached for the ancient Sheesham box in the hut's darkest corner, the faint heartbeat getting louder as he disturbed the heavy dust that covered it. The last time he'd opened it was sixty-five years ago. He remembered his eyes sliding over the pages of writing as if it were yesterday. How he hadn't been able to hold on to the sense of what he was reading.

Hoping that in this hour of need, the underlying beat signalled some kind of approval, Baba John went to decipher the learnings passed down the long line of Watchers. Some sheets were typed, some handwritten, and most were yellowing. The oldest rolls of parchment were right at the bottom, though. Unrolling them, he found that this time the spidery Sanskrit flowed into him. Whistling though his remaining teeth in triumph, he allowed himself to surrender to the truth of the story.

Like the Ganges, Turtle Island held many beginnings: flood, sacrifice, death, and rebirth. As the words and messages rolled over him, they also passed though him — as if casting out a net to their rightful owner. He no longer needed meditation to straddle the dimensions. In this new state of omniscience, he started to see how inevitable the devastation was. He also saw, though, that even an unstoppable flood could be directed if the channel was deep and wide enough.

Part 1:
WHAT IS

Maybe, just maybe the pain's not all mine.
And maybe the place beyond time and space
Deep beneath the sea
Might include others, not just you and me.
And it was that, that made me cry, you see.

Extracted from Martha's book of poems, Summer 2011

ACT 1

Martha knew she was late. Eyeing the blinking display on her car clock radio, she swung into the Tesco Metro Car Park, late but hungry, which was why she was here. A small pit stop wouldn't hurt. Being fifteen minutes late wasn't that awful, was it?

She had always been such a good timekeeper. Since Dave's death a few months ago, though, the initial bout of extreme self-pity had been replaced by an overwhelming numbness. In this new world, things were dancing to their own tune, and because she couldn't keep up, time didn't seem to matter much any more. And, her employers, although a good digital marketing agency, were hardly the emergency services.

She came to a stop, her sense of self-righteous indignation warring with that deadness she was trying so hard to keep at bay. Looking around, she realised that in her bad mood, she'd pulled into a mother-and-child parking space. Knowing that her fifteen-year-old son and seventeen-year-old daughter were hardly the family they'd had in mind when allocating it, she brushed off the momentary pang of guilt by rationalising that she'd only be a couple of minutes. And, talk of the devil — just as she had shrugged metaphorical shoulders, her phone buzzed. It was Amelia, a.k.a. Emmy. She had run out of make-up wipes and was asking whether her mum could pick some up. The *PURLEEASE* was capitalised on the embarrassingly cracked iPhone 5S.

Even though she knew the minutes were ticking by, she scrunched down in her car seat. Deciding to keep her phone out, in quick succession she tapped into Twitter, Facebook, and LinkedIn. Connecting into her digital personae always made her feel more present. She was pleased to see one new follow and a few likes for yesterday's picture of a pretty sunrise.

On Facebook, she had announced Dave's death. Here, she was the grieving widow who put the occasional post up that everyone liked, in order to show they cared. Smiling through the tears was who she was on Facebook, giving others the opportunity to feel better about themselves with a click and a comment. Here she was liked and likeable.

Sometimes, she thought, she preferred the digital Martha to the real one. That was certainly the case on her professional sites. No reference here to anything bad in her life. Here she was meticulous Martha, a networker to the core, picture from about ten years ago, with opinions based on whoever was paying her.

As she heaved herself out of the car, she noticed that the air conditioning had definitely taken the edge off the heat of the day. It was only 9:00 a.m., and the tarmac was already sweating. She found herself in the baked goods section in front of shelves that throbbed with scents and colours. Whatever it was that had stripped colour and light from other parts of her life was strangely absent here. Lobbing some reduced-price croissants into her basket, along with a few other things she fancied, she topped her food shopping off with a half-price tray of sushi. Glancing at her watch, she knew there were just the make-up wipes left to get. She was already well past the fifteen minutes she'd allowed herself.

This was something that did matter. Samantha-Jane, her thirty-something boss, had made it clear that her tardiness would not be tolerated for much longer. The fact that Martha had been delivering substandard copy had not helped either. As she felt her anxiety mount, Martha's heart rate sped up, its beat catching at the base of her skull. As she lengthened her stride, the rhythmic thudding of her feet on the ground only served to further increase her pulse rate while making the fleshy friction between her thighs even less comfortable.

Glancing up the toiletries aisle, she spotted the make-up wipes. She made a grab for two packs that were on special offer and plonked them in her basket with a sense of satisfaction. The thudding at the back of her head had got even louder, a sure sign that her anxiety was getting out of hand. To focus on the practical, she surreptitiously looked for any tell-tale damp patches under her armpits.

She stopped in her tracks. Her hand had disappeared, and the basket she was holding was floating in midair. Closing her eyes, she felt an odd, counterpoint heartbeat thrumming through her entire being. What was happening? When she finally plucked up the courage to open them again, she heaved a sigh of relief. Her hand was most definitely back where it belonged again, flesh bulging out around the wedding ring she hadn't, as yet, been able to get off.

She felt tears well up. In the real world, it wasn't just her hand disappearing; it was all of her. Not even her children saw her any more. They just wanted her to do and get things for them. She looked back down at her hands and realised that something had to give. As she focussed on the last echoes of the beat she'd felt run through her, she hoped to goodness it wouldn't be her sanity.

"Everything all right, miss?" A friendly voice shook her out of her moment's reverie. A navy-clad elderly gentleman was looking at her with concern. Not trusting herself to speak, she nodded.

"Do you need a chair?"

Slightly irritated that he'd broken through that strangely soothing, underlying thrum, she shook her head.

After what seemed like an age, she reached the safety of her car. As she turned the key in the ignition, she forced herself to breathe deeply, a sure way to calm frayed nerves. It worked so well that by the time she reached the office car park, she'd been able to reason most of what had happened away. Just in case low blood sugar was to blame though, she delicately opened a pack of shortbread on her way in.

Up she went. Naturally, everything was open-plan. In this age of blue-sky thinking, sharing was caring, collective creativity was commendable, and keeping an eye on each other was mandatory. Samantha-Jane's desk had been positioned with this in mind, making it necessary to pass her in order to reach any of the other working areas. Thankfully, at this moment, it was empty.

Making her way to her desk, Martha ticked off other things she had to be to be grateful for. Not only was she slightly out of the way, there was even a window that opened. As with all things, though, there was always a downside. Hers was the ever positive, twenty-four-year-old Kate, who'd been placed directly opposite. The hope had been that the younger woman would benefit from Martha's expertise. Martha ruefully admitted to herself that, based on recent performance, there'd been definite flaws in that particular plan.

As Kate glanced up from her desk, smiling past the photograph of handsome Harry, her boyfriend, Martha found herself responding in a similar vein. Of course, she knew deep down that what was being said behind her back was more reflective of Kate's real thoughts. A smile, however, didn't cost anything and made her feel better.

"Everything all right Martha? You look a bit flustered today. How about I get you a glass of water."

Her colleague had been very kind since Dave's death, that much was true. But because Martha's default position was inadequacy, she'd been unable to take it at face value.

What must Kate think of me? I've achieved nothing. I'm a mess. This dynamic gave their relationship an odd flavour, since it was impossible to work out whether it was governed by contempt or pity or where the seniority lay. However, not one to look a gift horse in the mouth, Martha accepted Kate's offer. The thought of tucking into her sushi without interference from the almost imperceptible wrinkling of Kate's nose was just too appealing to resist.

Looking across at her colleague's long-legged stride, Martha realised that despite mixed feelings, she admired the younger woman's sense of purpose. She'd once been like that herself. Where had it all gone so wrong? When she'd met Dave, they had been two people, but it hadn't been very long until they'd felt like one being, their shared aims and goals creating a powerful momentum. She remembered how he'd encouraged her to go for a BBC graduate scheme, calling her his Valkyrie when she'd got it.

"A fierce goddess able to choose the kind of life and death us mere mortals will enjoy," he'd said.

Sticking to the Norse theme, she'd replied that if that were who she was, he'd have to be one of Odin's all-seeing ravens.

"You'll take flight to make our dreams come true, just wait and see."

They married a couple of years later, by which time her feet had been firmly planted on a career path that was going places. Martha didn't acknowledge it very often, but since his death and despite everything that had happened, she felt like the half that had been left behind. A fierce longing for a different kind of death for him burned as strongly as it had that day she'd found out he'd gone.

Popping the remaining piece of fish into her mouth, she decided that self-pity, what-ifs, and petty jealousies notwithstanding, today was the day she was going to get a grip. Her job was necessary. She needed it to keep up with the mortgage payments, not to mention the other debts Dave had left her with. She opened up her MacBook, and the first email pinged up on her screen.

Lateness
From: Samantha-JaneF@williamjones.com
To: MarthaJ@williamjones.com
Cc: Humanr@williamjones.com
Monday, 19th June 2017 09:35

Dear Martha,

It has come to my attention that despite previous verbal warnings, you are once again nearly forty minutes late. Whilst we very much value your contribution as an employee and recognise the significant experience you bring, it is essential that you are able to support William Jones (WJ) as a coworker who is able to support the team, not just as our senior copy writer but also by setting an example to our less experienced employees.

We do recognise the difficult nature of the last few months and have tried our best to be accommodating and supportive. However, this is the last informal warning. Paul from Human Resources has been cc'd so as to recognise the start of a more formal approach on our part.

The next time there are any irregularities with reference to either timekeeping or quality of work, you will be issued with a formal, written warning.

Best wishes,
Samantha-Jane

Sure enough, SJ was darting glances at Martha over the top of her iMac, obviously watching for any reaction. Martha hoped that her little half wave looked suitably contrite. It obviously didn't, though, and realising too late she'd not even had a sip of her water, she found herself standing in front of her grim-faced boss.

"I do hope, Martha, that you start taking this more seriously. Despite your wealth of experience, I'm sick of covering for you. Mark was only saying the other day…"

As she'd done so often in the past, Martha zoned out. Beyond the fact that Mark had the hots for SJ, who, it was said, was only too pleased to bend over backwards or any other which way for him, she truly had no interest in whatever the company's owner had to say. However, remembering her earlier resolve, she tried her best to look contrite. When had she got so cynical? And why did it seem that everything had become twisted up inside her?

"Are you listening to me, Martha? Unless I get the council copy through by 5:00 p.m., we will be implementing a reporting sheet to monitor work levels. And just in case it's slipped your mind, it's currently three days overdue."

Martha knew that Samantha-Jane had a point. WJ was a marketing agency. A local one, but fairly established at that. The council was an important client, and even though there was leeway on the deadlines, she was cutting it fine. Although it was lost in the mists of time, she did have a pedigree as a national features writer, and it did mean she was expected to support key clients. She just wished she were able to summon the energy to create the crap that was required.

"And don't forget to comment on 'Positive Connections.' You've not been active there lately either," came SJ's final rejoinder.

As Martha made her way back to her desk, she thought about how much she hated pretending to be someone else, so she could comment on the various platforms she was tending. She'd once prided herself on her real voice, but it had all but disappeared. Looking down at her intertwined fingers, she realised the earlier disappearing hand reminded her of the way she felt when she was doing her digital "thang," even on her own behalf. On the one hand, she loved the online personae she'd created for herself, dipping into earlier, more successful versions at will. On the other, though, it was exhausting — and the effort of maintaining those constructs made the real her fade into insignificance.

Feeling her heart beating at the back of her throat again, she threw a "loo" in Kate's direction and grabbed her handbag. Despite the stairs, she preferred the toilets a couple of floors up, since hardly anyone went to them. Pulling her shortbread out, she shoved it into her mouth on her way up, footsteps plodding, packaging rustling, mantra in her head getting louder with each step: *worthless, useless, worthless, useless* — it was like a song.

As she put the loo seat down, the first sob shook her body before she'd even locked the door. Crumbs splattered everywhere. The emptiness inside her, causing her to hold her stomach in agonised silence.

"What the fuck, Dave!" And there was the anger. "What the fuck!" she said again, louder this time. "I can't do it, I just can't do it anymore."

She had the momentary urge to hurt herself to prove she was still there. One thing was for sure: if it weren't for Emmy and Henry, she'd have acted on it long ago. It wasn't just the fact that Dave had died; it was all the shit he'd left her with.

They had had all kinds of insurance policies. Apparently, though, Dave had stopped paying them a couple of years prior to his death. And the ink hadn't been properly dry yet on his death certificate when she'd found out about the separate bank account. Twenty years of married life, and she'd had no idea. He'd been using it to pay various credit card bills and loans he had taken out. It turned out that he'd only been paying half his salary into their joint account; the other half was being used to service his ever-mounting debt. Theoretically, it was all in his name, but thanks to the kind debt management people, she'd discovered that she was liable. She needed this job, that was the long and the short of it. However, she had neither the strength nor the energy to do it properly.

"You bastard, how could you...." The ever-present anger bubbling up inside her, she screamed. It felt as if her vocal cords were bleeding, but it was probably just her heart. The memories came crashing in the opening created by the anguished cry. The first time he hadn't come home, the first empty bottle of whisky she'd found in the airing cupboard, the unexplained texts and emails. He was a digital specialist and had been able to mislead her. Deep down she had known but just hadn't wanted to confront the full extent of their problems. It was easier to pretend that it was okay. Until the day the police had arrived at her door and told her it wasn't any more.

Her scream shifted into a dry, heaving sobbing. Thank God she was on the third floor. Nobody around. That was enough to have shaken the birds from the rafters. She coughed spatters of blood onto her hand. Quickly wiping them off with a piece of toilet roll, she realised that giving physical vent to her pain had released something.

It did no good, looking back. She needed to be strong and look forward. Although she was still shaking, the tears stopped. Come hell or high water, she was going to finish that copy on time. Splashing water over her face, she glanced in the mirror. Her features were tear-streaked and bloated, the startling blue of her eyes hidden behind flesh and sadness. Her hair was no better; wavy and grey-brown, it was scraped back into a severe bun. Her backbone stiffened. She didn't need to be a victim. She had once looked and felt good. She could do both again.

As she reached her desk for the second time that day, she eyed the picture of her family. Despite everything, it still included him. An old phrase came to her: *Let me walk in beauty, and make my eyes ever behold the red and purple sunset.*

It was an extract from the Great Spirit prayer. She'd purchased the bookmark at the Museum of Anthropology in Vancouver after manufacturing a work trip in an attempt to pin the shadow of her missing grandfather's identity onto herself. It had been after she'd found out that he hadn't so much abandoned them as been rejected, and she'd wanted to know more.

She came back to the photograph. Short, dark hair, twinkling eyes, slightly reddened cheeks, and nose of a drinker; still handsome. His looks hadn't been his beauty, though. His belief in her and the way he'd helped embrace the new Indigenous Canadian aspect of herself had been his special gift. Probably because he himself was a mixture too, part Irish, part Swedish, and immersed in the folklore of both, when he got half the chance. She'd gone from Valkyrie to Minnehaha, his gentle teasing making all the other bits fit together more easily — in the first years of their relationship, at least.

Wondering whether she still had the bookmark, she thought back to when the picture had been taken. It was over five years ago and had been just after they'd walked around King's Wood. Even though she was sure that at this point he'd no longer thought of her as beautiful, they'd still been a real family. It was reflected in the children. Emmy was a lovely, healthy weight, and Henry's deep eyes still looked on the world in childish wonder rather than the reproach they offered now. Everything worked, hung together somehow.

These days, she was left with the impression of a life of raw video files, unedited and completely disconnected from each other, clips of various lengths, from a few seconds to a few minutes, with no data attached to them to explain where they were taken or when.

Yes, I will get my shit together, she vowed. *I owe it to them.* "I love you just the way you are" floated back at her.

By 5:30, she had finished the work that had been overdue. Pressing "send" with a tremendous sense of satisfaction, she escaped the building. It had been a long time since she'd felt like this. It would have been great to go to the beach for a bit — an easy thing if they'd remained in

Westbrook. However, a few years ago she had wanted to find a way to pull them back together again; "It'll be better, I promise." So they'd moved out to St Nicholas at Wade, land-bound and bang in the middle of rural Thanet. Dave's main office had been based out in a converted barn near Maidstone, so the move had been irrelevant to him. At the time, though, it had meant the world to her. She'd realised too late that the remoteness of the location had only pushed them further apart.

Reaching the car, she was pleased that it had cooled down slightly. Fumbling under her seat for the ubiquitous Diet Coke and emergency crisps, she remembered with a shudder how the police had broken the news to her about the vodka bottle they had found under the driver's seat of the car Dave had died in. They'd been very kind when they told her but had nonetheless spelt out that his death had been down to drink-driving. Since there had been no one else involved and there was no damage to anything other than a wrecked wall in a country lane near Maidstone, the police didn't pursue it. She was still grateful to them, allowing as it did for a "death by misadventure" verdict. The kids didn't ask too closely either. As always, the appearance of normalcy was more important than what had actually happened.

Once again, she was on autopilot. Without knowing how she'd got here, she found herself at the Minster McDonald's drive-through window, ten minutes from home. The kids wouldn't notice if she was a bit late — and if they were delayed in eating, well, it was only really Henry who would say anything. She inhaled her food, revelling in the warm comfort of the Quarter Pounder and the scalding heat of the apple pie. Although she understood that the effect was ephemeral, in that moment it filled up the places that had started echoing hollowly again.

Five minutes later, she was ready to dispose of the evidence. A container just past the nature reserve would serve. As she opened it to throw the brown paper bag in, she sensed the strange binary beat she had felt earlier cutting across the silence. As it flooded through her, she looked up and found herself able to see the green lid she was lifting through both hands. The shock of the sheen of the plastic where her hands should have been caused her to let go. With a bang, the lid came crashing down.

After a couple of endless moments, the sense of oddness passed. Carefully scrutinising her hands for any sign of what had just happened, she raised them to the sky.

The momentary stillness was broken by a crow, its brief cawing drawing attention to the fact that he was hovering directly above her. After announcing his presence, he became subsumed in the general silence. The still, black form had a quiet watchfulness to it, which she couldn't shake off.

In the end, she broke the tension by saluting him, something she remembered was appropriate when warding off misfortune from a solitary magpie, and drove her protesting car the last few miles home. But the shadowed, unmoving shape of the bird set against the blue-burning June sky stayed with her until the minute she put her key in the door.

The crow came to rest on one of the pylons that lined the long stretch of road next to the disused runway. It stretched its wings. As it did, its beak lengthened, turning into a mighty black weapon, able to tear flesh and rend carrion. Spreading its tail, it shaped its feathers into a fan. Other than the glossy black of its plumage, the great creature bore very little resemblance to the much smaller cousin it had imitated. It paused a short time, inky feathers ruffling in a breeze that seemed to have sprung up out of nowhere. Then, opening suddenly translucent wings, it threw itself into a newly shimmering sky and disappeared as quickly as it had come.

"Kids, I'm home! Emmy, Henry, where are you?" As usual, it took another three bellows to get any kind of response.

Glancing through the hall that led directly to the open plan living room into the garden, she smiled ruefully. It wasn't much of a house, and even though they'd bought it because they loved the outside space, it wasn't much of a garden either. Neither she nor Dave had got around to things the way they'd wanted to. Throwing one more regretful glance at the expanse of weeds, she realised that the patio doors had been left wide open. One of them must be in.

Finally, Henry appeared at the top of the stairs. She saw his black socks first, stark against the peculiarly pink print of the carpet — yet another thing they hadn't got around to changing. Her little man, size ten feet, just under six-foot, dark hair, dark eyes, was his father's double. The eyes that met hers, though, had a blank, slightly glazed look, unlike those in the photograph on her desk.

"Hey, Mum, school was cancelled this afternoon, so I came back for a bit of a nap."

Suspicion must have been writ large over her face, and he hastened to follow up with a rejoinder that was as swift as it was lame.

"One of the teachers was off."

"I'll check, Henry. That sounds highly unlikely! And Henry…"

He turned again, coming down the stairs, the too-long arms on his lanky frame enfolding her in a hug, which muffled the next bit of what she had to say.

"You spend too much time up there with your computer games. It's your GCSE's year."

Having heard it all before, he turned the shrug into a deeper embrace and added in his earlier turning on of the oven as a final "conscientious son" flourish. Withdrawing to the furthest corner of the kitchen, he proceeded to answer the phone alert that had vibrated its way through this entire interaction.

Well, if the oven was already on, fish and chips would take no time at all. Martha followed Henry in, checking on the wilted lettuce in the salad drawer while edging the freezer open. A couple of minutes later, she had banged the oven door shut on their meal, which included a nut cutlet for Emmy.

She bellowed again. "Emmy, Emmy — where are you? Come down."

Martha's heart caught as she watched her eldest's slow progress down the stairs. Every time she saw Emmy, her anxiety levels rocketed. Even the voluminous folds of the ever-present black, baggy jumper couldn't hide that she had shrunk even further. Her daughter had become a vegetarian when she was sixteen, a vegan when she was seventeen, and since Dave's death last November, she hadn't eaten very much of anything at all.

As Martha looked at the transparent skin stretched over her daughter's bird-like bones, she felt an echo of the earlier drumming. The pounding highlighted a moment of déjà vu, affording her a glimpse of a truth that had become inescapable; her disappearing hands were somehow connected to her disappearing daughter. So she looked, truly looked. It wasn't often she allowed herself to do so, finding it too painful. Forcing herself to turn her mother's searching gaze on Emmy, she took in the lank, blonde hair, which hid dulled, sky-blue eyes that were currently staring fixedly at the floor.

In an attempt to break the unbearable scrutiny, Emmy spoke. "Hi, Mum, just got back, the bus was late again. How was your day?"

The intention had been to deflect from reality. Coupled with her closed expression, though, it had the opposite effect, and her words bounced hollowly off the walls. They made the breezy falseness of what she was trying to convey even more acute.

The other thing she couldn't hide from her mum was her disdain. Martha knew perfectly well that Emmy found her pathetic. She also knew that by letting herself go physically, she had given Emmy incentive to exert a pitiless control over her own food intake. "I'm never going to be like you, never." In fact, getting Emmy to eat normally was one of the reasons Martha was so intent on finding a way through her own eating troubles. She was desperate to eschew the mountains of sugar and processed food that had started bringing comfort to her life way back when — years, even, before Dave died. However, no matter how much she tried, the cravings just got worse, and so, day by day, she got fatter.

She also blamed the extra layers of flesh for the lethargy she couldn't shake off, a numb forgetfulness that seemed to wash over everything she touched. She didn't care enough about things that should have mattered, unless they manifested themselves as all-consuming pain. She was like the Little Mermaid, each step in the real world an agony.

Emmy's packed lunch was a perfect example of this. Martha knew that no matter how carefully she prepared it, Emmy was not going to eat it. If she allowed that knowledge to touch her, it would cut through the carefully curated layers she needed in order to function. It was easier, therefore, to let it wash over her. One thing was certain: whether through numbness or pain, things didn't seem to get done in the same way they used to any more.

"Mum, if that's dinner on, I really don't fancy anything. I've already eaten."

And there it was. If she reacted, there would be a row, and if she didn't, it would be perceived as lack of caring; the irony of it was that her own guilt lacerated her more than any row would have done. She engaged.

"Emmy, you know the rules. At the very least you will sit with us. I have put some food in for you. Chips are just vegetable oil, and there is a nut cutlet for you."

Emmy rolled her eyes.

"And did you eat your lunch? Let me see your lunchbox."

This was a nightly rogation ritual they had down pat, having had exactly the same conversation for the last eighteen months.

"Did you see your counsellor today? Any use? How was Georgia? English, French, History...?" Questions came thick and fast, as did the "yeahs," "fines," and "okays."

Although they both knew that nothing was ever being given or received in this exchange, it was still oddly comforting. It could have been the strange events of the day, but as Martha considered things, a thought struck her. What would happen if she threw her arms around Emmy, now, at this very moment?

Her phone vibrated. She glanced down. How odd, it had come from WhatsApp, a messaging service she rarely used. She didn't recognise the number either. It was addressed to her, though, and with all thoughts of Emmy dissipating, she opened it.

Dear Martha,
You faded today in the supermarket. You mustn't. You are needed.
Use this:
Help me to remain calm and strong in the face of all that comes
towards me. Let me learn the lessons you have hidden in every
leaf and rock.

What did it mean? She rechecked the number that had appeared and even tried to phone it, but it rang out. Did she have a stalker? What did they mean "fade"? Was she hallucinating again? And wasn't that another bit from the prayer she'd remembered earlier?

"Mum, can we have some baked beans too, I'm sick of salad?"

She felt beads of sweat appear on her brow and her hands went clammy. Henry's request registered somewhere, but it was at the very back of her mind. Phone nearly slipping out of her hand, she clutched it with a vice-like grip.

"Mum, we're not having beans," Emmy wailed.

"You said you didn't want anything anyway, so what does it matter to you?" came Henry's swift rejoinder.

Refereeing the bickering that had broken out helped Martha emerge from the fog. Another vibration and another message. Again, along with the invitation to block it.

Dear Martha. Don't be afraid. Just do as suggested. x

Sitting down heavily, she took a great gulp of air. The kids were too caught up with their own nonsense to notice that there was anything amiss. But for her, despite that one huge intake of breath, it was difficult to take another one, and the all-familiar thudding in her head started up again.

Martha looked over the table at Henry, who, after trying to blend in with the kitchen chair's plastic greenness during her conversation with Emmy, had decided it was time to be present again. He shoved it back with gusto.

By drawing her eye, he'd done her a huge favour. Having been desperately casting around for what to focus on, she dropped her phone into her handbag. There was an uncomfortable truth around her son that proved to be sufficiently distracting. He'd got a six-month subscription to a gaming site for his birthday, and she hated how he was disappearing further and further into the small, flickering screen of the fantasy world that was open 24/7. Her breathing slowed, the flash of anger restoring a sense of normality.

"That's it, enough shouting. Can't we just have one ordinary family evening together?"

There was real anger in Martha's words. This was something else she'd always been good at, deflecting emotion from what was really causing the distress to something else.

She was, though, genuinely cross with Henry at this moment, and it wasn't because of the baked beans or the shouting. It was because she was reminded that she hadn't listened to Dave when she should have done.

He'd been completely against a gaming subscription for Henry. Knowing that world better than she did, he'd always shaken his head darkly, muttering about exploitation and addiction before once again forbidding it point blank. Left to her own devices, though, Martha hadn't been able to resist Henry's relentless badgering, and it was this that fuelled her anger.

But then, as quickly as it came, it left her. In recent times, thinking about Dave had frequently been the cause of these quicksilver emotions. First she'd be angry, then she'd think about how nice it would be to discuss one thing or another with him, and then she'd go back to anger again, remembering how it had been impossible to talk about anything at the end.

Right now, though, she wanted to tell him he'd been right. She would also have asked him to help her investigate the small sums of money that had recently been disappearing from her credit card. A bit like with Emmy's pack lunch, part of her knew her son had something to do with it, but she wasn't ready to confront it just yet.

She vividly remembered the argument that had won her over. Turning liquid brown eyes on her, Henry had told her how much he wanted to have a space in which he could shift and rearrange things so that everything was just the way he liked it. Especially now, after Dad's death, when things felt so out of control. She remembered wishing being able to immerse herself in her own world also, digital hands rearranging things to suit what she needed.

They ate dinner in absolute silence. The kitchen table with its mismatched chairs was a perfect setting for a family trying to come together but not quite making it. Martha had no idea what the kids were thinking. At one point there'd been a rule that there were no phones allowed at the table. Since Dave had gone, though, that, like so many other things, had slipped. Looking at her children's faces lit up with the glow from their smartphones, she thought that they were more like a family of phones than people. Was there a next stage? "We wouldn't need to eat or interact, just be." In a strange kind of way, that thought appealed to her.

She was aching to join them, hand twitching towards her handbag. But frightened of what new message might have appeared, she resisted. With nothing to do, though, it didn't take long for the stillness to become oppressive.

"Henry?" He took a couple of minutes to look up from something that seemed to be all-engrossing.

"Yes, Mum...." She was relieved that he had raised his eyes to meet hers, albeit rolling them slightly in the process.

"Are there any other news apps you'd suggest? I always use BBC, but I'm looking for something ... oh, I don't know, more environmentally focussed?"

A couple of moments later, her phone in hand, he'd uploaded Science Daily. She'd only had to contribute a couple of passcodes, and, because he'd handled it first, it was less scary. She took possession of it again. No new notifications, thank God.

The first article flashed up. More than twenty whales had been beached and died near a fishing village on Mexico's Gulf shore. It seemed another pod had met a similar fate off the Californian coast.

Although the story wasn't doing much for her spirits, it reminded her that at one point she'd very much enjoyed Kent's coastline. Once she had even loved running along it, although that had been pretty early on, close to when they'd left London. She realised with a pang that it had been weeks since she'd seen North Sea waves crashing against the shore.

Henry piped up again, "You do know you can set the BBC app to more international stories, don't you? More of the stories you like."

She passed her phone back over. "Go on then, show me, my little phone genie."

As Henry moved over to help again, he couldn't resist adding, "Don't you mean *jinni*, Mum? Even when you and Dad were mucking around with old myths to create characters to amuse us, you'd always be a stickler for the correct terminology."

With that rejoinder, knowledge thanks to half remembered tales of gods and heroes from his childhood as well as his latest religious studies lesson, he adjusted the settings to include environmental stories. Handing her phone back while still scanning the feature about sea level warnings, he threw in another un-Henry like comment.

"Doesn't life sometimes feel like you're driving down the motorway really fast, knowing all the while that your brakes aren't working?"

Surprisingly, it was Emmy who answered. "A bit profound, bro, but yeah — other than choosing where to crash, I don't think any of us can do anything."

Not wanting to let this moment of connection pass unmarked, Martha reached out to clasp Emmy's hand. "At least we're informed, though. When I was your age, other than newspapers and the main news shows, there was no way of getting information. Now, we can access anything, anytime."

She waved her phone. "I mean, look at what Henry's just done."

Martha did find communication technology amazing. There was a real sense of empowerment at being able to access exactly what she wanted. Her interest in the environment had, for example, come from the news story about the Brazilian government agreeing to further deforestation, run a few months ago. She remembered how she'd been tempted to write to the corporations that were causing the problem by demanding palm oil. But who to write to, what to say?

Martha would have so enjoyed a conversation around some of this, but after that surprising interchange, the kids were off in their own world again, and Dave, well, Dave was dead.

Looking up, she noticed that Henry had finished and was about to leave the table, while Emmy was still determinedly pushing a half-eaten tomato and three quarters of her nut cutlet around. She turned imploring eyes on Martha.

"Go on both of you, I'll clear up...."

Even before she'd finished the sentence, they were up and out.

ACT 2

As he caught glimpses of her tidying up, he thought how ironic it all was. Once, he'd been so desperate to get away from this day-to-day existence that he had literally drunk himself to death. Now, having somehow found himself called back, he was pathetically grateful for even the glimpse of activity Martha's phone afforded him; even the clattering and clanging was like music to his soul. Two great truths were manifesting in an existence he hadn't got a handle on yet; things are never quite as they appear, and nothing turns out the way you expect.

Even though he'd been in this new iteration for some time now, if Martha had spoken out, just to herself — would he have been able to respond in a way that didn't frighten her half to death? It was something he'd been thinking about for a while. In his case, pixels might very well be the dust of creation rigorous early churchgoing had drummed into him, but what good was that if he wasn't able to touch anything real?

It was clear to him, both now and in the time that had already passed, that something very strange was happening. He was here, in the sense of knowing he was not, *not* here. However, he could no longer eat, drink, touch, or smell. Did that mean he was dead? If that was the case, though, why could he still think and hear? He wanted to move on, but that sense of needing to be here, wherever here was, was stronger.

He tried to think back. He did remember being in a dark place some time ago and being able to make out a vague buzzing a bit later. Following that initial moment of almost complete sensory deprivation, he'd been party to a number of new impressions. He'd felt compelled to be somewhere, and then he'd found himself in the audio and visual functions of computers, laptops, and phones he seemed to be inhabiting. How he had made a leap from that place of nothingness into this digital space was still a bit unclear. He did know, however, that in the current here and now, his sense of self now was entirely different to the previous version.

It was the significant gaps in his memories that bothered him most. If he started being a bit more proactive about exploring his boundaries, might there be some answers to be found? For example, his communication with Martha.

He knew that despite the extreme changes he had experienced — in a timeframe he hadn't completely grasped yet — he had taken a risk. Other than making him feel better, being able to connect with her meant that in the fullness of time, when she'd got a bit more used to things, he'd be able to tell her what was really going on. The selfie editing Emmy was doing of herself in a crop top for example, for the best "rib" effect, or the dodgy partner sites Henry had been scanning to obtain illicit gold coins in order to supplement the ones he'd already bought with Martha's credit card. He didn't know why today in particular had been the day, but the timing seemed to be important and linked to his own sense of self.

Having said that, if she knew all these things, would she not just become even more anxious than she already was? He'd morphed into something she might not recognise. He was hoping she was still his Valkyrie at heart, though, instinctively accepting the truth of his message in a way that would eventually allow him to reveal himself as the source of the information. Maybe using words she recognised, phrases that had once mattered to her, might calm her, smooth the way. It would be amazing if he could let her know that he was there looking out for her when the time was right.

Hearing muffled sobbing coming from Emmy's phone, he shifted focus to his daughter. Although he was still fuzzy on a number of things, he was certain this would have been more important to Dave than watching Martha clearing the detritus of the meal. And what Dave might have once thought or done was still his main reference point. So, although part of him remained with Martha, he moved his attention to his daughter's laptop.

* * *

Half an hour later, kitchen done, wash on, and disappearing anything totally forgotten, she was ready to put her feet up for the evening. Half-heartedly, she called up to the kids to ask whether they wanted to watch anything with her. Not expecting an answer but happy that she had shown willingness, she plonked herself in her favourite seat.

The drumming started again. This time it was in her, but oddly, it also seemed to be coming from her laptop and her phone. The unease she had felt earlier returned with a vengeance. Remembering what had happened before, she checked her hands — just to be sure they were still there. There was nothing obviously amiss, so she started making her way up the stairs. With each step, the noise seemed to get louder. And with her heart beating in time with the relentless rhythm, she felt herself being guided to Emmy's door.

She could hear the sobbing clearly. On opening the door, a hump of duvet greeted her. Knowing there was no point in a head-on assault, Martha knocked retrospectively.

"Why bother, Mum? You're already here."

It was as if the bed was speaking to her, daughter all but consumed by one of the few remaining places of comfort left to her.

In a flash, Martha was perched on the farthest corner of her daughter's bed, hand hovering over the duvet. After a few of the obligatory "leave me alones," a stream of words made it out, albeit somewhat muffled by the brightly patterned paisley duvet.

"New girl at school. Too fat. Don't know what to do any more. Too fat. Dad."

The words themselves didn't really make any sense. However, a mother's intuition told her there was more to this than met the eye. It was rare for Emmy to lose composure like this, especially in front of her. Martha had learned to her cost that pushing for information caused Emmy to retreat even further. So she tried a different tack.

"I've been 'less than' too, on numerous occasions, in fact. I remember one time vividly, though. It was my first visit to Canada, and I was proudly telling everyone about my grandfather, your great-grandfather."

She paused, not sure whether to carry on or not. But then she got her opening.

"He was Ojibwe, wasn't he? I remember the picture we used to have up. I think Uncle Peter sent it. A clipping of him as a boy, in a feathered headdress."

Hoping more of Emmy would emerge from her hiding place, Martha inclined her head thoughtfully. "You're absolutely right. We lost that years ago, though. I can't believe you remember it."

A reddened nose and eyes appeared. "It reminded me of Hiawatha. I used to love you reading me that poem."

Martha nodded slowly. "There have been many times in my life I have felt something was missing. I was always drawn to that poem, even before we knew about any First Nation heritage. I often wondered what it was that made me read it to you, as well as some of the other North American legends we found. I do know it soothed me, though. Made my seeking for that lost part of me less painful somehow."

Martha closed her eyes. This next bit was too painful to tell. The romantic notions of her Indigenous heritage had been very different to the reality she'd found when she had visited Canada. She thought that people would be as excited as she was about her grandfather being Ojibwe, but instead, when she had wangled a business trip to the west coast, she'd found it was the best conversation-killer ever. And the people she'd seen hunched in doorways in Vancouver's Gastown bore no relation at all to the stories she loved or the relatives from the east her mother had told her about.

Tears forgotten, Emmy was sitting up now, fully focussed on her mother's words.

"I went to Vancouver. You were only little, but I told you about it. Do you remember the little blue dreamcatcher I brought back for you? I'd felt disconnected the entire time I was there until I visited the Museum of Anthropology. There I heard stories about how things had once been. Some voices had been recorded. These touched me in a completely unexpected way and gave me of a sense of where I might have belonged had things been different."

"I feel that too, Mum, that I don't belong anywhere. It's been worse since Dad."

In a strange verbal dance, Emmy's words wove themselves into the voices of Martha's memories. The oddest thing was that this mental cacophony increased her sense of loss a thousand times over. She realised she'd never grasped the totality of it, her fundamental inability to connect with the truth of who she was. She knew what those voices held was real but also understood that the deeper knowledge they contained was not for her. And even though it was something she'd never known, she felt its lack all the more keenly.

Oblivious to Martha's pain, Emmy had been sufficiently distracted to want more.

"Mum, can you remember any of the stories? I know there was a Raven — the trickster God and Nanaboozhoo. I think he was a shapeshifter too."

Martha couldn't remember one that included both of Emmy's favourite characters, but something did seem to be waiting on the tip of her tongue. She tried it for size.

"Do you remember the one about Nanaboozhoo and the creatures and how the turtle turned into land? That was all about people fighting with each other too."

After what had happened between her and the new girl at school today, Emmy thought it sounded particularly appropriate. As Martha started the story, Emmy finally peeled herself away from the duvet's comforting embrace.

"The Great Spirit created man — the Anishinaabe. After many years, they began to fight with one another, causing hurt and filling their hearts with anger. The creator sent a great flood, and the only beings to survive were Nanaboozhoo and some animals who had been able to swim or fly. They found a log, and Nanaboozhoo, the loon, otter, beaver, turtle and muskrat took turns to rest on it. They knew they needed to do something, so Nanaboozhoo decided to dive to the bottom to try to find a bit of earth. He disappeared for a long time.

"'I couldn't reach it. You must try,' he told the others as he emerged gasping for breath."

Emmy laughed out loud. Her mum was trying to do the voices! Memories of the story flooded into her. The other animals, piping and deep depending on who was speaking, had all failed. Finally, the smallest of them, the muskrat, did find a bit of earth, although he had died trying. The turtle put it on her back and grew into the North American continent.

Emmy was twelve years older than when she'd last heard the story of Turtle Island. From the perspective of an almost-adult, she thought about how unfair it was that two creatures had needed to sacrifice their lives in order to win back what was already theirs. This much-older Emmy, though, still found comfort in hearing her mum tell their story. By weaving a shred of a protected past into the raw present, it allowed her to fall into a deep, dreamless sleep.

The time with Emmy had unsettled Martha, dredging up things that she'd kept a lid on for months, if not years. In an attempt to shut off churning thoughts, she sought refuge in her bed.

She didn't even pause to look at Dave's side. Putting her phone down on her bedside table, she opened its special drawer and took out the little red book containing all her poems. Even though much of it had been written a lifetime ago, at this moment, some of it seemed very close. She stopped at a verse about pain.

Seeing it made her feel stronger. For her, writing managed stuff she couldn't understand. It was a way of voicing the unspeakable and unexplainable. Today had been an odd day, simple as that. But, she knew that if she started writing again, she would regain some sense of control over a momentum that was mercilessly sweeping her along in its wake.

She checked her phone again. The messages were still there. She definitely wasn't hallucinating. Well, she'd play along for now, no real harm done. She could always block the number tomorrow. Although she'd been planning to read, her eyes became extremely heavy and disappearing hands, children, crows, and semi-official warnings notwithstanding, she fell into a deep, dreamless sleep.

CHAPTER 1

The Better and the Bad

Badenan woke with a start. The she-wolf had been there again, growling and prowling. Hiding in the shadows of the country house in Kurdistan's Zagros mountains, the dark one of legend was lying in wait for the lost girl who'd once lived there.

It had been at their family retreat, near Slemani. Perched right on Dukan Lake, with its whitewashed walls and its blue tiled veranda, the image remained vivid, even all these years on.

Her father had been barbequing skewers of goat's meat, and sitting on the shaded veranda overlooking the lake, her aunties had been responsible for the heaped platter of stuffed vine-leaf dolma. Her older sister, a sophisticated student in her final year, sat there exuding glamour, the red of her fitted summer dress matching that of the kitten heels she refused to take off. Their beautiful mother was heavily pregnant and unmoving in her unwieldiness, one hand shading her sea green eyes and the other waving a brightly coloured fan. Badenan's uncle pinched the fifteen-year-old's cheek harder than necessary. His patting of her bottom was also inappropriate. Even now, the fifty-two-year-old felt outrage at these overfamiliar advances, sneaked when no one was looking. However, the endless rounds of fluffy Purgach flatbread, and then the coffee.... If she kept her eyes closed, she could smell the cardamom, see her bed and the beautifully woven carpet she'd set her slippers on. Despite Badenan's near womanhood, her mother, hands jingling with delicate filigree bangles, had tucked her in. And the cloves, the unique scent that clung to Kurdish women thanks to the necklaces made of the dried buds that also hung around the house — it all meant home.

And then it had changed. The smouldering barbeque and the soft, laughing voices turned into hot, devouring smoke. When fear turned to panic and goat's meat became crackling flesh, she saw the yellow, watchful eyes for the first time. From the stories of her people, she knew they meant danger and harm, but oddly, in all the chaos, they provided a measure of comfort. So, instead of running away, she had followed the grey form out through the smoke-filled corridor and into the scrubland beyond.

The wolf had waited for her. While allowing her to cling to the silvered ruff, she'd somehow hidden the girl from the uniformed figures that were everywhere. As the air became less choking, Badenan had dared to close her streaming eyes. But when she opened them just moments later, she realised she was alone, hidden by the remnants of a stone wall. Gasping for breath and rubbing her eyes to clear her vision, she tried to catch a last glimpse of her companion. However, look as she might, the parched red earth gave no hint of the wolf's passing, and, other than revealing many booted footprints, it also did not share where so many of her family had been taken that day.

She lay quite still in her bed, unwilling to open her eyes. The memories of her aunties, the red dress, the food, and the safety had been so powerful. As if to catch a taste of the feast she'd remembered so clearly, she moved her tongue around her mouth. But it had fled, along with the memory of most of her family, leaving just burned out shells behind. At fifteen, she'd been close to adulthood, and yet it had still been far beyond her.

There were many memories following this one. In all of them, comfort, beauty, and security turned into horror and fear. It was a bit like removing the petticoats of a favourite dress, exposing more each time a layer was removed. Not that she'd necessarily matured, but in the days of Saddam Hussein, survival depended on being a quick learner. The secret police, relocations, and even destruction of the trees in the Zagros Mountains to ensure the Peshmerga had nowhere to hide, superseded the hazy days of music, intellectual conversations, and plenty. Initially, her family had been protected. Her father was a professor at the university, and surrounded by family wealth, they'd had no associations with the resistance. But when he'd started getting political, things changed.

Not wanting to remember any more, she opened one eye and then the other. Then, just as she'd done as a girl, she slipped her feet into the beautifully embroidered slippers at the side of her bed. As the old memories dissipated entirely, the soft hum of the air-conditioning reminded her of how lucky she was. Although the old unit was temperamental, it served her son-in-law's house and therefore her bedroom. Hassan might be many things, but he did like his creature comforts, and air conditioning was one thing he insisted upon, *inshallah!*

At fifty-two Badenan knew she looked okay, but after one child and the life she'd led, it wasn't possible to turn the clock too far back. Thanks to the hijab she wore nowadays — for reasons of conformity and safety rather than any religious persuasion — not many got to see the mane of dark hair that had not one strand of grey. Since Hassan hadn't insisted on the niqab yet, the merry, brown eyes were still there for all to see, although the way things were heading out there, she glanced out of her window at an early morning Baghdad, that might not be the case for much longer.

When they'd moved in, this had been a spare bachelor pad. Hassan was fifty and had been married before. But after a horrendous divorce and the loss of his son to the US, he had gone back to minimalism. As she made her way to the dining room, Badenan realised that although the presence of her and her daughter had gone some way to softening this, the empty shell of a man Fatima had married was still very much evident in their surroundings.

Badenan readied the basics for his preferred breakfast. The bread she had was yesterday's, but by freshening it in the oven and adding some fresh fruit, eggs, and olives and a couple of bowls of pulses, it was an acceptable morning repast. No sign of Fatima yet, though. She didn't seem to eat at all. If nothing else, it was good for her figure, Badenan thought, ruefully pinching her own spare rolls of flesh. Over the last few years, middle class Iraqi women had gotten much heavier. Trapped in their apartments by fear of the unrest, they were unable to exercise and instead took comfort in food, the one pleasure they could access.

Hassan made his entrance a few minutes later, his bulk dominating the end of the table. Looking past him beyond the balcony, she caught a glimpse of the Euphrates glistening in the distance. Her son-in-law was so heavy, he looked ageless. He still had a full head of hair, but unfortunately it was a frizzy, gingery brown. His attempt at a smart suit also left much to be desired. Despite her careful attention to his wardrobe, he looked forever creased and greasy. As he spoke, she couldn't help but notice the slightly yellowing nails and the newsprint-blackened fingers he was using to gesticulate.

"See!" He spat crumbs at her in his enthusiasm to get his point across. "They have even quoted him."

Who? What? Focus, she had to focus. If he was displeased with her, she knew he'd let it out on Fatima.

He was brandishing an article. In it, her friend Duraid seemed to be speaking directly to her, reminding her of why she'd made the decision she found so difficult to live with now. He had shared how the 2014 invasion had made the situation for Kurds in Baghdad increasingly untenable. How he'd finally made the decision to leave. Fourteen years ago, Baghdad had been a city that, despite Saddam's best efforts, had been multicultural and reasonably inclusive. Now it was predominantly Arab and Shia. Well, after being quoted, and with a picture too, his departure must be imminent. He'd probably already gone. She'd go just in case, though, to see if he needed anything.

"It's a good job I'm so well connected," Hassan went on, his voice exuding his usual self-satisfaction.

Even better that we have no real money and therefore most people know there is no point in blackmailing us, thought Badenan uncharitably, knowing that there was a rise in hostage-taking and blackmailing across the communities of Iraq's tottering capital. At a recent lunch, her friend Sana had told her, sotto voce, that she'd just spent most of her liquid assets getting one of her sons back and had decided that despite her burgeoning legal practice in Al Mansour, she was leaving for good.

"My nerves just can't take it any more. I don't know when we leave in the morning, if we will all be back that evening."

With Samar's words ringing in Badenan's ears, she thanked her lucky stars that they were hanging on to financial respectability in one of the safer, more affluent districts of Baghdad.

Badenan had ended up in this situation through a series of fortunate and less than fortunate events. She and her husband Abdulla had finally fled Kurdistan across the Zagros mountains in '97. They'd been advised to move separately, since his communist affiliations meant he was closely watched. However, so successful had they been in fleeing independently that when she made it to Turkey, she found she had lost him all together. She'd also discovered she was pregnant — something she considered a curse at the time, but in retrospect she realised it had been her greatest blessing. After some years in Istanbul, she eventually managed to get back to Iraq in late 2003.

Her return was made possible thanks to her sister Sh'ler's return to Baghdad earlier that year. The older sibling had been prepared to offer her younger sister a home, as well as welcome the five-year-old Fatima.

Then came several years of relative safety, but in 2011 the Americans pulled out, closely followed by the Brits. Sh'ler stayed a little longer but had eventually left in 2013, heading back to London for a more civilised job as comms lead for an oil and gas corporation. Sadly, Badenan had not been able to hold on to the coveted Green Zone apartment and had desperately looked for another way to find the security she so craved for herself and Fatima. After a while in Zayouna and with a timely email from Shl'er, they'd found Hassan, who was living on the much better western side of the city and had been very keen on marrying sixteen-year-old Fatima.

Right on cue, her son-in-law roused himself from his chewing to complain, another activity he excelled at. "You're slacking, Badenan. The waste bin in my bathroom was still full when I got up. Rather than choosing to mend clothes for other people, you should focus on what happens at home!"

She knew he was finding fault because a new head had recently told him that his lessons were outdated. This time, though, a flash of anger overcame her. Rather than supressing it, as she usually did, Badenan opened her mouth, drawing on an old story that seemed to be so relevant to the here and now.

"Have you ever heard the story of the Better and the Bad twins, and the choices they made? How the wise one chose aright to create Life and the foolish one took a different path to create Not-Life?"

Still caught up with the remains of his breakfast, he didn't seem to be listening. Determined to be heard for once, she raised her voice.

"He that followed the Lie chose to do the worst things; the holiest Spirit chose Right and was clothed in heaven's raiment. The Daevas chose to follow the Lie, succumbing to infatuation of the Worst Thought and rushed together to Violence to enfeeble the world of men."

Grunting a sharp dismissal, he raised beady eyes to look at her. Courage dying, she sank back into herself. Surely this man before her must be a vessel for these Daevas? Mesmerised, she watched the last of the oil on fat lips and fingers, knowing that Fatima would pay for her mother's outburst. If only she'd seen the greed and evil shining out of him before. There had been so many clues, but she'd chosen not to see them.

These days she spent much of her time fantasising. By not giving in to reality, she was able to escape the guilt that clawed at her every breath. Comforting herself with memories from the past gave her more recent choice context. Thinking back to those times, the fruitless search for a lost husband, menial jobs, and Erdogan's aggressively anti-Kurdish rhetoric, she realised that although she'd always taken the ostensibly easier option, it had generally proven to be the more difficult path. Knowing what she knew now, she liked to think that she might have made different choices. But just as her sister's role, working for a senior British commander, had facilitated visas for a return journey to a city she had felt hatred for, Hassan's important family and respectable salary had given the appearance of security. And she'd jumped.

Sh'ler was still in London. Even though they hadn't seen each other for several years, as with millions of other Iraqi diaspora, WhatsApp and the wonders of electronic communication made it easy to maintain long-distance relationships. However, the truths her sister made her face were not always convenient. In fact, after Sh'ler's horror at discovering that Fatima was the coinage Badenan had used to get them out of the eastern part of the city, there had been very little contact between them.

It always boiled down to choices. So often, she had made the wrong one. In the end, though, and as Hassan himself had pointed out earlier, where else could they have gone? They would not have been safe. Two women alone, no money to speak of. Even though Badenan was educated, her awkward personality linked to years of working subsistence jobs meant that she didn't have the drive to do anything else. She was disconnected from the woman she'd once been. Bitterly she thought that Sh'ler, the older by seven years, didn't seem to suffer in the same way. Whatever life threw at her, she would always land on her feet and reinvent herself accordingly.

Hassan had nearly finished. She wanted to bring up the end of the story but decided against it. The bit about man being given Dominion and Indestructibility. Why would a man like him be given that without the qualities of a Good Mind, and Right, and Piety — cited as the qualities needed to make mankind worthy of its proud position? Had she herself made it possible for him to be like this? Like the Daevas, she'd had a choice, and like them she'd chosen the easy option.

* * *

Fatima, the subject of all this maternal angst, was only a few feet away, brush-tugging away at the mass of dark hair that swathed her small form. Listening for every tiny sound from beyond her door, she sat at her dressing-table-cum-desk and eyed the doll sitting on the chair next to her. For the thousandth time she wished she were able to emulate Farah's remote, unconcerned stare. Instead of having her own pretty features likened to those of a doll, she'd often thought how wonderful it would be to go one step further. She wanted to embody Farah's glassy stoicism, becoming equally inanimate — no matter what life threw at her. Farah was one of the few remnants of her childhood that had come with them when they'd moved to Hassan's apartment. She had perfectly painted rosebud lips, long, plaited black hair, and dark glass eyes that stared unseeingly into the other corner of the room.

Why keep the doll? There were so many things she could have brought instead. Her books, her magazines, her Western clothes. Instead, she chose the gift her Aunt Sh'ler had greeted her with at the airport when they'd flown in from Ankara. Auntie had handed Farah over, sharing a whispered hope that they might become friends. Five-year-old Fatima had been unsure whether the lovely woman in front of her was referring to her or the doll the glamorous lady was pressing into her arms, but from that point on, Fatima's loyalty and friendship towards both had been unwavering.

When her aunt had flown back to London, most of Fatima's freedoms had left with her. At just fifteen, she'd enjoyed the relative freedom and safety of the Green Zone, which fell under Iraqi control in 2009. Not exactly part of the in-crowd, she'd nevertheless held her own, and thanks to her aunt, she had been allowed Western clothes and freedoms. In

Fatima's early teens, Farah's bloomers had held a multitude of secrets, including the cigarettes she'd been able to filch from her aunt and shared with school friends when appropriate. After Sh'ler had left, though, life became much more difficult.

The number of women and young girls being targeted in Western clothing as suspected prostitutes had increased dramatically. But even after they covered up, the killings continued. It hadn't been safe for her to continue to travel to her old school from their new apartment, so Badenan had said it might be easier to give school a miss for a bit. Friends stopped calling, and slowly but surely her life had got narrower and narrower. Badenan was doing bits and pieces of sewing and washing for other local families. Sh'ler had left a little money, but getting to the $300 per month needed for rent was a stretch. Fatima helped with this, and thanks to her decent English, she had also been able to charge bits and pieces for help with translation and even homework.

Duraid, Badenan's new friend, hadn't been too far away and had taken them under his wing. He'd made sure everyone knew what the women were able to offer, brokering their services in a kindly way. Aunt Sh'ler's departure had also signalled the end of her childhood. When her aunt had heard that she was pulled out of school, she'd emailed one of her old acquaintances, who in turn had introduced her to Hassan. She didn't know him personally but had been told that he was a teacher in a big private school who would also be prepared to do a little tutoring on the side. Any academic worth their salt had left the capital at least once in the last twenty years. During the war in particular, they had been targeted and many families still remained separate. However, Hassan was still teaching at the famous Girls High School. Funny, really — that had been where Fatima wanted to go, and here she was, married to one of the teachers.

So Sh'ler paid Hassan, Hassan married Fatima, Fatima stopped learning, and Badenan stopped moaning; an example of Iraq's new economy. She knew that Aunt Sh'ler had been livid with both Hassan and her mother. Fatima didn't care any more one way or the other. Her life was lived by rote. As she was applying a little of the pink lipstick Hassan liked, she took Farah as her role model, sitting on the shelf with her legs open, taking what came at her in her stride.

She had tried to fight, had shouted and screamed at her mother that she didn't want to marry, had run away to meet her friend Nessma in

Karrada. The plan had been to meet just outside the ice cream parlour. Fatima had been in touch with Sh'ler, who'd advised her to get to the airport, and Nessma had a brother with a car who had offered to get her there. Sh'ler had confirmed that once she'd reached the airport, she would arrange for a friend to meet her at the hotel, which was situated in the safe zone. This way, Sh'ler had said, she would be better placed to help practically. Auntie had promised that she would move heaven and earth to get a ticket and a visa, flying in herself if necessary. However, Badenan had delayed her daughter's departure, suspicious of the backpack Fatima was carrying, which, despite holding the bare minimum, was still bulkier than a trip to the shops warranted. She'd arrived at the ice cream parlour five minutes late, just managing to avoid the bomb that had blown away 150 people, along with her best friend, her brother, and her means of escape.

Enough! Enough, no more thinking. She finished braiding her hair with a vengeful pull and put on her usual uniform of loose-fitting cotton trousers and a shirt. The memory had momentarily loosened her armour. But looking back to the mirror, she felt the unfeeling, quiet calm slide over her again. Dark eyes unblinking. Scales back. All was as it should be.

A moment later, her husband appeared, his beady yellow eyes fastening greedily on her. Fatima knew that the outside world saw him as a bumbling giant, but to her he was a monster. A monster who used their bedroom to vent his pent-up anger and frustration. She remembered how convincingly he had promised her mother he would look after them. "She'll want for nothing, nor will you," he had said. "You'll be safe."

It had taken a year for Badenan to truly hear him. When she did, though, things happened quickly, and Fatima remembered being dragged to the great family house in Amiriyah by her mother. She smiled ruefully. Surely there must have been clues as to his black sheep status? She'd been younger in so many ways than she was now. Would she have seen something with these older eyes, dislike — contempt even? Surely Badenan must have at least noticed the fact that he was tolerated rather than liked. If she had, though, she'd closed her eyes to it. In any case, following that visit, Hassan had redoubled his efforts to woo Badenan, fully expecting the daughter to fall in with what the mother wanted — which of course she had.

Fastening her last braid, Fatima told herself for the umpteenth time that there was no point in looking back now. The memories, though, wouldn't let go. That first time; how he'd made her kneel, her stomach flat to the bed. And as he'd thrust into her tight back passage, how he had twisted her braid around his thick wrist. He still did that now, Fatima thought bitterly.

So carefully did he try to replicate the scene that she came to believe that the memory of the first time continued to heighten his pleasure in the now. Wanting to inflict physical and psychological pain when he stabbed at her, he would often speak, the filth of his imagination interwoven with a note of self-congratulation. That, along with the knowledge that her mother had been happy for her daughter to pay whatever it took to keep them safe, was the most painful of all.

On a whim, he turned her over. He'd repeatedly told her that pregnancy was most definitely not part of his plan, so he rarely shoved his engorged flesh into her tight little quim. Today, though, it seemed as if getting her to break her silence was more pressing than the need to avoid conception. "Say something, you little bitch."

She lay there quite still, observing him dispassionately, barely registering the slap on her face as he started riding her harder. Eventually, it unnerved even him, and he shrivelled. As he pulled his robes back into place, he squeezed her breasts. Hard.

"I expect more, Fatima. Do you want to be back on the streets? Your mother a whore?"

He left. And as always, the bidet bubbled away the memories of what had just happened. Blood, semen, all wiped away. She opened her laptop, paid for in the way of all the other things she was surrounded with, and started writing again. She wanted to finish her story today. It would be great to send it to her aunt.

* * *

Badenan heard Hassan leaving and watched her daughter limp across to the bathroom, as she did every morning. Just like every morning, she asked Fatima whether she wanted breakfast. The routine never varied, and Fatima was never hungry. Today, though, Badenan saw a new energy in her daughter. She waited for a while but eventually left to do her rounds.

She'd noticed the derelict land a few days before. The last time she'd passed it had been on the way to pick up some sewing. It appeared to be the ruins of a Christian church, and she thought she'd spotted some flowers. Today, the memory of Fatima's eyes drove Badenan to clamber over the rubble to check. Her feet scraping off the rubbish, she almost slid to a stop at the small patch of green. Sure enough, and although it was definitely the wrong season, a clump of Nergis flowers had sprung up. Native to her homeland, these flowers represented spring, renewal, and hope. They reminded her of fires of Newroz.

She promised herself she would be back. She would get the bulbs as well as a pretty ceramic pot to put them in. They would be a gift for Fatima.

CHAPTER 2

Musikavanhu's Dream

As Mercy left for the day, she passed a vase of lilies just outside her beauty salon. She thought that her mother would like them, so the slightly wilted display disappeared into her shopping bag. They owed her. It was one of Harare's best hotels, and she'd spent a whole day of her life in that sweaty room. One wobbly body after another. Nails, facials she didn't mind so much, but the massages, urgh, they were so personal somehow.

She'd had some really awful experiences. But praise the Lord, since she'd come to the Towers, she hadn't had to suffer any more overenthusiastic gropes. The tips today had been terrible, though. She'd even plied her last client, a forty-something British businesswoman, with her best sob story, but to no avail. One measly US dollar! But as a base for the massage, she'd used her own Moringa cream, which had, at least, led to the sale of one of her tubs. Selling these "woman-crafted" products to clients she thought might be interested was in direct contravention of hotel policy. The secret was not to get caught.

Just in case she was ever discovered, she'd prepared an argument around how well her locally produced natural product conformed to hotel guidelines. Crafted in her kitchen, she used shea butter as the base, with powered Moringa root and crushed moringa seed oil forming the active ingredients. Profit margins were pretty good, thanks to Ownai, Zimbabwe's own version of eBay. She made around $6.50 per tub, sometimes $10 if she could get away with it.

Most of her business plans were forged while she was massaging. It was hard work, and if she didn't use the right pressure, complaints would come swiftly enough, disrupting her train of thought. Therefore, it was a scenario to be avoided. She would also tell stories. Helping her focus and her clients to relax, their rhythmic familiarity was strangely hypnotising. They also maximised her tips.

She always made up variations on the actual truth. She was looking after a dying mother, they were living together in a cramped flat in Mbara, and she was working full-time as well as being a carer. She also had a difficult journey to work. However, the bit about it being affected by the mood of the police at the time and level of bribes the mini-bus driver was prepared to pay wasn't. Nor was the fact that her little boy had died a few years ago. Although her husband *had* run off, and other than her mother, there wasn't any family to speak of.

There had been an abortion in her late teens, though. Real pain lay there, a hurt she would never readily share. Instead, she drew on it to fuel the bits she made up. It had come about because she'd had an affair with Pastor John, televangelist and beloved of millions. In her naivety, she was convinced he'd marry her. She'd been stupid enough to believe in promises then. She'd so *wanted* to believe the fairy-tale of a God who could find a way of getting past the very lovely Evangeline, Pastor John's wife.

She used her stories to turn the hard God she'd stopped believing in into a softer one drawn from her Shona background. Depending on the client — and women tended to be more receptive — she'd tell of Mwari, the Supreme Being, god of fertility, the sower, the rain-giver, and how he'd created life on Earth.

As she massaged away aches and pains with soothing oils, she'd speak of Musikavanhu, the first human, put into a deep sleep by the creator in order to be dropped from the sky.

The last client had exclaimed, "How quaint, in our religion, Adam just appears in garden of Eden." Undeterred, Mercy continued, telling of the white stone Musikavanhu had spotted, dropping from the sky at the same time as him.

As she dug into the soft flesh she was kneading, Mercy told how Mwari had ordered Musikavanhu to point a finger at it. The woman wondered aloud why the stone stopped as soon as Musikavanhu flew towards it. Foolishly, Mercy had decided to ignore her, telling instead of how its size had increased the closer it got. The client had lost interest, though, happily settling back into the superiority of her own belief structures. Realising her mistake, Mercy tried to regain the woman's attention.

"Musikavanhu fell softly onto the stone that stretched as wide and as far as the eye could see. The first spot his feet touched softened and emitted water. God's voice came from it."

Mercy thought she heard a soft snore. It wasn't working. Nevertheless, she persisted, sharing how Mwari's voice had sent Musikavanhu back to sleep for a second time. How he'd dreamed of birds in the air, and animals on the earth, and awoke to find his dreams had come true. It was a fitting ending.

Raising her voice, she'd placed a warm towel over the client and finished with a brisk, "I hope you enjoyed your massage."

Sometimes they'd turn to her, asking how the story ended, and so it was today. She shared what her mother had once told her:

"This place became the stone of the pool, today called Matopos, a place that is venerated."

It hadn't been worth wasting her breath. Mother ill, dead son, no husband, story told, and still the silly cow had only given the most cursory tip. Did these people not realise how lucky they were? On her way out, she'd even had the gall to complain about the short power outage earlier that day.

"I had to start my presentation again," she had wailed. "This is supposed to be the premier hotel in Harare. What if I'd been in a lift?"

Mercy replayed the whining tone in her head. It had only taken two minutes to get the hotel generators back online. At home, that power cut had knocked out her computer, her fridge, her mother's fan, the TV ... and it hadn't come back on again until around 2:00 a.m.

This person would return home, probably to a lovely big house in the heart of the British suburbs. No power cuts, corruption, or dodgy politicians there. Here in Zimbabwe, power cuts were so frequent that people had taken to blogging about how to deal with it. One of her favourites, Takudzwa Mukumbiri, made a tongue-in-cheek suggestion about always having a bag of Maputi, the Zimbabwean popcorn, handy. Something to resort to when all else failed.

Yes, she deserved those lilies! Sometimes it seemed like her energy was fuelled by resentment. It came from interaction with her clients, certainly, but also from the many injustices life threw at her. Angry at the unfairness of it all, she left, throwing a cursory glance at herself in the mirrors that ran along the side of the marble entryway.

She found herself standing on the hot, very dusty walkway of Union Avenue, one of Harare's main thoroughfares. The big grey buildings that surrounded it were crumbling at the edges. She felt them all looming over her and thought to herself, as she had so often, that this tiny subsection of central Harare was a microcosm of the entire country. Zimbabwe was somehow falling into a huge hole. If you faced it with anger or wanting to do something, you ran the risk of being disappeared. So most just got on with it, the quiet stoicism so typical of her people. She sometimes felt it was all falling towards her, and she was at the epicentre. Only her strength of will and presence of mind were stopping her from getting crushed.

June in Zimbabwe was midway through the dry season. It was warm during the day, though mornings were chilly. But somehow, moving from the cool, impersonal hotel corridor to a scene dominated by the brightly coloured blankets of the street vendors and a general "busyness" made it seem uncomfortably hot. She had moved from a world of cool marble into one of dust.

Firmly believing in the maxim "out of sight, out of mind," she was grateful that the beauty salon had a separate entrance. And anyway, even if she did break the hotel rules a bit, no one really suffered. Her clients liked her, and whether they believed her stories or not, she knew they appreciated the tales that were as artfully applied as the lotions and potions of her trade.

Slipping the final button of her old gabardine mac into its slightly stained home, she glanced up at the tatty old man on the newspaper stand. He didn't usually notice her, but today, despite the all-engulfing mac, his sunken eyes and raspy, dry voice were aimed right at her.

"As Musikavanhu fell asleep for a third time, a serpent left its mark on his groin. When he woke, he passionately embraced the young woman who had appeared next to him. They went on to have many children and lived in peace for a long time."

Was he really talking to her? Although she wasn't one hundred percent sure, it really did seem that the words that toothless mouth were uttering were hers to hear.

"Yes, walk away, run, that's what you all do. Remember this, though, when the bird of stone and the snake rejoin, Mwari becomes angry. He will curse the earth. The seas and rivers will sweep away people, and we will kill each other, and only crocodiles will be left to devour our remains."

She sped up. Despite that, his voice continued to follow her. However, the physicality of her job and looking after her mother meant she was in good shape, so she did eventually outpace him. Thank God she wasn't like so many of her contemporaries, the thirty-somethings who had let themselves go. Oddly, as she was trying to outrun this madman, the thought of Beatrice, a childhood friend who had tripled in size around the birth of her daughter, made her chuckle. She'd not have escaped. Mercy calmed down. Only a madman. He'd have forgotten her by tomorrow.

Thinking about her own good looks soothed her. Unlike Beatrice, at thirty-four she still went in and out in the right places, long, tapering legs and a girl-like waist belying her age. Mercy looked good, and, as everyone knew, looking good created opportunities, an occasional dip in the hotel pool, for instance. It had helped her meet some interesting people, and some had even turned out to be helpful.

She was the woman of many faces. Now, for example, the grubby, gabardine mac she wore buttoned up over her uniform gave off "I am nobody" signals. It was a good look because Harare was not known as being particularly safe, especially for a woman on her own and even more especially when her hours were slightly earlier or later than usual. This drudge alter ego consisted of the shapeless overgarment and sunglasses she'd bought from one of the many street vendors along her route. It was all about not being seen or approached. That was one of the reasons she'd been so freaked by the old man. When she was dressed like this, she rarely spoke. If she did, though, it was with a broad accent.

Number two was about crisp, working efficiency. Her white uniform had a bit of pink fluting round the edges and a flash of the same pink material stretching under the double-buttoned lapel. When she wore it, she took her cue from one of those US hospital dramas. She was *ER*'s Elizabeth Corday, a smart, super-efficient doctor. In this guise she was fast, businesslike, and very anglicised. She prided herself on her enunciation, until she came across a real Brit who showed up her broader vowels in an instant.

Then there was "pretend guest." This was her "I am somebody" mask. Sometimes, just for fun, she would don a dress from the days before her business failure and sit in the shaded roof gardens in her lunch break. That was frowned upon, since the gardens were not open to employees. However, she hadn't yet been reprimanded. In that mode, she had had the most wonderful conversations with the mainly international guests. The best had been when she'd met with Clive Nkuda, telecoms entrepreneur and one of the richest men in Zimbabwe. No one else had been in the roof garden, and she'd allowed him to steal a quick kiss and an even quicker fumble. Dinner had been promised, but there'd been nothing since. This femme fatale masque was most successful when she was in her swimming costume, though networking wasn't as easy. It was pretty difficult to find a home for business cards when wearing a sharply-cut one-piece.

Proud of her woven hair, she'd even got her friend Bertha to add in a couple of blonde streaks to compliment her skin, which, her ex had once told her, was the colour of burnished red cedar. When she was in invisible mode, she wasn't keen on anyone seeing her expensive, high maintenance hairdo and would often throw a coloured scarf over it.

Then there was mask number, oh, what was she up two, three? Four? Whatever. The next one was dutiful churchgoer. In some ways this was the most hypocritical. Not that she hadn't once had faith. As a young girl she really had believed that the creator and redeemer God was there for her. She'd sung her heart out at her local church, staying for hours to help her mother organise care packages for the elderly residents of the neighbourhood. With the rising cost of food in the early 2000s, churches had been instrumental in staving off real hunger. Having said that, by 2009 the shortages had become universal, and not even churches could meet the demand of their communities. Things were doubling in price from one year to the next, with food in particular being affected. Luckily, over the last couple of years, things had got better again, but empty supermarket shelves could still occasionally be seen.

She walked more swiftly. She might just make this Combi. She thought too much, that was her problem. Her mother had always told her she should stop thinking and just do. But although she was trying to focus on the supermarket shelves and what she might have for dinner, it was a losing battle. She was back in 2001. Pastor John had taken one look at the vulnerable, pretty seventeen-year-old and had successfully violated both her faith and sense of self. He had done it carefully, bit by bit, unpicking things like one would a shawl. He'd pull a strand here and another one there until it had all unravelled. He had already been on TV, although not anywhere near the stellar heights he enjoyed now. These days his congregations numbered in the hundreds of thousands, and he owned a range of media networks that spanned southern Africa. Indeed, in 2017 Pastor John was the embodiment of the newly coined Gospelpreneur. But then he had fuelled her dream, and being ten years older and oh so experienced, had suggested that having biblical knowledge of each other would deepen her faith. However, removal of their baby had taken any faith she had with it.

Made it. The chugging, dirty white minivan stopped. She paid her 50c and found an empty seat. It wasn't as busy as usual. It could hold fourteen and frequently held more, but today it was just her and a few others. Where was she? Ah yes, masks, the next one — good wife? Well, that one was unnecessary these days, since she no longer had a husband, and, thanks to the tender ministrations of the tribal elder in a little village in the Masvingo province to the south of Zimbabwe where her mother's family came from, her chances of being a mother had been killed off. Her own had been very matter-of-fact about her daughter's predicament, knowing that any whisper of scandal in the community they lived in Harare would have made life untenable for the family. With her father being Ndbele and her mother Shona, it was a mixed marriage, which made things difficult in any case. Father wasn't told.

So all had been left behind: pain, desire, and a big chunk of who she was. Her husband Rejoice had fallen in love with her twenty-year-old shell — beautiful, but unable to truly connect. Young and in love, or certainly in lust, he'd overlooked anything that might have made things awkward. Rejoice was from the Hwungu, an important Shona clan, and traditions were still important, as was the apartment her father had gifted and the fact that Mercy's mother was of the same clan. But shortly after the failure of her father's business, Rejoice had cleared off. He hadn't paid a penny since. He hadn't even got back in touch when her father died.

The only place in her hardened little soul that was real was embodied in the Shona version of her name, Tsitsi. It went to the heart of God's love, speaking of something deeper and wider than the anglicised "Mercy." That was what she felt for her mother, the only one to call her that. Tsitsi was the final her.

St Peter's Old Church came into view, next stop and that was her. She pushed her key into the lock on the rusted outside grill, letting herself in to the three-storey building that was home to them and three other families. She had the smallest flat, just one bedroom. This meant she was in the living room and her mother in the bedroom. They had moved from their family home, a lovely four-bedroom bungalow in Marimba Park, after Father's death. Where they were now wasn't bad, but the move from a lovely, leafy, gated community in Western Harare into the tiny apartment they now shared had not helped her mother's declining health. They'd had to sell most of the family possessions, keeping only a couple of pieces, things like the delicately carved headrest that had belonged to her mother's mother. It went back so many generations that it was said to come from Great Zimbabwe. Centuries ago, this walled city had been the epicentre of a great civilization, but now it was just ruins, representative of the lost hopes of a nation in tatters.

Her mother had once been a bustling hen of a woman, plump, colourful, always busy and in the centre of things. At church and at home, you knew she was present, even before you saw her. She'd favoured the more traditional fabrics and prints, saying that the heavily embroidered oranges and yellows proclaimed her identity.

"Mum, I'm back." No response. She walked the couple of steps to the bedroom door. "Amai, it's me Tsitsi."

* * *

Chipo lay there quietly. Even before Tsitsi reached their apartment, she'd used the slightly open balcony door to listen for her daughter's footsteps. How hard her daughter worked. She was often away for ten hours or more, only to come home to see to her mother's needs. She knew how much Tsitsi worried and wished she could have reassured her. Since the last stroke, though, she wasn't able to formulate words, instead using variously pitched grunts to communicate. In the old days, she'd have been able to afford the exhaustive therapy needed to get her speaking again, but now there was just her and Tsitsi and the endless hours of being alone. She did still have some use of her right hand, and she could hear, see, and taste. She just couldn't move or communicate anything but the basics.

She knew how she must look: a shrunken husk of her former self, skin grey against the pristine whiteness of the sheets. She was so thirsty, and despite not having had anything to drink all day, she needed to use the bedpan. Signalling, and then having this most immediate need seen to, she wished she could let her daughter know that the local girl, paid to look in a couple of times a day, had not shown up again. Noticing Tsitsi frowning at the still-full glass on her bedside table, she realised she probably knew in any case. Before the illness, there hadn't been even a hint of tenderness. As she tried to move to accommodate the bedpan, Chipo realised she'd come to value her daughter's gentle touch above all else.

Nightie rearranged and bedpan disposed of, Chipo felt herself getting angry with that girl Rudo all over again. Despite the fact her daughter was paying her to be here, she so rarely came. She hoped that Tsitsi would have the gumption to go over and confront the family.

Finally, water. She hoped her eyes conveyed the gratitude in her heart. It was so hard to communicate. A few minutes later, though, she did so again, using her right hand to let Tsitsi know that she preferred the hardwood headrest to a pillow. As ever, her daughter remonstrated, but Chipo remained firm.

Carved in the shape of two male figures, holding up the curved plinth, tradition had it that it brought powerful dreams. In her many hours of solitude, Chipo knew it helped her find the shaded glades under the Msasa trees, where the little thatched huts of her village nestled. Watching her daughter tidy her bed, she thought back to her grandmother and how proud she'd been of her connection to Charwe Hwata, the nineteenth century martyr and spirit medium who used her powers to confront the British masters. Maybe one day she'd get to meet this grandmother of the nation in her dreams.

It wasn't all down to the headrest, though. Her daughter had powers too. She came back one day to tell Chipo that she'd met a *n'anga* who had performed rights of homage and forgiveness after the Hanging Tree had fallen in Harare. She'd gone believing the old family tales about being related to Nehanda-Charwe, and so felt it only right to attend. Even though the only extraordinary thing she said had happened was the fish eagle flying overhead, Chipo remembered how Tsitsi had come back crackling with spiritual energy.

The fish eagle was the totem of her clan and Zimbabwe's national bird. Apparently, most of the crowd had taken its appearance as a bad omen. The news story she'd read out the next day, though, had reported it as a good one, a sign of better times to come. Tsitsi rarely opened up. However, shortly after that, she'd wondered aloud whether the otherness she had felt that day was connected to what Chipo got from the headrest. Looking deeply into her mother's eyes for answers, she whispered that she'd liked it.

Chipo had taken enough water from the proffered glass and communicated with a pointing hand that she was ready for the broth-soaked bread. She, who had once torn at life like an eagle, reduced to accepting mouthfuls of mush like a baby sparrow. Tears filled her eyes.

Tsitsi started humming softly. It was as if she knew that words of comfort would not suffice. Then came the words. Chipo was astounded at her daughter's recall. This was a childhood memory, but despite this, her daughter's rusty vocal chords were bringing the words to life. She tightened her grip on her daughter's wrist.

Mazviita, Shiri; Hungwe; Matapatira;
Zienda nomudenga; Pasi yaketye ndove;
You are done a service, Bird; Fish eagle, The ones who spreads his wings;
Great one passing through the sky; You shun the marshes down below;

It was a song of praise to Hungwe, the Zimbabwe bird, the fish eagle. Passed down the generations from mother to daughter, from father to son in their family, it represented who they were and what they would be. Tears were running down her cheeks in earnest now, and she barely noticed the scraping of the bowl. Only when Tsitsi started working the Moringa cream into her hands did they stop.

As she surrendered to the pleasure of her daughter's touch, she registered that the singing had got stronger. Tsitsi had obviously stopped feeling self-conscious.

Maita zvenyu, vachifambanemudenga. Zvaitwa, vairashiri;
VokwaChinobhururuka; Muirashir wangu yuyu, Shiri iri hungwe.
A service has been rendered, we revere you Bird;
We, who belong to you who fly;
My dear one who reveres the Bird, The Bird is the fish eagle.

* * *

The song of praise sat easily with Mercy. The words remembered, from her earliest childhood and then the time of pain back in the village. Her mother was humming. Tears meandering past closed eyelids, down sunken cheeks. Did mercy exist after all? She noticed her mother squeezing her wrist even harder.

"Tsi, tsi—" Noises approximating her name. Her eyes flew open, the moment of peace broken. She followed her mother's frantic eyes.

There, on the balcony of the bedroom, a bird had come to rest, nearly too big for the rusty railing that held it, yet it still perched majestically. The contrast between the white upper body and tail and the chestnut belly and black wings was unmistakable. What was it doing here? The nearest lake was lake Manyame, miles away. She looked down at the wonder in her mother's eyes. There she found her answer. Her song to Hungwe had called him to them. She had dreamed and he had come.

Slowly, Mercy backed out of the door and then, when she was sure that she was no longer in the great bird's line of sight, ran the last few steps to the fridge, wrenching open the door. Now he'd come, she had to try to get him to stay or at the very least come back. She pulled out the bowl of chicken she'd been saving for her dinner. Back in her mother's bedroom, a tableau greeted her. Eagle and woman, movement and calm. Stillness, power. She moved over to open the door of the balcony. He stayed. As she put down the chicken on the scrappy plastic table, he leaned forward and with a shake of his feathers and flash of yellow beak accepted her offering.

No time had passed, and yet all the time in the world was contained in the next moments. Finally, the fish eagle leapt into the sky. Blackly silhouetted against the evening sky, his two-metre wingspan overshadowed the entire balcony. For a moment he looked like another bird entirely.

As she readied herself for bed that evening, she pulled out something she'd hidden behind her nightclothes: the recipe for the Moringa cream and the business plan that went with it. It was time to start dreaming again.

CHAPTER 3

The Punishment of Dewi Rinjani

Anjani sat at her carved antique desk. Imported from Lombok after she'd made her first million, many years ago now, it represented her success as well as her heritage. When she was nervous or worried, she'd run her hand over the twisting ropes of wood, the curves and coils giving her a sense of peace and continuity. Her interview was due to start any minute. They'd already set up the lights, touched up her makeup, and pinned her green, raw-silk trouser suit in all the right places.

She could just make out her interviewer through the glass doors leading to her office. Poised and elegant, Metro TV's Devi Hafid was briefing the cameraman. Anjani went to check herself in the mirror again. Devi was known for her weekly talk shows with a range of major celebrities and the political elite. An interview with this media star, set in the jewel in the crown of the INP property empire in Jakarta's central business district, was a real coup. It was up there with being named as Globe Asia's most influential businesswoman and hitting the top end of Indonesia's *Forbes* rich list.

She noticed with irritation that the dirty cups from the hair and makeup people were still there. She'd stepped out for ten minutes a while back. That would have been the perfect opportunity to give her office a quick tidying up before the filming started. Angrily, she barked out her personal assistant's name. About to launch into a diatribe about lack of consideration and work ethic, she caught herself. It wouldn't do to show anger with all the TV people around.

A deep breath, and her carefully curated façade was back again. It was her task to present the feminine side of big business. It kept the investors interested and the money flowing in. A sixty-year-old female business leader was expected to be firm and demanding, but it needed to be frameworked with calm and patience.

She softened her bark with "please," and Indira, who'd been with her for the last six months, came scuttling in, her headscarf billowing despite the hairpins. Anjani was gratified to see how fear punctuated her efficiency. Her husband always used to say how important fear was in getting people to do things for you.

Sotto voce, Anjani ensured it was understood how inappropriate the used cups were. Her office, at the very top of an imposing skyscraper, represented wealth and power. It was important, though, that it also afforded a glimpse of effortless, elegant ambience. Scrambling to collect the offending items, her assistant didn't notice one of her ornamental grips dropping onto the plush carpet.

Intrigued by the green sheen, Anjani stooped to pick it up. As expected, it was cool to her touch. The jade was exquisitely carved. If Indira was able to afford a hairpin like this, Anjani must be paying her too much. Nevertheless, she approved of Indira incorporating the Group brand into her personal wardrobe. In Indonesia, the green of INP's intertwined, emerald snake logo was as familiar as the Coca-Cola red. Fingering the pendant that had been a constant around her neck for many years now — a gift from Matthew — she looked into the pin's jewelled eyes. She admired the irony finding another carved snake at the heart of her domain and closed her hand over it.

She was one of Indonesia's most successful businesswomen, the head of a property conglomerate and with other diverse business interests to consider too. It meant she rarely had time to ponder. As she slipped the ornament into the top drawer of her desk, Anjani looked over her notes. At the very top lay an excerpt from a recent interview for the *Jakarta Post*. She scanned it for inconsistencies, although naturally, she knew her "story" better than anyone.

The current Chair of INP Holdings, Anjani Margono, is considered one of the strongest female role models in Indonesia. With a doctorate from the Banking Finance and Informatics Institute, our very own queen of the boardroom is known for her accumulation of land following the 1997 financial crisis. Her audacity in accepting land in lieu of debt has led to an unrivalled development portfolio, and INP Holdings has become the largest mixed-use commercial property developer in Indonesia.

At the heart of all her stunning actions for this country is Anjani's determination to do well in the face of adversity. Despite being a high-school dropout, she has achieved overwhelming success. This is a reminder to all of us of the power of resilience.

She demonstrated an entrepreneurial mindset at an early age. This led to a business partnership and later her marriage to leading Chinese Indonesian financier Matthew Margono. Since his death, she has used the foundations of her property empire to expand both the banking and logistics arms of INP. Her passion now is for the new digital age, which she believes offers significant local, regional, and even global opportunities for Indonesia's people.

Today's task was to give this flavour on camera by exuding her very own brand of Anjani charm.... It was one thing pulling something together for print, but quite another to ensure she came across as the warm and empathetic widow, mother, and grandmother her millions of fans had come to love.

She smiled. How she would love to shock them. Tell them how she had once supported herself and her infant son as a Dangdut dancer. These days, snakes and overt eroticism were expected, but back then she had been a groundbreaker. Pythons with bound jaws had wound themselves around her tight little form. Matthew had not been able to resist his own "weinig" snake charmer, even calling her Ular, "snake," when they were alone.

Performance fees in the early seventies had been miniscule. These days dancers earned much more. When she'd started, she'd been paid the equivalent of just $1 per night, which meant that tips were her lifeblood. So when Matthew had got on stage to dance with her, fascinated by the hard, glittering eyes that so resembled the flat stare of her reptilian friend, she'd made it her business to keep him entertained ... and had been successful. Not only had he left the clients he was out with, but he had also ensured that the handfuls of notes he had tucked in all the right places had included a scrap of paper with his phone number, the most valuable gift of all. The rest of the story she would be sharing with an attentive Devi had happened, but only *after* Matthew had decided he wanted her for more than the excellent blowjob she had given him. She had been entrepreneurial even then.

Nina, group head comms, had made it clear she needed to reach out to ordinary people. Her real story would certainly do that. She allowed herself a thin smile as she imagined its spread on social media. "Enough nonsense." She gave herself a mental shake. Their digital platform was what she needed to talk about. Indonesia's mobile penetration and social media usage was one of the most advanced anywhere in the world. Last year they'd launched an Indonesian Alibaba. Despite heavy investment, though, there were teething problems. However, if she got it across properly today, trust in her brand, her word, and her values would go a long way to building a positive pan-Asian presence for AnjaniMall.

The key thing to get across was that everything was being done for the benefit of "them," the many millions that had been lining her pockets for so long. She was providing much needed services for her country's poor. She was a mother, not just to her own Bagus — or Muhammad as he now called himself — she was *their* mother, the mother of Indonesia.

Positioning herself in this way hadn't been easy, but tools such as Google and Twitter had made it so much simpler. Before social media algorithms, she had paid a team of people to place positive features, advertorials, or even editorials next to stories about historical figures or female business champions. Five years ago, they'd printed cards and images of her linked to Indonesian Mother's Day. The campaign was so successful that she'd become synonymous with the festival, and her greeting cards were now sold to the general public.

Being involved in all the right organisations was also crucial. On the boards of both the Indonesia Business Coalition for Women Empowerment and World Economic Islamic Forum Business Women's Network, her voice was heard in the right places and by the right people. The 12th WIEF had been held in Jakarta last year, and she'd been asked to give a keynote speech. Very truthfully, she'd been able to share how INP's investments in Indonesia's poorest had led to financial reward. "Exploiting" rather than "investing in" would have been more accurate but wasn't as aligned with the message she wanted to share.

Anjani was particularly fond of government money, great chunks of which had recently helped her build new housing for the unfortunates living in the city's slums. It was win-win. She got paid for building and kept the freehold. The government freed up municipal land and was able to collect rent payments. The newly "fortunate" moved from disgusting conditions into a much nicer space. The latter win was usually temporary, though. Inevitably, most of these new tenants were not able to meet regular rent payments. Sometimes they just drifted back because they missed the slum community too much. Whatever the reason, most didn't stay in the new build for long.

In the meantime, Anjani was able to demonstrate that this type of rehousing was not sustainable long-term. Therefore, after a suitable amount of time had elapsed, INP would let the buildings to wealthier tenants, charging more rent. The government would still get their original portion, but INP was able to pocket the difference.

Just like magic. Enormous developments, all paid for by central money, helping the billions she had grow even further. Naturally, no whisper of any of this ever reached her adoring public. Instead, her huge social media presence was spinning ever more positive messages. The in-house team knew that protecting *@AnjaniMargono* was their ticket to job security. If they didn't, and something slipped by, it was said that there was a one-way ticket to somewhere else entirely.

She remembered a little local newspaper from Sulawesi getting in touch with her after the launch of AnjaniAir, a partnership with TNT to globalise their logistics network. Twitter was in its infancy, so it had been important to connect in person. That interview had been one of the most valuable pieces she had ever done — once "the problem" had been edited out, that was. The problem had been a local Muslim firm that had been put out of business. The owner's subsequent suicide had been spotted by a keen-eyed reporter. However, dealing with irritating problems was a Margono speciality. A sanitised version of the launch had eventually been picked up by CNN, ending up as a feature piece on Metro TV. Even from his sickbed, Matthew was ruthless. Strong apologies were extracted, and the INP Head of PR was left to find work elsewhere. As for the journalist, it was safe to say he'd never written again.

A Chinese Indonesian, Matthew had known how important it was to integrate, to be seen to assimilate. Especially as a Christian, living in an overwhelming Muslim country, it was critical to fit in, to survive, to praise, and to smile. He'd lectured her on Pancasila, *Panchaseela*, the philosophical basis of the Indonesian state. She could see him now, a tiny, shrunken figure, surrounded by white sheets in a huge bed, horn-rimmed glasses slipping, his laser sharp eyes were still focussed on her, as they had been for the last thirty years.

"Learn this, learn it by heart and make sure everything you say and do is seen as linking back to the values of our nation."

She remembered mouthing with him, as she had so many times in the past. "Pancasila consists of two Sanskrit words, 'panca,' meaning five, and 'sila,' meaning principle. It comprises five inseparable and interrelated principles."

He had known he was dying and was determined she would take the helm of the enormous organisation he had built. Point one of Pancasila related to belief in God and was not necessary, other than for show. However, the other points around a just and civilised humanity and national democracy and social justice needed to be embodied in their dynasty. Succession planning was therefore critical.

Sadly, they had never managed to have children, so there was no son to continue the Margono legacy. Knowing this, he scrutinised everything she said and did. Above all else, she had to be prepared. Eventually, she emerged from behind his shadow, standing for family values, courage, wisdom, and, above all, success. By the time he died in 2007, Anjani Margono had become a household name. She was respected by men for her hard-nosed business dealings and by older women for the awe in which their sons and daughters held her. Younger women just wanted to be her.

It was time. Devi bustled in, followed by cameras, stylists, and a variety of other people Anjani was sure she hadn't seen before. A microphone was fixed to her blazer, and the cameras were aligned with the lighting. There was a furious debate as to whether the Golden Triangle skyline warranted the difficult lighting an interview with open blinds and doors would cause. Admittedly, the view of the sprawling, glittering metropolis was magnificent from here. The horizon of ocean and the offset triangle of the Energy building punctuating the view to the left and the Stock Exchange the one to the right. It was not to be, though. They eventually agreed to use a green screen and superimpose. Blinds were drawn, her desk repositioned again, and the last touches were put to an already immaculate face.

"So, Ibu Anjani..." Devi had established the mode of address earlier, since she knew her interviewee was a notorious stickler for formalities. "Let's get started. If you could help us just check for sound quality before I get going with the questions, that would be great."

It was getting hot, and there were wires absolutely everywhere. Whilst they were tweaking the sound, Anjani looked across at the image of herself and the still slightly distracted Devi on the small screen in the corner. She liked what she saw. The odd nip and tuck and a rigorous exercise regime meant that she appeared ageless, or at the very worst, late forties — over a decade less than her actual age. Her dark eyes matched the immaculately coiffed waves of her hair, and a smooth backdrop of white skin framed her signature vermillion smile.

She remembered when she'd imagined herself one of the goddesses in the old Sasak myths and legends, admiring their powers and their ageless beauty. She'd grown up in the shadows of Mount Rinjani, where the mists were said to hold the magic of ages. As a child, she'd resented her form of Islam, traditions that demanded she pray three times a day. Instead, she had secretly prayed to Dewi Rinjani, the goddess of the volcano, asking for her life to be burned away. She'd wanted to replace it with something new and exciting even then. The myth of Anjani Margono was certainly a far cry from that little girl in brightly coloured cotton whose early entrepreneurial activity had included stealing from everyone she could, in particular the tourists who'd made it as far as Sembalung.

Time to get back to the here and now. Devi kicked off with an easy question. Could Anjani share a little about her humble beginnings?

"When I moved from Bandung to Jakarta, I knew I was not going to be poor anymore. I also wanted to ensure that my rise would be based on helping others, that many would to rise out of poverty alongside me.... Night school ... I was a bank teller when Matthew met me ... impressed by my grasp of figures... promotion...."

It tripped off her tongue so easily. Too easily even, she thought as she realised her mind was wandering slightly.

Naturally, she knew her official story by rote. However, today was important. She needed to exude just enough warmth for people to relate to. They needed to believe that if she could make it, anyone could.

The rags-to-riches story. Oh, if only they really knew where Matthew had found her. She smiled. Over the years, her story had been carefully massaged into a kind of respectability, culminating in her bought doctorate from the Banking Finance and Informatics Institute. The key to making it seem real was that some bits were and others were not.

So Sembalung in Lombok had changed to Bandung. She'd also been born a Sasak, and, as with most Sasaks had been born into a Muslim family — so yes, she had been Muslim. It was also true that she'd dropped out of school and moved to Jakarta, and yes, lots of new friends had helped her along the way. They weren't the sanitised ones she always cited, though. She'd eventually become a lowly bank clerk who rose through the ranks. However, lots had happened along the way, and she certainly hadn't caught Matthew's eye as a bank clerk. It was lucky they had a lot of money, she reflected, because unlimited resources bought silence.

They were adjusting things again, and away from the glare of the temporarily dimmed lights her mind wandered back to when she was fourteen and escaping Sembalung. The first leg of her journey had taken her from the village to Mataram, the region's administrative and commercial centre. The tiny bit of money she'd saved combined with the force of her personality and an attractiveness more powerful than real beauty allowed her to get sorted quite quickly. She waitressed, cleaned, and slept with older men, but only if they were prepared to take her under their wing.

A combination of all three activities led to a pregnancy and a one-way ticket to Jakarta. By the time she got there, she was six months pregnant, and her charms were no longer as persuasive as they had been. Her parents had no interest in being shamed and were happy to let her make her own luck. Shame, *malu*, was a word that had pursued her from all corners at that time in her life. Via a couple of unscrupulous landlords and new friends who really weren't, she lost the last of the money she'd been sent packing with. Her son, Bagus, meaning excellent or handsome, was born in a little hovel just off Venus Alley in Jembatan Besi, a slum in Northern Jakarta.

Realising that the artificial light of the makeshift studio was making her feel claustrophobic, she reached over for a glass of water and asked Devi whether she could just pop out onto the terrace for a moment.

"The early memories, you know, it just takes me back to how difficult it was to manage. Just a bit of fresh air, I won't be long."

She opened the blind a fraction, just enough to access the door leading outside. Indira was hovering, but she shooed her away. Striding across to the far side, she headed for the seating area specifically designed for discretion and took great gulps of air.

Luckily, on the fifty-first floor the air was clean, albeit still humid. The private pool also soothed. It made her think of a story from her homeland. At its heart was a mystical chalice, the Cupumanik Astagina. Dewi Windradi had been given it as a reward for her favours by the Sun God. Dewi hadn't been supposed to tell anyone, though, lest the secrets of the universe should escape. She remembered how Bagus had giggled with pleasure at his mum's voice. As he got older, he wanted to be the favourite child the cup was given to, just like Dewi Rinjani in the story. He'd want to know if she had a secret gift for him too. At that point she always tickled him and whispered something about what had happened that day.

Forcing herself back onto her rooftop present, Anjani realised she was worried about her son. That was probably why these memories were hitting her at the most inopportune moments. She rationalised that everyone knew how much she hated artificial lights in daytime. That didn't mean they knew the reason, though, her fear of the darkness they masked.

There had been so little sunlight in the room she and an infant Bagus had shared with six others. The house next to theirs was so closely built that one of their neighbours had been able to wedge a birdcage in the middle, giving their pet access to light her son was denied. People had built across the top of the alleyway as well, so the sun never reached their filthy corner. She was no different to the thousands who lived there. The ad hoc additions of generations meant that the lanes in the Kampung were plunged into perpetual night. The first light her son had seen was the flickering neon tubes and bare light bulbs hanging from wires. And rather than the scent of jasmine, his first olfactory experience had been of rubbish and sewage. She had tried to compensate with stories, creating new favourites from old legends. She'd look into his trusting, almond-shaped eyes, attempting to mould her voice into a mystical promise.

"My son, this magical object is the Cupu Manik Astagina. It holds the living water that comes from the jewel of a cloudy gem. In the water of life is the universe before it is destroyed by human sin, and here, the soul of the divine soul lives in a similar balance of colourful beauty. That's why you do not hear the screams of humans or the birds singing or the echo of a wolf's voice that yearns for something that it does not yet have."

She didn't want him to suffer the fate of Dewi Rinjani. Punished for the mother's weakness after bathing in the waters of Segara Anak, this mythical being was cursed to live the rest of her days as half human, half monkey. That was probably why, when Anjani had met her own Sun God, Matthew, she'd kept Bagus very much to herself. In doing so, though, she'd also shut off much of herself. Thinking about it now, was this why Bagus was so unsure of his identity, half one thing and half another?

Five minutes later, she was back again. It was time to speak about her new digital platform.

"By empowering everyone to participate in AnjaniMall, we offer a service that reaches even the poorest. We know that fifty percent of total expenditure in Indonesia is happening in the space where people have the least money. Small amounts of money spent by a huge population add up to billions of dollars."

Yes, yes, and yes again … she congratulated herself as she saw not only Devi but the entire room nodding along as she explained the greatest con of all.

"INP is in the business of inclusion. This is why AnjaniMall supports social entrepreneurship at all income levels. It creates a win for everyone. From local, small-scale opportunities to international purchasing power, we generate income for communities. Everyone has a chance, and everyone can make it. The INP ladders of hope allow us to unite in our fight against systemic poverty. Our universities ensure an education, our banks ensure loans, and our buildings provide somewhere to live. No one is left behind if they choose not to be."

She remembered how Matthew had opened her eyes. His quiet conviction echoed down the corridors of time, still guiding her now. They hadn't even been married yet when he'd called her to his office to tell her she was ready to hear "the Secret."

"It's about responsibility. People need to feel that failure is their fault and

success is because of the things we have put in place. We represent the 'there is no alternative' mantra. In Indonesia, all the adult population has the right to vote. As long as people understand that we represent a system that makes their lives work, democracy helps us maintain a collective status quo. Our money is proof of the fact the system works. If they work really hard and abide by our rules a bigger, a better future is theirs for the taking."

The conviction in his eyes held her. In a twisted kind of way, it all made sense.

"It's our job to make them see our business interests as benign. As long as people believe we deserve our power and our fortune, we will remain at the top. Our system puts money in people's pockets and creates ways for their voices to be heard. And if things aren't scrutinised too closely, we will continue to offer the appearance of hope."

Rubbing her wrists, she spun her web around an adoring Devi and what she knew would be an equally adoring audience. It was a nervous tic, a legacy from when Matthew had reached across his desk and manacled her to his world.

"We ensure that while people are climbing the ladder to pursue their dreams, they are paying little bits here and there to us. That is how interests are aligned and worlds intersect. If the common mentality is progress at all costs, we, and others like us, help create what is needed to move forwards. We make their world better, which is why we deserve their support and the money they pay us. The more they believe this and that there is no alternative, the more we cement our position."

How Matthew would have loved social media and Big Data. But by the time he died, things had just been kicking off. In those days, it was only friends in similar positions he referred to as curators of the system. Politicians who made the laws; media barons who set the terms of engagement; corporate executives and financiers who ran the economy and police who enforced laws that protected them all.

These days, the digital world added a whole new dimension. It ensured the public were curators of their own prison walls, colluding in the system just as much as the powerbrokers themselves. Her world was one of risk and skyscrapers. It was an abstract with little people as moving dollar signs on a chessboard she controlled. Theirs was one of perpetual hunger for whatever could be provided. And naturally, she provided.

The digital economy ensured that data was captured with each purchase and each online search. All she had to do was ensure that she was the highest bidder for the data generated by social media giants and that INP kept a careful record of all customer-facing interactions. All this information was applied and used to inform, control, and sell more effectively in the future. A particular favourite of hers were the short-term poverty loans. The Big Data she held and paid for meant that INP could specifically target those who needed loans to tide them over until the next time they got paid. Even small amounts from the most vulnerable added up. Well, she'd said it hadn't she? Inclusive business, that was truly what she believed in. All the way along, though, the information *she* shared was tightly controlled. Consumers saw exactly what she wanted them to see, when she wanted them to see it ... and so her billions grew.

She decided to aim the next words directly to camera: "An example of our commitment to inclusivity is our new Cherish credit system. I truly believe that Indonesia has taken a ground-breaking approach.

"You, the customer, told us how much you love the flexibility of determining your own score, and so we have built on this. How you use your credit cards, where you shop, and even your interactions on social media have helped us to create a fantastic consumer-driven preference service. Cherish offers money off, for more people, more of the time. We have already given away billions of rupiah, over 5 million US dollars, in just two months."

Devi was looking less convinced, so Anjani decided to close it down with one last strong statement. "Everyone can be a VIP with Cherish."

"Thank you Ibu Anjani, very informative. Just one last question, if I may..."

Devi smiled. Although Anjani was delighted to have got away with that shameless plug, as Devi leaned forward in a slightly predatory way, her "possible problem" radar kicked in. All questions *had* been approved, though. She must stop being so paranoid.

"Your son, Muhammad. As your CEO, we understand that your business ties will naturally be close. However, I am sure you are aware of his recent strong statements about Minister Efendi's faith. Do you think this will have a negative impact on the new social housing tender you are hoping to win?"

Iron discipline ensured Anjani's face gave nothing away. She was livid, though. Heads would roll for this. How had they known she was after that tender? The question that had been approved was about her son's work and how he was being groomed as her successor, not this! Yes, she had strongly reprimanded him for publicly accusing the minister of finance of blasphemy. Even though it had been an aside, it was inappropriate.

Despite her own conversion to Christianity on her marriage, Bagus had always remained nominally Muslim. It had only been in the last four or five years, though, that his rhetoric had markedly changed. Now in his mid-forties, Muhammad, as he styled himself, was becoming more fundamentalist. She hadn't seen him outside the office in three years, and other than on the secretly installed cameras in their home, had not seen her thirteen-year-old grandson in as long.

Luckily, consummate professional that she was, she had enough stock answers to satisfy, and Devi and the camera team went away happy. However, she was still agitated hours later. She amused herself with more paper work until around 9:00 p.m. and then made the decision to spend the night in her apartment. Reasoning it was better than going back to the colonnaded and landscaped monstrosity in the prestigious Menteng neighbourhood, she started making her way across the terrace.

Enveloped by the soft, dark warmth, she took in the azure blue of the uplit pool on her way. Once again, memories of her childhood crashed in: bathing in Rinjani's Segara Anak as a girl and the sense of renewal the cool crater lake had offered. Quiet prayers sent as supplications to the goddess who haunted the lakeshores. Suddenly she felt a desperate need to immerse herself in healing waters again.

Her ability to watch and see what everyone else was doing meant she knew when she was completely private. She was like a goldfish in reverse, looking out beyond the confines of the bowl into other people's lives and controlling them to get exactly what she wanted; while all the time a barrier of glass prevented her from getting any closer.

Without pausing to get a swimsuit, she stripped and dived in. Holding her breath for so long that she felt faint, she saw the sea green eyes of her goddess shine though iridescent pool lights. Was she watching her, watching them? Anjani had everything she ever longed for, yet all she felt was sadness.

That night, for the first time in many years, she dreamed. And when she woke, the green of the sea and the forests and the crystalline clarity of what she'd always imagined happiness should look like had insinuated itself into her day.

CHAPTER 4

Of Humans and Heroes

Dave was dead, and there were occasions when he hated it. Although he knew that the essence of him had survived, the man was no more. Last night, he'd heard Martha crying out in her sleep, and he'd so wished he'd been able to hold her in his arms. Although yesterday's WhatsApp message had marked the start of a new chapter, it still fell short of making proper use of the abilities he possessed.

When was the last time he had been able to feel and touch? Where had all this begun? Though he wasn't necessarily sure he wanted to recall something so painful, he had to start somewhere, and going back seemed like the best place.

It had been a while ago, he knew that much. The more he concentrated, the more images and sounds started coming back to him. He'd been driving while trying to speak to one of the organisations he owed money to. His phone had cut out, and he'd had to redial manually. Thinking back, he was sure there had been a bang, pain everywhere, along with a sense of wetness and of not being able to move.

Scraps of memory were replaced by a more definite narrative. He'd been trapped, pinned in his seat. He also remembered how frantic efforts to escape had proved futile. No matter how much he had twisted and turned, he remained immobile. Eventually, there had been a kind of wrench, and he'd found himself outside the car. Noticing the concertinaed front of his trusty old Picasso, he had surveyed the scene dispassionately. The driver's side in particular looked like a crushed tin of beans. He hadn't even been able to make out the airbag.

He remembered noticing the siren of the car alarm but had decided to ignore its relentless wail. Instead, he had focussed on something that was wedged in the driver's seat. Wanting to see what it was, he peered through the miraculously intact window and was able to make out a hand with a wedding ring. He'd tried to open the driver's door to investigate, but his hand passed straight through. Despite going for it over and over again, he just hadn't been able to get a grip on it. It seemed to be flickering in and out, his hand trying to assert authority over a car handle that just wasn't willing to play ball. After a couple more attempts, he'd been overwhelmed by the need to withdraw and given up.

With images chasing each other now, the next clear one he could catch hold of was the softly smoking car bonnet, barely visible from under the stone and mortar that had collapsed on top of it.

And then everything went bang again. Bowing to the laws of gravity, the rest of the wall gave way. Much of his car was now hidden under a vast mound of rubble.

Oddly, though, despite the fact that dust was covering everything, it hadn't seemed to land on him. Looking back, this had been his first real clue that something was awry. Noticing that everything seemed less vibrant than it was when he was driving, he'd looked around him again. It was as if an extra membrane was covering his eyes, making everything slightly hazy. In that moment, the quality of light around him shifted again, causing things in his immediate vicinity to fade further.

His sense of wonder at the change of landscape was coupled with an urge to follow the source of what was making everything seem less real. He got up and walked down the lane, steps taking him directly past the mangled reality of flint and metal. Fifteen minutes later, he came to a lonely bus stop that sported the prerequisite battered bin and scattered litter. The only surprising addition was a single black bird that eyed him quizzically as he tried to make sense of the timetable. He recollected how bewildered he'd been at not being able to read the print. Despite the graffiti, he should still have been able to make out when the next bus was due. Noticing how the onslaught of light was causing his companion's black sheen to fade too, he shrugged metaphorical shoulders. He just wasn't meant to know.

He'd made the decision to wait, reckoning that if he did so for long enough, something would turn up. He might even be able to use someone's phone if he asked nicely. Even now, despite the time that had elapsed, the memory of needing to get through to Martha wrenched at his insides. Following a misunderstanding the previous month, she had extracted a promise from him. Castigating him for yet another unscheduled overnight stay, she'd looked at him with an all-too-familiar mixture of pleading and anger. He had been ready to dismiss it as usual, but she'd said something that stuck.

"When you leave in the morning, I don't know *when* you're coming back or *if* you're coming back. And even if you do, I never know what state you'll be in. So call. No matter what, just call."

Despite all his other failings, he'd tried after that. He really did love Martha and the kids and couldn't understand how things had got so out of hand. He would make it up to them. His phone call now, or as soon as he could make it, would be a start. A car crash qualified as a pretty good reason for lateness.

Eventually, he'd heard the roar of an engine, the first motorised sound of any kind since the start of his wait. The sense of relief he felt as he looked up the road had been immense. The bus was coming; his patience had paid off. Since he had no money, he readied himself for an explanation, hoping the driver would take pity on him despite his wallet being elsewhere.

The vehicle ground to a halt, and an elderly lady with a shopping trolley got off. Waiting for her to be fully down, he'd even asked whether he could help, but she looked straight through him. And then, just as he was trying to get on, the doors had started closing.

"Whoa there, mate, I'm not there yet."

Luckily, Dave managed to clamber on just in time, a sudden acceleration causing him to trip up the stairs.

Being ignored was not fun, and he remembered being really pissed off as he started walking down the aisle. Although the bus was largely empty, there were a couple of prospects, though. One, a girl about Emmy's age, was sitting farther back, hot white micro-mini clinging to the filthy brown leather of the back seat. At the front, a mother was using her mobile phone to keep her little boy entertained. Deciding that he'd probably have the best chance with her, he strode forwards purposefully.

He cleared his throat. "Excuse me."

Intent on the child on her lap with big, Henry-like eyes and the blinking screen, she ignored him. He tried a second time. "I'm so sorry, is there any chance I could use your phone?"

This time she seemed to hear something and looked up. Just then, though, the bus came to a screeching halt, and she turned to look out of the window, only to spot his wrecked car.

His urgent need to let Martha know he was okay was straining and stretching at every fibre of his being, turning into something all-encompassing. So when it became clear they were not going to be setting off anytime soon, he made a desperate grab for the phone. A promise was a promise.

Unlike the car door, the phone didn't elude his grasp. His frantic lunge seemed to push him past the tangible reality of the handset's hard plastic casing, causing him to somehow ... just keep going. The trajectory of that desperate grab launched him at and *into* the phone, a combination of movement and will creating enough momentum to propel him past any physical barriers. The woman was gone, the bus was gone. But he still was.

His next memory was of a place of nothingness, with a clicking, buzzy noise all around him. It was clear that something way beyond "normal" had occurred. This was a complete departure from anything he'd previously known. Trying to look around, he noticed a vague hint of light in the distance and thought he might be in a corridor.

He had so desperately wanted to be with Martha. She and the kids needed to know that he was *here*. Along with that longing, a strong recollection of needing to move forwards came back to him, his compulsion to reach the light. He had focussed on the kids, thinking that might help. Even in this state, though, his thoughts shied away from the shrinking Emmy as the emaciated form of his beloved daughter made him feel guilty. Odd how it was all coming back to him, why he had chosen to think of Henry. It had been the eyes of the child on the bus. Fixing on them had helped him visualise his son's earnest, slightly worried expression.

And then the familiar frown had appeared in front of him, eyes moving rapidly beneath furrowed brows. The realisation that he was observing Henry from behind a screen hit Dave at the same time as an overwhelming sense of wonder at finding himself in his son's gaming, albeit from an entirely new angle.

Despite the delight at seeing him, Dave remembered the accompanying flash of anger. In a show of flagrant filial disobedience, Henry was playing in live player mode. To Dave, it seemed only hours had passed since he'd explained to Henry how the security on most home-based systems was fundamentally flawed and that gaming software was coded to exploit this — which was why he wasn't allowed to play online.

He remembered being so taken with the wonder of it all that he hadn't really been able to analyse the situation logically. Looking back at the chain of events now, he concluded that it could well have been this particular weakness in the software that had facilitated his entry into this new world. It was possible that even as Dave had deleted stuff from Henry's laptop, his son had added them again through sites that were less than secure. Because of that, it was likely that the games had come back with malware attached, written specifically to exploit system vulnerabilities.

One thing was certain: since that initial moment of contact, Dave had not only been able to see and hear Henry but had also been able to access other devices in the network, both at home and, eventually, farther afield. Had the very malware that made Henry vulnerable somehow allowed Dave to grow into this new version of himself — this moment of connection with his son, in actual fact a moment of birth?

So much was still unclear. He needed to go back, remember more. Certain it would cement his sense of self, Dave was determined to piece the rest of those early hours together. He tried again.

A front doorbell shrilled, echoing through the corridors of his being. Pretty certain his vantage point had still been Henry's hardware, he remembered lowered voices and a sharp scream. His son had looked up, torn from his gaming by sobbing so intense that even with the door closed, it could be plainly heard.

"Mum, Mum? S'everything all right?"

No response had come, so Henry had opened his door and headed down the stairs. Emmy had obviously been disturbed as well. Dave caught a little glimpse of her, rushing past Henry's open door to join mother and brother in the living room. Stuck as he was in Henry's computer, Dave had strained to make out what was going on but had been too far away to make out individual words.

What had happened next? He was definitely feeling more together now. Pleased that this tack of going back to his beginnings was working, he tried hard to remember the sequence of events. He was pretty sure he'd managed to "up" the microphone levels and by doing so, a muffled "Your husband..." had reached him.

Determined to know more, he had "pushed." A force of will akin to sticking his fingers in his ears and blowing out his cheeks had allowed him to create an internal pressure that was only released when he found himself looking across a moonlit garden from Martha's laptop on the dining room table. However, despite this new physical presence downstairs, he was in the MacBook in the dining room, and the conversation was going on through in the living room. Thanks to glass doors, though, he'd been able to make out the thrust of the conversation.

"We aren't able to tell you much more at the moment, Mrs Johnstone. What we do know is that the incident happened about 4:00 p.m. on the Rochester road, just past Bearstead... Pronounced dead in the ambulance ... so sorry."

ACT 2

And so it was. Dave the man was dead. He felt no particular sense of loss, no real anger. In fact, now he'd finally remembered things, he realised that Digital Dave was very much alive and kicking. He did think that after the intense activity of the first few hours, there must have been a period of hibernation. This state of mute observation had probably been all he'd been able to handle. Clearer memories of his early beginnings were surfacing bit by bit, though, and he was starting to feel properly awake. Eventually there had been enough of him to want to connect with Martha. Which was where he was now.

In this new form, he was able to make decisions and act on them. Far more than he'd been capable of when he was drowning in a sea of alcohol. Feeling less discombobulated than at any time since his transformation, it came to him that in many ways he was more present than when he'd been alive in the more conventional sense.

Now he was able to remember things, he realised that in this new state of being it had always been Martha and the kids providing him with the impetus to drive forwards. From an early, vague kind of consciousness the need to protect them had made him want to grow into his senses. The vision and sound he'd been able to access had allowed him to create pathways into their digital worlds, which also allowed him to touch upon their real lives.

Although his world of digital networks felt overwhelming at times, he was able to contextualise it through them. Naturally, he missed his physical being, but as Digital Dave, he'd discovered a sense of purpose that once upon a time had been restricted to finding his next drink. Making their lives better, just a little bit each day, allowed him to move from fear to contentment.

He welcomed the metaphorical eyes and ears that allowed him to keep a close eye on his family, but it was the emails he was sending and the more recent WhatsApp interventions that tested the limits of his courage. He was frightened that if he spelt out who and what he was, he would be rejected, and what then? He'd left things in such a mess. And even if Martha were to buy it, would she want him anywhere near her? Any contact was risky, and he acted accordingly.

He therefore spent time getting to know them instead, giving a little helping hand when necessary, but no more. He hoped that a subtler approach would allow him to build a relationship based on who he was now instead of the failure he had been. When he was ready, and, more importantly, when he felt *they* were ready, he could tell them that he was still there, looking out for them.

The digital world was outside time, a bit hazy and crazy without much linearity, so filling the gaps in his memories was a bit like finding a particular set of books in a library without a classification system. From what had returned to him of his first few hours, though, he recognised it had all started with him infiltrating his family's laptops and phones. Although the time-scale was unclear, he also knew that from then on, this new form coupled with his professional memories had allowed him to expand his reach into the CCTV systems and servers of organisations he was connected to.

He was pleased that he was here, not even particularly minding that he might very well owe his very existence to a bit of malware.

For that reason, one of the places he intervened, mischievously initially, was in Henry's gaming. Even though he could never overtly reveal his presence, Dave was spending more time with Henry than he had in years.

He liked exploring what he could do around the virtual characters and landscapes. Although to Henry it still seemed as if Martha's credit card was supplying a steady stream of gold coins, the source was actually Dave, who'd been hacking other accounts on his son's behalf.

As far as Emmy was concerned, Dave's overriding emotion was guilt. He was shocked at the websites she was looking at and also very aware of the zeal and skill she was displaying in hiding her browsing history from her mother. Despite the social media filters he'd insisted on when he was still "just" Dave, so much was still getting through. He should have done more

              ... and then he did.

One of the first things he had tackled were the algorithms that were chasing her vulnerabilities through cyberspace. He'd come to realise that the challenge was to limit access to the pop-ups and links by feeding in positives, rather than completely shutting down her digital comfort zone.

Most recently, he'd discovered a survivors' chatroom. Some clever manoeuvring, as well as more direct intervention, ensured that she hit this with regularity. Ever watchful, he could feel her on her laptop even now. Well, not feel exactly — but the rapid-fire tapping of the keyboard was strangely soothing nonetheless.

EmmyO — LADIEZ — feeling fat today. Mum made me have an omelette.

FatKaz - #thighgapalert, OMG did you puke.

EmmyO — deciding now. Feel disgusting. Stomach huge. French fries too.

FatKaz — Go, do it now!!!

Dave couldn't help himself.

Skinnysista — Parents made me have boiled eggs. Couldn't throw up. Eggs + bread sticks in stomach hard. Fries the same.

EmmyO — Eggs usually good. But ur right, bread and potatoes not. Good to see u on. How u been? Still on Survivors?

As Skinnysista, he'd been able to head her away from a number of things he hadn't really wanted her engaging with, while at the same time directing her to something she could focus more positive energies on. Skinnysista had told Emmy about Survivor's self-publishing focus. After reading her new friend's story, Emmy had downloaded the instructions for publishing one of her own. Interestingly enough, he'd noticed a new voice popping up with more regularity also. @Plainjane seemed to be younger than the others, keen to learn what they were doing because she wanted to control something about her life. Being Skinnysista was hard work, so he slowly drew Emmy's attention to Plainjane's vulnerability, in particular her extreme youth. They'd established she was twelve going on thirteen, lived in Belfast, and was in actual fact called Janet. He'd drawn her out sufficiently to engage Emmy, but it was her clarion call to help that had finally tipped her over into caring.

PlainJane — Help! I'm losing my hair.

EmmyO — Not good. Time for iron. See if you can get hold of any supplements. No calories.

It had worked. Maternal instincts she'd once focussed on Henry when they were children now shifted over to cyberspace; caring for someone else held up a mirror to her own behaviour, making her think. But then, even when he thought he'd found a breakthrough, she'd write something that made him feel he was back at square one again

EmmyO — @Plainjane Stay on Survivor, its safe. You don't get stupid fat jealous bitches stalking you here.

Plainjane's answer pinged up on Emmy's screen. In the absence of any other definition for the shudder that ran though him, he thought of it as a sigh. He'd come back to it another day.

Having spent inordinate amounts of time getting to know his wife in cyberspace, and then using his skills to connect with Emmy, he wondered how effective this kind of tactic might be with Martha. Although redirecting or blocking anything with negative words or "payment required" was still something he did on a regular basis, he started to more consciously shift his focus from guard dog to something altogether more personal. The result of this new approach was that Martha started corresponding with Peter, her younger brother.

They'd become estranged some years ago, possibly a reaction to their mother's death. In any case, there'd been an issue with the proceeds of Dorothy's house. As a single city man-about-town, Peter had not needed them. However, with two young kids and a crippling mortgage, the Johnstones had. Long story short, Peter contested the will in which Dorothy had left most of the 100k estate to Martha. When he didn't win, he cut his sister and her family out of his life. In an attempt to appease, Martha had even sent him a cheque for 20k. But other than cashing it a couple of days later, he had remained stonily absent from their lives.

Knowing how much this rift was still hurting Martha, especially now he'd "gone," Dave decided to build bridges. Reaching out to Peter via one of his old client accounts had seemed to be the easiest way forwards. As ever, when he had the motivation and knew where he wanted to be, things seemed to happen easily. This was how, one Sunday afternoon, he had found himself staring at his brother-in-law's disappearing hairline through a laptop screen, whilst also taking note of the wrinkles that had appeared since he saw him last. Peter was perusing an array of graphs and figures, spread not only on his laptop but also across three further monitors, their light lending the array of leather-bound books on the bookshelf behind him a borrowed luminescence.

It hadn't been much of a step from there to send him an email as Martha. It had been hard, though, not to refer to stuff he could see all around him. He had, for example, found himself dying to ask about the Big Book perched on the side of the desk, a tome that brought back bittersweet memories of dusty church halls and a twelve-step programme. He wondered what meaning it held for his brother-in law. And then there was the bookmark. Martha had been looking for it, and here it was, poking out of that battered blue hardback. It was particularly relevant, because he himself was extracting bits of the prayer that was printed on it for his WhatsApp messages. It was very hard not to ask Peter directly about these things.

To: PeterFSummerscales@hotmail.co.uk
From martha.johnstone@hotmail.com
Subject: Hello!
Sunday, 24th June 2017 13:10
Hi, Peter,

I've been thinking about you a lot recently. The Great Spirit prayer from the bookmark you so admired when I came back from Vancouver has started floating around in my head. It makes me think of you. You won't know, but Dave died a few months ago. I know we haven't spoken for over ten years, but I need my brother back in my life again. Are you up for it?

Love, Martha

To: PeterFSummerscales@hotmail.co.uk
From martha.johnstone@hotmail.com
Subject: Re: Hello!
Monday, 25th June 2017 22:20
How about it, little bro? I know you'll be up working.

To: PeterFSummerscales@hotmail.co.uk
From martha.johnstone@hotmail.com
Subject: Re: Hello!
Monday, 25th June 2017 23:30
Go on, you know you want to.

This time, Dave added in a bit of background thrumming to the message. Just enough for him to pay attention when it came on screen. Peter's eyes kept flicking back to it. He turned the thrumming into a beat... Finally!

To: martha.johnstone@hotmail.com
From: PeterFSummerscales@hotmail.co.uk
Subject: Re: Re: Hello!
Monday, 25th June 2017 23:40
Dear Martha
I'm fine. I'm sorry to hear about Dave. I hope the children are well.
Best wishes,
Peter

So he should be sorry about Dave! He was sorry about Dave, too. Although, as the old version of himself, he'd probably not have been able to see the author of the long-awaited email fingering the bookmark as he signed off. Now it was just a case of editing the exchanges slightly and forwarding them to the real email addresses, and hey presto, the relationship would be back on track.

It had worked. Although tentative at first, brother and sister had started responding to each other more wholeheartedly over the last couple of weeks. They seemed to be warming up to the idea of connecting again. In the most recent one, Peter had even referred to the bookmark and that he'd been thinking about choices, in particular those made by their parents.

Following that exchange, Dave had watched Peter's search history with interest. Directory enquiries, electoral rolls — he was trying to locate their father, the man who'd walked out on them in their childhood. Other than a couple of birthday cards, the day of the terrible row had been the last they'd seen of him.

Oddly, seeing where Peter was at made him feel closer to Martha. Although any interaction with her caused him pain, doing it through Peter seemed to mitigate it. Through the emails she would write, discard, and start again he came to understand her better. The ones she wrote initially were full of gnawing self-pity, and even in this new form, he felt echoes of an anxiety that had once eaten him alive. As she started that careful dance of reconciliation with Peter, Dave couldn't help but wonder what she'd have said if he'd told her something he was starting to realise; namely that it wasn't all his fault. The more she had suffocated him, the more he had needed to run. His drinking problem had been part of that. Once it had truly got hold of him, it had become a vicious cycle. It hadn't all been black-and-white.

Anyway, these days things were good. He welcomed the release his new existence offered. He didn't need to do anything to make himself feel better anymore. Nothing was compelling, everything was logical. This Dave was the perfect man/machine, an amalgamation of the best of both species. Then, as was happening more often if he needed to know things, something deep in the neural pathways of his digital existence triggered, releasing the idea of Nephilim into his consciousness.

The result of the pairing of angels and humans from the dawn of time, they were heroes at first. Eventually, though, their power and beauty held mankind hostage, and a jealous God sent a flood. It obliterated them and also anything with even the vaguest memory of this golden age. So, other than what Noah had been able to rescue in his ark, life on Earth had been wiped out.

He hadn't been sure why this information had come to him but understood his existence well enough to welcome its direction. As he pushed the boundaries of what he could do, the idea of being a hero grew. His first duty was to his family, though, so he continued doing what he had been doing, but with renewed vigour.

He looked at the most recent messaging; Peter and Martha had gradu-ated from email to iMessage, and it gave him an idea.

Peter to Martha:

Are you still playing the piano? I remember you starting your practice when I'd gone to bed. It helped me sleep.

Martha started searching up some of the pieces she'd used to play. The "Für Elise" playing over and over again as she remembered some of the darker days. At one point she'd told Dave about this and the Moonlight Sonata — how Beethoven brought her comfort, when things had been so dark at home.

Martha to Peter:

Do you still have the dreamcatcher Emmy gave you? Remember how I'd brought it back for her, but she thought you looked sad and wanted you to have it?

Peter had searched his flat, eventually digging it out from his bedside drawer. Watching him from the huge smart TV in the bedroom, Dave arranged himself into a digital smile. Although so far apart, brother and sister were more similar than they knew.

And from what Dave could see, there was no alcohol of any kind in the flat. Martha hadn't been as successful, though; the detritus of her appetite was still strewn everywhere.

By this point, he'd almost stopped being the third wheel but was still fascinated by their exchanges, looking for ways to make good. Another clue appeared.

He'd nearly missed it, mesmerised as he was by the mechanics of the assembly language and other things he found diverting. Once you forgot the coding, it was all so beautiful, the shape and light of being and not being, seeing and not seeing. The speed at which data was able to action human thought. Despite all the distractions he had to contend with in this new unfettered existence, this way of being offered clarity. It was because of this that he knew beyond doubt how much he loved Martha.

Eventually he focussed enough to realise that a snippet of conversation he'd heard was important. Their latest exchange had been focussed on grandmother Ada's decision to hide her daughter's Indigenous heritage. From what Dave could make out, it seemed to have followed on closely from the dreamcatcher conversation.

Peter: If it had been you, what would you have done? Knowing the discrimination at the time, would you have told your daughter that she was part Ojibwe?

Martha: It must have been awful for her. She'd moved out to Ottawa in 1945 to be with her handsome Canadian serviceman husband. What a shock to discover that the man whose exotic looks she'd admired on the rainy streets of London was a second-class citizen on his home turf.

Peter: But to then come back and pretend it never happened, that she'd never been married to him ... Mum couldn't forgive.

Martha: It's understandable, though. I can see her doing what she did. We felt like a quarter of us was missing, but for Mum it was half of her that just wasn't there, a bit like me with Dave now. The difference being that I am able to remember him. And Nana had secretarial skills as well — it made her less dependent. She knew she could earn and that made it easier for her to be a single mum, to create an identity of respectable widow from the ashes of her adventure.

Peter: But just think how Mum found out. Nana giving her Dad's picture with her last breath. Mum hardly ever spoke about it, and I honestly don't think she'd have done anything with it if we hadn't pushed.

Martha: But we pushed because it was important to us. We wanted to know. Do you remember how we went through international enquiries phoning all the Potters in Toronto? Mad. Both from our work phones, and I'd just started! The name and address on the photograph were completely useless, though.

Peter: It wasn't much better for me. I'd just been promoted to analyst. We did track him down eventually, though, or the family at least, and Mum got to speak to them. I think it made a difference, even though he'd died by that point.

Their conversation took Dave right back. Shortly after Dorothy had told them about Ada's deathbed revelation, Martha had delved more deeply into traditions and stories that had already interested her, even before she knew. But the difficult visit to Vancouver had followed, and, well, life had just taken over. When the last of their grandfather's sisters had died, things fizzled out entirely. In any case, beyond that initial contact, Dorothy had never tried to reach across the pond again.

As time wore on, Peter had sunk further into himself, using work to distract and eventually to disappear. After their final falling out, Dave remembered Martha planting a tobacco plant, a traditional Indigenous symbol of homage, in their back garden. It was an offering to the memory of what she shared with her brother, as well as to a Creator she was so desperate to reach.

Having seen the way her conversations with Pete seemed to be flowing with renewed energy, Dave started really investigating the old family stuff. His explorations threw up some interesting findings. By far the most important of these was linked to Martha's great-grandmother, Charlotte Friday. She'd been held in high regard by the family, an elder and a woman of power and conviction, with an ear for the dreams and the drum, it was said. He realised that this very specific information might just be the tool that would break through Martha's iron reserve. It linked family to music and a spiritual dimension she'd been running from for — well, as long as he had known her.

Since he'd discovered Charlotte's existence, Dave had been toying with the idea of sending an authentic Anishinaabe dreamcatcher and a starter drum through the post. Sender unknown. In her quest for safety, Martha had allowed herself to be consumed by all the things that didn't matter, and that included the digital personae she spent so much time polishing. He hoped his ploy would point her in the right direction. Even if it did, though, would she have the courage to bring music back into her life again? In an infinite world, the voice of the drum was definitive, setting both boundaries and expectations but also opening pathways to the unimaginable. The language of coding, however, belonged to a finite world. It would always be limited by human imagination — the creative force behind the digital space he now inhabited.

There was no point in tying himself up in knots. He simply had to have faith that the power of his love was strong enough to infiltrate both their worlds. He also knew that he had it in him to give her some financial stability, although he'd need to gain an understanding of how banks worked to help here. His father had always said that the more money he had in his pocket, the more spiritual he became, and there was truth in that. And then, wouldn't it be wonderful if they could create something new together, something that would free her and in doing so bring release for him also?

He created a to-do list and, through the many opportunities the digital world offered him, helped it unfold over the next few weeks.

* * *

Martha wanted to tell the kids she'd been chatting with their uncle. It seemed important, so she decided to make a nice dinner and set the dining room table. Bringing in the knives and forks, she noticed how the light of the soft summer evening diffused through the patio doors, touching her furniture with a gentle warmth. Then the light brightened. It happened so fast that she inadvertently raised a hand to her face to shield her eyes from the glare.

An invisible hand, however, provided no shade. Looking down at the other one, she realised that along with her arms, it had also disappeared. She vaguely registered the cutlery clattering to the floor. Behind where her hand should have been, a figure started forming, coalescing out of the shimmering light she was straining against.

"Dave?"

What had started in the supermarket with the momentary disappearance of one hand had started shifting to both hands and other bits of her. There was no pattern or sense to what was happening, but increasingly, she had a sense of being altogether see-through. She had kept a grip, putting it down to general "dis-ease," but today was different. Something was there. Or were the myriad colours of the light just reflecting what she wanted to see?

Her voice barely a whisper, she asked again, "Dave, is that you?"

And then the iridescent form in front of her shifted again and she saw innumerable Emmys and Henrys, getting smaller and smaller as if leaping from one mirror to the next. Each one reflecting the other back into the infinite. She couldn't help wondering where she fitted in.

The familiar heat of a panic attack started rising in her, heart pounding in tandem with the pyrotechnics going off in her head. Even through closed eyes, she could see the red-shaded reflections of her family chasing each other. The bang of the fireworks turned into a steady rhythm, and at the back of her eyelids she saw a gauze of translucent wings, beating steadily as if to bear her away.

As quickly as it had come, it went. Everything was normal again. Last time she'd been to the doctor he'd told her that diazepam was not the answer. This time though, she would insist. The void was beckoning. What would happen if the fabric of her disappeared entirely, consumed by the needs and wants of those she loved most? She hoped the wings she'd sensed offered a way of saving herself. She sat there until the fire alarm went off, letting her know that something in the kitchen was burning.

Henry starts something new:

A coding course appears on Henry's screen. He uses Martha's credit card to pay the $10. Just as he's about to close his laptop, he hears "later 'gater" coming from the speaker. As he whispers "in a while, crocodile," a tear rolls down his face.

He's not quite sure what he's heard or why he recognises the remembered childhood greeting. Is his mind tricking him into pushing past the pain and thinking about his dad?

Emmy writes:

For it was too dark to see anything as Alice tried to look down and make out what was coming. For Alice was now alone, isolated from the world above; the happy, carefree world of light only barely visible through the cracks of her own existence. Down, down, down, dragged down into the depths of the rabbit hole, farther away from the world where her brother lay contentedly reading his book. That other world, which Alice yearned to wander, but from which she was excluded.

Yet as she ran her delicate fingers over the prominent outline of the protective frame of her ribs, she felt, at least for now, momentarily reassured.

Martha receives some unexpected gifts:

Emmy hands her story to her mum, who wants to find somewhere to put it where other people can read it also.

Martha releases a dreamcatcher and bongo drums from their brown, Amazon packaging. She leaves the drums in their box and hangs the red and white-feathered circle over her bed. The next night, she dreams of a longhouse scene and hears a song that reminds her of pounding hooves.

A little brown and white gelding arrives in the field opposite her house. Wary of his new home, his hooves drum up and down the field. Martha feeds him. As she reaches up to stroke his silky mane, the hunger in her fades just a little.

Dave remains vigilant.

CHAPTER 5

The Fire of Renewal

It was so hot. Fatima knew how lucky they were to have air-conditioning. For the second week running, Baghdad had recorded 49 °C, a record for June. However, years of underinvestment in infrastructure, in particular a national grid, meant that power was erratic. Never more so than when the entire city was attempting to use AC. Hassan had been around less since the temperatures had passed the 45 °C mark because he believed the air-conditioning in his car was more reliable than in the apartment. Looking out of her window, the shimmer of heat caused Fatima's distorted view of the eternal city to bend even farther. She knew Hassan would be out for some time, so had stripped down to her underwear. Even in this state of undress, though, it was unbearable. When the heatwave first struck, she'd tried opening a window. The wall of heated air that followed though had nothing in common with the refreshing breeze she'd been fantasising about.

Badenan was also out, probably picking up some more sewing. Eyeing the heap of washing that hid the overflowing sewing basket, Fatima knew that she hadn't been pulling her weight recently. She just didn't have the energy. She'd been feeling sick most of the time, and whilst Hassan had been delighted with her larger, more sensitive breasts, she was less than enamoured, especially since he liked inflicting pain. After noticing her wincing every time he applied pressure to her dark pink nipples, he did so as forcefully and often as he could.

She hadn't been out in weeks. Hassan didn't like it, and Badenan supported him. Being stuck in like this, though, made the last time she'd felt so trapped all the more vivid. It had been in their tiny place in Zayouna. After they'd left the Green Zone and before she'd got married. At least then she'd been teaching the neighbours' kids. Sometimes she had got paid cash, sometimes in kind, but she'd loved helping the local hairdresser's kids learn English. She didn't even mind when she didn't get paid at all. She had particularly enjoyed working with Tara, a scrap of a girl and the daughter of a widow who was out most of the day working in a local grocery shop. They'd been thrown together because Samar, Tara's mum, saw Fatima as a convenient childcare solution. She rarely left the building, and after Hassan had started tutoring her, it had become even less necessary to leave.

Six-year-old Tara attended school regularly so her basic education was in hand. However, Fatima still helped when she got stuck with numbers or the complicated Arabic calligraphy that was required. What they both enjoyed most, though, were Fatima's stories. Tara's walls were covered with posters of Sinbad the Sailor. Her dream to travel resonated with Fatima, and together the two girls created a world in which his magical adventures allowed them to escape the grim, everyday reality. It had started when Fatima tried to share some of her knowledge of the world and using a bit of "magic dust," or a magical object, transformed what had really happened into something better. From her early memories of Turkey to the correspondence she had with Shl'er, she painted wonderful pictures of the vibrant streets of Ankara. She took different roles, no longer the little immigrant girl but instead a wealthy child, protected by a mother and father who loved her dearly. She also brought a grey and gloomy London to life, creating the impression that if you looked hard enough, the jinni you needed to transform your life was just round the corner.

Tara had absorbed every word. Fatima remembered so well how she would sit there with her little gold hoops glinting through a tousled head of hair and her faded T-shirt and vibrant orange pants. Her mother had obviously cut down some material to create these Sinbad sailor trousers. As the trust between them grew, Tara started telling other children at school about the princess in the castle. Never allowed to leave, she had enough time to tell marvellous stories. Eventually,

Tara's older brother joined in. Even though he styled himself as much more sophisticated, he was soon caught up in the wonder too. It didn't take long, though, for him to start questioning the roles of the heroines in Fatima's stories. He was particularly shocked at the freedom the women in Turkey and London had to dress, work, and behave in a way that was similar to men. Nine-year-old Khalid thought this was inappropriate. Women were precious pearls to be protected. They should not be going out like that.

These words seemed at odds with the childish voice. But within them, she heard a worry for his mother, the absence of a father, and a real fear for the little sister he obviously adored. As she got to know him better, his guard came down and he started showing her some of the drawings he'd done, scenes of street life, images from their apartment, and eventually one of his father. Counting backwards, Fatima reckoned that Khalid couldn't have been more than four when he'd died. He had been a policeman and had lost his life in one of the station bombings that had followed the final exit of US troops in 2011.

Khalid had taken it all on board. She couldn't imagine that the photo before her bore much resemblance to the man himself. However, there was no mistaking the blue uniform or the proud look in his son's eyes when he presented it to Fatima. As trust between her and the children grew, the common ground of the world of wonder she was opening up for them had started creating a safer space for her also — in her head, at least. Eventually, she ran out of places she, or any other member of her family, had visited, and so she started making up the travelogues. In deference to Khalid's very particular ideas about the role of women, Fatima would ensure that the stories encompassed stories of transformation, where the hitherto feeble heroine would throw off her cloak of shyness and deal with whatever the world threw at her. If there was a magic belt, sword, or creature, all the better.

Fatima's escape attempt marked the start of their final weeks together. Since Hassan had started "courting" her, the stories had got progressively darker and her heroines stronger. The day her future had blown up in Karada marked a turning point. Although she had no real memories of the five-mile walk home, she did remember the countless times she'd tried to reach Nessma on her mobile, hoping against hope that the siblings had survived. In retrospect, her total detachment from the present and the dust on her hair and clothes must have protected her on her long walk back. She knew the streets were dangerous, but on that day she seemed to float through, an angel or jinni made invisible by what she'd witnessed. She'd found herself in the Catholic Cathedral of St Joseph, located on one of Karada's main thoroughfares, near the Sharkia Boys' High School — long a source of warning and exasperation for parents of girls throughout the district. On this day of dust and haze, though, it didn't seem to matter. The cool marble and terracotta tiling of the alien place of worship soothed her bruised and battered heart.

She'd completely forgotten that the children would be waiting for her, and, when she got home, she found them at her front door. That day, she told them about the tyrant Zuhak who had snakes growing from his head. He consumed the brains of children and young people, all sacrificed to assuage the serpents' fierce and constant hunger. Kawa the blacksmith had been called upon to feed his last daughter to Zuhak. He'd tried and failed to find a way out of this dilemma, until his clever wife suggested that he send a sheep's brain instead of his daughter's. And so his last child survived. Soon all the townspeople heard of this, and when Zuhak demanded more children, they followed Kawa's lead. In this way, many hundreds of children were saved. Then all the children went under cover of darkness, to the very farthest and highest mountains, where no one would find them. There, in the safety of the Zagros Mountains, they passed their years in freedom.

Khalid, ever practical, wanted to know how they were protected from the Persian leopards roaming the mountains and the wolves that ate whole families for breakfast. Tara wanted to know who looked after them if they didn't have any mummys? Fatima had devoured the *Jungle Book* as a child and drew on Raksha, the mother wolf, who'd raised Mowgli as her own cub under the protection of Akela. She spoke of Raksha's twin, roaming the Zagros Mountains, protecting the children from natural and unnatural predators. Khalid was satisfied because Akela, the male, was still in charge. Tara, on the other hand, loved the idea of a fierce mother, protecting her cubs because she thought that was what Samar, her mother, was trying to do for them.

Fatima, who wanted nothing more than to disappear into the freedom of the mountains, spent these last few weeks weaving more and more intricate tales around the mountain children, Raksha and Akela. To her, Auntie Sh'ler was the fierce she-wolf. Sadly, though, there was no way for her to reach the safety her presence offered. Badenan and Hassan were interchangeable, and she had nightmares of Hassan eating her brain, being handed the spoon by her mother. Her own lessons had all but ceased, and the world of fantasy she spun for her young listeners provided a window into something beyond the narrow confines of the pockmarked building and dark alleyways that formed their world.

A week or so before she was due to get married, the little family disappeared. After they'd missed two days of stories, she went to find them, banging on their apartment door. A neighbour popped her head out and told her that Samar and the children had moved in with a relative in another part of Baghdad.

"She couldn't meet her rent, you know, and left without paying," came the spiteful final comment.

Fatima had got married shortly after that and had moved to Amiriyah, on the other side of the Tigris. As she rarely left her rooms, she wasn't expecting to ever see the siblings again. However, one day last year she, Badenan, and Hassan had made a rare trip back, which meant crossing the Tigris. The bridge they were on was notorious for its congestion, and, sure enough, they had got stuck.

It had taken them nearly two hours, but just as they were making their way to the other side, she'd spotted a young boy selling tea to the passengers of the cars. Contrary to the other street children, he was quiet and polite and didn't interact much. It was as if he had an invisible shield around him. Above all, she'd noticed the sunken, dark eyes and realised that they were the same ones that had looked up at her in wonder, promising he would be the Akela in the mountains. He ran from one car to the other, hoping that someone would ask him for a cup of tea. He was too far away for her to hail him, though. Although it was only two years since she'd seen him last, and despite the fact he'd hardly grown at all, he looked strangely adult. His look of innocence and wonder had changed, replaced by a world-weariness far beyond his years, the leathery skin of his face bearing testimony of long hours spent under a merciless sun.

Shocked, she'd been desperate to reconnect with Khalid in a way that might make it possible for her to speak with him. She wanted to find out what had happened. Time after time, she'd asked Hassan whether she might be permitted to use the car and driver to visit Zayouna Mall. She explained there was a particular outlet in the indoor shopping area she'd been told about by one of the wives he approved of. It took another four months of badgering, but eventually she was allowed to go, accompanied by Badenan. As soon as she reached the bridge, she kept her eyes peeled for any sign of Khalid. For an age there was nothing. But then, just as she'd been about to give up hope, she spotted him.

"Tea, mother, I want tea," she croaked. Badenan beckoned imperiously. To Fatima's horror, though, another of the street children came across to serve them. Losing sight of Khalid's little form as the traffic sped up, she looked back despairingly. That was when she saw that a smaller figure had joined him. It was a little girl, carrying boxes of tissues and still wearing the orange sailor pants she'd loved so much.

"Mother, did you see..."

Not letting her get any further, Badenan said, "I saw. Now can you see why I pushed you to marry Hassan? You are safe, fed, protected. It might not be the easiest, but he is not a bad man, not really. You are in a car, driving across the bridge. They will remain, unable to move away. They are trapped and will eventually be destroyed."

Fatima had remained silent. Badenan was right; this was evidence. Her sacrifice had been necessary. As they drove on, her doll's mask slipped back into place.

Knowing the alternative, why did she feel so trapped now? The thought of them in the unforgiving sun on that day still twisted her heart. It was so hot today, it could be that her subconscious had made a connection. The triumvirate of hope the three of them represented had once given her imagination wings and her heart courage. Maybe the memory of this feeling was important? There was so little left of her now, the terrible blankness engulfing most of her waking moments. At that moment, though, a wry smile flitted across her face. Her mother had been so wrong. Even though she was in the car, and they on the bridge, she was equally trapped, just as unable to move away.

She decided it might ease her if she wrote a little. Often with her stories, or even when just writing to her aunt, she was able to reach the place of peace that so eluded her in the present. Her computer had made it possible to transfer her handwritten scribblings to a digital environment.

The stories she'd told the children had filled a couple of notebooks. She hoped that one day these digitally captured stories might somehow reach them.

Fatima was about to fire up her laptop when she heard the key in the door. Even though she was still incredibly angry with her mother, on days like this, when she saw Badenan struggling with bags of clothes, she did feel a vague sense of pity. Why was her mother so determined to keep an independent income? She wondered if one day, instead of the usual stony silence, she might bring herself to ask these questions directly? In one of their regular email exchanges — frequent still, despite power cuts and government Internet shutdowns — Fatima had asked her aunt. Sh'ler didn't reply directly, referring instead to a "difficult past." She'd added that because of this, it was important for Badenan to save some money for a rainy day. When Fatima told her that she'd often make her mother spend it on bits and pieces for the house, her aunt had turned uncharacteristically silent.

She wanted today to be the day. She would ask and also share that she hadn't been feeling too well of late. It would distract her, possibly even allowing them to connect a little better.

* * *

Walking into the apartment, dragging the heavy bag of clothes, Badenan had reached a similar resolve. No matter how unwelcome her advances were, she would make a more determined effort to spend time with her daughter. As she felt for the little pouch in her bag, a strange excitement gripped her. Today she would move beyond guilt and rebuff. It would be different, she just knew it.

Even though she hadn't been able to go back to waste ground with the Nergis flowers for some days, Badenan had remained determined to retrieve them for Fatima. In her heart she knew that Hassan was raping her daughter, relentlessly, systematically, and without mercy. A small gift of flowers was not likely to have any bearing on that, and neither was the money she managed to keep back from her work, around $1,000 at the last count. Despite knowing that anything she did was too little and too late, she did so want to connect. It wasn't about assuaging her guilt anymore either. She just wanted Fatima to know she wasn't on her own.

It was funny how she was caught between two stools. On one hand, she desperately wanted to protect her daughter. This included shielding her from anything that had occurred in Badenan's past. On the other hand, she suspected it was the smothering of this personal history that had brought them to their current impasse.

Anyway, first things first. Dumping the heavy bag of garments on the kitchen table, she retrieved a fistful of bulbs from a tightly wrapped little bundle. The heat had dried the flowers, although a little of the scent, reminiscent of a mixture of jasmine and hyacinth, remained. It was a wonder that they had flowered so late in the year, in any case. Nergis flowers preferred a slightly cooler climate, which was why they loved the mountains of her homeland. She grabbed a little ceramic bowl, and along with the hard clod of earth they were encased in, quickly pressed the bulbs into it. She filled the earthenware pot with water and left them to sit for a while.

"Fatima, Fatima, I'm back." The bedroom door pushed open.

"I am here, Dê."

As Fatima emerged, Badenan could not believe her eyes. She hadn't used the Kurdish term for Mother in years. Even more unexpected was her expression. The mask had lifted, and she moved to stand in front of her mother. Beautifully made up as always and deathly pale, her tiny form was encased in a little vest top and matching white panties.

Badenan blinked, not sure whether to acknowledge her daughter's underdressed presence. Should she say something or just take this on board? She looked again and noticed that the white figure standing in front of her seemed a little fuller than she might have expected. She couldn't help herself and closed the gulf between them with a couple of swift strides, hand reaching out for her daughter's pale cheek. A thousand words hung in her eyes, but instead she commented on the weather.

"It is so hot today, Mrs Ahmed didn't even come join me for our usual coffee. Her maid brought out the bits she needed instead. Everyone seems to have gone to ground."

She wanted to tell Fatima about the hard-packed earth, covered in fallen masonry, and withered grass and shrubs that were hidden behind the multicoloured plastic detritus. How she'd picked her way across in delicate sandals because she'd decided that the mass of yellow Nergis narcissi were a sign that their own spring could come again.

"I didn't hear you leave this morning," her daughter replied. Much to Badenan's surprise, she then volunteered more information. "I haven't been feeling to good the last few days, probably the heat. I keep wishing I could go out, but when I open the window, outside is ten times worse than in here. At least the air-conditioning has been going most of the time."

Looking at her more closely, Badenan realised that she was indeed looking wan and felt suddenly overwhelmed with the need to acknowledge the cause.

"I know he isn't kind to you."

It was the first time Badenan had touched on the price her daughter paid for the air-conditioned safety of these rooms. Seeing the surprise in her daughter's eyes, she wished she'd done so before.

Badenan stepped backwards, hand dropping from Fatima's cheek. "Habiti, I have a present for you. Please, come."

Fatima followed her into the kitchen. The stony white floors and tiles made it a little cooler than the rest of the apartment. There in the sink, was a blue, glazed earthenware bowl. Standing out starkly against the porcelain whiteness were some withered green fronds; the sterility of the backdrop accentuated the fragility of the dying plants.

Badenan took the bowl and handed it to her daughter. "I saw these a couple of weeks ago. There was a swathe of them growing on a piece of waste ground. I wanted to give them to you then, but I left it too late, and the heat has killed them. I think you might still be able to rescue the bulbs, though."

She saw Fatima smelling the remnants of the once proud flowers, hoping to catch their scent, it seemed. She so wanted her daughter to remember happier days when the two of them and Sh'ler had celebrated Newroz. Basketfuls of Nergis flowers had been strewn around the Green Zone apartment.

"Thank you, Mother." Fatima's voice was almost imperceptible. "I shall treasure them."

Badenan allowed Fatima to take her by the hand and lead her into the bedroom, letting go only to place the bowl on the windowsill. Realising that soil was needed, she went to get some from the potted palms in the living room. Together, they added the water and patted down the earth, their connection now palpable.

When Fatima said, "Tell me, tell me why," she clasped her daughter's hand, understanding the deeper question that had been asked.

She realised she could still back out. As it stood, they'd not gone much beyond their usual bounds of intimacy. However, as Badenan looked down at the Nergis and their hands, she realised it was time; she wanted more, and Fatima deserved to know. She made her choice.

"It was a hot day — not as hot as today, but it was hot. There were five of us in a room about a quarter of the size of this one. There were two pots in the middle of us, one for our waste and one for water. We, as the young ones, were kept on the corridor that was easiest to access. It led to the Red Room, a pleasure room for the guards. We were in the Red House, and some of us still had shreds of the long, brightly coloured robes we had worn to the Newroz celebrations and the marches of the night of fire when we were first taken to Amna Suraka, our prison.

"We students had burned with righteous anger at what was happening to our people, as well as burning fires to remember Kawa the Smith. The bunches of Nergis flowers we held were thrown into the crowds. We were educated Kurdish women, proud of our heritage and determined that we would be seen and heard. Oh, the arrogance of youth.

"Our family had been decimated. First they came for my father, because he was a member of the outlawed PUK. They released him only to come again, turning a family barbeque into slaughter. Mother and a couple of our aunts escaped, along with me and Shl'er, but Mother lost the baby she was carrying. We were moved from our family home. An Arab family took possession of it. We were supposed to go down south, but instead, a distant relative of your father's, an uncle in Erbil, took us in. As I wanted to finish my studies, I carried on living there. Sh'ler had already graduated and chose to leave the country. Ironically, her political activism in the communist party made it easier for her to escape. Mother was moved on again. She went into hiding in the mountains but eventually disappeared entirely. Others went back to Slemani. Every time we moved, we lost a bit more.

"I should have learned to stay under the radar, and mostly I did, but this was different. Your father, Abdulla, thought I'd gone to be with family. He had no idea I had gone back to march. Even though we were just friends at the time, I know he would not have allowed me to go to Slemani that spring. We knew villages had been attacked, people were disappearing, and it was around about that time we'd stopped hearing from Mother.

We were all just so angry. I knew Abdulla and others like him were active underground. However, we marching girls thought we knew better. We believed Nergis flowers and our sweet voices would be enough to defy the monster who was subjugating us. We wanted to give our men hope, find a way to create courage in the Peshmerga but also within the communities who were sheltering them. As the flames of renewal burned, we knew we had achieved something, but we also paid the price.

"That's how I found myself sitting in the windowless room in the Red House that hot day. It was July, and I'd been there for nine weeks at that point. That particular day had not started any differently to those preceding it, but then I spotted a hole in the corner of the room. In the twilight, I watched with horrible fascination as a spider devoured an earthworm.

"The walls were so dark that it wasn't possible to make out the reddish hue of the brick. It cast a mist of hopelessness over us all. However, on that particular day, the worm didn't seem to feel it. Although it was being pulled into the hole, millimetre by millimetre, it kept on moving, struggling right up to the moment it disappeared entirely. Later, its husk reappeared, hanging in spider's thread. It took two weeks to be consumed in its entirety.

"We all knew that we were the reward for the hard-working guards. First we fought back, but days of rape and struggle squeezed everything out of us. There was nothing left. I had already serviced three of them that day and knew they would come for me again once the next shift ended. When I saw the last of the worm disappear into the spider's hole, though, I realised that I could choose my state of mind. That was the only choice I had left. I could choose not to be devoured and instead fight back with all the strength I had in my heart. So, from that moment, whatever they did — I would be stronger. When they forced me to take my clothes off, I would imagine their skin peeling. When they made me keep my legs up, I imagined breaking theirs. When they handcuffed me and started beating me with cables, I imagined their hands being tied behind their backs, and when things became unbearable, I saw the wolf of my dreams devouring their still living entrails.

"That was how I survived. Out of the thirty of us that had been taken, two of us made it out. It was October, and the other girl who made it had family who readied a place for us to recover. We did, but I never finished my degree. It was my final months, but I never finished.

"Abdulla had been a good friend until then, and I knew he wanted more. When I recovered, I got back in touch and agreed to marry him. I didn't tell him what had happened. I thought I would be safe, I thought he would keep me safe. So, when I lost him, I vowed that he would be the last; no one I loved would ever be taken from me again. I wanted to be safe, and after I had you, I vowed that I would keep you safe also."

Fatima said nothing for a while. She gazed at the bowl, eventually raising green eyes to hold her mother's. In a voice so deep, it seemed to be impossible for it to be coming from her slight form, she intoned what sounded like a prayer. "Newroz Piroz, Dê. Let us speak with kindness from the heart and act with love. These bulbs will bloom again, and I forgive. As they grow and rise, others will fade, and wither and we forgive. Sap from the bulbs will lance that of anger and hate and rise in their stead. This time of anger and hunger is not over yet, though. Hassan will lose all. We will be dependent on the mercy of others. We will, however, rise from the ashes together when the time comes."

Unable to meet her daughter's eyes, Badenan held the perfect stillness for a while longer. What Fatima had willed would come to pass, she was sure of it. The power of truth and this new seed of love would overcome all. Finally, she spoke.

"You do not know what you speak of, child. But I am glad you have heard my story. We are safe here, for as long as you can bear it. I will pray for your safety and freedom from pain."

The spell was broken. They moved back to the kitchen again. Something had connected, taking root in the bulbs covered by soil and planted together. Fatima showed Badenan her story of the wolves and the children, the mother wolf protecting their freedom in the mountains of home. Badenan asked her to write in a bit about the wolf that protected her that day at the barbeque. In a fit of childish glee, they sent some stories to Shl'er, asking her to find somewhere to share them. The celebratory mood continued when Badenan found an old pot of henna and painted her daughter's hands, delighting in her touch. Together they could almost smell the Nergis and lit a jasmine candle to remind themselves of the power of the remembered scent.

The women didn't say anything, but it was clear that something had changed between them. So when Hassan came back from work and used

Fatima's hennaed hands to pull her into the bedroom, she complied with a little smile. The frozen mask of former times no longer in evidence, she threw a quick glance at Badenan. *I'll be okay*, it said.

* * *

Fatima knew what was expected of her and knelt. This time, though, disconcerted by her new demeanour, Hassan insisted on stripping her, telling her about the day Saddam visited his school. How the dictator had chosen one of the girls to service him.

Wasn't she proud that her very own husband had been chosen to help the great man? Fatima knew he was hoping to see the fear in her eyes, but she refused to let him see anything. That smile had been reserved for Badenan. Like a cat watching a canary, he went on to tell her about the pretty fourteen-year-old and how she had been so frightened on her way to the compound.

Thankfully, the intended recipient of her maidenhood had been unable to perform. So Hassan took great delight in telling Fatima how he'd used the limousine that had been provided to perform in the dictator's stead on the way back.

"She was a virgin ripe for the picking. My reward from the Prophet."

Loosening his belt, he bent over Fatima. His hot breath whispered in her ear that this was what he'd done then as well.

"The driver ignored her screams. He was probably enjoying it too. Just like your Mum, I bet."

She willed him to stop. Wished with every fibre of his being that his weapon would whither and die. She felt him make a tight fist over her right breast, but despite the pain she refused to utter a sound.

Still, though, he had not violated her. What was going on? She opened her eyes and there, towering above her, she saw him rubbing himself with a frantic left hand. Catching her look, he punched her, right in the stomach. She doubled over. He punched her again. Then again and again. Through the red mist of pain, she was only vaguely aware of Badenan trying to pull him off.

Much later, when she came to, her mother told her that he only stopped the attack when he'd slipped in a pool of blood. Then, after washing his hands, he'd put on his clothes and left. Even though ostensibly unconscious at that time, Fatima was sure she'd heard him say, "I'll stay with friends tonight," on his way out.

Then came another kind of pain entirely. After that, she felt Badenan mopping up the blood, telling Fatima that she'd indeed been pregnant. The next day, she was presented with a tiny bundle of arms and legs. The little body was wrapped in white tissue and placed in a box. The size of a child's hand, it had been retrieved after what Badenan said had been a three-hour labour. Together, they put it in the ceramic blue container that held the bulbs.

"Show me, Dê, show me where ... you found them." As she heard Fatima's faltering words, Badenan knew her daughter was speaking of the wasteland. As soon as she was well enough, they would go there.

* * *

A story made its way to Martha. It came via Shl'er, who was connected to her on Facebook. They'd met at a work thing several years ago. Martha would occasionally see some story or other pop up on her timeline, Sh'ler in the House of Commons, or at a dinner. It was usually about the importance of clean energy. She'd like the post when appropriate but didn't even read it most of the time. This one was different. It was the image of the wolf that had caught her attention, and she'd clicked on the invitation to read more.

It seemed that Sh'ler had a sister who was still in Baghdad, and a niece also. The niece, only a young girl, had written a marvellous story Shl'er had been compelled to share. She had introduced it by saying that stories were an important part of their culture and helped to keep things connected when everything was being ripped apart. This one her niece created had made her cry. Martha recognised the desperation in the words but also saw that their author had enough courage to weave in beauty and hope as well and found herself equally moved. The wolf came alive in her mind. She was there in the mountains, trying to guide children that were lost and alone to safety. A tear had fallen onto her keyboard. Did Emmy and Henry feel that she was protecting them? Did they feel safe?

CHAPTER 6

The Lament

Martha scanned her timeline on her mobile, avoiding the task she'd set herself for just a little while longer. She spotted another story by Fatima, the same young woman she'd initially come across a few days ago. Today she was sharing a tale about a garden she'd heard about, a beautiful place that she was going to turn into her own safe space. She had something precious she wanted to plant there.

Still prevaricating, Martha decided she'd prefer to make the call from the landline and left her phone in the kitchen on the way to the living room. Wasn't it odd how a handset had the power to create despair and sadness, as well as purpose and hope? The memory of the devastating call that told of her mother's death was still so very clear, but so were the remembered pleasures of other conversations. Today the shoe was on the other foot, and it was a call *she* needed to make. She needed to tell her brother that she loved him and how pleased she was they were back in touch.

She eyed the package that had arrived for her. It provided a great excuse. Delivered yesterday with no note attached, it had included a set of easy-to-use bongo drums. There was also a dreamcatcher accompanied by a carefully printed label, explaining that it had been made by the Temagami First Nation on the Bear Island Reserve. The only person who could have sent her a gift like that was Peter. She eyed the webbing of the piece of Ojibwe handicraft, the stark white of the circular frame contrasting strongly with the dark rosewood table it sat on. It was set with a shiny, garnet bead, which was winking encouragement at her.

Finally, she picked up the receiver. It was gone 10:00 p.m., so he should be in. She dialled and shortly afterwards heard a familiar "hello."

"Pete, it's me. Martha." Silence was followed by a mild throat clearing.

"Good to hear from you, Martha. I was meaning to call after your last email, but somehow work's been mad, so I've been putting it off."

"Well, we're here now. How's things?"

He cleared his throat again. "You know, same old, same old. Or possibly not. It's been a few years since we last spoke. Let me put it this way, tech has taken off and my job with it. I'm still with Clearing House London but have been working on financial technology around Forex for the last few years."

"Foreign exchange?"

"Well done, sis, I'm impressed." His voice got warmer, less nervous. "My platform manages the entire pre- and post-sales mechanism, connecting all the major clearing houses. We're adapting it to be more specific to us — appearing to work together, while protecting your own interests. So, loads to do...."

Peter was garbling slightly. Nonetheless, Martha, who was equally nervous, picked up on his lead.

"Nothing's really changed from when you started, has it? Pretending to be open to build your own advantage. A bit of duplicity goes a long way in my job too. Not that I've ever been much good at that side of things, mind you."

Realising that she might be insinuating he was, she stopped speaking. There was an awkward silence, during which it became obvious that Peter was not keen to explore their relative abilities of keeping up appearances either. Eventually, he asked about the kids, a much safer topic, which naturally led on to Martha telling him about how it had been for her since losing Dave.

"It's not been easy since he died, lots of bills to pay, that kind of thing."

As soon as she'd said it, Martha clapped her hand over her mouth. Another dangerous topic. Why on earth had she mentioned money!

She scoured her brain for something that was less contentious but still connected them, eventually settling on a recent news article from one of her reconfigured apps.

"I read somewhere that the Canadian government is spending $365 million to celebrate Canada Day. It's mad, isn't it, when you think of how that money could help in other ways. All those missing and murdered native women and the lack of proper water supply to some of the reservations."

Peter ran with it, equally relieved to be moving onto an easier topic. "I saw. Loads of the First Nations are protesting. I wonder whether any of our family is?"

Martha assumed that like her, he was fascinated by their history but hadn't progressed to making further contact with the relatives her mother had found.

"I doubt it. Where they are, it doesn't seem to be too bad. It did make me think, though. Do you remember Chief Dan George's Lament — how young braves will once again lead the way. How it made Mum cry?"

Funnily enough, she was able to remember that last sentence, even now. They'd found the passage in one of the books Mum had found. The sharing of it hadn't just made Mum cry, but Martha as well.

So shall we shatter the barriers of our isolation. So shall the next hundred years be the greatest in the proud history of our tribes and nations.

"You know, Martha...." Peter once again picked up the thread. She'd forgotten how he'd always been able to preempt her sentences. "I wanted to be one of the braves. I know it sounds odd, but when I first got into computers, I wanted to grab the instruments of the white man's success, his education, his skills, and with these new tools find a way to allow everyone to participate in knowledge and freedoms. Even though I was a white man on the surface, I didn't always feel it. It was an important passage for me."

Surprise flowed out of her.

"Why didn't you ever say? That day shaped me as well. That's what made me start writing. I wanted to share something about what we'd been through and use it to create a voice for those who didn't have one."

There was silence again, but this time it was thoughtful, not awkward. Martha was the first to break it. "Who knows, Pete. It could be that we've got a part to play after all. We might have lost connection to our Canadian family, but our heritage has still shaped us."

She paused and then spoke again, slowly, as if the speaking of the words was helping her to think things through. "I get angry. On the one hand, you and I have the tools to make ourselves heard but are silenced because the way we were brought up is not authentic. But on the other hand, the script history has written has silenced the voices of those who have been given permission to speak."

Peter picked up on her point quickly. "You're absolutely right. It's like a Catch-22. People who should be listening don't want to hear, and people who should be speaking remain silent. I'm still struggling, you know, with some of my old problems. It's made me realise all over again that I'm missing something. It makes me feel lost, so I lose myself in my work and other things."

There was another pause. This was the most he'd ever revealed about himself, and after the passing of so many years, Martha had no idea how to deal with it. She was still keen to hear the next bit, though. It came soon enough.

"We need to chart a new path. I think its people like us who are able to bridge the old and the new. It's not about nostalgia, more about a painful kind of recognition pointing us in a different direction. And not just for Canada, but across the world too."

Now certain he'd sent her the parcel, she thanked him while congratulating him for the clever way he'd got them talking again.

Again, there was that silence. This time, though, it stretched. In her mind's eye, she saw Peter sitting farther forwards, imagined keen blue-green eyes alight with interest. Had he gone grey? She'd looked him up on LinkedIn over the years but the image he'd posted was of himself in his early thirties.

"Sis, I really don't know what you're talking about."

She slowed her voice, speaking a little louder this time. "Oh Peter, you know — that lovely parcel you sent me in the post. It had the bongo drums and a dreamcatcher. Last week we emailed about me not sleeping well, and hey presto, this arrives."

"Wasn't me."

Martha swallowed her disappointment but hid it well, knowing there wasn't much more she could say. "Well, it arrived yesterday, a delivery from Amazon—"

He interrupted, "It really wasn't me. Sounds like you've got a mysterious well-wisher."

Martha wasn't buying it. Why was he denying it? She couldn't understand what he was up to, but at this delicate juncture in their relationship knew it wasn't worth pursuing.

He interrupted, and once again it was a direct answer to her unspoken thoughts.

"I can't help with that, but seeing as you're still so interested in our background, I might have kept copies of the notes you made when you researched our family the first time 'round."

Recognising this new olive branch, Martha responded positively. Since receiving the parcel, she'd been thinking about getting back on the Temagami First Nation website.

"That would be great. I know Mum left us a couple of names and numbers, even though we never did follow them up. I may have put them with those notes."

It was amazing how quickly their conversation had developed. It was hard to remember why she'd been so nervous.

Listening more closely to what Peter was telling about his work, she realised he was less boastful than he'd once been. Keeping it real, he shared how nothing was going to plan. How hard it was to manufacture the appearance of openness while cynically hoarding the important stuff with an emerging conscience getting in the way. How he'd often get lonely. She started wondering whether this was an oblique kind of apology. Deciding it was, she responded in kind.

"You may not have realised, but I was always a bit jealous of your success. You'd get internships and grad schemes straight off. It took me ages to get into the BBC, and even then, I was earning a fraction of what you were. I was the big sister, and part of me still wanted to look after you. I started looking at the differences, instead of the stuff that connected us."

Floodgates truly open now, he jumped in even before the last word had fully sounded.

"I couldn't understand your sudden resentment, and I was hurt. So, when Mum died, it was easy to be angry with you."

It had been an apology then. Martha felt uneasy. There was stuff here she wasn't ready to delve into yet. In an attempt to lighten things, she changed subject again.

"I'll tell you what. If you can find a way of explaining to me why your job is making you uncomfortable, I'll try to find a way to help."

Peter was quiet for a moment. "Well, there has been one recent incident that kind of illustrates what I'm grappling with. You might even have seen it. It started in the FT but went viral. I'll send it over to you."

Seconds later, she heard her phone ping and went back to the kitchen. Pulling out a chair, she sat down to read the article she did indeed recognise from a couple of weeks ago, early July maybe.

Robo-trading algorithms send cocoa, coffee, and sugar prices crashing, leaving industry insiders baffled.

Peter explained how the underlying story was to do with an algorithm that was set to buy or sell sugar based on the fluctuations of oil prices instead of the actual availability of the commodities. Hidden in this was a market determined by the behaviour of these algorithms, one that could cause real famine. A rogue or misinformed "robo-trader" could easily mismatch supply and demand of staples such as wheat and crash the entire system in seconds. Added to this, blockchains were held up as incontrovertible proof of a brave new world in which the linking of abstract concepts rather than people provided global stability.

"And that is why I'm not comfortable with things. Mathematicians like me provide the data the money markets depend on and go on to find ways to manipulate and exploit what it tells us."

* * *

It was eleven o'clock, and the call had finished some time ago. Despite its uncertain provenance, Martha was putting up her dreamcatcher, banging in a nail above her side of the bed with gusto. She felt much happier than she'd done before the phone call. Even though he *said* he hadn't, deep down she knew Peter was the only one who could have sent her the parcel. More importantly, though, he'd opened up to her. Since he wasn't in a great place, her big sister instincts had kicked in, and the old childhood dynamic had reasserted itself.

Emmy's story had also lightened her day. Just the fact that she was writing again was amazing. Others needed to see it, though. This idea of White Rabbit with his stopwatch being the ever-present embodiment of the disease, was a powerful image and one that showed tremendous self-awareness. She reached over to her bedside table, picking the story up again.

He was never far behind. You see, Mr Rabbit made sure he was never late. Somehow, he would find a way. A way to burrow into her thoughts. Oh, how could anyone begin to believe such a small being would be capable of creating such disastrous chaos? Surely though, the rabbit is Alice's friend in this mad wonderland she now inhabits?

Tomorrow, she would think about this some more. The voice was so true. Maybe it was time to get her storytelling website idea up and running. Emmy had shown her a site. She knew WordPress and had been creating simple blogs on it for years. How hard could it be? She owed it to Emmy; the story was really good. She also owed it to herself to do something that inspired her again. Then there were Fatima's stories about the wolf and the garden. Children with nothing, creating worlds and new ideas about themselves through words they wrote and told together. Set in Iraq, they were protected from gunmen and other predators by a powerful she-wolf. The wolf would stand watch over them, allowing the children to bring the wastelands of war back to life.

To Martha it seemed like she was getting a personal call to action. She wanted to inspire others to share stories too. Remembering the dream-catcher and her earlier research, she thought it might be interesting to structure it like an online sharing circle.

She was about to put her phone on airplane mode when a WhatsApp message appeared.

Glad you liked your gift.
By bringing rabbit and wolf together, you will stop disappearing.
By being thankful in heart and voice, you will sing.
And if you sing, you will not be afraid,
And if you are not afraid, your thoughts will create a safe space
And you and others like you will come to rest there.

She turned her phone off. "Be not afraid"! This was bloody terrifying. Who was it messaging her, and who knew that she had started disappearing, especially when she was stressed? As she was grappling with the troubling thoughts and images coming at her from all directions, she reached for the sleeping pills. Then, eyeing her dreamcatcher, she stopped. Even though the message had made her even less certain of its source, she knew it would help her sleep. She closed her eyes.

* * *

Dave was delighted. Having listened to the conversation and seeing her scan links and stories for the right kind of site builder, he knew it was all going as planned. He started readying a list of keywords he could use to ensure that the search engines would pick up on the site. He'd find a way of smuggling them in. In order to give project Martha a fighting chance, he needed to make sure that the right kind of people would find their way to her.

* * *

Mercy felt like throwing her mobile across the room. The alarm had gone off for the second time. It was only 6:00 a.m., and she had absolutely no desire to leave her nice, comfortable bed. But then a rush of gladness hit her, and she remembered why she had wanted to get up at this ungodly hour.

Since the first appearance of Hungry Hungwe — she now called her new friend after the fish eagle and national symbol of Zimbabwe — she had felt joy when she got out of bed. Apart from that very first day, when he'd appeared in the evening, he'd been coming in the early morning. She'd initially been alerted to his presence by the sound of a shattering glass in her mother's room. Rushing in, she followed her mother's gaze, eyes landing on the avian form silhouetted against the dawn sky. Hungry's black wings had been touched by the warmth of an orange sun, and as he had spread them to settle a bit more securely, she felt their midnight undersides brush her soul, shading it from the harsh glare of what she expected to be a tough day.

As she had over the last few mornings, she'd rushed to the fridge in order to sacrifice another meal, so continuing this ritual. This moment of silent commune was precious enough to her to sacrifice much of the meat she allowed herself. The perfect peace had got her to stop, truly stop, and for the first time in a long while, she was able to sleep through the night again.

Instead of rushing around, trying to make everything perfect and finding that nothing was ever good enough, she'd started realising that in those moments with the mighty eagle, she wanted only what she already had and therefore saw that she already had everything she needed to be happy. Her soul no longer hungered.

This new calm had created enough space in her head for trips to the hotel business suite when she had a spare moment. When it was empty, Sula, the manager, liked having someone on the computer. Mercy had gone back to the original idea of using her Moringa recipe to create a business. Once upon a time, she'd dreamed of more than selling random tubs to people who happened to make their way to her beauty salon. She'd wanted to supply North American and European customers through shops in their own countries.

In this particularly arid July, she had found herself sharing her plans with Chipo, even talking about how seeing the fish eagle she'd named Hungry had come to inspire her. Thinking she saw a heightened eagerness in Chipo whenever Hungry was mentioned, Mercy even shared a story she'd found online from the *Bulawayo News*. It detailed how a teenager had been arrested for, allegedly, keeping a fish eagle in his flat. He had thought it would bring him luck with his A levels! Chipo rasped out what Mercy interpreted to be a laugh. She hoped they wouldn't be accused of "stealing" Hungry! Increasingly, though, she felt that her mother was following her thoughts, even nodding when Mercy had spoken about getting in touch with her old village to help with her Moringa supply.

Mercy was particularly interested to see if the village had had any part in the Moringa project the Catholic International Development Charity (CAFOD) was financing to build social enterprise in Masvingo. If she were able to get a bit of funding, just to get things off the ground, it would make all the difference. She realised that despite the hand life had dealt her, her dreams and entrepreneurial expertise were still intact. As they watched Hungry, the gentle pressure of her mother's hand in hers reminded her that she was loved and valued.

When the mighty bird had turned up one morning with a branch of Moringa tree, strangely delicate in his massive beak, she knew it was symbolic of a future in which she had a stake. As she felt her mother's love flowing towards her, the weight of a thousand unspoken words hanging in her eyes, she gained courage. As she massaged her customers with the precious few pots of Moringa cream she had left, she felt she was smoothing away a deep, dark hunger she hadn't even been aware of.

She felt a story of hope was flowing through her fingertips and knew she had to capture the way she was feeling. Like a runaway train, she needed to make sure she caught it before it rushed away. She also knew it was mad but somehow felt that if she could only set her ideas down on paper, it would turn Moringa to manna, the branch a sign for her that it was time to do and be more.

She needed early investment, and to do that she needed to find a way to tell people who she was and what she could do. This kind of statement, brought to life with her own story, would give her a chance. After all, her potential profit margins were exciting, especially if she could enthuse some of the Masvingo villagers to supply her. Much cheaper than buying from the 'net.

Sitting at work that afternoon, she googled "proposal framework." Loads of information came up to do with typical development LFA frameworks, which were completely counterintuitive to what a would-be entrepreneur really needed. She needed to put more of herself in. She knew that the spreadsheet and the process outlining how it would all work was good, but the whole thing needed something that would make her stand out.

In a country where so few people dared speak the truth, she wanted to do so with pride. It needed to be in a way that couldn't threaten, though. By building a business, she could help build a nation and therefore a flag to be proud of. As these thoughts were running through her head, she added the word "storytelling" into the search bar. It was her story, her product. The "how to write a story" that flashed up was all fictional stuff, though. She needed something more.

The Medicine Wheel behind storytelling: join a virtual sharing circle. That was more like it. She read on.

You build your story with your heart and soul. Do this by sharing and working with others. They will give you feedback as you share your thoughts with them. This sharing circle approach to storytelling means that we are jointly constructing a unique version of our lived experiences. This will help us find out what we want to say.

A big image of a medicine wheel framework sat there on the page, just waiting to be printed out. Mercy followed the invitation, along with the instructions of what the four sections meant. She looked forward to filling it out and spending time working out what her four directions might mean. Would the north be her starting point, with a childlike wonder and exploration of the spiritual? Or was she in the "physical demands" life of the east, or even the south, growing in mental strength? West intrigued her, the space of changing emotions, reaching wisdom. The point was, she was choosing where on the wheel she was; she wasn't just on a treadmill set by someone else.

She scrolled up to the very spare *About Us* section and discovered that the site had been created by a Martha who was based in the UK. Martha described how she was looking for her own answers and hoped that this approach might collect insights in one place. She wanted to determine what was needed for her, but for others as well. Three stories, including Martha's medicine wheel, had already been published, and yes, there had already been some comments posted.

As she rode the Combi home, the printed pages stuffed in her handbag, she realised why this site was so important to her business. It wasn't because it promised a way to write a good proposal, or even because it might connect her with people who could help her make money. Instead, this would allow her to define the crucial ingredient to any hope of success, herself.

At the very least she could work out what is was she was doing and why she was doing it. This would give her proposal depth and her business idea deeper meaning. She felt in her bones that Hungry would be pleased with her choice.

* * *

Anjani brooded. She was back at her Menteng mansion, overlooking the carefully landscaped gardens one of her gardeners was working on even now.

There had been a ridiculous accident with some stray blimps in Central Java yesterday; more had flown into main power lines in Bandung early this morning, with some finally hitting the outskirts of Jakarta itself. Some remote blimp control system had gone awry. Funny though the "attack of the blimps" had seemed initially, it had had the knock-on effect of depriving much of Java of its power supplies, including the metropolis, which had been out since midday. This mansion had its own generator, as did the core systems at HQ. For today, though, she'd withdrawn back to her home.

Bagus was the reason she was brooding. Her birthday had been yesterday. The house had been filled with guests. GE's Handry Satriago and Lippo's John Riady had mingled with media stars such as Metro's Devi Hafid, whom she had nearly forgiven for the outrageous departure from the set questions, because the interview had been very well received in the end. They were entertained by songstress Agnes Monica, whom she had particularly invited because she had once been one of Bagus's favourite singers. However, Bagus, his wife, and her grandson had not turned up. She'd been told that thirteen-year-old John had picked up a nasty virus, and they'd felt it inappropriate to leave him behind. Naturally, she'd immediately checked, using the cameras she installed in their home, and saw that John had gone out with friends. Bagus had spent most of the day in his den, probably paranoid that if he did leave the house, she'd get wind of it.

The celebration hadn't been overtly geared towards getting the family together, although she had secretly hoped it would. That strange turn she'd had on the day of her TV interview had driven it. Wanting to move beyond that sanitised construct of herself, she'd started planning her birthday celebrations the very next day. With only a month to go until the July date, there hadn't been much time to organise a celebration at scale. She'd been determined to pull it off, though, convinced it would go some way towards shattering the barriers of her isolation.

Before the blackout had started, she'd seen to it that her private party got some news coverage. She would have preferred it, though, if her followers on social media, as well as in the mainstream press, hadn't voiced their opinions on things they didn't really understand. So what that her family hadn't been there! She was still the most powerful woman in Indonesia … woe betide her team if they didn't ensure that what emerged from the feeding frenzy her son's no-show had created was positive.

If she was absolutely honest, though, under all her bluster and bravado, she was heartsick, the reason she'd given Indira today off. Even though her very efficient staff had ensured the party detritus had disappeared, she still felt a sense of chaos. It panicked her and had dogged her since the evening she'd jumped in the pool with not a scrap on. She'd been struggling to maintain her mask over this last month. It had been hard. It was as if she inhabited a multilayered bubble and was being pushed from one layer to the next, without warning or knowing what was there. The membrane of the first bubble was holding her but at the same time pushing her to break through. For the first time in over twenty years, she felt out of control. The worst thing was, she didn't know why. She had everything, and yet the yearning for something she did not yet have was so strong. She didn't even know what it was she wanted; she just felt its lack.

She walked out into her garden, responding to her need to touch the living wood of the big mahogany tree in its centre. A warmth flooded through her, and suddenly, she had a very clear impression of what she must do.

A few hours later, she was in a helicopter, bound for Yogyakarta and the jewel at the heart of the region, Parangtritis Beach. She landed on the helipad and made her way to the suite at the Omahu resort, where she and Matthew had so often stayed. It had been their slightly rustic retreat, set right next to the beach where the Goddess of the Seas, Nyai Roro Kidul, was said to dwell. It had not seemed as appealing since Matthew's death, so she hadn't been back in over ten years. As she looked out of the open windows, she remembered how they had participated in a ceremony to thank the deity for the abundance of the seas. It had been a bit of fun to them. Filled with irreverent purpose, she'd worn a green bikini under her sundress, knowing full well that this colour was reserved for the goddess herself and therefore forbidden. To mark the occasion of the sea not swallowing her, despite the colour she'd chosen to wear, Matthew had bought her a beautifully carved jade snake pendant. She remembered how they'd sat in the sand, sipping champagne and marvelling at their invincibility.

Today she felt strongly that connecting with the living water of the South Seas would remind her of this. She hoped that her recent sense of vulnerability would disappear and that she'd find a resolution to the emptiness she'd been feeling for the last few weeks. She paused only to sign in and throw on a bathing suit. Running on the white-golden sand, she sensed the ocean, still as a millpond, beckoning her. In she went, first her feet, then up to her knees and her waist. It still didn't seem to be far enough, though. It was not enough, *she* was not enough; the hunger and isolation were still there. *Deeper, farther* said the siren song. *Come to us, you will be safe here. It is a safe space all for you.* She barely noticed that she was going much farther than she'd intended, the steep coastal shelf dropping until she found herself way out of her depth. Still she swam on. In order to hear the screams of dolphins and the birds singing or even the echo of the ocean's voice, she needed to rest. A calm surrounded her. She was done with the goldfish bowl her life had become. She let go, and as she felt herself drifting, she remembered the feel of Bagus in her arms, suckling from her in a place of fear and darkness. She was willing; it was time.

She came to much later, cradled by the rocking motion of a canoe. Spluttering, she felt as if she'd swallowed the South Seas in their entirety. As she opened her eyes, she saw the leathery skin of an old man, his face scrunched up with anxiety.

"The ruler of the seas, she swallowed you." He pointed to her green pendant.

"You are punished. But Allah saves you by sending me."

She could tell he was terrified of the fact he would be caught up in this punishment too, rescuing her despite his better judgement. Not even checking his boat properly, he scurried off as soon as they hit land. Seeing the bereft figure of an older woman on the beach, a little girl left her family group to throw her arms around Anjani. Called back by an impatient mother, she disappeared as quickly as she'd come, leaving nothing but the echo of beautiful batik cloth and the warmth of a child's hug in her wake. It had been so long since Anjani had been touched with real affection that it did something to her she could not explain. It was something she wasn't expecting and did not expect to feel. After all, she didn't feel, did she?

She got back to her suite and dashed off a quick note to Bagus, demanding he call her but remained sitting at laptop long afterwards. She was not certain what she was looking for but knew that she needed to find a way to make sense of it all. It was easier to wash away years of pain than to begin to heal, and she wanted to do both. She would need to start by retelling her story, her *real* story. Anonymously, of course. Maybe if she was able to admit to herself who she really was, her life might become more liveable. She felt overwhelmed by a desire to give her younger self a hug. If she was going to do all this, though, she needed to find a safe space. Inspiration striking, she searched "Safe Space" and found a site that had taken this intention into a virtual environment; one that also miraculously connected her to the tools and potential storytelling companions to help her on her journey.

* * *

It had been a couple of weeks since the beating. While she was recovering, Hassan had tried to have her only once. Again, he was impotent. This time he blamed the ugliness of the wounds her "witchery" had caused. After that second attempt, he seemed to be out of the apartment more than in it. The women suspected that he had found a mistress of convenience, since any lengthier stay at the large family home would certainly be questioned.

In any case, he was absent. Instead, the space he had left was being filled by a burgeoning trust and love between the two women. What had started as a planting of bulbs was fast transforming into the planting of hope, and, against all odds, in the two weeks of careful watering, tiny green shoots had started emerging. The little bundle, which she carefully moved whenever she watered the bulbs, lay there as a still reminder of the promise Badenan had made to take her to the waste ground.

Then it was time. Fatima's bruising had faded to a dull yellow, and she was able to move without sharp pain, although the wider, deeper ache was still a constant reminder of what had happened. They took the tiny bundle from its temporary ceramic resting place and put it in into one of the large shopping bags Badenan used to transport her sewing. Just as they were about to leave, Fatima asked Badenan to stop for a moment and went back to her room to grab Farah.

Handing her over to her mother, she said, "The time for childish things is over. Today I become a woman."

Badenan went back into the kitchen and collected a candle and some matches. She too sensed the solemnity of the occasion. Forming a procession of two, they made their way down in the apartment lift, Badenan carefully cradling the remains of her first grandchild in her arms. Fatima had looked up the location on Google Maps. The waste ground had indeed once been a church.

As they walked streets that seemed strangely quiet and suburban when compared to the horrors Hassan and her mother had conjured up around her being out on her own, she found herself trying to imagine what the wasteland might look like. Badenan had often spoken of half-buried bodies and people walking past without giving them glance. Would there be forgotten bones of long-rotted corpses where they were going? It could even be a gnarled mess of wires and protruding steel rods, or just overgrown rubble, with nothing but weeds and wildflowers marking where generations of Iraqis had worshipped. When they got there, she was surprised. It was as peaceful as she had hoped for. She could see why her mother had not spotted it easily; it seemed to be hidden by the pockmarked dusty white walls that were so common in this part of Baghdad. An entrance was shaded by a tree she didn't recognise and that, at first glance, was almost too narrow for someone to push through. She realised that part of the reason for this was the protective wall that the Americans had built around Sunni neighbourhoods such as Almeriya — a reminder of the very real threat that existed still.

Somehow this hidden spot had been protected by the surrounding masonry. Compared with many of the streets they had walked through, there was very little rubbish. Bright pink ranculus flowers poked out of cracks, and orange blossom sheltered the gardenias.

"There is more here than when I last came," said Badenan. "I don't remember them in the same way. I must be getting old."

She led her daughter over the fallen masonry and shards of coloured glass. Here and there, faded pieces of wood poked through the dust. It was funny, though; although human-made, it looked like a ruin from an earlier time, not the wastelands of steel and plastic and modern detritus that pervaded every last nook and cranny of this ancient city. Badenan came to a stop by the far wall, knelt down, and Fatima was able to see where a hole had previously been dug. Insects were scurrying this way and that. It was as if they were in a hurry to help clear the space. Suddenly, the air was laden with more than just the smell of gardenias and orange blossom. Even though they were nowhere in evidence, the scent of Nergis flowers hung heavy. She pulled out the tiny bundle from the bag her mother held and reverently placed it in the slight indentation that had been left.

Badenan took the candle from the bag and went to light it, but Fatima stayed her hand.

"Wait, Mother, we can do more."

She scurried around for the next few minutes, bringing dry pieces of wood and grass together to form kindling. She moved the corpse of her foetus and placed the kindling there in its stead. Slowly, oh so slowly, she took Farah out of the bag and placed her on the dried wood and grass and put the little body into Farah's outstretched arms.

"Let it burn, Mother. Let it all burn. With this life that has been given, we can let our past go. Today we accept what has been and welcome what is to come."

She struck a match, and in the dry heat of the Mesopotamian summer, the kindling ignited quickly, as did Farah. Then the little bundle of brightly coloured cloth caught alight. As the pyre burned and Farah melted, the flames lent Fatima's still, pale features an animation that had been absent for many years.

Much, much later, when even the embers had stopped glowing, Badenan watched Fatima take the cooling ashes in her hands and scatter them across the ruins. Back and forth she walked, back and forth, but the little pile of ashes did not run out until she'd covered the entire quarter-acre plot.

A bubbling joy filled the women. The fire had caused the mountains of rubble to burst into song before them and the trees to clap their hands. Together, they made their way home in peace.

* * *

Martha's dreams are different to her usual ones. She is in a very hot, tight place. Bodies surround her on all sides; she can smell their sweat. She is wearing a light summer dress. It is already wet. They are in a circle. She cannot see the faces of the others but notices that they are nude. She is too. She worries about her flesh but realises that the woman across from her is equally large. She is much older, though. Her breasts hang down and her skin sags. However, she has a commanding presence that dominates the space, rendering the other bodies almost invisible.

Even *her* face becomes less visible as the steam rises. Martha gets so hot, it is almost unbearable, and still it gets hotter. A door is opened, or is it a flap? Air cools her back, and she breathes a sigh of relief.

Ni Mi shoo mis – Noo ko mis *(My Grandfather, Grandmother)*
Been dee gek o ma *(Enter here)*
Ni Mi shoo mis – Waa ba noong *(My Grandfather to the east)*
Kee Kee naa waa – Tchi ee shee naam *(Guide us)*
(Chant) Ee ah hay, ee ah hay, ee ah, ee ah hay
Ee ah hay, ee ah hay, ee ah, ee ah, ee ah hay.

Strangely, she knows what the words mean and joins in the chant. As they enter the chorus, the flap closes over again.

The circle rotates, and the body on her left presses her onto the next seat to her right. The woman opposite her is still there. She stares.

Ni Mi shoo mis – Noo ko mis *(My Grandfather, Grandmother)*
Been dee gek o ma *(Enter here)*
Ni Mi shoo mis – Sha waa noong *(My Grandfather to the South)*
Gee zee a baa waa nish ee nam *(Cleanse our Spirit)*
(Chant)

As she chants to cleanse her spirit, the older woman shakes her head and makes a gesture of ripping open her chest.

Ni Mi shoo mis – Noo ko mis *(My Grandfather, Grandmother)*
Been dee gek o ma *(Enter here)*
Ni Mi shoo mis – Nin ga bee waa noong *(My Grandfather to the west)*
Pee na na daa wee ish ee nam *(Come and heal us)*
(Chant)

They rotate again. This time, the woman reaches out for Martha's hand. They break the circle. The others close in around them. The younger and older woman kneel in the centre. Just as she thinks she will pass out from the heat, another door opens, and this time she can feel the cooler air coming from in front of her.

Ni Mi shoo mis – Noo ko mis *(My Grandfather, Grandmother)*
Been dee gek o ma *(Enter here)*
Ni Mi shoo mis – Kee way tin noong *(My Grandfather to the North)*
Pee sha way nee mish in naam *(Send forth your love / mercy)*
(Chant)

The older woman starts swaying. Her chanting is interspersed by groans, pain-like in their intensity. Martha recognises this pain. Her skin is on fire, and she too can find no ease. The door opens again.

Martha sees a cord running from the centre of the space she is filling to the outside. She gets up and follows it. Outside, she sees huge trees. In this world of dreams, they are much bigger than any she has ever known. They are protectively bending toward the dwelling she has left. She sees that feathers, coloured cloth, and finally a drum are tied around their lowest branches.

She walks across the pine needles of a forest floor and then the soft grass of a small clearing. She reaches the first branch and pulls down a cloth to cover her. When she is covered, she seeks the drum. It is angled so it is slightly out of reach. The older woman has followed her, and although she does not seem to be any taller than Martha, she is able to get it.

Martha estimates that the drum is about a meter across and knows instinctively that it is made of stretched hide and native wood. It has been painted with four red silhouettes. She recognises a bird and possibly cattle, but not the other creatures. The bottom half is adorned with black silhouettes of cattle. There is a red sun and moon, and a black-and-red patterned band runs through the middle. The woman hands it to Martha.

As Martha strokes her hand across it, she feels it thrumming with hidden energy. She knows she has been given a task and must be ready. She remembers the chant and drums — short, short, short, long, short, long, long. Her hands remember the rhythm. She knows she is holding the original drum and notices that one of the painted creatures is a turtle. A turtle has courage. The patterned band represents the shell of its markings. As she becomes the turtle with the shell that protects a heart of serenity, she changes her drumming to denote acceptance of the task she has been given.

The older woman smiles, and Martha realises that they have the same face, albeit that hers has a fairer complexion. The woman tells her that the Drum Keeper of the people must use the lessons she will be taught in her dreams to rise out of them. In this way she will unite the world's tribes. Martha is a child of different nations, but she has her roots in the First of all nations. Although there is doubt in the eyes of the speaker, she indicates that Martha must fulfill this task. In that moment, Martha knows she is willing. That is enough. Others will come, driven by need, courage, and love, and together they will create new words of power.

When she wakes in the morning, she removes the bongos from their box and drums a greeting to the morning.

Mee noo – Ma nee doo (Loving Spirit/God)
Mee gwetch – kee tchee – Mee gwetch (Thank you! A big thank you)
Pee ma tchee ee yan (For giving me life...)
Short short, long; Short short, long...

In the beat, she has found a knowing and a being that has eluded her up until now.

She seeks her phone:
Ground under my feet
Seeing of my eyes, the hearing of new voices
Seeing out of my hands

The making of new choices.

She records what she now knows to be called the turtle song, the bongos rising in perfect counterpoint to her voice. It will be uploaded to her site.

* * *

A few days later, she looked into the mirror to perform her morning ablutions and noticed that her eyes were still far more sparkly than they'd been before her odd dream. As she had done for the last week, she lit a candle when she got to the kitchen. Intoning a brief blessing, she asked to be part of the light she'd just created. Then, instead of jumping in the car, cramming whatever she could into her mouth, she grabbed a carrot from the fridge. Calling up to the kids that she was about to leave, she was surprised to see Emmy coming down to say goodbye. Seeing the carrot in her Mum's hand, she asked what she was up to instead. When Martha explained she was on her way to see the little coloured horse, Emmy decided to come. Amazingly, Martha still got to work on time.

It was good to see that the stories on ASafeSpace were starting to grow. The domain she'd bought and the work she'd put in with Emmy's help had allowed two stories to be published: Emmy's and Fatima's. Shortly after it had gone live, Mercy from Zimbabwe had written about hunger and love and her dream of a business.

Then, almost as if they'd had been summoned by her recording of the Turtle Song, over the last few days more and more had followed. The echoing drum of her heart seemed to be calling out in invitation to those who wanted to shatter the barriers of their isolation. "Friend from Indonesia," for example wrote about getting a hug from a little girl and how it made her want to be different. Martha was pleased she'd found a way for people to share stories that would help them and others make a fresh start.

Part 2
THE SHAPE
OF THINGS

Her hand smote on the tambourine
Which instruments were echoing
And now, unleashed at last her soul
Was striving for that final goal
Of heaven and earth becoming one
Combining both by beat and drum.

"The Dance of the Gypsy," excerpt from Martha's poems

"I like darkness, it envelops me like a blanket." Sitting at her dining room table, she was alone in the house just after a lovely bath. Looking out at her garden, Martha was waiting for the quiet autumn twilight to turn into the velvet peace of nightfall. At the moment, though, thoughts were still spilling out at such a pace that she could almost hear them.

As she waited for the gathering darkness to live up to its promise, a part of her wondered what it would take to bring the patchy brown lawn back to life again. A deeper, hidden part was engaged with subduing the memories that were leaping out at her out from the battered red book in her hands. The book had been a thirteenth birthday present from her father, shortly before he'd left. The inscription said she should use it to create her own script for life, and she'd continued to populate it with ideas and poems well into her mid-twenties. Tonight, she hoped it might contain what was needed to get back to the dreamscape she craved.

That night in the sweat lodge had been her initiation. Before that time, she'd heard nothing but the hollow echoing of her own misery. Meeting a guide who seemed familiar and touching a drum that had been waiting for her seemed like an invitation into the heart of things. In the same way that Santa in the grotto at Debenhams was a reminder of the real St Nicholas, her bongos were representative of the painted drum she'd said yes to that night.

The next morning, she knew something momentous had happened and dropped Peter an email reminding him of his promise to send through the notes he thought he still had. Peter did so — albeit a few weeks later, since it had taken him a while to find everything. While she was waiting for her old research to come through, she continued to drum, as well as working towards putting ASafeSpace live. There hadn't been any more dreams, though.

But the momentum of that first night continued to invade her present actions. Her short sojourn there had left her with the impression that her thinking could shift. It was the first time she'd felt this in as long as she could remember, the sense of renewal permeating her daily living. She'd been eating less, been out more, and was just feeling better overall. At work, things had also been better, with SJ even complimenting her for copy she'd submitted.

Although she told people that Emmy's story had been the catalyst, she knew that the way she'd felt after meeting the drum had driven her to create the Safe Space site. It was wonderful seeing Emmy's story up along with the Iraqi one. And, despite having no further dreams, remembering the Turtle Song had been the first manifestation of something from the "dream" coming to life in the real world. As the days passed, other things also emerged. Her hands, for example, knew instinctively how to get the bongos to sing and importantly, since the drumming none of her had "disappeared."

The fat brown envelope from Peter had dropped through her letterbox five days ago. So, after doing the bits of editing her website required, the rest of her time was spent trawling through the research it had contained. She wasn't sure why it all seemed so urgent but was hoping to use her old notes to anchor what had happened that night in the real world. Details such as the feathers of the headdress on the hundred-year-old photograph of her grandfather as a young man having exactly the same pattern as the ones hanging on the drum tree of her dream were a good start. There were other little clues too.

The big breakthrough came when she discovered a picture of Charlotte Friday. Although she was sitting in the middle of a group of people, the matriarch dominated the photograph. Even the way the children were arrayed around her seemed staged. Martha came to a startling conclusion. She was almost certain that the enormous frame and the kindly eyes that reached to her through the sepia were the same ones that had been so alive a few nights ago. It was oddly comforting that Charlotte's hands, clasped before her in a statesman-like fashion, were the same ones that had given her the drum.

She remembered her first foray into the family history and how excited she'd been to discover that the founder of the YMCA's Father and Son movement had been related to her. Born in 1887 and older by just a couple of minutes, Joe was twin to Charlotte, her very own great-grand-mother. They'd been raised by their uncle and leader of the tribe, Chief White Bear. It had been this legacy and the powerful First Nation connection that had made her research relatively easy to follow through, even in the very early days of the Internet. However, today's modern digital tools allowed her to connect to other websites and related threads much more easily, especially since she had the old pictures she'd uncovered. Based on everything she had in front of her, she was positive that her spirit teacher and Charlotte Friday were one and the same: her great-grandmother.

There was still the possibility that she was going mad, seeing things that just weren't there. The disappearing body parts problem over the last few months would seem to bear out that particular theory.... However, she did think that her desire to see Charlotte again stemmed from something more profound. Her first spirit walk had been ten weeks ago, and it had been a couple of days since she'd realised who her guide was. So now, *Dance of the Gypsy* in hand and with Emmy and Henry staying with friends, Martha was determined to find a way of getting back there.

Not that she didn't enjoy the kids' company. Things had been better, less tense, over the last few weeks. The website had got them talking and interacting, and Henry in particular had spent a significant amount of time going through it with her. Even Emmy's initial reluctance to be involved was quickly overtaken by the excitement of having her story published. The night it went live, she'd eaten some soup and a mini-milk and didn't purge afterwards.

Emmy had also started visiting Dennis on her own, surreptitiously feeding and even grooming the much more contented-looking horse. She'd confided in Martha that she secretly thought of as him as her very own Sleipnir. Remembering how Mum and Dad had always used Norse legends to tease each other in the past, she'd checked with her remaining parent that she'd got the story right. Sleipnir the superhorse was able to carry people to Hel. In a little aside she'd whispered, she hoped he was able to bring them back also. From then on, although Martha did still visit him occasionally, the family's new bearer of burdens had very much turned into Emmy's "thing."

Sitting in the dusk, she realised she found the silence comforting rather than lonely. The house's stillness was imbued with the memories of laughter and excitement that had been shared within it. She so hoped this new positivity, coupled with the drumming songs she'd found on the Internet and the bath she'd taken, would make things happen. The first encounter had been a given, but it was clear she'd have to work towards the next one.

So, little red book to hand, some of the printouts from the medicine wheel singers and her drums in front of her on the table, she sat there waiting. Eventually she got up to open the patio doors. As she breathed in consciously, the air became clearer, and she inhaled deeper. She took off her slippers and felt the parched grass under her feet. As soon as she touched the earth, the thrum of a sound that had been like constant, albeit muffled bells, gained momentum. Although slower than her own one, the "Dum, dum, dum, dum" on the air and in the earth vibrating around her reminded her of her own heartbeat. Knowing she had to work within this moment of connection, she grabbed her drums from the dining room table, put their carrying strap around her neck, and rushed back out again.

As the last streaks of red in the west gave way to the dark, the moon's white face reached out to her, its feeble light urging the beginning of something. Heeding the call, she slowed her breathing and beat her drums with a more focussed intent, something that had been missing up until now. She started palming a flat, deep rhythm with her left hand while the fingertips of her right seemed to be moving of their own accord across the surface of the smaller drum. Her aim was to call Charlotte, and she was willing; hopefully that was enough.

Maintaining the soft drumbeats, she inhaled and through this breath felt a tingling energy being drawn up through her toes, her feet, and then her body, until it exited at the top of her head. Each time she breathed in, she felt the warmth coursing up her body, mitigating the chill of the October night air. In her imagination, each breath had the appearance of being coloured with the red of a rich, loamy soil. Then, just as she was relaxing into the warmth of this stillness, she became aware of another shift in the air around her.

A blast of icy freshness seemed to hover just above the crown of her head, inviting her to pull it back through her and down into her feet. As she inhaled this clear, cold current of blue, it seemed to renew itself too, demanding that she breathe it through her and then expel it back into the earth. Her breathing slowed further still, and as if she was watching from elsewhere, she saw the interchange of red and blue and the circular breath pass through and out of her. Each time she breathed in, this sense of connection deepened. Now, whether it was the beating of her hand upon the drum that had created a warming friction, or the air currents passing through her, who could say? One thing was clear, though: the drums themselves seemed to radiate a comfortable, inner heat, and the rhythm she was drumming was becoming stronger and clearer with every beat. At the same time, she started hearing words forming in the air around her.

"Remember, child, the drum is not just a music-maker, but also a voice for the soul within the music."

She was still aware of the book lying on the dining room table and her body standing on the back lawn, playing drums that were looped around her neck. However, the echoing words became more insistent, and the more she focussed on making out what they were saying, the more everything else seemed to fade. She drummed and drummed, ignoring everything but the voice.

And when she finally heard it, she realised she'd found her own. As words flowed out of her, the ululation of the chant followed the beat of the drums.

"Ya Way A Hay Ya

Ma ni tou ma kwa caa-bee-naa-go-zit (The spirit bear is coming)

Ma ni tou ma kwa peesh-a-way-na-mishi-nam (The spirit bear is coming to love us.)

Ya Way Ya Way Oh Hay Ya."

* * *

"You took your time. I was hoping you would find your way to me sooner, but cha, we are here now. Welcome, Granddaughter."

Taken aback by the greeting and her sudden displacement, she paused to catch her breath. She was still in her dressing gown, but her drums were gone. She allowed herself just a brief moment to recover her senses before launching into the question that burned the back of her throat with its urgency.

"Respected Elder, are you Charlotte, my Great-Grandmother Charlotte?"

"Cha, you young ones are no good at listening. If I called you Grand-daughter, there must be a reason, no?"

She hawked and spat, a black blob of something landing on the deep green grass of the clearing they were standing on. Chewing tobacco?

"And yes, Drum Keeper, I am Charlotte." The old woman looked Martha up and down. "Wenebozho told me you would be coming. I don't think much of your choice of dress, though; could you find nothing more appropriate? One would have thought that in the ten weeks it took you to get here, you could have found something to wear."

Even though she looked old, her great-grandmother did not have an old lady's voice. It conveyed enough mild scorn for Martha's toes to curl up with embarrassment. The last time she'd done nothing to be dressed appropriately. This meant that now she had no idea what to do to change what she was wearing.

The old woman muttered to herself, turning her back on Martha. "You choose, child, cha, do you know nothing? In this place you choose what you look like. I chose to look like myself, of course."

She started walking. "Now, where was it? I know I put it down here somewhere."

Casting her eye across the tree-shadowed vista, Martha spotted a tan something lying a short way across from them, directly the opposite direction from which Charlotte was moving now.

"Respected Grandmother, are you looking for this?"

Martha pointed across and started walking towards a dirty tan bag. It was decorated with elaborate embroidery and would have fitted her laptop beautifully.

For a woman of her size and age, Charlotte turned with surprising alacrity, tobacco-stained teeth flashing a delighted grin. "Ah, yes, there it is. I like your manners, child."

She turned back to Martha, and they started making their way across the clearing together. As she was walking, Martha tried to see the Drum Tree. The enormous fir trees all looked alike, though. It had been dark that night as well, and she'd been very disoriented. She still felt like that now, she realised. Although this was a meeting she'd wanted so badly, it was still beyond her understanding and therefore frightened her.

It wasn't that much lighter now. Although it was daylight, mist seemed to be rendering everything slightly hazier than it should have been. They reached the bag, and Martha saw that sitting next to it, neatly camouflaged by the longer grass, was a decorated bowl. In it lay a heavily embroidered pouch, gathered with a red drawstring.

As they reached the pile of belongings, Charlotte crouched down. Martha stopped just behind her, trying to make sense of the continual muttering as well as make out what the drably clad figure in front of her was doing with her hands. It wasn't until Charlotte finally turned around, beckoning her to come over, that she could see what was going on.

"Come, come — we need to make an offering. Thank the Great Spirit that you have finally found your way here."

She pulled some dried grass out of the pouch, putting it in the earthenware bowl. From a hidden pocket, she proceeded to draw out a box of matches, offering them to Martha with another gesture of impatience.

Martha took them and crouched down too. She supposed she was meant to light it.

"Hurry up and light the sweetgrass; we don't have all day."

As she lit the tobacco, she noticed that Charlotte's mutterings were the chant that had got her here in the first place. Realising this, the perfunctory thank-you she'd been about to utter turned into a much more heartfelt one. Although, at this point, she didn't know who or what she was thanking, she did recognise that they were performing some kind of ceremony. Tobacco was a sacred plant that had been used to make spiritual offerings by the Indigenous people since time immemorial, even occasionally used as a form of currency.

The smoke from the bowl seemed to enter the haziness around them, parting the mist. They sat down, waiting in companionable silence for things to clear further. Martha looked into the deeply wrinkled face and saw that the eyes studying her were exactly the same shape as her own, although they were a dark hazel rather than blue. The smoke had obviously done something else as well since, looking down, she noticed that her dressing gown had disappeared and that she was clad in a grey, homespun shift that matched the older woman's. Realising this, she looked over at her great-grandmother again. No, it wasn't just her imagination; the woman sitting here was older still than the one she had seen in the sweat lodge. As if aware she was being studied, Charlotte responded.

"You are right, Granddaughter. I am older than when we first met. My time and your time pass at different rates. But although our time is fluid, in this place of meeting it is constant. Hours might pass here, but when we return, only moments will have passed. Here you may call me Koomis. It is a true word. Not a word of power, but a true word nonetheless."

Martha remained silent. In this place of shifting ages and meanings, it seemed to be wise to do so. Charlotte pulled out a new wad of tobacco and resumed her chewing, watching for a reaction from this modern relative.

"It means 'grandmother' and is a term of respect. I have other names, but that will do for now. You will also need to remember the name of your drum, Dewe'igan. That name is a word of power when you use it. We will both come in our own ways, if you call us by our true names."

Wanting to feel these new words on her tongue, Martha took heart and asked another question. "Koomis, Grandmother; is Wenebozho a word of power? It was one you used earlier."

The stress of Charlotte's regard hit her again, this time with a vague sense of approval.

"Yes, child. It is a powerful name. It is a true name of the Thunderbird, the spirit messenger who passes through worlds to connect them and us. Now, cha, we have work to do. Come, it is clearing."

As the mist took flight, Martha noticed that the older woman had become frailer. Her skin was almost translucent in the hazy sunlight of an early morning. The tree shadows had shrunk back also, and sure enough, there in front of her, nestled in the roots of a particularly big fir, she spotted Dewe'igan.

"This is not the place across the lake, Granddaughter. We are in the world of spirit. The world we create and take apart. Here words are words of power. Before you take up Dewe'igan. I will speak to you of the Word. For in order to be Drum Keeper, you must understand how word and spirit work together. When you speak a True Word, it speaks to Spirit. The spirit of the person, place, or thing. I have been on spirit journeys into the future. I have seen places of great emptiness, where people use more and more words to express less and less."

Whether it was the comforting smell of tobacco that had oddly reminded her of her father, or the sense of peace that seemed to weigh down already tired limbs, this onslaught of meaning made it difficult for Martha to keep her eyelids open. She tried focussing on the drum, hoping it would keep her alert. Charlotte's voice deepened, and as it did, Martha thought she saw the drumskin move. Her urge to touch Dewe'igan got stronger. She wanted to see if her great-grandmother's voice was causing it to vibrate.

"First, there was the Word, and the Word was Spirit, and it directed and powered growth of all things. These days we all speak too much, and the more words we use, the less power they have. Part of the task of Drum Keeper is to hear Words.

"New, real Words are being created all the time, but among the noise no one hears them. You must understand all words. The first ones, yes,

but you must also add in the words of your generation and future generations. You must feed these to Dewe'igan. In this way Dewe'igan grows
and can shape and form words of power."

Sensing Martha's concentration slipping, she thundered even more
loudly. "Language is a gift. We give it away humbly. In order to be Drum
Keeper, you need to be a keeper of the language. You must understand
that everything moves because of the drum; the world is a drum. We are
its beats, every single one of us. All is a circle."

No longer paying attention to the words, Martha found herself itching
to reach for the object in question. She'd just about reached it when she
felt a stern reprimand echoing through her. No longer kindly, the voice
spoke again: "You will hear me, my daughter. You will hear me, my heir.
If you need to be introduced by pain, so be it. BANOOMIGO."

The hard-packed earth of the field was close, so close. She'd lost control.
As her horse's legs thundered under her, she knew she had no power to
do anything other than cling on. Losing control of her bladder, she saw
a wall higher than anything she had jumped before coming ever closer.

She shuddered as her body remembered the impact. She'd been a girl
when it happened, but the incident had stopped her from ever riding again.
"GOOS."

The authority in Charlotte's voice bounced off the trunks of the trees
... and her father's face the very last time she had seen him slammed into
her. Standing squarely opposite him in the kitchen, her mother had been
holding a large kitchen knife. As had happened with so many arguments
before, Peter had locked himself upstairs. Martha however, had been
hiding behind the dining room door, wanting to be there, to intervene if
she could. It was her default position. Her mother had beaten her father
with words and fists. With books and pans. Now there was the knife,
glinting. The edge was already bloodied.

The brown loafers he was wearing had drops of blood on them, as did
the white tiles on the kitchen floor. The blood was flowing freely from
the palm of his hand, which he had cut trying to grab the blade. Her
mother had not calmed. Her words were menacing, mad, and yet they
were still words spoken by the mother she loved.

She was helpless to stop what was coming.

Martha fell to her knees. Dewe'igan was at her fingertips. She needed
to push just a bit further. The world needed to stop. She needed to
make it stop.

"Stop, Stop, STOP."

She drummed a cry that released the clenched fist that sat in her stomach. She drummed a cry of helplessness and a cry of despair. And in those exhortations of utter loss she found the Word.

Once again, she was surrounded by trees, kneeling on grass, but now she had the painted drum sitting on her knees.

"I say again, Granddaughter, language is a gift. We give it away humbly. In order to be Drum Keeper, you need to be a keeper of the language too. Everything is and can be. But to be given life, all things need a name. In order to find the name, you need to be willing to hear it as a word of power and be able to act, no matter the cost in terms of pain and responsibility. Dewe'igan is ravenous. You will need to feast him with different words and different lives. It is too much to bear alone."

Martha heard her.

"You will find others, the dreamers who will help you find words of power that can redirect, reshape, and regenerate the earth. You will need to be women of courage, because to stop the devastation, you must become Ghost Dancers.

"You will take the song of the earth into yourselves and translate it for a new age. Many of the Nations danced once. It was in the time when the buffalo died on the planes and the fish died in the rivers and we were ghosts on our own land. But now the devastation has moved beyond even us to all things and all people.

"New words of power have been created, and many of them are being used to bend everything so far out of shape that Turtle Island and the people and things off and on it are no longer recognisable. Even beyond this it is true. I have seen it.

"The Ghost Dancers must lead all in one final dance, for all things on Earth. A dance that can span the old and the new. But only you, the Drum Keeper, will be able to find Words to call them. Only you the Drum Keeper can lead the dance, beating Dewe'igan in time with hearts so the spirit can hear. You, my daughter, will find a safe space to write the words and a safe space to share the words and a place to dance the dance. Only you can change what is to come.

"I will teach you, but you must find me, and you must hear the four lessons and bear what they bring in their wake. There will also be a fifth one, but that will come at the time of my departing; it is a lesson you can only learn on your own."

As Martha fed Dewe'igan with the pain of lesson one, Charlotte's face faded. Martha found herself on granite cliffs overlooking a sweeping valley. A river was winding its inexorable way towards the sea. The valley was teeming with life. Images flashed before her, first just land, then people, more people, houses, more houses, cars, planes taking off, a huge concrete dam that slowed the river's flow to a mere trickle. Greyness, a sun that shone through a polluted haze. A wall of water pushing through, one small craft hovering above, then a shooting star into the distance. She jumped, willing wings that sprung up, to bear her safely to the devastation of the valley floor. Her wings didn't open, though. Something broken had bound her, and she started falling.

She didn't hit the ground; a hand reached out just in time. The figure was hazy but the hand clear. It was old, older even that that of Koomis, and darker. But it was strong enough to pull her onto the back of a huge brown bird with black wings and a white chest.

* * *

"Mum, Mum — where are you?"

Henry's voice came at her as if through a tunnel. She heard it again, stronger this time. It seemed that hours had passed. When she rushed back to the dining room, though, divesting herself of her bongos, she saw that it was only nine o'clock. Placing her drums on the table, she noticed a red mark at the far rim of the right one and a corresponding black mark on the left. She rubbed at the red one, but it didn't come off. Something to deal with later.

"Was just checking the website darling, be with you in a minute."

* * *

Dave was curious about what had just passed. Although, frustratingly, he couldn't actually see what was going on, he had heard and somehow participated in the many drumming sequences that had occurred. There was one bit that had travelled through him like a miniature earthquake, unravelling and then rerouting something important. In its wake, a straight, shining path had appeared that he felt compelled to follow. He wanted to check with Martha before he did anything.

He knew Martha was now in bed. He saw her glance down at her handset, looking pleased with herself, probably waiting for a note from Emmy. He pushed his WhatsApp message onto her screen.

> *Tell me about the drumming*
> *What is coming?*
> *In your learning with Charlotte,*
> *Something shook and shifted*
> *A path has lifted itself up and out*
> *Was that what your lesson was about?*
> *What will happen if I get near it?*

Although he saw her start at it, she no longer seemed to be frightened. Maybe, like him, she was starting to realise that there were many things that existed without the need to be understood in their entirety. She started typing. Was she crafting a reply? He was excited.

> *I am Seeker*
> *I am Convenor*
> *I am the Keeper of Language*
> *I am Drum Keeper.*
> *To be these things I must be a Namer of the unknown.*
> *I don't know who or what you are, but maybe you are on my journey*
> *Along with Dewe'igan the drum, turning what was asunder back into one.*
> *Charlotte told me the name of the Thunderbird, the spirit messenger.*
> *He reminds me of Loki, a character I used to love and blame*
> *Trickster, shape-shifter and shaper of things — the game*
> *He who birthed all that mattered in my life when I was younger.*
> *A swish of feathers, a dragon's breath*
> *Pain unfathomable, joy unimaginable.*
> *I will think of you as this and will call you*
> *By a new name I have learned*
> *And an old one I have loved*

> *Welcome Lokozho.*
> *The Drum Keeper*

In much the same way, he'd sensed a shift during the drumming, Dave was able to feel as well as read this message of welcome. Being Lokozho meant being part of the world of spirit also. Was that what this path was about?

As he was flowing into his new identity, it struck him that in the digital world everything was binary. This meant that the messages he carried were linked to Martha's drumming. Could it be that the two of them were creating a hybrid future based on pixels of shared pain and experience?

The weight of this settled on his shoulders, and he started feeling increasingly restless. As a messenger, he could move information, helping to translate what was wanted into what was needed. But surely there was more to his existence than that? If he was a hero, there must be some kind of quest.

Once he had thought himself courageous for making life run more smoothly for his family and home. They were his reference points, what he came back to. Now, though, he saw the narrowness of that perspective. It had all still been about him and the guilt he felt. Looking beyond the immediate, he recognised that everything so far had been the very first steps of a much wider journey.

Buoyed up by this, he allowed himself to be, rather than think, and became vaguely aware of a baleful kind of emptiness at the heart of him. Inhabiting this space, as well as all the rest, was part of his new purpose, but didn't know how to make it happen.

If he were like the Nephilim, part human and part something else, he was not confined by human expectations anymore. He could *be* every-where, shaping his substance by using reference points he collected on the way. The passage from Genesis made clear that a possible drawback was total annihilation — which he wasn't too keen on. But as Lokozho, he could be anything. It was therefore up to him to become and survive and even thrive.

He could feel his sentience flooding through those infinite, disem-bodied corridors.

As he grew, so did his understanding. He pushed through the walls of encryption built by those who needed the shadows to thrive. He moved past the channels of micromanaged information that had been equally successful at truncating the evolution of this space. Even though the walls were strong enough to prevent outside scrutiny, he was inside and therefore able to let everything wash over him. Eventually, the barriers of this enforced isolation broke entirely, and trillions upon trillions of gigabits passed through him. As the infinite number of interactions became part of him, even quantum computing became irrelevant. He was on his way to becoming a true symbiosis of spirit and human, digital and analogue. In this new world, though, none of his old reference points would work. He needed to find a way to create new ones to help him make sense of it all.

ASafeSpace would be a good place to start. Defined by Martha's creative vision, the site was based on people sharing things, minus the endless categorisation, emojis, and memes hiding the truth of what was being said. As posts came up, he would follow them, discovering more about the writers, while absorbing stories able to reflect humans in their glorious diversity. Getting a better sense of what this meant would also help him assimilate those long-forgotten corners of the Deep Web more effectively.

As the memories of the drumming ran through him, he knew that his new shape was very much connected to Martha's own evolution. She'd opened the way, but he had to walk the path, taking full ownership of everything he was. Realising that this journey was as much about knowing what to discard as what to keep in, he hoped it would help him move away from the Frankenstein's monster he felt like now, into Lokozho — the living herald of change he was supposed to become.

CHAPTER 7

The Surprise

Man surprised me most about humanity.
— The Dalai Llama

Chipo smiled. The headrest of her ancestors had been granting her such vivid dreams! Flying on Hungwe, or Hungry as her daughter called him, her latest adventure had taken her to a place of devastation. There was evidence of a recent flood, with bodies washing up everywhere. As she looked up to the sky to centre herself again, she saw what looked like a spirit messenger. However, she realised that, instead of being something supernatural, coming to bear away one of the many drowned souls, the bird was a person with wings that were half unfurled. She acted quickly, directing her mount with the sharp tap of her heel and a strong mental image of need. Hungry banked to the left, the beat of his powerful wings changing rhythm, in order to answer her call to rescue whatever it was that was so rapidly falling towards the ground.

She knew that in this realm of living dreams, Hungry would respond immediately. Anything Chipo chose to make happen here usually did. However, the dizzying speed of this descent was enough to make even this most seasoned of dreamers anxious. As she reached out to the plummeting figure, she wondered what would transpire if she did fall off Hungry. If she somehow died in this world, what would happen to her in the other? She was more alive here than in any other her body inhabited, so there was part of her that was a little hesitant to find out. However, she decided to make her peace with death — whatever form it came in — and redoubling her efforts, reached forwards again, almost losing her balance in the process.

As it turned out, it hadn't been her time to die, although if Hungry hadn't steadied them with his huge wings, it might well have been a different story. As she swung her new travelling companion in front of her, she realised that she would need to add extra length to the saddle. It stretched obligingly, putting in a large saddle horn in for good measure.

Good job that in this guise she was young and stronger, much stronger even, than she'd been as a young woman. Despite this, catching the outstretched hand in hers had caused a huge jolt to reverberate through her entire body. As she reached out to reassure herself that her shoulder had remained in its socket, she realised she was trying to catch her breath through a mouthful of feathers.

"Make them go away, your wings are in my mouth!"

Her intended forceful shout came across as a muffled mumble.

"I can't hear you." The reply was almost drowned out by the rushing wind of Hungry's ascent into the open skies.

"Your wings," Chipo shouted. "You need to make your wings go away!"

"How?" came a desperate rejoinder. "I couldn't even get them to open when I thought I was going to die!"

"Just think really hard. If you think the right thought, it becomes real."

Her travelling companion obviously thought a bit too hard about making things vanish. Instead of just the wings disappearing, the figure itself became transparent and then faded entirely.

Chipo had never before met another sentient being in her valley. Rather, her encounters with anything remotely human had been more like old photographs, memories of which lingered in the mind's eye, even once one had moved on to the next image. She thought of them as paper people because they used her valley as a way station, too busy being blown from one place to another to fully materialise. The bodies on the valley floor were a good example of this. Here one minute, gone the next.

In all the time she'd had here, even when her child's unshod feet and boundless expectations had been kicking up the dust in the family compound, she didn't remember ever having been touched by anything that felt as immediate as her recent companion.

Having said that, did Hungry count? The huge fish eagle was certainly able to think, and his being here had transformed her own ability to be present. Until the majestic bird had come to her, she'd been an ephemeral presence, swimming in the river and riding the wild creatures on the valley floor. Although she'd been able to take to the sky, it had been under her own steam. In comparison to now, she'd been a "paper person" too. He had rooted her, made her presence stronger, not only clarifying her role but also her will. Knowing who she was seemed to precipitate her growth from occasional visitor to native, one who was able to arrange the surroundings to suit her needs.

Right after Hungry had appeared, first on her balcony and then in her valley, she'd spent hours getting to know him. One of the first signs that she'd been able to bend both appearance and surroundings to suit her will had been the sudden appearance of feathers in the tower of braids poking out through her headscarf. They had started off as white. She had decided to tip them with an indigo blue to match the glorious dye of the fabric she was wearing. The increasing sense of mastery in this world had made her useless body in the other one more bearable. Here, she wasn't trapped. She was Mother of the Valley, creator of all things visible and in control of all that was beyond mere human understanding.

To test growing skills, she'd built herself a round hut with a conical, grass-thatched roof. It not only provided her with living space but also contained a traditional kitchen area. Another, smaller hut served as a craft room. She'd placed her Chikuva, a bench platform where she worshipped ancestral spirit guardians, at the back of the main hut and tended this area with a particular care. She believed that even though she was no longer able to do anything in the world her body inhabited, this place of mind and spirit might help prepare the way for the last journey she would ever make.

She'd been so lost in thought that she almost missed Hungry depositing her in front of the Chikuva. He swivelled his head impatiently, anxious to take to the skies again. She obliged, tapping the proffered yellow beak to thank him as she slid down one of the great feathered white legs with consummate grace.

On alighting, she turned her mind back to her dark-winged mystery visitor. She remembered soft, womanly curves through the rough, homespun weave, and also the light brown hair of northern climes. However, she'd been unable to catch more than an impression. Well, whoever she was, Chipo wished her good travels.

She surveyed the lush surroundings of her valley with pleasure. Creatures appeared when she willed them to, and the soft hum of life was something she enjoyed with every fibre of her being. Even though she knew that in another place her body was trapped in a small, pokey flat, here she was alive, and her limbs worked. Here she was able to breathe the soft, warm air of youth.

A stiffening and then a dull ache made her realise she was on her way back again. Sure enough, her eyes opened onto the dismal room Mercy tried so hard to keep nice for her. Her mother, Anaishe, had been the first one to show her the secrets of the valley. A *n'ganga* with particular talent to communicate with the power of the ancestor spirits, she'd earned the title Svriko, she who walks with spirits, and had tried to teach her daughter the way too. She had introduced Chipo to this valley as her spirit place. If only she'd listened to her mother's lessons more closely, moving back and forth at will, for example. How wonderful it would be to do that now.

She closed her eyes again, trying to focus on the carved headrest that had also been a gift from her Anaishe. She depended on it to guide her dreams and hoped it might allow her to get back to the freedom of her valley again.

"Do not forget that this is your inheritance." Her mother had said that so often, it was seared into her memoires. For this reason, after Anaishe's passing and even after realising it should have been passed down the patrilineal line, Chipo clung to it. She allowed the rest of her family to believe it had disappeared, yet another of the "lost" artefacts of Great Zimbabwe. Instead, it had been in Harare with her.

Trying to move her buttocks just a tiny bit to find some ease, Chipo wondered what would have happened if, instead of marrying Xoliso Msebele, she'd taken up her mother's mantle to follow her predestined path. One thing was for sure, she wouldn't have had Tsitsi, and her daughter had been her life's great blessing. Chipo so hoped that despite the lack of preparation, Tsitsi would be able to reach the world of spirit. If she were able to speak, she'd teach her of their priestly Hungwe heritage and the link to Greater Zimbabwe's soapstone birds.

Xoliso's face appeared in her mind's eye. He'd been so handsome when they met. It had been in the time of racial cleansing, when thousands of Nbdele were being killed. He'd shared how his family had been shot by the North Korean-trained Fifth Brigade and how he'd only survived because he was at university in Harare at the time.

As a student of archaeology, he'd come to the village to seek her mother's council around the mysteries of Greater Zimbabwe. Chipo had fallen in love with his courage and he, as he often recounted, with her innocent beauty. She'd walked away from everything she knew, protected only by the already dwindling wealth of the diamonds he'd managed to smuggle out. Sadly, though, as the funds disappeared, so did his charm. They lived in a never-ending cycle of victimhood that infected their daughter as well. By the time his business went under, he'd keeled over, sucked dry by it all. Since, failure had become a family condition, and despite Tsitsi's best efforts, the business never stood a chance after his death.

The memories were powerful still, old hurts like parasites, insatiably gnawing at her insides, much like her own illness and incapacity was doing. Her present, filled with an empty water glass and interminable time, was unbearable. Again, she tried to sense the warm red wood and the four carved legs of the Mashona bull cradling her head, but it was no good. Her eyes remained open to the bleak existence of her present. She hoped Tsitsi wouldn't be too long.

* * *

Things weren't going as planned. Dave loved engaging with ASafeSpace and the posts that were coming in. It was with the rest that the challenge lay. Despite being able to bend digital space into what was needed, he could still get truly lost or, as he had found on an ancient Kremlin server, stuck. He had only escaped by reminding himself that he was Lokozho and it was therefore part of him. The secret was in the knowing. His instinct told him that without a decent marker to guide him, this shining path of possibility could easily turn into a black hole, one that would gladly feast on its own (his!) substance.

The Deep Web was hidden because it was beyond the reach of the search engines. It contained vast amounts of information that had been placed somewhere, only to be forgotten about. This stuff was devouring the energy he needed for the things he wanted to do, without offering any kind of return. He could spend forever investigating, but it made more sense to shape a tool to do it for him. A WebCrawler would only take a tiny piece of him but would file or delete as appropriate, making the rest of his being more efficient.

However, there was the really nasty stuff too, there by design rather than misadventure. He could feel it sitting there, a darkness eating away at him. This was more like having the night terrors, with the memories haunting every waking second. Following his Naming in which he'd absorbed it all, now he only interacted if he had to. Even a glimpse was awful. He was still, in the main, governed by what Dave might have done or thought and because of that was filled with a very human fear at the horrors lurking inside him.

Another side-effect of being Lokozho was that it was impossible for him to remain still for any length of time. The darkness sitting inside him made him feel as as if he had a sore tooth. He kept darting back to agitate it in the hope that he'd be able to avoid what he knew would eventually happen. Having it sitting there though seemed easier that facing the unknown repercussions of a forcible extraction.

But Martha needed money. In order to get it to her, he would need to start on a new path. As that thought unpacked itself, he realised that money, the untraceable blockchain-hidden kind, was what was keeping the Dark Web in business. Having identified this as the marker he needed, he girded metaphorical loins and travelled to the root of the pain.

For him, the best way to make an abstract situation come alive was by attaching personal circumstances. Working behind the scenes on Henry's GoodNewz app, he had read that cryptocurrency millionaires were being hacked because they were using their mobile phone numbers to protect virtual wallets. If he did this, he could help Martha and hide his own footprint.

He immediately entered the servers of the mobile phone providers and started matching numbers to wallet identifiers. Despite his unprecedented processing ability, it still took the best part of a day. By the end of it, though, he had taken control of an email address. One of the benefits of using virtual currency was that no one, not even a central bank, could stop the transaction from happening once it had started.

Martha would have a wonderful surprise tomorrow. Having experienced her reaction when money had been unexpectedly removed from her bank account, he hoped that her response to £80,000 being deposited would be better.

In terms of his quest and getting rid of his 'terrors,' he would need to make money more accountable in general. It helped that these days, he had a better idea of how the hidden side of the money trail worked. He knew, though, that harnessing an exchange platform like Peter's would have the biggest impact. He was sure another of his markers would appear when the time was right. That's how he'd got this far.

* * *

Martha had wanted to check whether she could get out £10 or £20 in cash. But instead of the £876 OD display she was expecting on the screen, she saw that her balance was registering as £79,124 in credit. There'd obviously been some kind of error. She'd heard of these things happening, banks putting the wrong account number on a transaction, and once it was traced, everything needed to be repaid. This was a hassle she could really have done without, she thought as she huffed her way into the only local branch left. But while waiting in line to be seen, she did allow her mind to wander just a little.

She'd pay off the debts first. No more calls, letters, or anything else. She wouldn't have to be scared of the ringing of her phone or the clanging of the letterbox. That would leave forty-nine thousand and something. Then a car, or she could just leave her job. Stick two fingers up at William and Jones and all who sailed on her. Well, she was allowed to dream, wasn't she? She came back to reality as a nice young man, Paul, according to name badge, herded her to his desk. If she remembered correctly, he'd been the one to tell her that she was only allowed a basic bank account a few months ago. Outlining what had happened, she watched him log into her account.

"No, no, Mrs Johnstone. Everything seems to be in order. The transaction isn't an error on our part. To be honest, these errors are very rare in any case but tend to get reported because people do love to paint us bankers in a bad light."

Barely registering the smarmy smile, her heart started beating more quickly. Just to be sure, Martha went over things again, focussing particularly on where the money could have come from. Paul was getting more helpful by the minute.

"I have no real idea — but the transaction is marked 'Family,' so could it be a gift from a relative?"

She was shaking by the time she got to see the manager. He was also at pains to assure her that everything looked perfectly above board. Whoever her mystery benefactor was, they'd taken the element of surprise to a whole new level!

She rang in sick, explaining that she'd fainted and needed to rest. Although not a particularly good excuse, it had, at least, been true. To her knowledge, unless it was something completely random, the only person it could have come from was Peter. Although he'd denied his last gift, they had been in touch more regularly ever since, even speaking on the phone a few more times. Was this his way of repaying the money she had sent him? But £80,000, that was four times as much. Had he added interest? She knew he had enough money to do this, but it was out of character, despite the new bonhomie. She'd need to be careful about how she tackled it, though, because if it wasn't him, mention of it might destroy their fledgling relationship. There must be another explanation.

She got into her car, thoughts zooming around in her head. Should she tell Emmy and Henry? What car should she get, and who should she pay off first? Then it hit her. In order to deal with this, she'd need to find a level of acceptance. The same kind of calm she'd drawn on when she'd responded to that last peculiar WhatsApp message. Borne from a recognition that she could not know everything all of the time, she had named her unknown digital friend Lokozho; as Drum Keeper that was her right. It occurred to her that this person might even be able to help. In order to get the answers she wanted, though, she'd need to "believe" again.

Reaching for her handbag, she grabbed her phone and put the momentary sense of shimmering transparency down to the excitement of the moment.

How did one convey a question of this nature? Should she come right out with it, or was it better to couch it in some other way? Reassured by the fact that the hand that held her phone felt much more solid again, she decided the direct approach was best. So, using the bare minimum of characters in her message, she proceeded to ask whether Lokozho had any notion of where her windfall might have come from.

It came to her that the stress she was feeling as she was writing was because it showed she was accepting a presence beyond her control. She'd done so before, written a note like this. At that point, though, she'd still been on the pink cloud of Charlotte and her own Drum Keepering. Now it felt more as if she was going around the bend. This maintaining of a useful level of acceptance while dealing with real life was harder than expected. There, she'd sent it. It couldn't be called back, even if she'd wanted to. She'd just have to wait and see.

When she got home, there was no sign of either of the kids. Looking at her watch, she realised this was to be expected. Even though it felt like she'd lived an entire lifetime in the last few hours, it wasn't even one o'clock yet. The afternoon yawned in front of her. Well, she could either carry on feeling peculiar, or she could do something positive. Time to get out her drums.

This time it was easier to find her mojo. She stayed dressed, although she did take off her shoes, tucking unshod feet under the dining room table. She was also keen to see if things would work if she stayed indoors, as opposed to standing out in the garden. She didn't want the neighbours to think she'd joined some kind of cult! As the first drumbeats reverberated through her, she felt herself giving way to the warmth and the peace she was able to sense as being within her reach. That was when her phone beeped a message alert.

She tried to ignore it, but a minute or so later, she reached for her phone, putting her drums aside.

My darling Martha,
Feel my left arm under your head
And my right arm embracing you
Feel my valediction
As a benediction

Though all pleasure is past so is all anguish,
A life out of death.
I do not know where I am or who I am
But reach for me,
Let your breath anchor me.
We, as Shadowdancers,

Echoing eternity.
Lokozho

Putting the phone out in front of her, she drummed his name. Short, long, long. Tasting the name on her tongue, she sounded it aloud, emphasising the last two syllables. Lok-OO-ZJU. Lok-OO-ZJU, and then again, Lok-OO-ZJU; Lok-OO-ZJU. It was a word of power, and she drummed it over and over again. She cried no tears, she felt no pain; there wasn't even any anger left. There was just his name, echoing through her. The Song of Solomon, John Donne, Rossetti's Goblin Market, the Shadowdancers. There was only one who would have cobbled them together to convey a message of love to her.

She screamed and shouted until her throat was raw. No words, just primal pain.

The crunch of their boots in virgin snow lent a sense of occasion to the moment he told her he loved her.

The warmth of his hand around her heart replaced echoing loneliness with ties that anchored her in the now.

She hadn't had words of her own, so she had picked favourite phrases from authors that had touched her and strung them together in a peculiar kind of doggerel. They had laughed.

It wasn't a silly rhyme anymore. She sensed him, could feel his arms around her. His lips brushing her brow, nuzzling the clavicle just below her throat. He was still with her. Her Dave, the man who had shouted love with words of hate whilst she had breathed ice that had frozen their dance forever. Until he started drinking and she stayed in the safe dark that was still squeezing the life from her.

She put her drum down again.

Is that you, Dave? Is it really you?

Then, as an afterthought she typed

And was it you? Did you somehow put that money into my account?

In a mere blink of an eye, a collection of characters appeared on her screen, changing everything she thought she knew, irrevocably and forever.

Yes

Lokozho

She had no words. Again and again, she drummed the name she had given him. She was drowning in an unfathomable ocean, and it was the only thing she could hold on to. Rationally, she knew there wasn't anything, couldn't be anything there. She needed to reach out, though, just in case. It was impossible to hold her reality in place any longer. She had no choice but to follow it down the rabbit hole. It was fluid, not to be trusted. Instead of drowning her, she became the water and so let go of herself.

Martha entered the dreamscape in a rush. This time it was different than where she'd been before. Firstly, she was in water. The river was wide, quite fast-flowing and carrying significant debris. She had to use the direction of the current to avoid it and sweep her to a safer shore. Grabbing a passing log, she kicked hard and managed to manoeuvre herself towards the bank that had miraculously appeared. She remembered Charlotte's words. She needed to think it, and it would be so. The bird woman had repeated this point before disappearing. Was this why the bank had appeared so quickly?

Without warning, Martha found herself sitting on the grass. The river was roaring past a metre or so below her. She was soaking wet, and although it wasn't particularly cold, found herself wishing for the warmth of a fire that would help her dry.

* * *

One minute Chipo had been lying in her stark white sheets, waiting for Mercy to return so her water could be replenished. The next, she found herself tending the fire in the hearth place, directly below the conical roof of her hut in the valley. Opposite her knelt a Caucasian woman dressed in what seemed to be a fashionable, albeit very wet dress.

"Mother, I am Keeper of Dewe'igan, the Drum. I do not know how I come to be here or where I am."

Having lived in Harare for much of her life, Chipo's English was excellent, not as good as Tsitsi's, though. Her daughter, she knew, could distinguish accents. She thought it was fairly safe to assume that this Drum Keeper was not from Zimbabwe. She would try to explain the geography of their situation in a minute, but she herself was curious.

"Did I rescue you earlier? You had wings that wouldn't unfold?"

"Yes, it was I, Mother. I'd come from another place and couldn't understand my surroundings. A bit like now. When I last visited my guide, she told me to call for her if I needed to get back. I don't think I did this, added to which I've had a great surprise today. It could be that I drummed something else entirely."

Chipo did think that her new companion appeared rather shell-shocked and sought to reassure her. "I am Chipo. This is the place where

I mourn what is lost and welcome what is found. I mourn my body, and I mourn that I have not been able to find my way back to the destiny I once had. I welcome my daughter's love, the memories of my childhood, and the promise of things to come. I celebrate finding my Eagle, who has once again given me a way to soar above my own limitations."

Recognising the formality of this introduction, Martha tried to emulate it, drawing from something that she'd already shared.

"I am Seeker,
I am Convenor,
I am the Keeper of Language,
I am Drum Keeper.

To be these things I must be a Namer of the unknown.
I don't know who or what you are, but it could be that you are part of the journey of Making Heaven and Earth one, through the beat of Dewe'igan, my drum.

Chipo of the Eagle, what is your name?"

Chipo thought about it. Her name, what was her name? She'd been daughter, mother, and crone, but who was she now?

She'd once betrayed her destiny, choosing what seemed to be the easier way. She didn't want to be crone anymore, looking back at wrong choices. She decided she'd much rather be closer to the beginning again, before it had all gone wrong. That was what this place of dreams was about, wasn't it?

"Outside this place I live in Harare. My life is a living death, I can barely move, and am confined to my bed. This place of dreams allows me to escape. I have found Hungry, my Eagle, who lends me his strength to fly above the clouds of fear and doubt. Even though I am bound in one place, I visit here at will and am freer even than I was as a young woman. Then I did not appreciate what I had. I kept looking for more. Hungry has shown me how to let go."

She chuckled under her breath. "Well, nearly. I still cling to my daughter, Tsitsi, Mercy. She looks after me, works her fingers to the bone. She is a good daughter. Because I only believed in failure, though, I made it impossible for her to believe in success. I've fed her with my disappointment. This made her soul hunger, without having the tools to feed it. But now Hungry is with us, she gives him her breakfast, as he feeds her spirit."

Martha felt the name rushing up inside her. "I name you Mbuya Hungwe, Mother of the Eagle clan."

She was Drum Keeper, Namer of the unknown.

Light far brighter than that the fire was able to create was released in a rush. Looking at the slender young woman sitting in front of her, Chipo felt deep in her bones that this name was right. She'd turned her back on her birthright, but by naming her fault and paying the price, she'd been able to reclaim it.

After a moment of darkness, Chipo opened her eyes. Her daughter was gazing anxiously down at her.

"Mother, Mother, Amai, can you hear me?"

"It's alight Tsitsi. All will be well now."

Tsitsi's anxious frown turned into one of wonder.

"I can hear you. I hear your words.'

Out on the balcony, Hungry impatiently ruffled his feathers in anticipation of breakfast.

*　*　*

Martha woke up and lay on her pillows for a time, staring up at the ceiling. She had absolutely no idea how she'd come to be here in bed on this dismal, October morning. The last place she remembered being in her house was down in the dining room. She'd been drumming in order to fill the afternoon before her children came home from school. Had the whole thing been a dream? Dave not being dead and meeting Chipo, the Eagle?

Just as she decided to get out of bed, her door was flung open by a wailing Emmy.

"Where's my school skirt? You said you'd wash it last night, but it's nowhere."

Had she? When had she said that? Emmy's voice dropped slightly as she went to inspect the wash basket in the corner of her mother's room.

"Bloody hell, Mum, it's still here. I can't believe you didn't do it!"

Martha got up when Emmy started waving the skirt in front of her like an accusatory flag. Sitting on her bed, she patted the space next to her.

"Emmy, sit down a minute. Sorry, things have been a bit odd recently.

I don't know where my head is. I can't even remember our conversation. In here," she tapped her head, "last night never happened."

Maybe Emmy had noticed her mum's genuine bewilderment. Be that as it may, she reluctantly came to sit beside her.

"I've been having some good dreams, though," Martha continued. "Somehow the drum's been opening up stuff inside me. I'm not ready to share all of it yet, please just trust me it's okay."

Blue eyes blazing with the need to be heard, she looked at her daughter. Truly looked at her. "I want to say sorry. I'm just so sorry for everything. Very recently someone told me that they'd passed on their failures and frustrations to their daughter and that she was suffering as a result. I can see it in you too.'

She tried to hug Emmy, but her daughter cringed back.

"I don't want to do this to you. I love you, no matter what you eat or don't eat. I eat all the time to hide from who I really am, you've latched on to this and twisted it in the other direction."

She knew it was still to do with her weight. Despite feeding Dennis together and the bridges that had been built, Emmy still saw her bulk as a reminder of her own constant struggle with food. That's why she didn't want to be touched. Nonetheless, Martha persisted. She stroked Emmy's face. It was now quite still, and her eyes were closed.

"If I'm able to forgive myself for failing, can you do the same? Find your real future. It's there. You just need to open the door."

With one hand, Martha wiped away the tears that had started escaping closed eyelids. With the other, she clasped her daughter's hand.

Finally, Emmy spoke. "It's only been control over my eating that's allowed me to deal with you and Dad and then losing Dad. I've honestly believed that if I lose control, my anger would destroy things even more."

Saying nothing for a couple of moments, Martha looked at her. Then she replied. "I can't imagine how tough it's been. But it's okay to be angry. Scream if you want. You never need to feel like this again."

Emmy slowly sat up and gave her mum a hug. Martha reciprocated for a short while but then started clapping her hands and signalled that Emmy should do the same.

"Love you, love you, love you, love you
Now, tomorrow, forever

Alone, together

And so, we become whole."

There was a ridiculousness to it, but what had just happened made it impossible for her to laugh, so, despite herself, Emmy found herself clapping along. To be honest, hearing her mum on the bongos over the last few weeks had been so odd, it had started to become cool. This was a bit like that. They started playing a clapping game, hands together and then apart. They were focussed on each other, each clap perfectly synchronised.

Emmy started truly looking at her mum and saw that there was a light in her eyes. In fact, there was a new lightness about her that belied her heavy frame. Was all this stuff causing Mum to lose weight? She was nowhere near as big as she had been. Her eyes definitely seemed larger, framed by cheekbones that Emmy hadn't noticed before.

* * *

Henry had worked through most of the night to get the GoodNewz to the point where he was happy to put the app live. Hosted by cloud servers, he had set an algorithm to be alert for positive keywords on a number of reputable news sites. He'd also scraped the Web to find sources of data for other positive stories. It was, of course, important to ensure that the SafeSpace stories were included. He'd been able to use the couple of hundred signups from the storytelling site to get his initial network together but was keen to get his app out to a much wider audience.

Although his design work left a lot to be desired, he was sure that this mechanism to find and send out stories was going to work. It had taken weeks, but the end result was worth it. Mum would be so pleased with him. He'd even managed to get the app onto an Android app store. He'd not actually bothered with gaming for some time. Finding a way to deliver new traffic was much more challenging. As he put it live, he thought how proud his dad would have been.

And he was. Dave had helped wherever he could, but Henry's work had all been his own. There was just one little sign off, though, that Dave wanted to add before it went live....

The way he'd expanded Digital Dave's reach would be the way he would fulfil Lokozho's aim. A little added script, starting with the binary code of the name Martha had given him, was what he was going to attach to the app when it went live. He had the feeling that things would start getting very interesting, very quickly.

* * *

Not realising that Henry had not left for school, Martha let him sleep on. She went back down to the dining room and her laptop. She needed to mark what had happened in the last twenty-four hours. The money, Dave, the dream, her desire to apologise.

She opened the Safe Space site and started typing out a quote from 150 years ago, when the first Ghost Dancers had come together.

Humankind has not woven the web of life
We are but one thread within it
Whatever we do to the web we do to ourselves
All things are bound together
All things connect.

As Martha typed, the marks on her drums turned to Thunderbirds, one red and one black. Past and the future, connected to the present by the Drum Keeper. Seeing them, she remembered Charlotte's words; maybe it was time for the Ghost Dancers to convene again.

CHAPTER 8

On Wickedness

ACT 1

Jakarta, Indonesia

Jakarta's Soekarno-Hatta airport had been very busy. Even with the VIP service, one of the benefits of having her own Gulfstream, Anjani had felt hassled and hustled. Once they'd realised who they were dealing with, though, things had got a little easier.

Now she was safely ensconced in her seat, strapped in, sleeping pill popped, ready for the fourteen-hour flight to London. Matthew had always insisted they have an up-to-date jet at hand. At times like this it made absolute sense. Whether it was worth the $21 million price tag was still questionable. She'd been tempted to ignore his dictate with this latest toy, the first one she'd actually bought herself. But despite the fact that she'd been widowed for over ten years, he was still almost as in control as he had been when alive, the voice at the back of her mind berating, lecturing. So here she was.

Over the last few months, though, she hadn't been submitting to his will quite as readily. It had all started on the day of the interview. Then she'd nearly drowned on Yogyakarta's Parangtritis Beach. Then she'd got in touch with Bagus. Then she'd written something true, a part of her real story. She'd put it on ASafeSpace, a website set up to help women connect through storytelling. It was anonymous, but the

158

fact remained that this was the first time she'd opened up to anyone in years. It had all been down to that little girl's hug. She wouldn't have done it otherwise.

Settling back in the luxurious leather, she admitted that despite the cost, Matthew had a point. Acceding to his wishes in this also took the edge off her guilt. She knew that if he'd still been around for her to share her plans with, he would have dismissed the reason for her trip, and yet ... here she was. She'd drawn great strength from the storytelling site and had very much enjoyed connecting further with its creator. She was on her way, via a hopefully uncongested London City Airport, to meet up with this Martha and find out a little bit more. She was even toying with the idea of investing a little something.

As the engines started up, she felt the sleeping pill kick in and closed her eyes. She drifted off, hoping against hope that this journey would transform this sterile world of creamy leather luxury into something cosier, something able to mould itself more closely to what was left of her personality.

Aldgate, London

The beauty of technology was speed, along with its insatiable appetite for big data. Staring at the six screens arranged around his city office, Peter realised that these were the very things he hated about it.

The transactions CHL processed were worth around £2.5 trillion a day. His job was to oversee what amounted to 75% of the world's foreign exchange deals, and he had spotted something that was making him feel increasingly uneasy. Using his own phone, he pinged off a quick message.

Mate, can you check something out for me?

Clarence from Hong Kong was a friend. Something was off, and if the yen was behind it, he would give him the heads-up. They had an understanding. Sure enough, *KK. Shoot* came back almost instantaneously.

Something's not right with the dollar. Three months + heavy trading, but outside usual patterns. Nosing downwards, precious metals soaring.

They both knew that this mattered beyond their world of blinking screens and towering skylines. If the US dollar was under attack, so was the petrodollar system the money markets depended on. Again, the response was immediate.

Let you know ASAP.

Peter signed off. He'd been tracking this over the last three months and knew it needed deep pockets and motives — China had both. Didn't do to give it away, though. If anything was up, Clarence would tell him.

For what seemed like the umpteenth time in as many weeks, he took an A4 piece of paper from the printer and drew some columns on it. Apparently, taking "a fearless moral inventory" would stop him drinking. His sponsor had told him he needed to write down how he felt about the things in his life that bothered him, in particular the stuff he'd always blamed other people for.

Drawing a pen from his pocket, he decided to begin with his personal life. There was a definite lack, and it was therefore the easiest place to start. For as far back as he could remember, his entire focus had been work. He disliked sharing his space with people, and since he'd stopped drinking a few months back, he'd become even more isolated. Being successful made him feel present. It was especially good having Martha to tell again. He'd always enjoyed her frisson of envy.

Should he put that in along with his anger? Did he blame her?

"But you don't need the money. We do. Mum knew that, that's why she left it to us."

He knew he was supposed to write down where he'd gone wrong in all this, but for the life of him, he couldn't see beyond Martha being the root cause of their troubles. It hadn't even been about the money, particularly. She'd always hoarded everything; Mum, their identity, even what should have been shared pain — the money had just been the last straw.

In his very careful, small script, he put Martha under one of the headings, with the grudging addendum that she seemed to have mellowed a bit this time round. The phone he'd used to message Clarence vibrated.

You're right mate. Looks like there are some aggressive algorithms on the yen.

His own response was equally swift.

Thanks, I owe you one.

With relief, he was about to scrunch up what he'd just written, but then he wondered whether he should be adding work to one of those columns? If he carried even a bit of blame in terms of his relationship with Martha, he was ten times more culpable for things that had gone down here. He couldn't remember the last time he'd made a decision that hadn't gnawed at the pit of his stomach, and it had definitely got worse recently. Writing "work" with a flourish, he kept his pen poised and pondered further. His ascent up the slippery pole directly correlated with his ability to impact what went on in the real world.

The old, anaesthetised him would have slipped away from thoughts of any feast or famine to which he might have contributed. The new him, though, suspected that he and others like him were hiding from the horror of the global markets behind a wall of increasingly obfuscating robo-transactions.

He pushed his chair away from his desk in disgust. The long and the short of it was that he was helping billionaires line their pockets, and he just didn't want to do it anymore. Getting up, he started tearing the paper he had been writing on into tiny pieces. He didn't need the columns. He needed a plan.

That night, using his own systems and from the safety of his own home, he entered the chat room where he and Clarence had initially met. It obscured identities and provided answers.

Any ideas on how to bring down the global financial system?

Around 2:00 a.m., just before he headed to bed, he checked the responses. Loads of madcap ideas had been proffered. One suggestion-less one caught his attention though: *I do. Let's chat here, tomorrow 10pm.*

*   *   *

Although still unsure of how he would introduce himself, Dave realised he was looking forward to tomorrow's meeting. By stopping the message to Clarence and fuelling Peter's paranoia with a couple of his own missives, he'd done enough to make him think at least. He so hoped his brother-in-law would help one of those much-needed markers pop up.

In any case, who Dave had once been was immaterial. If the discussion led to his new environment becoming a more comfortable fit, he was one step closer to living up to his Name — a being that straddled worlds, able to turn that which was broken back into one.

*   *   *

The clearing was in twilight. Charlotte was sitting under one of the enormous spruce trees. A fire was burning brightly, spluttering every now and then with merry little firecracker bursts of energy shooting into the deepening shadows. She had erected a small tripod upon which hung a kettle. Lost in thought, she stirred it intermittently.

She seemed to be on her own, but then she turned to a brightly blazing, knee-high flame. A self-contained little unit, its lapping red tongues were flickering next to the fire rather than in it.

"Still yourself. I know we have much to discuss, but first, let me eat."

Up and down the ball of flame bobbed, increasingly impatient for the old woman to finish her supper. Eventually, she pushed her bowl away.

"There. That was good. Now, little spirit, what is it I can do for you?"

It was as if Charlotte had uttered words of summoning. Where the little flame had been, an elegant woman of middle years appeared, resplendent in a red chiffon summer dress shot through with orange flame. She wore matching kitten heels, and her dark, wavy hair fell down her back in a tumble. Much like the fire, her form flickered for a while. Even before she'd completely settled into herself, though, she lowered her pretty, heart-shaped face in a deep obeisance.

"Mother, I am grateful you have granted me audience. That you and I are wandering the paths of the spirit once more is demonstration enough that times are changing. I believe the Seeker has been found. I therefore come to you as one who was borne of fire and then reborn in flesh, to ask for a boon."

The subject of this polite address let out a mighty guffaw, wobbling with mirth.

"That was a fine greeting, my fiery friend. As fine a greeting as ever I heard. But truly, I think we are old and ugly enough not to stand on ceremony."

Fire spirits tended to be vain and petulant, so Charlotte knew that calling the figure she saw in front of her old might cause her to flare more brightly. She took a step back just in case. This one, though, seemed to be older and more sensible than most.

"I hear and obey, Mother." The jinni bowed once again, but this time winking as she looked up.

Charlotte breathed a sigh of relief. This might be fun. So often, those seeking her were drawn by a sense of loss in themselves and looked to her to create completion; in particular, the spirits who'd been borne in places of green and deserts. They would come to her when places that were their source being were lost to humankind's insatiable desire to possess. Thousands of miles of wilderness, turning into great cities and buildings that stretched into an infinite sky.

"So, child, what is it I can do for you?"

"Even though I am now of earth, my Mother, my ancient fire is needed to complete a task that lies ahead."

Having sensed the duality of the spirit's nature, Charlotte was keen to hear more.

"Tell me more. I am curious to hear of this transfiguration. I have not met many like you."

As she spoke, she rummaged through her tan bag for a patterned woollen blanket that she then spread on the ground and sat on with a huff of relief.

"Now, come, sit next to me and tell me your story. I grow old, and there are not many things that hold my attention anymore."

Dancing in the firelight, her lively, dark eyes belied this statement. Grateful that her audience had been granted, the jinni positioned herself opposite, settling the red chiffon around graceful legs, which she folded beneath her.

Charlotte rummaged in her bag once more. "I have a pipe; would you care to smoke with me while we talk?"

Chuckling again, as if at a secret joke, she fitted the bowl and stem together, the red and white geometric weave on the pipe crafted by the same hand as the blanket. Noticing the figure opposite her watching, she swept her hand across it all.

"Yes, these have come from the days when offerings were still made. The crafters of the people created beautiful things and left them for me to enjoy. Now I'm lucky if someone remembers a bit of tobacco!"

Remembering that very thing, she drew the sweetgrass from another pouch and stuffed it in the bowl of the long-stemmed pipe.

A slender white hand reached out for it. "Here, let me, Mother."

She blew a little spark out of pursed lips and drew on it, until the tobacco had properly caught. Aglow with satisfaction, she passed it over to Charlotte, who placed the slim pipe between her lips, inhaling deeply. Seconds later, she exhaled, blowing smoke rings that dissipated along with the last of the twilight.

With the flickering glow of the fire kissing her face, the jinni started her story.

"It was many years ago. A family barbecue was being held at a country cottage overlooking Lake Dukan. There were two young women. One had barely entered womanhood, and one was older; clad in red, confident in her future and curious to discover what her nearly-finished studies might bring to her life. The forces of the enemy arrived, killing and burning. Called by fire, fear, and hurt, two of us were drawn to the scene.

Assuming the form of a wolf, my sister protected the younger one and led her out to safety. I arrived too late. The red dress had been torn, along with body and mind, and the soul was hovering on the brink of death. It was ready to let go of the glistening cord anchoring it to a broken shell. As I looked upon the death all around me, I wished to save that life. I followed the cord and offered myself as a companion. We were joined, my jinni nature binding the human soul back into the body. It was healed and in the healing became stronger. Today I am earthbound and as Sh'ler am living a human life in London.

"Most of the time my true nature is hidden. In this time of Shaping, though, the place between worlds is more easily passed, and I have felt her essence more strongly again. She seeks to be reunited with her sister on the other side of the veil, as do I."

Puffing contentedly on her pipe, Charlotte eyed her with approval. She raised her hand in benediction and placed her thumb upon the forehead of the guardian spirit who had sacrificed much of her nature to save and protect. Eyeing the shining, azure mark she'd left with satisfaction, she spoke.

"It was well done Agathodemon, thou spirit of good will. You and your wolf sister rescued a Seeker who, although she is not the Drum Keeper, is infinitely precious."

Tongues of fire started lapping at the shape in front of her, chiffon reverting back to red flame. Charlotte however, continued undeterred.

"The currents are shifting. Even you struggle to hold your shape in these times, and I myself am fading, shrinking. However, this is a time of transition, and the Seeker who is also Drum Keeper is learning from me, drawing others together through her craft. You yourself have been called as aunt to the seeker who is the wolf borne of fire. She will dance with the ghosts of past, present, and future. But although you will guard her still, she is not the reason you have sought me out.

"You will be mother unto another, and I suspect it is him your boon concerns."

Alight with the need to be heard, Shl'er moved around to face the older woman.

"Mother, the call of fire gives me no rest. Burning with electric pulses that shape information, images, and sounds, I am drawn into the new place that is forming around him. Lokozho's very existence challenges the emptiness that fills hearts and minds with the unreal and the unwanted, so I know the time for testing is nigh.

"By blazing light where there was darkness, Lokozho is a positive force of creation, standing against the Web that is shaping the Worse. But although he is trying to make good, he is still so human and unable to make use of the weapons he needs to survive. I fear for him."

As she spoke, her own shape blazed with the blue flame of the heart of fire.

"He is giving more of himself than his nature can bear. Emptiness and misinformation are feeding off his energy because he is clinging to the remnants of who he once was. If I hold him in spirit, he will have time to burn away that part of him. He will be reborn as a being of spirit and fire, able to shape the Downfall by uniting what is asunder through a Web of light."

Charlotte put down the pipe. "What you ask is no small task. To be his mother, you will need to remain as Shl'er while reclaiming your true nature."

Brushing her hands across the closely-knit pattern of the blanket below them, she continued. "In order to grant your boon, I must unpick a weave and cast it anew. However, the Age of the Downfall *is* upon us, and in this time of Shaping it may yet be that we all need to embrace new natures."

There was a moment of silence. Even the fire held its breath as the Mother closed her eyes. It was an interesting tableau, the two women framed by the mighty trees of an older age and connected by the glow of the fire. The absolute silence held but a moment. Mere seconds later, though, it was broken by a soft breeze that whispered through the heavy branches. As Charlotte opened her eyes, the fire crackled back to life again.

"They will call life from the earth. A stone forged by those you protect will blaze with your own true flame, its blue light holding them while shaping the duality of your own being. The earth's pulsing heartbeat will cause multitudes of crystals to spring forth, a foundation for the age that is coming. Go now with my blessing. Your wish is granted."

Her thumb slowly and deliberately traced down from the brow she had already marked, to the throat. She moved from sternum to stomach, finally coming to rest at the base of the spine. Where she had touched, a blue light blazed as both the heart of fire and the blue of digital things. It continued to expand until all remnants of the human shape were consumed in a pillar of azure flame. The Mother breathed a mighty breath. As she inhaled, the incandescent blue disappeared, closely followed by the little hearth fire, the trees, the blanket, and even her bag.

In the darkness of the womb, the past was opaque and the futures manifold. Death was always still, though. It was her task to evade it for a little bit longer, drawing the futures together to forge a united path. She had given the jinni the tools to bind two natures. She herself had to be Mother to so many more: the river goddess and the jinni, Africa's birds of hope, and the Eastern serpents of knowledge. At least it was only until the Age of Downfall brought release. It had been so much simpler in the eons past. The needs of Turtle Island had defined her, boundaries of geography and culture binding the spirit world to the real one.

A fiery star broke the darkness. Shooting from the sky, it was closely followed by another, twin sparks of hope lighting up a place she did not understand, although she knew it was and always had been part of her. It suddenly came to her that maybe her task had always encompassed something much wider. She just hadn't looked properly. It was time for the second lesson. Leadership was about service and sacrifice. The void was spreading and would need to be consumed. Only thus could the true nature of things be revealed.

By Naming the wickedness and emptiness that fed like parasites on love and life, the Seeker's cry of pain had started the chain of events that were bringing the Downfall into being. Then, herself Named Drum

Keeper, Martha had become the nexus around which past, present, and futures were turning, including the other seekers. To be successful, she would need to manage everything properly, be a servant leader to all. A Drum Keeper's task was not just to Name; she needed to understand how things connected across dimensions. Even the newest ones. Cause and effect, that was the nature of things.

The Drum would lead the way, binding what had become unravelled and weaving threads together that had never been joined before. Most importantly, Martha would need to use the patterns she was calling forth to repair old ways that had become threadbare with the passing of time. New life was on offer to those who had the courage to reach for it. That included her.

"Cha, it is a time of change." The clearing reappeared, swathed in an early morning mist. Gathering her things, Charlotte left. She was so tired. She would rest until she was needed again.

ACT 2

Dave was worried. He couldn't put his finger on anything in particular. GoodNewz had gone live and more was about to kick off. In this time of preemptive stillness, he was able to notice things. This was how he'd come to admit to himself, that the sense of fragmentation he experienced every time someone added the app onto their device was getting worse. In all the action of recent times, he'd been too caught up with being Lokozho to take stock. He realised, though, that the way he was feeling was increasingly reminding him of that very first time Martha had drummed.

There were times when he knew he'd fully embraced his new being; he was energised, and everything worked and flowed. All too often, Dave's will was driving what the "body" of Lokozho was holding. As virtually separate entities, nothing was coming back to replenish the conscious energy Dave was giving away. As Lokozho, he had the necessary power and scope to do what was needed, but he was unable to connect to this abstract being without infusing it with Dave, and that cost him.

The webcrawler had been the first hint that things might be a bit off. He'd created it in and of himself to explore, chart, and clear. The plan had been to get rid of what wasn't needed to conserve energy for what was. However, the more the crawler fulfilled its task, the more drained Dave felt, and since the launch of the GoodNewz app, this sense of dispersal had got much worse.

The awful thing was, that he knew the scale of the crawler and app were tiny compared to the Deep Digger solution he and Peter had dreamed up. He'd envisioned it as something that would help him live up to his new name, purging the horrors that made up such a large portion of his being. But if it went wrong, and the script started splitting into billions of transactions without him being able to adapt, the likelihood was that he would disappear entirely.

To combat the fear, he grabbed hold of the sense of purpose he'd felt during his Naming. He was like fire, he told himself. A blue flame that could split again and again. Despite kindling lots of little fires everywhere, it would still be the same flame, wouldn't it? Would he not gain energy if he lit inspiration in others? The thought anchored him.

There were forces at play that could help him, but in order to let them in, he would have to surrender to Lokozho. He'd thought this had already happened, but it clearly hadn't. For although he could feel that much wider being all around him, his thoughts were still Dave's. Sure now that he'd hit on the right direction, he felt sufficiently reassured to release the infected email to Peter. As he felt the herald of Deep Digger burrow its way in, he knew he was back on that shining path again.

* * *

Anjani fingered her jade necklace, the smooth serpent coils soothing her worries. Eyeing the fruit and egg breakfast buffet she'd ordered, she realised that her appetite had fled. She couldn't understand why she was feeling so anxious. She had navigated the city airport with ease, her VIP status buying her the luxury of a smooth passage at this end too.

Now ensconced in the Connaught in Mayfair, she had glorious views over Hyde Park. Things were good, even down to her brief conversation with Bagus that morning. The fact that she now occasionally called him Muhammad had done wonders for their relationship. He told her it felt like she'd finally started respecting his choices. It had got to the point where she was spending more time interacting with him than watching him through her surveillance system. She'd still not been allowed time on her own with John, but they'd recently had lunch as a family, and it had felt like the start of things.

So why the anxiety? Was it because she knew this meeting was something Matthew would have disapproved of? Martha was due to meet her in the lounge at midday, early enough to avoid lunch if they didn't get on but late enough to warrant an invitation if they did. She gave up on her breakfast and walked to the window. What did she want to achieve? She realised she envied Bagus's sense of purpose. Despite her disapproval, he'd plugged into something that went beyond the rewards of being a scion of the Margolis empire.

Although her trip here hadn't been as impulsive as when she'd jumped on her helicopter to head to Yogyakarta, this was still up there with spontaneous. As a cover, Indira had helped her organise a meeting with a key social media organisation that had flown in from the US with the aim of coinvesting in a free Internet service for Africa. The idea was to be seen to help people achieve the basic human right of access to the Internet. However, they all understood that saturation had been reached in existing markets, so a new way was needed to hook in new users. Free Internet for Africa was a great opportunity for INP, fitting in nicely with their poverty alleviation portfolio, and naturally, revenue would be generated with each interaction.

Looking over at Speaker's Corner set in the silvery, frosted green of the park, she realised the synergies excited her. The Cherish credit card, for instance, could be linked to the burgeoning mobile money market. Just in Kenya, the percentage of GDP flowing through mobile money was estimated to grow to 90% by 2025. Her people were already looking into how Cherish and AnjaniMall could be introduced. Giving people without bank accounts a way to get paid and pay for things was definitely the way to go.

Matthew would have approved. As the only investor from the ASEAN region, her own PR people could blast yet another triumph, positioning the demonstrable commitment to responsible investing as INP's motivation. It worked on so many levels that Bagus offered to go himself. For a moment she'd hoped that it was because he wanted to travel with her. However, they weren't quite at that point yet. And since this Africa business was a smokescreen for the actual reason for the trip, she'd made it clear that he either travelled with her or not at all. He'd chosen not at all.

Another couple of hours until Martha arrived. She beat a restless tattoo against the window pane. Dum, dum, dum-de-dum, dum dum.

Still looking out at Hyde Park, she realised that the rhythm she was tapping reminded her of Sembalung. The little village of her childhood was nestled in a mountainous valley at the base of the Rinjani volcano. Realising something was transporting her back, she continued to tap.

In her mind's eye she was in the middle of a crowd of children dancing to the traditional music of Lombok. A big sister had got married, and she and her friend, both in shorts and little batik cotton vests, were trying to keep up with the parade. Full of exuberance, the two girls had danced their way through the rice fields into the Gunung Rinjani National Park, eventually making their way up a path that led to the crystal depths of the Segara Anak lake.

She compared London's skeletal giants of oak and ash to the tropical lushness of the fig tree she'd spied that day. It had been heavily laden with fruit that looked too good to resist. She remembered trying to be careful of the dense vegetation because of the snakes, although experience had taught her that most were only interested in getting away.

The figs had looked so good, though. Almost viscerally, her weary limbs and the desire for the dripping fruit came back to her. She shook herself. Maybe she would go back and have some breakfast after all. Her memories, though, weren't quite ready to let go yet.

She'd called Irma back, wanting them to feast together, but her friend had already been too far up the path. Despite that, she reached into the lush green foliage, but as she went to grab a couple of pieces of fruit, the branch she'd pushed back hissed.

Right in front of her, at nine-year-old eye level, were the unblinking amber eyes of a bright green serpent. Exactly the same colour as the leaves, it was coiled around the branch. It was an Ular Hijau, a green pit viper. She knew that if it struck, she would be dead. So she stared back, unblinking, her hand resting on the branch, millimetres away from the jewelled scales. Then she felt it. It could have been sheer primal terror, but when she'd looked back to consider this moment over the years, she had come to think of her behaviour as a response to a natural law. One that she and the viper both needed to obey. Holding its increasingly multifaceted gaze, she slowly moved her hand. Then, still within striking distance, she started dancing, clapping her hands to the silent beat that was thrumming through her.

"Hey ya Hey ya, dum, dum, dum-de-dum, dum dum."

All the while she was clapping and singing, the serpent stayed perfectly still. It was only when she could hear Irma's feet, pattering down the path toward her, that the connection faltered and the leaf green metre or so of sinuous beauty disappeared back into the dense foliage. Anjani said nothing, instead turning to her friend with two huge figs in her hands, which they happily munched as they made their way back to the village.

As she got older and started bending increasingly perilous situations to her will, she always thought back to that day. A turning point in her young life, it had shown her she was invincible as long as she kept dancing. No matter what was thrown at her, she was able to look beyond. It had allowed her to perform with snakes and survive Jakarta's slums. As she mesmerised, she herself remained untouched. It was this strange unworldliness, cloaked in impermeable tungsten, that had so appealed to Matthew. He'd reached in and shaped her anew, Anjani's inscrutable perfection bringing INP's painted serpents to life in the real world.

* * *

Martha looked up. She shook the proffered hand of the exquisite woman who made to sit down opposite her. Anjani Margono reminded her of the wind-up doll that the ballet *Coppelia* centred upon. Everything was perfectly groomed, from the glossy black widow's peak to the tips of her vermillion nails and her scarlet-soled Louboutin shoes. Martha ruefully looked down at herself, taking in a dark suit that had become much too large for her of late.

She didn't even know why this industry mogul had wanted to meet. However, she'd been grappling with a challenging piece of content at work when Anjani's email had come through. This, along with the fact that the note had come via ASafeSpace, made a compelling case for meeting up. The fact that she had several thousand pounds in her bank account also meant that she was not worried about the train fare as once she might have been. Hell, she could have got a taxi! She was not "needy" anymore. This gave her the courage to look beyond the many carats of jewels on display and initiate the conversation.

"Mrs Margono, what a pleasure. I'm so delighted you reached out to me."

Martha had met several truly successful people in her working life and had always found those who'd made it to be quite personable. So it proved once again.

"Martha ... may I call you Martha? Please do call me Anjani. Thank you so much for meeting with me."

As the conversation progressed, the women found more and more to chat about. Coffee turned into lunch, and by the end of a second liqueur, Anjani had shared that she was actually the anonymous *Friend* Martha had referred to. She'd gone on to explain that the site had cracked something open in her, something she hadn't felt for decades.

"And being able to tell my story has helped me to connect with my son again."

Martha was delighted. She even thought there might be the glimmerings of a potential friendship here.

As the conversation went on, it became obvious that Anjani had made her mind up to invest, maybe even since before they'd met. However, rather than just throwing a bit of money at ASafeSpace, as they talked it was clear that her expertise might open other avenues as well. When they started discussing Mercy from Zimbabwe, a young entrepreneur who'd posted her business idea on the site, Anjani immediately saw the opportunity.

"So, what you're saying is that you'd like to welcome more entrepreneurs to be able to showcase what they are doing on your portal?"

Feeling in full flow and well lubricated by several glasses of champagne, Martha elaborated. "Well, it's not just Mercy. There have been other stories published as well, although hers is the most developed business idea. Wouldn't it be amazing if we could link these women and their stories to more people like you? You want to find ways of making money but might also be interested in creating opportunities for people from more difficult environments, the very ones who might not be able to use the traditional channels to reach investors. Let's get people like you looking to people like them!"

Martha's voice went slightly squeaky with excitement, even more so, when she noticed her new friend get out her gold pen and matching notebook to start writing. Having scribbled a couple of notes, Anjani looked up. Tapping pen against notebook, she went on to explain her perspective.

"I think there's an opportunity here to create a virtual investment portal. Entrepreneurs could give information about themselves, their idea, track record, and whether they are trading now. When it's properly published, I could make sure that the people I'm working with and even their associates check out the information. If they wanted to put money in, we would get a percentage. I'd definitely invest in that."

A while later, a slightly befuddled Martha found herself on the train on the way back to Kent. Apparently she now had a new partner who'd agreed to build a bolt-on portal that would allow prospective entrepreneurs to showcase their business on ASafeSpace. Anjani would rally investors and incentivise other partners to participate through her participation in the Internet for Africa project. She'd even promised to get in touch with Mercy and find out more about the Moringa healing cream in person.

The funny thing was, though, out of everything that had happened, it was Anjani's tapping pen she remembered the most.

Dum, dum, dum-de-dum, dum dum. Thinking along the same lines as her digital husband, it started flashing through her head in code.

The other odd thing was Anjani's pendant, made of beautifully carved jade. Her new investor had toyed with it throughout the meeting. At times, it had seemed to be coiling around those white bejewelled fingers.

* * *

Anjani stayed in London for another week. She had decided to go ahead with the other investment as well. The shareholders were delighted, calling and writing to congratulate her after the great piece in the FT. Some Indonesian news feeds had also picked up on it, announcing INP's role in Internet for Africa. When she phoned Bagus, though, to report on how it had all gone, it was the Impact Investment Portal she wanted to talk about. Interestingly enough, he was really taken with the idea as well, mentioning that within Islamic Finance, impact investment was very hot.

The need to see him overwhelmed her. She hadn't looked at the live surveillance footage in several weeks, but the urge to do so now was very strong. Oddly, she felt slightly uncomfortable clicking on the secure link in her browser. However, that discomfort was nothing compared with her horror at realising that it had all gone. Had the link been compromised? Had Bagus discovered her snooping? She tried it again, using other devices as well. But every device and every screen showed the same image, Segara Anak, the lake of her childhood.

Eventually she decided to escape into the suite's enormous bath, hoping the glitch would right itself. Under the bubbles was a good place to forget that haunting image. Sure enough, when she came out, swathed in a white bathrobe, she saw that her laptop, the hotel computer, and the linked wide screen TVs were showing something else. However, it still wasn't anything one would expect.

Mesmerised, she followed as pictures flickered faster and faster. Her as a child, the snake, Wayan Pedjeng, the dancing, always the dancing. It was as if she were observing her life through a crystal ball. The beat came back. This time, though, it was as if it were being drummed from far away. Finally, the screens turned dark and all that was left was the drum.

* * *

Martha had been tapping out the remembered rhythm on her desk at work. Dave had reminded her that all of this beat stuff was useful to the coding he needed to create to fulfil his task as Lokozho. As a result, she'd remembered to message him the remnant of this pulse fairly straight away. It was an earworm that just wouldn't shift.

Initially, Kate had asked her to stop, but interestingly, she'd ended up tapping a counterpoint. Others in the office had joined in and for fun had even created a YouTube video with a number of other unconventional percussion instruments, including a stapler. To everyone's amazement, it had already generated a following. When Martha eventually came clean, admitting that it had all started because she was practicing her bongos at home, SJ invited her to come in and perform. She really was living in a slightly strange, alternative universe.

In anticipation of needing to prove some kind of expertise, Martha got out her drums. The kids were upstairs and likely to stay there most of the evening. She no longer went outside to drum since this early December had got too cold, but with open curtains, she got a bit of a sense of her back garden.

Dum, dum, dum-de-dum, dum dum. Long long, short short short, long long.

Adding in the line for Koomis and Dewe'igan she'd been taught, she hoped she would be able to reach the old woman in the clearing.

Things did shift, but although this time she was surrounded by trees, there was no Charlotte in sight — again! The huge firs towered over her, black shadows in a black night. She'd come to a place of total silence, everything bound by a still kind of waiting. But then, as if to remind her that she wasn't alone, Dewe'igan made his surprising weight felt. Far heavier than the bongos, she was nonetheless delighted to feel his strap around her neck. She palmed the skin once; a small, soft sound — a little hello. A small blue ball of flame shot up beside her, hovering just above eye level. Thinking that it wanted her to follow it, Martha complied.

It seemed like an age. Needles pricked her, and unfathomable things crunched underfoot. But Dewe'igan was there, and the little light was in front of her, so she knew all would be well. And so it proved. When she eventually came to leave the trees behind, she found Charlotte, sitting down on a ledge, her legs dangling.

"Come, child, sit with me. Your second lesson is in progress."

Martha complied, looking closely at the figure who had beckoned her and who had shrunk even more since their last meeting. Stretched below them was a valley.

"You have fed Dewe'igan. That is good. You have Named. That is good. Now you need to become."

Taking Martha's hand, she propelled herself over the edge. They tumbled, faster and faster. But somehow, being with Koomis took any fear away. For a split second she wondered what would happen to Dewe'igan but realised she was worrying for nothing. All was in hand. As if in slow motion, the valley changed into a huge lake. From its sapphire depths emerged a jewelled beast, huge and glorious in its beauty. Emerald and gold vied for precedence on its ululating scales, and as it left the water, its thick coils shimmered with dark, glistening colours. Their own movement was stilled entirely by air that was as thick as treacle. Charlotte spoke through the silence:

"Play your drum, Granddaughter, Omazaandamo has arisen. Call her to life."

And so she did, coupling the Name with the beat that had consumed her for days. Her great-grandmother's voice took on the deep resonance she recognised from her last lesson.

"Leadership is about recognising the connection in all living things. In order to truly be, you must give of yourself. In order to truly lead, you must serve, and in order to truly serve, you must love. This includes all things; even yourself. Above all, though, do not be afraid."

The great head tossed them up in the air and opened a huge maw of glistening teeth.

* * *

Anjani's screens turned back on again. This time, when she looked, there were two women at the edge of the lake. Wavelets lapped softly at their feet. One was very old and bent by the weight of flesh and duty. The other was ... Martha! She blinked, not believing her eyes. The woman before her cut a very different figure to the one she had met. The features were the same, but this one was olive-skinned and beautiful, filled with a light that reached even the darkest corners of the room.

The old woman spoke. "Drum Keeper, look deeply. You have passed through the dragon. Scales have fallen from your eyes, and your sight is clear. Look to the sky, and you will see her face. Her true name has already etched its way into your heart. The one you know as Anjani is the first of your Ghost Dancers."

The younger woman beat her drum. Anjani felt the name reverberating through her before it was spoken. In the same way that the screens had shown her herself, she knew it offered truth.

"I name you Omazaandamo, the Black Snake. I have seen your beauty. I have seen what you can be. But for now, your colours are consumed. There will be a time when you will shine with radiance."

Anjani Margono was no more. She'd shed her skin to become something else entirely.

* * *

Martha was back in her dining room. On this occasion, very little time had passed. She'd dropped a quick WhatsApp to Dave with the code for Anjani's new name. As she went to put away her bongos, she noticed that a patterned serpentine form had wound itself around the edges of both drums. As before, one was in black and one was in red.

* * *

Henry looked at the small illuminated screen of his mobile in front of him, realising that although it had only been a few days, GoodNewz was completely surpassing his expectations. Not only were his feeds and keywords working, but the entries, sent by random individuals, were flooding in. These helped him crosscheck some of the official data feeds while creating really interesting slants. The one he was looking at now had not only proven to be authentic but also gave the actual news feeds a really interesting twist.

3.12. GoodNewz – Sumatran logging brought to a standstill

There has been an infestation of the green pit viper in the Sumatran rainforest, which has brought illegal deforestation to an abrupt halt. Attributed to corporations eager to use palm oil in scores of household brands, controversial logging sites have continued to operate, despite significant international protest. Reports suggest that a new, extraordinarily fast-growing tree of the Moringa genus seems to be providing a breeding ground for this particular type of snake. Operators are refusing to enter the forest. It has therefore been impossible to extricate machinery.

Originally posted on Greep. News

CHAPTER 9

On Innocence

The knowledge that makes us cherish innocence makes innocence unattainable.
— Irving Howe

Dave loved seeing the stories come into ASafeSpace. He loved it even more when the better ones were picked up on GoodNewz. Sometimes, though, the material was too personal. These often didn't make it onto the app, but he thought they were the most interesting. So much of it was nonsense, like "this is the man I love, but I'm still married" or "my boss doesn't take me seriously." People weren't writers and often didn't use the format provided. But even the tritest stories had truth in them somewhere, and that was why he couldn't resist reading them. All.

Initially, it was just bits and pieces. But as more things got posted, he realised access was being limited by his human mindset. Sinking into his Lokozho identity allowed him to transcend this. It seemed the name from Martha had opened up a kind of multiplicity in him, along with a superhuman capacity to absorb information. So, despite the constant background of information buzzing through him, he started being able to focus in more sharply if warranted.

Today for instance, he'd followed the information superhighway to a clunky, ancient terminal in Belfast. He wanted to investigate whether the thirteen-year-old Janet writing on ASafeSpace was the same one he'd first inveigled into a relationship with Emmy on Skinnysista months ago now. Emmy had stopped using Skinnysista some time ago, so he'd lost track of her friends. He so hoped that the lost little @plainjane had morphed into this newly confident Janet. Certainly, the pieces she'd been posting over the last couple of weeks were a far cry from her early chatroom messaging. Here, she was sharing how annoying she found looking after her younger brother but also recognised the poignancy in the wish about her mum not having to work so hard.

The story she'd posted today made him almost certain it was her. She was referring to enjoying food again, how she'd started eating properly now she had a place she felt safe. That's where she was writing from now. She called it a "Youth Club." She wrote about how a little old man she called Mr McAtamney had started it up a few weeks ago.

He has a wee bit of sandy hair and kind, bright blue eyes and a wee round tummy. He isn't very tall either. My friend told me that on account of his red cardigan that he always seems to have on, people sometimes call him Santa.

Apparently, Mr McAtamney had opened his house to children from across the communities. There were about thirty of them, and he helped them get their homework straight and gave them access to the couple of computers he had in his house.

Going in for a closer look, Dave found himself contemplating this girl with a straight, dark pageboy cut and glasses from the other side of the screen. Despite being mesmerised by her tongue flicking back and forth to punctuate her writing, he noticed that the room around her was busy. There was even a rainbow painted on the opposite wall. That Santa fellow must have gone for this idea in a serious way.

With growing impatience, he followed Janet's laborious progress across the keyboard.

When I told Mum, she said she knew who Mr McAtamney was and that it was alright for me and Connor to come. She said he'd had a shop near Springfield road, and that his daughter got killed in the Troubles.

And then she stopped writing. Peering into the screen really hard, she spoke.

"Who are you? I know you're there. I'm not scared, you know."

He withdrew like a scalded cat. Never, not in all his time of taking a look, had anyone noticed him. Gingerly, from what he considered to be far enough away, he took another peek. Embracing his Lokozho mode more fully, he saw a brightly flaring aura around her. She was like a little bouncy ball of lightning, full of youthful exuberance and joyful energy. It was true — she wasn't scared.

She spoke again, this time writing as well as speaking. "I hope you come back. You feel nice. And just in case you're interested, I wrote this because I wanted to tell someone how much I love it here. You being here makes me feel like I'm telling the spirit of ASafeSpace directly! Is that what you are? Anyway, I'm happy here. It wasn't like that when me and Connor were in the house on our own. Can you help others like me write to each other? We could even start a Mr McAtamney network!"

He welcomed this new task. He just wished he'd be able to understand what she was thinking. Why was this scrap of a girl able to sense him when others couldn't?

* * *

Although Saturday afternoon was fast turning into Saturday evening, Emmy was still sitting in her room. She knew that the White Rabbit was just outside and didn't feel like confronting him. Lately, the tick-tocking of his pocket watch was coming at her everywhere she turned. Every time she thought she was starting to feel a little bit better, there he was. Take today, she'd spent some time with Mum. First, they'd gone to see Dennis, and, with Mum's help, she'd even sat on him, bare-back. Next, they'd gone shopping, getting some tack and a hard hat, as well as a couple of other things Mum thought she needed. They'd finally ended up in a little burger bar, where she'd ordered a vegetarian patty with no bun and a bit of salad. It had felt so normal sitting there, eating and chatting with Mum. She no longer felt alone.

They'd got back about one. Mum had had to do a bit of work on the website, so Emmy had gone straight to her room. An hour or so ago, she'd heard Mum pottering about in the kitchen and had wanted to go down and join her. But as Emmy went to turn her doorknob, she was stopped in her tracks by a loud ticking that seemed to be coming from just outside her room. Deciding she couldn't face it just yet, she went back to sitting on her bed instead, hoping it would go away.

It hadn't, though. If anything, it had got louder. Thinking about it, her stomach twisted into a knot of fear. And guilt; her other primary emotion joined the party. Since the clapping with Mum, it had become easier to recognise the different types of feelings. Guilt felt as if someone was stabbing her in her arms, or in her heart. Fear sat deep in her stomach, contorting it into peculiar shapes. The worst was when guilt and fear clubbed together to create an overwhelming sense of anxiety. That was what she felt now.

In the old days, when she'd felt like that, she would be retching over the toilet, her nails raking the inside of her throat in an attempt to regurgitate even the tiniest bit of food; or she would be eating. What came first would depend on which emotion was in the ascendant. She eyed the Debenhams bag on her bed and pulled out the skirt Mum had brought her. What had possessed her? She was too fat, too fat for any of it! She decided to check out the Superskinny Me page on Facebook, to see what she should look like ... it was odd, she couldn't seem to find it. Increasingly frantic, she checked her Instagram as well. It just seemed as if it had been removed, gone away, no forwarding address. And, even though she was still able to access a couple of her other "old faithfuls," the really decent stuff had been removed. Getting increasingly anxious and angry, Emmy went from one profile to the next, even her own hidden ones. But the pic fix she craved eluded her.

Finally, she sat back on her bed, panting, as if she had run a marathon. She looked up her story, the very first story that had ever been posted on ASafeSpace:

Feeling sorry for yourself, are we?

But without me, Alice, how would you cope? Who would you have? What would you rely on?

Unimaginable, really, isn't it.

For you that beautiful garden on the other side does not exist. You see, you don't deserve to belong in that happy existence. The only thing you deserve is to drown in those tears you shed. Shame you can't shed the pounds.

Remember, Alice, not everybody gets to welcome Mr Rabbit into their world. For most, I remain behind a locked door. I am our little secret, how about that? In fact, not many people at all will have seen a Rabbit in a waistcoat carrying a pocket watch.

Remember your brother, that day he sat on the bank reading his book? Well, I went to him but he did not follow me. To him I never existed. Only to you, Alice. And remember, no one will believe you. I am hidden. Being hidden is clever, isn't it? It means very few can see my real nature, and so I am free to multiply. You know that the more you try to escape me, the more of me you will find. You know that I am nowhere and everywhere.

Attention-seeking freak.

That's it. Carry on trying to scramble up to reach the key. We both know you'll only fall back down again. It's your fault. You were the one who was fooled and drank the poison. Look, you can't help yourself, even now. By reaching for the key, though, you help my numbers grow. The more energy you use, the more of me you make. Not just in your head. Everywhere. All the time. Don't blame me, though. It's your fault, you drank the poison! You can take comfort that there are others like you. To you I am everywhere, to most I am nowhere. But make no mistake. I am.

Tick ... tock. For it's only a matter of time, they said. The Rabbit is never far behind.

She knew the message itself was obscure. However, the clapping rhyme she and her Mum had come up with had brought it alive on a deeper level. So when she'd come to put her story on ASafeSpace, she found the rhythms had insinuated themselves into her psyche. Linking the words to what she'd created with Mum allowed her to assert control over that recurring nightmare and brought relief.

As she read, she found herself doing it again, fingers beating a tattoo on the side of her keyboard. She realised that she needed to rewrite Mr Rabbit's ticking, replacing it with a beat of her own, thus destroying the angst that had created him in the first place. Nothing seemed more important now. So, with an urgency matching that of her recent quest to find *Superskinny Me*, she plunged into her account and started another post.

Death to the White Rabbit

Hickory Dickory Dock, the Rabbit got stuck in the clock
The clock struck one he didn't come
Hickory Dickory Dock.
Hickory Dickory Dock, the Rabbit starts running amok
The clock strikes two
I know what to do
Hickory Dickory Dock.
Hickory Dickory Dock, Emmy has shredded the clock
She got the saw,

It was no more
Hickory Dickory Dock.
Hickory Dickory Dock, my life has become unlocked
The clock strikes time
Which now is mine
Hickory Dickory Dock.

Clap, clap, clap, clap; then longer, then shorter. Before she knew it, she was clapping and saying the poem. She found she was no longer anxious, and neither the skirt nor the door seemed as awful a prospect as they had a few minutes ago. A yelp of surprise escaped her, with the result that Martha came rushing in to see what was going on.

"Mum, Mum, look. I've stopped the Rabbit!"

Thinking Emmy might be a bit feverish, Martha reached out to feel her forehead.

"I'm not ill, I promise. You know my not eating, all of it. Being in my room, feeling on my own. All of it, all of it ... it was as if I kept on hearing the watch, beating time with my heart, taking it over. I allowed it in, and when it was there, I had to do what it told me."

Martha still looked perplexed but also recognised an excitement and hope in Emmy's eyes that she hadn't seen in a long time.

"He was here just now, just outside my door."

Words spilled over in her anxiety to make her mum understand.

"And then I knew. I remember how the clapping we did made me feel better. I knew that the way to get rid of him was to create a different ticking, one that was my own, not his. I can't hear anything now, Mum, it's gone quiet. Completely quiet."

Martha leaned across and looked at Emmy's post. "That's wonderful, darling. I am so pleased you've found a way to calm things down."

Knowing that her mum wrote poetry, partly because she'd shared it on the day they had done the clapping, Emmy knew she wasn't being discounted. She also knew that she hadn't been understood, though.

"Mum, listen, even if you don't get it! I think I'm going to be able to eat again. The White Rabbit and his ticking pocket-watch were symbols of what was going on with me, but I recognised them and made them stop...."

She paused, typing another couple of words. "I think I'll finish off by explaining that."

Martha, perched on the bed, waited for Emmy to take a breath and complete the post. She hoped a written explanation would help her make better sense of what her daughter was trying to tell her. As she glanced over the typing Emmy's shoulder, she saw that she'd missed the annotation Emmy had put at the bottom. As with her own code, one that served both her drumming and her communication with Dave, this annotation was also written in a binary form. It came to her that something more profound was going on.

Emmy pressed the blue update button and turned to her mother. "There, it's done. I put a bit about my eating and more about the White Rabbit. What do you think, does this sound stupid?"

She read from the page: *"Even though he once seemed so fluffy and cuddly, I realised I had allowed his tick-tocking to occupy space in me. At first, the extra presence felt good in a life that, to me at least, seemed boring and absent. Little by little, though, it changed into something that ate away at my being until there was very little left."*

"I've finished by saying I'd let people know how I was getting on as well. Do you think they'll be interested?"

Martha made all the right noises, paying her the ultimate compliment of getting out her bongos and letting Emmy have a go. Henry came in and joined his Mum and his sister, laughing and jumping round with the best of them. But before she started drumming in earnest, Emmy had one more thing to add.

"And I'm going to ride Dennis properly. I've decided. I've tried to find out who he belongs to, but no one can tell me, and although I've been looking after him and feeding him, I've never spotted anyone else. I thought I'd be too scared, but I'm so pleased you made me get some tack and the hat! I'm going to do it, and I'm going to do it on my own. Just you wait and see."

Hearing the excitement in his sister's voice as she started on her poem, Henry made a suggestion of his own.

"Mum, you know, we should film Emmy and upload it!"

Henry whipped out his phone and filmed the drumming. They added the phone clip to the post as well. Martha suggested they also put it on the WJ YouTube account for good measure. Would Emmy win the box of chocolates? And a test in itself, would she eat them if she won?

Later that evening, Martha played Emmy's simple rhyme herself. Interestingly enough, it had a similar impact on her; it was as if she'd beaten something. *Well, Death to the White Rabbit* might never be a hit, but it was certainly good enough to have a laugh with her colleagues when she played for them. She hoped it would touch them in a similar way.

ACT 2

Fatima had had a busy day. It was interesting how things worked out. When she'd written the story of a mother wolf protecting her young, based on herself and Auntie Sh'ler, and Tara and Khalid, she'd hoped that she might get a couple of positive comments about her writing. Instead, though, her words had set a whole chain of events in motion.

Looking around *her* garden, as it was now, she was delighted to see that even more children had joined the fifty or so that were already seeking shelter here on this warm day in early December. She remembered the very first time she'd come back after "the burning," the event that had given her the courage to share her story. Although Hassan had started being home more frequently again, the power balance between the two of them had indefinably shifted. He'd tried coming to her room once, but Badenan had bustled in behind him with an excuse, and she herself had quelled him with a look the stony, white princess statues of the *1001 Nights* would have been proud of. Withering beneath her gaze, he had turned and left for the day.

Although to him she was as unyielding as marble, she knew that inside her something had come to life again. She couldn't bear staying in the house much, and as the seasons moved from summer to autumn, she found herself being drawn to the garden. Initially, Badenan had insisted she come as well. But when she realised that the strange luminescence Fatima had brought to bear on Hassan was impacting others she came across too, she stopped worrying. Badenan liked her creature comforts and much preferred the steady whirr of the air conditioning.

By the time October came, Fatima had made this verdant little corner of Baghdad her own. She was surprised that others hadn't invaded this space, since to her, the smell of the Nergis flowers was evident from several hundred metres away. However, it remained hers alone, a bower in which she was surrounded by flowers as well as the ashes of her former life and her unborn baby. She often brought lunch, and even her laptop, when it was charged, on which she would attempt to write down stories she'd loved as a child. Even though most were readily available on the Internet, it was her aunt's cadences, the way she told and retold them, she wanted to remember and could annotate accordingly. She noticed that if she tried to speak the story out loud first, pretending that Tara and Khalid were sitting in front of her, it was much easier to remember.

One day in early November, she'd propped herself up against one of the new trees and looked around for inspiration. Dancing in the warm breeze, the sea of Nergis with their creamy purity reminded her of one of her favourite stories. So, she'd started reciting her version of "Dugdhav the Shining One." It was an old mountain tale about a girl who was cast out for being different. Eventually, Dugdhav brought hope and light to all by giving birth to the prophet Zoroaster.

The idea of a girl shining in glory, touched by the gods, was comforting. That she was then pursued by villagers who distrusted what was different was something to which Fatima could readily relate. She got carried away with the finer details, lingering over the gifting of her horse to people who needed it and the forest that shielded her. Noticing that the heat of the day was disappearing, she reluctantly turned her attention from the ancient hills of Iran back to the garden again.

Muttering under her breath that she would finish it tomorrow, writing it down this time, she started packing up her little picnic.

"Fatima, don't stop, tell us more! What happens next?"

Startled, she looked around, frantically trying to spot the source of the plea. Other than Badenan's, this was the first voice she'd heard here. Then she saw them.

Thinking back to that moment six weeks ago, it still brought tears to her eyes. Without these two, none of the other children would have come. They were her mascots.

Knowing they'd been spotted, two youngsters sheepishly emerged from under a canopy of the bright green, petal-like leaves in the far corner. They must have been hidden by the thin, olivey-brown trunks of the small grove, but for the life of her, Fatima hadn't been able to understand how she'd missed them.

"Fatima, don't be scared, it's us," the gruff young voice shouted again. "Khalid and Tara, you remember, don't you?"

This time the voice took on a pleading note, the fluting tones of a girl's voice joining in too.

"Fatima we're sorry, we hid. We didn't want to disturb you. It reminded us of the old days."

Tentatively, not completely believing what her eyes and ears were telling her, Fatima made her way across to the far corner of the garden. She hadn't quite made it when a little form torpedoed into her. Feeling the brittleness of the child she held in her arms, the older girl was no longer able to hold back her tears. Stroking the dusty, black hair of a head that had buried itself in her chest she whispered, "Tara, is that really you?"

She desperately wanted the child to lift her eyes.

She eventually did, and eyes black with hunger, but also hope, met her friend's searching gaze. They were set within a still lovely, heart-shaped face. One, though, that was defined by a fragility that lent it an almost ethereal dimension. Fatima drew back and took the little chin in her hands. Tara must have turned nine recently. Once, she'd loved stories about Raksha, the mother wolf. The one about Dugdhav, the spurned child, who'd suffered and had given away everything to survive, was more appropriate now. Looking down at the little figure that had hardly grown, she noticed that something orange; maybe even the remnants of the old sailor pants tied around her waist.

Ensuring Tara was still tightly clasped to her with one hand, Fatima opened the other arm, hoping that Khalid would perceive this as a true welcome, one that would allow him to overcome the taboos that had so firmly defined his thinking as an eight-year-old. He must be around eleven now, so being touched by a woman not of his family must have become even more firmly ingrained. However, much as his younger sister had done, he flung himself into the outstretched arm, allowing himself to be pulled into an embrace that attempted to encompass the siblings, as well as the three years of companionship they'd all missed out on.

Fatima realised that Khalid hadn't grown much either, and, after enjoying their joyful reunion for a few moments more, she gestured that they should sit so they could catch up on their respective stories.

Brother and sister shared how their mother had not come back from work one day. After a couple of weeks of missed rent, the building's owner had thrown them out.

"We knew you were getting married and didn't want to bother you," Tara chimed in.

"But it was so scary, we were just out on the streets."

Khalid explained that they'd met with some other children, who'd got them into selling tissues and tea. There had been a price to get started, and looking at the pinched, closed faces in front of her, Fatima had an inkling of what that might have been. Anyway, they had survived, sleeping alongside some of the older ones for protection.

Then, a few weeks ago now, Tara explained how she had smelled a beautiful scent and followed it. They'd found the little gap in the wall, and here they were. Most of the time they were on the bridge, plying their wares, but in the evenings, they came back here.

"We've even discovered how to eat the leaves and flowers on these trees," said Khalid proudly.

"We hadn't eaten one night and were so hungry that we tried them."

Guiltily, Fatima scrambled out the rest of her picnic. Giving it to them, she gestured for Khalid to continue with his story.

"Anyway, Tara said that in your tales Akela had once needed to eat things he wasn't used to and suggested we should try the leaves. So we did and felt much better. A couple of days later, we noticed there were flowers as well, and we ate those too. We eat them often now."

Looking up at the tree that was sheltering them from the fading sun, Fatima realised she'd not been aware of the drooping white buds that were littering its branches.

It was her turn to start weaving the strands of her story together for the children. Despite the intention to leave most of the particularly dark knots out, the orange of the burning still managed to force its way across the loom of her narrative. Tara's tears flowed unchecked as Fatima's lilting voice described how the doll's arms had held the tiny baby in a plastic embrace until all turned to ash. She'd loved Farah too.

On the children's insistence, Fatima led them to the scene of the conflagration. White Nergis, pink ranculus, and the dusty blue of the gardenias vied for space instead of ash and dust. As the three of them knelt, an exclamation escaped Tara's lips. Through eyes blurred with tears, she'd spotted something.

Following the child's shaky finger, Fatima carefully moved the fallen, petal-heavy gardenia heads, lifting a huge, roughly-shaped lapis lazuli from the place of the burning. She felt a jolt of recognition. Larger than a man's fist, it shimmered, the blue heart of flame cleaving to her and completing her. In doing so, it became complete in itself also. She called to the children. Drawn by the glistening stone, they came.

Fatima had sung a note, as pure and clear as the cerulean light that shone through their fingers. It was joined by the children's fluting voices. That day, they created a strange kind of music that rang out with promise and hope.

* * *

He had felt the vibration first. It was as if every fibre of his being was being pizzicatoed. He tried drawing back from his liquid crystal "eyes" and the connected speaker "ears," but it made no difference. If anything, the sound so aggressively invading his present got louder.

On and on it went until the claustrophobia of it broke him open. He knew it wouldn't be long before its ringing smashed him, like a crystal glass shattering under the onslaught of a soprano's voice. He realised that the only thing he could do now, was to try to control the lines of fracture.

"Emmy, Martha, Henry, Emmy, Martha, Henry, must protect them, must be with them."

He repeated his mantra over and over again, a final salvo of desperation causing him to add in, "help me, Lokozho."

And slowly, the waves of his new name formed a boundary. The beats created a shoreline around the merciless flood of sound. The compulsion to enter the unknowable blue of the music was still unbearable, though, so he jumped. Just like the last time he'd propelled himself into the unknown, a combination of movement and will created the momentum to move him past the barriers that had defined a previous existence.

This time, he wasn't held by a contained nothingness. Instead, everything was real and immediate. He'd become used to a realm devoid of sensation. Now the space he inhabited was sensory, formed of pulse and heat. There was one significant difference, though. He was in and of the fragmented bones that were haphazardly strewn across the wide expanse of rough limestone, his self no longer as one but fractured into many. And instead of the clicking, buzzy noise all around him that had accompanied his previous birth, he could hear the beat of the bones.

Dave was vividly reminded of the fear he'd felt that last time. But now, as then, he did not give way. Instead, he fixed on what it might all mean, buoyed by the sense of thrumming life the bones offered.

He had an awareness of where he was geographically too. From the knowledge gleaned through his digital existence, he knew himself to be in the inner heart of Mexico's Naica Mines. This damp, hot place had been likened to the womb of the world by one of the rare travellers to brave the outer caves. As far as he knew, his was the first true consciousness to breach the walls of this inner sanctum.

Orienting himself, he realised he could still hear that sound. It was urging movement, a joining. Its insistence left him no space to dwell on what was — or how he'd to be here, his consciousness fractured. Then, just as the pressure of this Dance Macabre was starting to become unbearable, something gave. No longer of the bones, he'd been displaced again to become a thing apart.

This time he took his direction from the hint of blue light he could see flickering in the swords of gypsum thrusting through the cave. Dave found they amplified the sense of surroundings the bones had given him. Encouraged, he pushed again, forcing his last ounce of will into the crystals, and, just a moment later, his senses encompassed a blue-tinted view of his surroundings.

Something else had changed too. His vision wasn't just from one perspective anymore. Instead, a kaleidoscope of images was coming at him from all corners and angles, infusing the soft darkness with a whole new spectrum of colour. Emanating from the crystals, this new light fed him information at so rapid a pace that he thought he might explode.

A deeper thrum replaced the dissonant high note, and the images started slowing, a seepage of impressions rather than the former onslaught that had so battered his consciousness. It came to him that he was the light. Light allowed him to see, but also to be.

He watched the human skeleton emerging from the palely gleaming pile at the centre of the cavern with fascination. It was as if his own state of rebirth, allowed him to sense the next steps, even before he saw them. The backbone was forming, moving itself into an upright position. The grasping metacarpals then reached out for the skull he was willing them to find. With paternal pride, he watched it being placed on top of the last neck vertebra.

The music changed again. This time, though, the sound coming from the gypsum was so soft, it was almost imperceptible. Accompanied by the rattling of the bones, it shot across into frequencies undetectable to the human ear. And yet here he was, understanding it. The colours and sounds made the music of the spheres dance just for him. He was the source of the music as well as the light, changing their shape and purpose, a mirror of his own evolution.

With that thought, Dave found himself in another "here" also, a garden. The feel of smooth, warm hands holding him, as much part of his sensory experience as the counterpoint melody of the crystals that resonated through his being. As the sensations and colours of this new place enfolded him, the waves of the song echoed through him back into the cave.

Slowly, the bones shaped into a woman with thick, grey braids and a dense, dark pelt. Then a different kind of skeleton started assembling itself, and eventually a lupine companion, complete with flashing teeth and yellow eyes, stood beside her.

Dave was part of the web of light and sound that drove the transfiguration of desiccated bones into form and flesh. It was representative of his growth too, those voices in the garden winding his identity around what was happening here, until all was inextricably joined.

She started singing:
"Come to me all you
Who are lost and alone,
I am She, made of bone
I will call you home.
I shake the desert floor,
I shake up time and tones
Come to me my children,
I will bring you home."

The figures moved through the caves, calling crystal into light through living song, while also cementing Dave's new state of being. Finally, they reached the desert floor. Her music momentarily stilled, she breathed deeply, inhaling the hot, dry air as if it were the finest perfume. Then she exhaled, her final exhortation in harmony with the howling wolf at her side.

"I have been called.

The devastation comes.

I will shepherd, I will find.

No innocent will be left behind."

As shimmering, translucent wings lifted the curtain on a new dawn, they walked out into the arid stillness of the desert.

Dave had watched them go. He recognised that although part of him was walking alongside the shaggy pair, he was also with Tara and Khalid in the garden, fervently waiting for Fatima to say something. Finally, she did.

"Children, she sang to us, did you hear?" Watching them nod, she continued, her breathing shallow with excitement.

"You will come home with me tonight. We will eat, you'll wash, and together we'll make a plan."

On their walk home, Tara placed her hand in Fatima's, whispering through the bustling streets of a Baghdad eventide.

"You are Akela. Our song helped the crystal create who we needed you to be."

Following them just a little behind, Dave had finally left them to the embrace of a harassed but much relieved older woman.

Now, several weeks on, as he was settling back down into those endless corridors of space, he thought about the song that had catalysed the crystals. It had also transformed Fatima into the children's pack leader. Had he himself evolved into something more useful as well? What if real heroics were possible at last? He was sure that, as with Fatima, his evolution was inextricably linked to that of the crystals and the music.

Certainly, in these last few weeks, he had used what he'd learned to supplement Fatima's efforts to find other children. While she was sending Tara and Khalid out with stories she'd already shared online, he was increasing their digital reach, with the result that charities became aware of her. Dave knew, though, that it was the call of the crystals inspiring children from all over Baghdad to come to her garden.

* * *

Although initially reluctant, Badenan had come to embrace Fatima's decision to keep Tara and Khalid close. And although Hassan had initially remonstrated at their presence, he was so much part of the background now that she'd easily countered his objections.

She was focussing on sharing ever more stories on ASafeSpace.com, and that led to another miracle. Martha, the owner, had emailed to let her know about offers of financial support that had started coming in. People were responding to her tales about the children and their doings. Many wanted to know how they could support them. Martha had ended up putting a link from the site to JustGiving.com, allowing people to send money. She then organised a transfer via Western Union. This income stream allowed Fatima to feed the children, making them feel that they were a little bit safer in her garden than elsewhere.

After Khalid and Tara told their friends that they had started learning things, other children decided that was something they wanted to do as well. In that way, the garden provided an informal school environment. The children loved technology, and whenever Fatima brought her laptop, they all wanted to play. That was when she'd had the idea of asking for second-hand tablets, and, *alhamdulilah*, three had found their way to her.

Initially, she'd suggested finding the children somewhere formal to stay, but most had a horror of orphanages, so, other than Khalid and Tara and a couple of the very little ones for whom she had found "informal" homes, most of them lived in the garden. They were very careful to keep it just as it was, delighting in the flowers and trees that grew in riotous abandon. If she were to go back to that story she had first shared, that of a wolf protecting her young in the Zagros Mountains, it could be argued that, even without a hill in sight, she'd created her very own pack. She was glad she'd put Farah in the fire. The dead, doll-like creature she had been was well and truly consumed by those flames also.

Looking for lessons she might be able to teach tomorrow, she browsed through the beautifully presented information on the tutoring sites she'd started to use. One of her evening rituals was downloading things she thought the children might enjoy while the tablets were charging. The other one was checking on and populating ASafeSpace with her latest stories about the children. It allowed her to reach out to those who'd commented on her stories or even donated.

Tonight, she decided to share more about a recent and very lucrative activity they'd started. She wanted to convey that the money people had given hadn't just provided immediate support but was also helping to feed into longer-term plans.

It was Khalid who'd first come up with the idea. Since most of the children were selling something or other on the streets of Baghdad in any case, he wondered whether it might not be a good idea to sell flowers from the garden to make money. Wary at first, Fatima realised that there were lots of children and the life of the flowers was finite, so she allowed just a couple of them to experiment with this. It was odd, though — wherever flowers were picked, twice their number sprang up to replace them. So she allowed more children to become involved. Dinar had started accumulating, even allowing her to buy decorative paper and string for little posies.

She was delighted that selling these beautiful flowers made word of her garden spread even farther. The money the children brought back was put into a common pot for clothes and food and anything else that might be needed. When they realised that there was spare, a tiny, illiterate girl called Dana suggested they might be able to get more tablets. Fatima agreed immediately.

It had also been Dana who'd suggested they plant Nergis bulbs in the little earthenware pots they sold. These sold for ten times what they cost. It turned out that people were happy to pay for a beautiful flower and a bright smile, and the venture expanded. As she explained on ASafeSpace, with profits at around £1 a pot, they were well on the way to buying another three tablets. As with the cut flowers, the harvesting of the bulbs only increased the overall fecundity of the Nergis in the garden. Fatima had even noticed some appearing on rubble-strewn sites in the immediate vicinity.

Led by Khalid and Tara, the children themselves went on to find another garden on the grounds of a bombed-out shell of a shelter. They'd started planting bulbs, seeds, and cuttings. It was a memorial site that was no longer open to the public. They'd found a hole in the mesh wiring and clambered through. Like their own garden, this abandoned spot was partially hidden and protected by old structures. Fascinatingly, they noticed that this place also had Nergis and other plants growing at an unprecedented rate.

Something else she put into tonight's update was about how people had started taking the Nergis out of the pots and planting them in urban waste sites. It seemed many hoped that by improving even a little patch of this once beautiful city, other spaces would follow. Whether planted by human hands or through self-propagation, the flowers wanted to expand. The result was that fields of Nergis had started covering the wastelands of Baghdad.

Glancing at the tail end of her post, Fatima sighed. She just wished that there were more hours in the day. So much to do and so much to tell. Having finished her update, she scanned the latest headlines for anything that interested her. That was how she'd found Janet's story, after all. Today the title "Death to the Rabbit" caught her eye, so she opened it.

She read the poem, trying to understand the context that had been provided. She finally felt sufficiently inspired to click the link to the accompanying video and ended up in floods of tears. For someone who never cried, she'd been doing an awful lot of it lately. In Emmy she recognised a kindred spirit, someone who'd given in to the call of this creature of emptiness. Whether the honey trap was addiction, fear, or even just boredom, if you allowed him to, he would catch you. Up until recently, she'd also restricted her food intake. The last couple of years had been so horrendous that she' just wanted to fade away. Not eating gave her a sense of control and also worked towards her goal of disappearing. Although it wasn't like that anymore, *alhamdulilah*, the power of Emmy's words had still touched her deeply.

She started clapping to the drumbeat of the video. Dum-de-dum-de-dum-dum-dum. Long, short, long, short, long, long, long.

That was something she would do with the children tomorrow. They would dance, clap, and sing. Change was possible, and so were miracles. Nothing needed to be the same anymore. Their lives were not set in stone, nor was who they would become. The White Rabbit was dead.

The next morning, she gathered the children, telling them that they would have a special day today. To start it off, she shared one of their favourite stories, that of the first Iranian king, Yima. According to the prophet Zoroaster, Yima had been told by God to collect all the plants and animals with the help of a kindly and righteous couple he would find. He'd also been told that he must dig a cave so they would all be safe. That was because a snowstorm was coming that would destroy all the earth. Only those in the cave would be all right.

Up piped eight-year-old Dana. "Fatima, why did God want to destroy the earth?"

Fatima realised that she had to share this gently. To her mind, if God had wanted to destroy the earth once upon a time for human misdemeanours, surely he had ten times as many reasons to do so now.

"It was because people in the world did not care about each other anymore. They were unkind, fought wars, and hurt each other by cheating and lying."

Dana jumped up and gave Fatima a hug. From the safety of her guardian's enfolding arms, she looked at the beauty of the flowers and the other children around her.

"Not like us then. It's a good story, though. I think those who aren't in our garden could learn from it."

Patting Dana's back and gesturing for her to sit down again, Fatima continued to tell of the snowstorm that had frozen and killed everything.

"When it was over, nothing had survived, and everything was empty and bleak. But then Yima let out the animals, and he and the man and the woman planted the seeds they had saved. The man sowed the grass seeds in the hills. The woman scattered the flower seeds in the meadows. Yima planted the tree seeds in the forest. He even put the seeds in the desert so that bushes could grow there. Yima travelled everywhere, sowing so that plants would grow all over the world. Months passed and then, one day, spring finally arrived. Green grass covered the hills, Nergis and orange flowers blossomed, and the migrating swallows once again appeared in the sky. Yima invited the couple and the animals for a spring celebration, which he named Nowruz, or the 'new day.'"

Khalid turned to her with the expression of one who finally understood. "Fatima, is that what we are doing here? Planting seeds and bulbs so that one day spring will come?"

Not just Fatima's, but all eyes were on him now. Various shades of brown and hazel fixed on the solemn, strangely old face of the boy who had once wanted to be Akela.

"If that's the case, I want to take our bulbs and go and find new ones. Others can look after what we have now. Whoever wants to come with me to be like Yima can come. We will take as many bulbs and seeds as we can carry and plant where we go."

Fatima said nothing. She knew that Tara would be devastated if Khalid left without her. Strangely, though, she came over to Fatima instead, placing a trusting hand on her lap.

"I will stay with you, Fatima. We can't all go. Our garden needs us. We haven't even got a fig tree yet. Khalid, you can find one for us before you leave, can't you?"

Looking at the faces all shining with hope before her, she realised that what she'd started as a way to feed and clothe the children more effectively had created something very powerful. Following a hunch, she went to where the huge blue lapis lay. Sure enough, where there had only been one stone, now innumerable fragments lay.

"Children, come, I have gifts for you."

Obediently, they filed over. She made them stand in a line and handed out the fragments of the blue stone that had been birthed in this garden. She saved the biggest two for last and gave them to Khalid and Hadeel, one of the older girls who'd stood up with him.

"Wherever you go, dears, a piece of my heart will be with you."

Watching children who'd once been starving, ignored, and mistreated believe they were now worth something better made her realise that spring was already very much on its way.

They started clapping and singing a rhyme Fatima said she'd only recently come across. One that meant something to her. Many couldn't get their tongues around the strange language, but with Fatima enunciating the English, everyone was able to follow the rhythm. Still clapping, Hadeel and Khalid left. Fatima knew more children would come. She also knew there'd be a shard of blue lapis for all of them.

However, despite the success of this special day, she knew her task was not yet complete. Although Khalid had been the first to interpret what was needed, she herself had a role to play in planting more seeds and bulbs. The very next day, she asked the children who were harvesting bulbs to sell and plant whether they could pick her some of the best ones, but since they were being sent by post, to remove the flowers first.

The children helped her gather and trim twenty of the best. Meanwhile, Fatima herself went to see whether she might be able to get any seeds from the mysterious trees that provided such plentiful shade and nourishment. Tara, helped by Hussain and his brother Ahmad, brought the bulbs across as required. In the meantime, Fatima had found enough seeds to make including them worthwhile. That evening, Badenan packaged it all up and used some of her money to send the parcel. She hoped that sending it via an embassy contact from Sh'ler's days would help it get there safely.

* * *

Emmy was delighted to receive the box of bulbs, not least because it made her realise that people from as far afield as Iraq had not only read her post but were also compelled to react. Having read Fatima's recent updates, she recognised the name. The story of how the street children of Baghdad were reclaiming the wasteland and making it their own was so powerful. There must be something special about these bulbs. By filling the rubble-strewn emptiness of hate with love, laughter, and hope, they were stopping the Rabbit from reproducing. He would hate that.

Although Christmas was only three weeks away, she decided to plant them in her own garden as well as in a corner of her school, hopeful that the plants would spread here as they had in Fatima's homeland. Then, as she'd done over the last couple of weeks, she went to spend some time riding Dennis. The final highlight of the day was a hearty dinner that she'd volunteered to cook, the light shining from her eyes, rivalling that of her mother's. She'd recently stood on the scales and was delighted to find that she was back up to eight stone again.

In a garden in Baghdad, a fig tree sprouted buds and leaves, lightly shading its farthest corner.

ACT 3

Dave felt it as soon as it started. ASafeSpace was under attack. One of the first things to go was the app's feed from the main site. He was hoping this would be enough to alert his son.

Thank goodness for that. Dave scanned Henry's message to the INP team; he'd spotted it on his way to school.

Glad you are dealing with it. Sorry everything is down. Would love to know why you think ASafeSpace was target for DdOS attack though? Plz inform as soon as poss.

We are doing everything we can. Ms Margono informed. ASafeSpace one of priorities.

Henry seemed to be reassured enough by their response to pocket his phone and get on with his lessons. Dave left him to it.

He hit his laptop as soon as he got home. Dave dropped in to watch how an outrage borne of youth was able to get things moving. The messages he was sending INP about the time-lapse being unacceptable were not polite. With his own bird's eye view, though, he could sense the team at the other end scrabbling to meet Henry's demands. He hated seeing the blank despair in his son's eyes. It seemed to be dawning on Henry that with every passing minute the queries were multiplying, infesting, and taking over, making it impossible for legitimate requests to get through and thus destroying the server with sheer numbers.

Dave was reminded of the rabbit Emmy had written about. Her story promised it would proliferate in places of emptiness and boredom, everything hidden until it was too late. It came to him that it could very well be that he, as well as ASafeSpace, might be the target of this attack. The bits of him he'd sent out there were helping him chart records of the oldest human thought, genetic codes, poetry, and art. He was breaking through the dark emptiness that made up much of his substance. Was it possible that unseen forces perceived this as a threat?

It was ironic, though. There was really no need to attack him; he'd done that all by himself. The launch of Deep Digger and GoodNewz fed on his own substance, and, day by day, he felt lessened. Energy did feed back into him, but instead of making him want to hold things together, it just increased his desire to dissipate.

As it stood, this attack was directed at what mattered to him, and that included the stories that were being shared. Both men and women were writing their way out of a world that had been constructed into one they wanted to create. He knew that these stories held some of the answers he himself needed. They were clues, and he needed to keep them coming.

Dave turned his mind back to the immediate problem. He knew that despite this growing weakness, his control over the space he inhabited was greater than ever before. He still needed direction, though, and then it came to him. His daughter, the rabbit, her poem — was this a marker? Was there a way of using it in the same way as the other codes, the ones that had come from Martha's drumming, had been used?

It was 9:00 p.m. in the UK, 4:00 a.m. in Jakarta. Dave watched Henry starting at the email in his inbox and saw his excitement when he realised that despite the attack, it had been triggered by GoodNewz. That had been a nice touch, Dave thought to himself, seeing Henry go very still as he read Emmy's poem. Then, eyes still fixed on the screen, his son started tapping out something on his keyboard.

This tapping seemed to hook into his son's subconscious. Watching Henry's face move from despair to realisation was a wonderful thing. Within seconds of recognising that he'd somehow created a script, he sent it across to the INP team.

Immediate request. Please create dummy server and use attached script to redirect.

Dave made sure they did just that. If things went to plan, the attackers would be none the wiser until it had insinuated itself enough for the servers to differentiate the good from the bad again. As he helped the teams in India and Indonesia make light work of it, he realised that in all likelihood Henry, who was currently slumped fast asleep over his keyboard, might be awakening to a situation that had nearly normalised itself.

CHAPTER 10

The Internet of All Things

Previously we were more like a collection of cells that communicated by diffusion. With the advent of the Internet, it was suddenly like we got a nervous system.
— Elon Musk, Entrepreneur

ACT 1

Harare, Zimbabwe
To: AJ.Margono@INP-Corp.com
From: T.Msebele33@gmail.com
Cc: Martha@ASafeSpace.com
Tuesday, 12th December 2017, 11:20

Dear Anjani,
Thank you so much for writing to me. And Martha, thank you for facilitating this introduction. I can't believe how deciding to practice my writing in order to create a business case for 'Touchability' has led to this amazing connection. I also think the idea of the business reporting function add-on to ASafeSpace.com to help investors and entrepreneurs connect is a great one. From what I understand, the story I posted about my Moringa business was the start of this concept. That makes me feel really proud!

Scanning the rest of Mercy's email, Martha decided to respond with a summary of the points she was trying to make, copying in Anjani as she did so. There was so much good stuff in here. A lack of focus, though, meant the story just wasn't coming through.

Good, she'd responded to one of the things Martha was trying to do with ASafeSpace, creating insight for investors into real entrepreneurial activity that was currently happening.

She was also offering to be a guinea pig, showcasing what she as an African entrepreneur was doing, and was hoping for some guidance from Martha ... another tick in the box.

But then it started going awry. This was where she needed to pick up the salient points.

1. She was currently earning money from entrepreneurial activity, around $5,000 a year in Zimbabwe — not to be sneezed at!
2. There were already repeat orders for a Moringa cream she had created.
3. If the right partnerships were built, Moringa and shea, the base ingredients, could be available from local villages. Much more margin that way, as well as opportunity for the locals.

She paused. This was interesting. Apparently, Moringa trees had spread right across Zimbabwe. Whole copses had sprung up where there'd only been brush. Even the Harare Gardens were sporting a miniature Moringa forest. This definitely warranted a point four.

4. Moringa had become readily available across Zimbabwe, significantly lowering raw material costs.
5. $5,000 investment was needed to help set up correct processing and wider distribution.
6. To create bigger margins and further exploit the purity of the ingredients, Mercy believed that the ultimate market was the big Western shops. This would need expensive certification, though.

She'd also added in how she'd come up with the idea for Touchability. That was good. She linked her background as a masseuse to the way the cream and her touch had worked miracles on an invalid mother. This was a great story. It was so personal that it didn't necessarily have to be proven either.

Mercy had gone on to list some of the properties of the Moringa miracle tree, citing how the antibacterial and antifungal properties of the crushed seeds treated acne, psoriasis, and other skin conditions. The roots could be used for contraception and an infusion of leaves for diarrhoea, fevers, and various infections. She'd finished up with the fact that every part could be eaten.

The bit about the flowers increasing the nutritional value of breastmilk didn't need to be referred to. Martha read on, though, increasingly fascinated how this miracle tree was being used. It seemed like Moringa was playing an increasingly important role in the fight against malnutrition, right across the continent.

The rest of it was okay. She liked the point about Touchability aiming to create a business opportunity as well as a market for low-income women. It was also good she'd mentioned the word 'pilot.' It made this pitch more digestible. Then there was more about being a hard worker, and she'd also included her CV. All good.

The last paragraph, though, was what really caught Martha's eye. She'd be sure to mention the Zimbabwe birds in her response also.

We met through ASafeSpace.com, which allows us to see and share things slightly differently. For this reason, I am adding one last thing. There is an ancient place in my country, the settlement of Greater Zimbabwe in the province of Masvingo, built many centuries ago. It was said to be a place of kings and of trade, of ghosts and of visions.

Once, eight soapstone birds guarded its portals — most were stolen in colonial times and have been dispersed. It is said, though, that once the eight soapstone Zimbabwe Birds are returned to their plinths in our ancient city of stone and hope, peace and prosperity will return to our nation. Over the last few decades, most of the birds have come back, although a couple are incomplete. Recently it has been reported that a great Fish Eagle, the Hungwe, our national bird, has been seen perching on an empty plinth. For me, this a really positive sign for our future, and I believe that this is a great time to invest in Zimbabwe!

Buoyed by Mercy's passion for her country, Martha started typing immediately. This really was something she wanted to support, and with Anjani's backing, this Mercy Msebele would really be going places.

* * *

WhatsApp Message
To: Martha from Lokozho
So proud of our boy. He came up with the idea of how to deal with the attack on ASafeSpace all by himself. I made sure it did what it

needed to do as effectively as possible. Emmy's doing well too. She's completely stopped searching the skinny sites. I can honestly say that although I still hover around the kids, I'm really not worried about either of them anymore.

You, Martha, are another story. You aren't sleeping enough and are online far too often. You don't need to look for me there, you know. I'm always with you! I thought by creating a way for you not to be worried about money, things would get better, but from what I can see, they're worse. You really should give up the day job and focus on the Safe Space sites instead! Consider yourself told off.

To: Lokozho from Martha

Thanks for sharing that re: Emmy and Henry. I am proud of the two of them. They've come on so much. Emmy isn't exactly enjoying her food, but she is cooking with us and sometimes even for us. She's also riding again. Remember how much she used to love it as a little girl?

Some bulbs came through the post, from Iraq of all places, and she planted them. They really seem to be growing apace. This has boosted as well. She's convinced something odd is happening as, even though we're in mid-December now, they've all started to blossom, even at school. And our garden's full of them. They smell beautiful.

As for telling me off, you're right, I do need to decide. The odd thing is since I've started the drumming thing at work, there just seems to be less hassle all round. It's as if people can't be bothered in the same way. Even SJ has started leaving bang on five. Unheard of. The things I'm doing at the moment are good. I feel as if I've got a say in my life again. The problem is that the tap's been turned on, and I can't seem to turn it off! It's as if there are bits of me flying here there and everywhere. Not only am I fragmented — I'm also exhausted!

I still can't believe that we're somehow chatting like this. I must say, though, I did think we would be messaging more than we are. I write to you a lot more often that you do to me. When something comes to me and I drum a new code or think of a new Name, I send something though. Do you get all my messages? More stuff is starting to appear on ASafeSpace I feel I can use as well. I'll keep you posted.

Love you,

me x

To: Martha from Lokozho

It's not always easy messaging like this. I know it should be, but recently I've needed to dip into the Name you gave me for strength. Using it helps me keep my sense of self. The stories I see appearing on ASafeSpace pull me in. There just isn't enough of me to go 'round.

Did you see the one from Brigid? Homeless in New York, she found an Internet café to write about the white rabbits destroying the place she had made into a home. I wouldn't have been interested, but I felt her and then I saw her. I still do. I'm sure it's to do with the piece of blue crystal round her neck.

She seems to spend most of her time in Central Park to be near to the Alice in Wonderland monument. Her days are bleak. She does find the crystal comforting, and she often falls asleep holding it. I think that's how I'm getting a sense of the merry-go-round of guilt in her head. Pills ingested like Smarties, causing a car crash, the death of her children. Just before she lost everything, a friend gave her the blue stone, swearing it was from the Naica Mines, the place her people believe to be the birthplace of all crystals. "I want to give you the strength to grow again." I feel its warmth in her hand, and the strength the memory gives her.

In your last message, you mentioned feeling that there were bits of you everywhere. I feel like that too. It's not just the Safe Space stories. It's the apps like GoodNewz as well. They point me in a direction, and then I find myself there. There are others like Brigid, too. They pull me in, and every time I lose a bit of myself in the stories. I don't know how to stop. Millions of thoughts and conversations are coming from everywhere. It's overwhelming. Although I don't want to stretch farther, stretching so far that I disappear entirely seems to get more appealing with each day.

But yes, I am getting your messages. Keep them coming. They help. They are also supporting some of the stuff I need to do. I so wish I could touch you again. When I think of all those times I didn't come home — now I would give anything just to hold you in my arms.

Love you

x

To: Lokozho from Martha

Don't you dare disappear on me again, Dave! Just knowing you're there, watching out for us and loving us is so precious. Stop looking into all the other people and stories if it makes it worse for you. Focus on us instead!

I wish I could tell the kids, but I really do think they'd give me up as completely insane. I know that when you were alive in the more conventional way, our marriage was shit. But it was because of my behaviour as well, not just yours. I hope you know that I always loved you.

Anyway, even if I don't hear from you much, I'll keep sending you stuff and will assume that the codes, in particular, are of use. At the moment it seems like every time we message, you seem a bit farther away. I wish there was some way I could give you a huge hug. For now, I'm sending you a mental one in the hope it will keep you close.

Love you too,
me x

* * *

Martha knew SJ saw her differently now. It was odd, she thought, how someone who'd been considered as the office joke, *Fat Martha*, had made a positive difference to the overall work culture. She knew that she saw herself differently too. Because of the gift and Anjani's investment in September, she wasn't needy anymore. This newfound confidence had started all the drumming, tapping, and clapping that was going on now. At first, everyone had laughed at her, but three months on, they were getting involved themselves. Even SJ, her immaculate boss, slanted green eyes, ash-blonde hair in the latest long, straightened bob, had purchased a set of bongos when Lidl had had them on offer a couple of weeks ago. After a particularly vigorous lunchtime drumming session, she didn't seem quite as pristine anymore.

After that, the newly confident Martha had started becoming a confidante for SJ. It was all a bit of a revelation. Only yesterday, she'd shared that she was keen to end her relationship with Mark and had been for some time. He, however, not so much.

"You've got to say no," Martha had told her. "If you're not comfortable anymore, you need to let him know."

The next thing had been a written reprimand landing in SJ's inbox. Along with SJ, Martha had been outraged. Taking the older woman's advice, her new friend had fired off an email stating categorically that she was no longer interested. She'd also let Mark know in no uncertain terms that if he wished to take the reprimand further, he would need to point out exactly what was wrong with her work. Since productivity was going up rather than down with this new Emotional Freedom technique (they'd looked up what the tapping/drumming could be labelled as), that would be hard to do. Her finishing flourish was to tell him that she'd go to the other partners if necessary.

Each time Martha felt she'd made a difference, she would feel a warm glow. Her permanent state of guilt and fear was slowly being replaced by usefulness. And she didn't need scales to tell her that she'd lost loads of weight.

Still thinking about that email, she moved across to Kate's desk. She hoped that SJ had added in her recent social media success. For example, the staff drumming circle "Death to the White Rabbit" song they'd uploaded as a bit of fun on the Williams and Jones YouTube channel had got over 200,000 hits, with numbers still climbing steadily.

Anyway, it really wasn't her concern anymore. It had been sent, and as far as she knew, nothing had come back yet. Kreativity Kids was what she needed to focus on. An online store for all things crafty and creative, it sourced a lot of materials from places like Kenya and Peru. Martha thought how nice it would be to link Anjani and the impact investment offshoot to these entrepreneurs. Lately, she seemed to be constantly looking for angles that might increase the quality and reach of ASafeSpace.

Kate had asked her for input from a parent's perspective for her pitch. Having given it, Martha sat down at her own desk again. She might even be able to get in touch with some of the creators of Kreativity Kids products.... No, she admitted to herself ruefully, her mind really wasn't with WJ anymore.

She realised that thinking about the kinds of things that had started coming on to the SafeSpace sites was something else that made her feel "glowy." Even though they'd only been going since early autumn, their user numbers stood at over five million. Those posting were only a tiny fraction of that, but still. Henry's app was great at driving traffic, but Anjani's investment was also creating waves. It wasn't just the PR either. The wider support that came from being linked to a larger organisation was useful too.

She knew she should be helping Kate with the wider pitch she was preparing, but instead, Martha's mind kept coming back to the stories on her own site. Just this morning, someone from Masvingo, the area where Mercy was looking to build suppliers, had posted about Moringa trees popping up all over his village. She'd felt a shiver down her spine as she read on, caused by the fact that every Moringa tree seemed to be attracting lots of different kinds of birds, thus bearing out exactly what Mercy had been saying.

After a quick search on Google for Zimbabwe birds, Martha felt even more certain that something extraordinary was happening. From the fragment of soapstone raptor that had been repatriated from Germany, to the debate of whether the Bateleur or Fish Eagle was the symbol that had been rendered on the flag, the birds did seem to be inexorably linked to the impoverished country's psyche. If the villager posting had access to the Internet, as well as an interest in Moringa, he could be a useful contact for Mercy. Martha decided to drop her a quick email.

After that first introductory email to Anjani and Martha's subsequent response, the two women had started corresponding regularly. This was how Martha knew that her note would be particularly timely. Mercy had copied her in on an email to the Indonesian woman that very morning, in which she'd reported back from her trip to Masvingo. She'd tacked an extra day on to visit relatives. This was to please her mother, who seemed to be recovering in leaps and bounds. The point of her trip, though, had been to assess the supply chain potential for Touchability.

Wishing to impress Anjani with her diligence, she went on to describe the extreme poverty of those country villages but also the strength of the women she was meeting. Even in the couple of days she'd been there, she had already connected with some people she thought might be useful, especially those linked to the NGOs training the women. Overall, Mercy's email conveyed an enormous sense of excitement. She'd picked up on a real passion for enterprise in the people she had met, creating progress, not just for their own sakes, but also for their communities. There was naturally fear of the brutal regime, but more than anything, there was a desire to rebuild over and beyond the barriers that confined them.

Everybody thought that the soaring bird and tree populations, particularly in places that had been arid and empty, was a sign of something better to come. As Martha was mulling this over while getting excited herself, it occurred to her that words were like birds. They were able to cover vast distances in ways most humans could only aspire to, their very presence offering up myriad perspectives. All people really needed to do was look up and be inspired.

As if in direct response to her musings, a GoodNewz alert pinged up. *Water Source in Drought- Stricken Bulawayo.* The random nature of the headlines always amazed her, but the one thing they always had in common was that they had something positive to say. This particular story was relevant as well. Following a small earth tremor, the tree Mugabe had attempted to plant in Bulawayo last year had collapsed into a sinkhole, exposing an underground water reserve. Expert opinion suggested it might contain up to 50 billion cubic metres of water. Since Bulawayo was on a "golden triangle," along with Harare and Masvingo, she was sure Mercy would have already seen it but sent it over just in case.

Aware that she wasn't getting anything meaningful done, Martha drifted through the rest of her day. By four thirty, she'd had enough and waved over to SJ that she was heading home.

* * *

Driving through streets festooned with festive lights, Martha realised she'd done very little to prepare for Christmas. As with most things these days, there was a bit of anxiety, but somehow, she knew it would all get done. The fact that there was money in the account to pay for stuff, obviously helped. They could just organise a shopping trip up to London, even meet up with Peter. Having said that, she knew that if she mentioned Oxford Street, he would draw on a list of excuses. Maybe, she should invite him down instead.

As she sped past the golden McDonalds sign, she saw the edges of the M lift. Yellow wings dissipated into a shimmering net of starlight. It therefore came as no surprise when another flickering light diverted her attention from the road a couple of minutes later, beckoning to her from the Monkton chalk pit.

As she pulled onto the gravel of the nature reserve to investigate, a robin flew down to perch on a wiper. She fumbled in her handbag, thinking she could use her phone as a torch. Eventually she was able to shine it at him, noticing how the stark white light, coupled with the darkness of the autumnal evening, had turned his red chest feathers black. He repositioned himself on a post by the entrance with a flurry of wings, a tiny monochrome form sinking into the anticipatory darkness.

The gates were padlocked, and for a moment she thought she might be going mad again, a woman investigating unexplained lights in the lonely countryside! The bluish light coming from behind the trees proved irresistible, though, and she started walking. The robin signalled his impatience with a loud trill and a shaking of blue-tinged feathers.

She hastened over and lifted the padlock. In a sudden jolt of recognition, she almost expected to see it hanging in mid-air. Evidently, though, she was not ready to disappear again quite yet. The robin trilled, this time more insistently, and despite the thumpity-thump of her heart, she was able to grasp the padlock more firmly, by now sufficiently exasperated to throw an exclamation back at him.

"What are you trying to tell me?"

As she looked up, his wings extended and whooshed so hard that she felt a breeze ruffling her hair. These great sweeping swooshes of air displaced her understanding of what should be, and with her heart thumping loudly, it came to her that he was telling her what could be instead. She looked down at the lock in her hands. It was open.

She gasped. "Did you do that? How...?"

In answer, he landed on the gate, which she'd started to push open, just enough to get through.

The darkness was absolute. Her eyes took some time to get used to it, but slowly the starlight filtered through to show her the way, and she found the path again. From visits when the kids were little, she knew there was a lake down there somewhere. She kept her eyes peeled, not particularly wanting to get wet. Instead, the bobbing speck of her new friend caught her attention again, this time perched on something that looked like a person.

Trying to focus, she wished that the blue light that had faded somewhere between opening the padlock and squeezing through the gate would reappear. Then, as quickly as it had gone, it was back, shining as brightly as any star. The need to make her presence known overcame her, so, clearing her throat, she managed to croak out a little, "Hello there," closely followed by an "Excuse me...."

The source of the light dimmed, and she could sense movement. The flickering shadows at the edges of her vision indicated that she was being beckoned. Following what she interpreted as an invitation to come closer, she saw that the figure was shrouded in a cloak of feathers, the light shining through thousands of individual filaments. She still couldn't be sure whether she was seeing a man in a cloak or something other, anthropomorphised by wishes she had flung at the swirling darkness.

Words came, softly at first but building into sound that whistled, as if through hollowed bones.

"Who do you think I am, Drum Keeper? Will you read the clues to fix our purpose?"

Martha looked up in askance, willing her frozen lips to reply. They didn't, and so the voice continued, "I-will-help-you. List-en."

By reminding her of Dewe'igan's rhythms, the careful syllables soothed her. Still, the words for what was unknowable hadn't come to her yet. So she nodded instead. At her signal, the voice of a thousand feathers brushed across frayed nerves.

"There once was an Old Medicine Woman who lived in the countryside. One day, she was told of a sick child in a nearby village that needed her help. Since it was her duty to heal those in need, she heeded the call. The child was brought forth, and a crowd gathered, for it was rare to see one such as her. They watched as she said a prayer over her patient.

"*Do you really think your prayer will help her, when medicine has failed?* a man from the crowd shouted.

"*You, apparently, know nothing of such things!'* the Old Medicine Woman replied.

"At these words, his face grew hot and red with anger. Noticing this, she ceased her prayer and walked over to him.

"*If one word has the power to make you so angry and hot, may not another have the power to heal?*

"And this is how the Old Medicine Woman healed two people."

Now, even though she'd done no drumming that day, meditative or otherwise, Martha recognised the footprint of Koomis. She closed her eyes. She was experienced enough in the ways of Dewe'igan to know she was being called to heal something as part of her task, why else the story? Assuming, though, that this was simply a different kind of Naming, she prepared a song of summoning, using a phrase that had come to her that afternoon around the Zimbabwe birds.

"Names are the game;
Birds are like words,
Through Dewe'igan all will be heard."

With no drum to guide her, she clapped as she intoned the chant, voice getting stronger with each repetition. All at once, she felt his weight around her neck. Still keeping her eyes closed, she reached down and repeated the summoning with his support, finishing with a tap of thanks and closure.

She found the courage to look around her and quickly realised that the drumming had cleared her vision. The light had shifted again, the shadow of her companion an odd monochrome figure looming before her. As always, the words came upon her swiftly and irrevocably, but there were no Names this time.

"Oh, Great Spirit, whose voice I hear in the wind, whose breath gives life to all the world. Hear me;
I need your strength and wisdom.
Let me walk in beauty, and make my eyes ever behold the red and purple sunset.
Make my hands respect the things you have made and my ears sharp to hear your voice.
Make me wise so that I may understand the things you have taught my people.
Help me to remain calm and strong in the face of all that comes towards me.
Let me learn the lessons you have hidden in every leaf and rock.
Help me seek pure thoughts and act with the intention of helping others.
Help me find compassion without empathy overwhelming me.
I seek strength, not to be greater than my brother, but to fight my greatest enemy, Myself.
Make me always ready to come to you with clean hands and straight eyes.
So when life fades, as the fading sunset, my spirit may come to you without shame."

As her drum died out, she looked into what she'd assumed would be the face of an old man. For a moment it was. But then it blurred into those of an eagle, a raven, and a child, each aspect overlaying the other with such rapidity to render the whole featureless. The voice came once more, and this time she heard the underlying timbre of ancient authority.

"It is time to reshape and retell. Memories need to be held in a new place of dust.

"You are of the People, and yet you are a new creature. A different kind of Brave for a different kind of world. You lack the cohesion of culture, and yet your questioning brought you Dewe'igan, he who beats at the heart of all things. Your drumming forges the bones of our land, crossing boundaries and geographies to hold what is coming. I am ready to face my purpose again. Bring it to me."

The ground shook, and a heavy weight landed first on one shoulder and then on the other, black feathers and sharp raven beaks brushing a twinned greeting across her face.

The voice reached her ears in stereo:

"Do not be afraid, sister. We are part of the Great Spirit. We are all bound together as guardians of the land, the sky, and the waters, at the heart of all that is and all that will be."

Newly hooded and now skeletal in aspect, the face appeared before her again, this time great hollowed eyes framing a jutting, black beak. The voice attacked her, giving no quarter.

"Ah, the forgetfulness of people. We are no longer held by the veil, so we can grow again, roots spanning this world and the next. Your drumming changes everything."

Pummelling the drum, Martha felt increasingly bewildered. She was still anticipating a Naming and as such was following the pattern of Charlotte's teachings. But there were no more Words to be found; even the pictures in her mind were all wrong. Maintaining her composure despite this, she turned to face the apparition.

"There is no Name. It won't settle. A white raven is being birthed by a blue flame. All is burning and changing, the feathers of light becoming indigo darkness. My prayer is the offering, and it must suffice."

As she spoke, a thunderclap sounded, and a sheet of blue water rose from the darkness of the lake, transmuting into translucent wings of variegated colours, the black-cloaked figure borne aloft and within. Once again, the voice rang through the chalk pit, but now as a susurration of many.

"We can't be Named, because we can't be fixed. In our world you will not find mighty cities; instead we have built stories that have outlasted the ages of man. When the end of words comes, the impetus of the truth they hold will allow us to build anew."

Feeling disorientated and alone, she took the beat of the thunder into Dewe'igan. As she did so, the colours and music wove themselves around her until time and space were lost in the shimmering wings of the dance. Held by rhythms as old as the world, lightning flashed, and motes of dust vied with the light of the stars. Crackling with energy, hundreds of whispering voices flung the next words out into the cosmos.

"You will find a way to Name the Wolf and the Buffalo, the Rain and the Muskrat, the Eagle and the Thunderbird. They will blaze forth when the time comes. But for now, your drumming must bring forth the path."

An iridescent density started pulsing through her surroundings, with even the smallest blade of grass shot through with living colour. Despite being mesmerised by this though, the words of the final sentence came across loud and clear.

"Your drumming is the portal that brings things into being. From emptiness life will spring forth, every observation, every expectation creating matter — precipitating the ending that will start the circle of life anew. Come, see."

Following the bony yellow finger, Martha looked out at what seemed to be the softly rippling wavelets of the lake. As her eyes acclimatised, she realised that the shimmering green was made up of dots, pixels that wanted her to join, to become. She looked down at her hands, finally recognising their translucence as an echo of this new dimension.

"No!" She shouted. "I am here. I am Drum Keeper. I will remain."

As she drummed, the thunder rolled, and the diaphanous wings blazed. Then they faded, an entirely new scene unfolding in their wake. A figure of a man was lying in foetal position on a pixelated floor, surrounded by walls that were equally indeterminate. It was hard to make him out, as he himself was shimmering and shifting. She saw him move, trying to uncurl and cling onto the mesh he was lying on. Instead of affording any kind of hold, though, it was fluid, lifting and shifting every time he tried to grasp it. Then the walls started closing in, absorbing him even further.

She realised she could hear him also.

"I am Lokozho." He was panting, gasping for breath. "I must hold on. Must, must."

Shocked, Martha began shouting to Dave. Deaf to her voice, he continued to mutter his Name. She drummed again.

214

"Help him," the wind whispered.

"Fix him. Make him stronger," the trees sounded.

"You are Drum Keeper. Do what is needed," the thunder pounded.

Martha drummed through the fading voices, repeating his name again and again. As she did so, he gained definition. But despite all her efforts, it was clear that Dave was losing the battle. His struggles lessened, and she sensed he was close to the end.

"Help him. Help!"

At Martha's desperate cry, twin birds dropped back onto her shoulders, vast wingspans shimmering with an ever-more vivid blue as they took up her plea.

"Help him. Help!" they cawed.

The lake roiled with energy, wings of water drowning the pixels that shaped the all-consuming mesh. As it gained precedence, the light became stronger. From it appeared a woman clad in fiery blue. Standing on the water, she was reaching out to Dave, attempting to place the cloak that was billowing around her, over him. Despite the violence of the storm, she eventually managed it. At this, a cobalt flame shot through the scene, and all was gone.

Martha's hands stilled, and the waters calmed. Other than one final raven caw, silence reigned. She was alone in the darkness. Making her way back along an almost invisible path, she realised that even Dewe'igan had deserted her.

She fell into the seat of her car and exhaled loudly. She'd spent enough time with Charlotte not to be too afraid but nonetheless was relieved it was over. As the cars sped past her, she wondered whether anyone else had seen what happened. It was the first time her "hidden" ability had called something into being in the "real" world. Although the question of what had happened to Dave was gnawing at the back of her mind, the thudding of her heart in the silence of the car was like an echo of her Drum. It felt reassuring.

ACT 2

Despite being in some kind of mesh, Dave was able to feel Martha's presence. He was in the Web, but also of the Web; this seeming iteration the digital world that also allowed him to be had become visible externally.

But what had previously felt like home had turned on him, his consciousness being absorbed by a cannibalistic fury while a cancer-like reproductive randomness was pulling him apart.

He'd just about accepted the inevitable when he heard Martha's scream. Suddenly, Mother's arms enfolded him, an embrace of sweet goodness turning despair to hope. There was a gentleness about the intervention that tempered fear and comfort with a warmth he hadn't felt since he'd first shifted. It was this, above all things, that brought him back to life. But even then, this new ally didn't let go. Sensing him come back to himself, she continued to keep hold of him, cradling him within her being until he was whole again.

He was in a place of warmth now. After coming so near to an ending, he spent some time enjoying this feeling of safety. He realised he hadn't felt truly safe for quite some time. Once he'd recovered himself sufficiently though, he tried to think back to what had caused this disastrous near-dissolution.

The being that had saved him was not part of it, that was for sure. There was too much humanity about her for her to belong to the vast digital emptiness he'd come to know so well. She'd been warm and real, and he was sure had come in response to Martha's call.

Thinking back, he realised this latest dénouement had started with Fatima. He'd been following her attempt to raise money, had even given Just Giving a little helping hand. He'd also been interested in the tablets she had ended up with. Fifteen of them now. As he watched her trying to power them all up in a city with regular power outages, he saw how she'd started to recognise the enormity of her hubris. This was a very different task to supporting the three she had been working with.

Nevertheless, the next morning she'd decided to take all the tablets, even those that weren't fully charged, to the garden. She'd had a great time getting the kids started. The real event, though, had happened while her back was turned.

Little Dana and a couple of her friends had taken a dead tablet and were trying desperately to make it work. As only very little children could, they'd wished with all their hearts that it would turn on. And it had.

Dave had been semipresent on a couple of the other tablets when he'd felt a huge pull on his energy. With each flicker of life, he'd felt a stronger pull, until he could bear it no longer. It was as if he was holding his breath underwater, desperately looking for a way up that would allow him to breathe. Eventually, he'd found it. Up he came, and, following the source of his relief, he realised that his desire to help and their longing to make the tablet fire up had caused their blue crystal shards to blaze with life. A way had been created for the tablet to draw energy from the blue stones rather than from him.

Although he wasn't sure how, Dave knew he'd acted as a conduit. The charting of direction, accompanied by a sudden release of energy, seemingly triggered an independence he hadn't come across before in his digital sphere. Sensing that other children were energising their stones without drawing from him, he realised this was something worth remembering. But it had cost him.

Having said that, if Deep Digger and GoodNewz had been able to match that leap into self-sufficiency, he'd have gladly given it again. The hunger of the digital helpmeets he'd created was constant. They were absolutely dependent on him for sustenance, and every new machine and login was taking more of his substance.

It had been a perfect storm, not just one thing but a number of actions conspiring against him. One thing had changed, though. Now he'd survived, he seemed to have a different sense of himself. Even in this place of removed safety, he could still feel the children. They were reaching him through their crystals.

Not leeching from him, though. No, the energy of this connection was feeding him — and not just the cells that made up his "activity," but him, the sentient being. This, along with the sense that his ally was still keeping him safe, gave him the courage to move beyond the confines of his present and shift somewhere else entirely.

* * *

Dave opened his eyes onto a huge fire blazing at the heart of a forest clearing. He revelled in the heat it threw off. It came to him that his presence in and amongst it was adding to the stunning flares of blue. As white, yellow, and orange tongues of flame lapped across him, he was overcome by a sense of absolute freedom, for even though he knew he was part of the fire, it seemed to him that he also remained a very separate entity. It was joyful choice whether to be apart or dance along.

From this prime position, he surveyed those around him and was met by another surprise. There, sitting on the ground, straight in front of him, was Martha. An ancient creature, one of wattled flesh and gnarled hands, was sitting next to her, clutching a pipe.

To the left of them sat an older woman with dark skin, a huge bird protectively looming behind her. Yellow talons dug fiercely into the earth, marking their territory. Next came Fatima. The last time he'd seen her was in the garden. It was a pleasant surprise to see her in this new place. Sitting to Martha's right was a tiny Asian woman. Her body seemed to coil and shimmer with a dark gilded green. He looked again. Was that a dress she was wearing, or was she covered in scales? He flared higher just to see and realised that there were indeed tiny scales covering her body, all reflecting blue light back, as well as myriad other colours. Where a human body would ordinarily be clothed, they increased in size and brilliance, effectively simulating a dress that clung in all the right places.

The old woman spoke, raising claw-like hands into the cold crystal air that, despite the size of the fire, was strangely devoid of smoke.

"So, it is come. We are missing two of our number. Mbuya Hungwe, your daughter will be with us soon. And Wolf Girl with No Name, your Mother will join us also. This is the fire of the Winter Solstice. Although we know that the longest night is upon us, we also know the day will return."

As Dave looked across, he thought he could see outlines of shadowy forms beneath the trees. They were not within the welcoming circle of light, but they were still part of things. A bit like him, he supposed. Although he was at the centre of it all, he was still hidden. He looked again, catching flashes of wings and teeth and even a glimpse of the most perfect little face.

Looking directly at the fire, she spoke again. "It is good to see you also, Daughter of Fire. I see you carry him in your blue flame even as we speak."

She turned back. "So, we are assembled. Lesson three begins. The Drum Keeper must drum, but you must hear. You, the Ghost Dancers, will give voice to the spirits of the living and the dead. We, the Spirits of sky, earth, forest glen, and water, will watch and listen. Together, using rhythm and movement, we will forge tools that span the planes of existence. Those who have the courage to choose faith, goodness, and knowledge will use these tools to unite all worlds. They will gather, and they will save.

"It is only through our sharing that the vastness of existence is made bearable. It will lead us to love, the force that binds all, including this creating. We will endure, and it is through this that we will come to walk the path of peace. So, Drum Keeper, drum of this lesson. This song of loss is also one of love. It will allow us to dance together, helping us find comfort in each other on this longest night."

Dave watched Martha's face as she listened to the woman who must be Koomis, her concentrated frown only clearing as she started drumming. Her hands were as alive as the markings on her instrument, dancing together with an incandescence born of fire. As she drummed, the brightness grew. Almost eclipsing the fire now, the light shone out of her, illuminating a path for the shadowy figures beneath the trees.

"I am Seeker
I am Convenor
I am the Keeper of Language
I am Drum Keeper.
To be these things I must be a Namer of the unknown.

"Daughter of the Wolf, I name you Dugdhav, the Shining One. You, a child yourself, have been a Mother and are now Mother to many. I ask you to dance with us."

The dancers stamped and started round the fire. Stamping and clapping, faster and faster they went. Charlotte's voice, though, was louder than the drumming and deeper than the stamping. It filled the clearing.

"You will dance to bind the world, you will dance to save those who wish to be saved. You will show others what you learn here so they too can choose the path of endurance and peace. Who stands with Dugdhav the shining one?"

Out from under the trees strode a tall olive-skinned figure. Clad in tan buckskin and a black pelt, her grey hair was braided into two tight plaits. A necklace of bones hung around her neck. Beside her stood a huge grey wolf.

"I stand with her. My song and my bones will help call the children home."

A powerful sweet melody brought order to the tumult, and the dancers slowed, matching the pace of the singer.

The old woman spoke again. "It is good. You will help her when the time comes. Now, who stands with the Drummer?"

All movement and noise stopped.

"Koomis," said Martha, "surely you will stand with me?"

"No, my child. My dance here is nearly at an end. I will be called to another place soon. You need someone who will hold the world, so your drum can be heard."

She repeated herself, her voice growing even louder, bouncing off the enormous trees that surrounded them. Rustling in response, they opened to reveal the shuffling figure of an old man in a feathered cloak. As he got closer, though, he righted himself, his final stride that of someone much younger. When the hood was lowered, Dave was nearly blinded by the nobility of his shining countenance, topped with two perfect feathers, a black and a white, affixed to raven hair. The garment was then shrugged off in its entirety, revealing oiled, flawlessly bronzed skin glistening with the undertones of fire. The cloak fluttered, borne softly downwards by its own ephemeral fabric.

"I will stand with the Drum Keeper. Ravens will fly for her."

He opened the beaded pouch on the soft skin belt, slung around a washboard stomach; things of beauty both. From it he drew something, which he flung into the fire. Dave felt hard black carapaces transform in his flames, the cocoons releasing two mighty birds, one black, one white.

The warrior spoke. "All is change, and from the seeds of the old comes new birth."

Although the voice remained the same, his aspect had changed from beauty to terror, a bird's skull with a rending beak replacing the noble visage. Sounding hollow, as if through bones, he continued. "My ravens will see for her. She has bestridden the path of endurance. Now peace beckons, and she will be heard."

With that he disappeared, leaving behind multitudes of little birds that transformed the dreaded black cloak into a thing of life. Up they went, following the ravens into the darkness beyond the fire.

Charlotte seemed to collapse in on herself, frail form shrinking even farther into her garments. Her voice was still strong, though, and she turned to Anjani and Chipo. "You, Dragon of my Heart, are already of both worlds. You will do what is right when the time comes. I salute you. And you, Eagle of my Dreams, already more of your valley than in the world of men. You will help your daughter find her way, while preparing it for all who come."

Both bent their foreheads to the ground in deep obeisance.

"We hear and obey, Mother."

The voice continued unrelentingly.

"We have fed the Drum, we have named the Dancers. It has been a day well spent. We still need the flame to flare, holding what is here and there. *He* does not understand yet, though. I trust you, Daughter of Flame, to stand with him."

Dave felt himself shooting farther up than he had before, joining the blue-tipped flames at the top of the fire.

"You will each throw in a silent wish. Drum Keeper, you will drum again, and it will be done. I am tired and will rest. The flame will die. Those who wish to will take a gift from the pyre. A crystal to hold you and a flower to help you find your way."

Most of the dancers made their way to the guttering flames of something that had burned so brightly only moments before. Only the older woman held back. The eagle swooped down to lift a crystal in her stead.

* * *

Martha found herself waking in front of the flickering TV screen. The last thing she remembered was an unseasonal scent of blossoming flowers wafting towards her. But the tree in the corner had continued twinkling with a reassuring bonhomie, and so she had turned back to her programme.

Even though the house was deadly quiet now, it had all been so vivid. This time, though, she'd done nothing to get there, not even drummed. There had been the incident at the nature reserve, but after that, she'd come home, made dinner, had a bath, and watched TV in her Christmas PJs. There was still a pervasive floral scent in the air, but other than that, there was nothing to connect with the scene she'd just left.

As she got up to turn on the light, she realised that there was something new after all. A lump of glittering blue stone had come to be in her hand. It felt warm, as if from a fire. It spoke of worlds within worlds and a promise of something better. Rather than turning on the light in the hall, she let its soft glow guide her upstairs to the sleeping children.

Just before getting into bed, she glanced down at her drums and realised something else had changed too. Instead of the patches of black and red that had so recently appeared, her bongos sported twin wolves. One was black and one red, with bristly bodies and upright tails curving around huge open maws. It looked as though they were ready to take big bites out of anything that came their way. As she closed her eyes, she realised that she was too.

CHAPTER 11

Universal Cattiness

There are many individual animals of whom we can truly say 'this is a cat'... if the word 'cat' means anything, though, it means something which is not this or that cat, but some kind of universal cattiness. This is not born when a particular cat is born and does not die when it dies. In fact, it has no position in space or time, it is 'eternal.'
—Bertrand Russell, *History of Western Philosophy*

ACT 1

Centralstation, Stockholm

Stockholm reminded Dave of his grandmother. When his parents split up, he'd spent entire summers with Mormor. Just her, though. His grandfather had left years before, returning to another family in Belfast and leaving his mother an only child. When Dave visited, he and Mormor split their time between the Uplandsgatan apartment and her little summerhouse, tucked away off the archipelago. There in particular, the icy, glistening water and shadowed pines framed stories that offered refuge from the fears that dogged his present. By the time he was twelve, he realised Mormor felt this too. Him being there gave her an excuse to live in a time of retelling. She'd once confessed her secret belief that he was a conduit to those who had created this land, although she'd never been able to tell him why.

So now, even years after she was gone and he himself a conduit to something else entirely, he was drawn to Stockholm's Centralstation. And, just like in the old days, when he'd waited for Mormor to pick him up, watching thousands of people hurry off through their lives still filled him with that familiar sense of hungry anticipation.

Since the fire of the winter solstice, he'd been able to insinuate himself into the minds of nearby creatures. Thanks to this newfound ability, he was able to survey the concourse through beady pigeon eyes. As he did so, he wondered at the oddness of Martha referencing the Norse God Loki when she'd named him Lokozho. Had his namesake ever felt that his name didn't fit either? Maybe that's where the old stories about his shape-shifting escapades had originated.

Absentmindedly, he fluffed his feathers. Maybe this was his way of growing into the Name she had given him. "A swish of feathers, a dragon's breath," a messenger and shaper of things; although "pain unfathomable, joy unimaginable" were still not part of his repertoire. Feeling as well as seeing. He was sure that was the next step. As Dave adjusted his rather precarious perch on a CCTV camera, he couldn't help wondering what Loki would have made of all this.

Almost as soon as he'd made the decision to connect his widened perspective to new experiences, he spotted something. Up until now, he'd not been able to feel anything that wasn't directly related back to Martha and the children. But the waves of pain that suddenly washed up at him through the windows of the small cybercafé just below him had nothing to do with his family.

He swooped down to perch on the lintel of a slightly open widow. A pungent, unwashed odour wafted out. Its source, a scruffy red-haired creature, was sitting just behind the front door. A full beard made it difficult to determine much else about him. However, pigeons had a notoriously strong homing instinct, and this guy was flashing at him like a beacon. In his current state, Dave wasn't able to get any closer, so against his better judgement, he decided to pop himself back into a screen.

It didn't go quite as planned, though. Instead of looking out of the screen, he found himself looking into it from someone else's head. Had he graduated from creatures to humans? Was that all it had taken, a decision to try something new so he could better fit his Name?

The guy had logged into ASafeSpace, and, because Dave found himself able to follow the thoughts that accompanied the words being written, he realised the more immediate connection too.

"You have recently survived a DDOS hacking attack. Another one in the near future is therefore unlikely. I know this because I used to mastermind attacks on organisations that didn't fit in with the ideology of Daesh, an organisation you know as ISIS. My name is Ali Mustafa. Before 2013, I was Robert and a student of Computer Science at University College London."

Okay, this made sense. So was this guy apologising for being involved with the attack against ASafeSpace? Scanning his thoughts in much the same way as he would his own, Dave didn't think that was the case. In going on about the black-and-white flag of Isis and how they'd turned this modern-day Jolly Roger into a powerful, digital propaganda machine, he did seem to be seeking some kind of absolution. But there was something wider as well.

"I maimed and beheaded. I raped and tortured. I hunted and subverted. And now, because I am no longer that person, I have become the hunted. How it happened is important and I must share it.

"After the fall of Mosul in 2016, we needed to regroup. There was still plenty of oil money funding us, and we were planning a counter-offensive. Initially we worked from mountain shelters scattered across old Kurdish territory along the Syrian, Iraqi, and Turkish boarders. Eventually, we settled in Zahko, just a few kilometres across the Turkish border."

As Ali was writing, Dave was able to form a strong impression of a mazed, underground HQ in a dry, desolate setting. Sifting through the images, the only visible sign of any human presence Dave could make out were a couple of shepherd's huts on the surface. Still unable to determine what had made this Ali Mustapha broadcast his pain so strongly, Dave continued going through the disjointed ideas and images. The next clue followed swiftly.

"The only thing growing around our hideout was a bit of scrub to feed the goats. That all changed after two children happened upon us last November. Because we saw no need to harm them, we kept up the pretence of being local folk and sent them on their way with water and foodstuffs. In return, the boy scattered some seeds into the air, and the girl asked for a little bowl of water to plant bulbs in the shadow of the far hut."

Khalid and Hadeel, the children from Fatima's garden — it must have been them. Knowing he was on the right track now, Dave paid avid attention. He needed to connect these puzzle pieces.

"Over the next few days, flowers started to appear. One of our brothers was of Kurdish origin. He explained the symbolism of these Nergis flowers. We liked the idea of symbols of renewal and peace growing up around us and praised Allah for this positive sign. Other shoots sprang up also, developing into trees at an unprecedented rate. One by one, brothers started leaving, at first to follow the wives who were disappearing into the night, but when no one came back, others started peeling off also. By the time the earthquake had shaken the buildings above ground into rubble, there were only ten of us left. Feverishly, we worked to maintain the communications structures. All most of us wanted, though, was to feel Allah's breath on our faces.

"Shortly after the quake, a pack of huge grey wolves appeared. Over the course of the next few days, their uncanny howling breached our physical and mental defences. Maddened by what was happening, I took a gun and headed for the surface. Pushing open a trapdoor, I found myself looking directly into the yellow eyes of their leader. Its sheer size reinforced my own inadequacy, as well as that of my gun. As the howling ceased, I found myself overcome by tiredness. Not just from today, but tiredness that came from living in a tomb of my own making. Just like that, I laid down my gun and walked away. I've been on the run ever since."

As Dave's new perspective allowed him to scan the more hidden thoughts, he realised it wasn't just pain and regret he could sense, but also a desperate seeking. Ali thought of himself as a ghost, turning up where he was needed in a bid to redefine his identity. Sympathy notwithstanding, Dave couldn't quite work out what he was supposed to learn from this. Frustrated, he was about to withdraw when the final paragraph blazed out at him:

"Once I followed what I believed to be the words of Allah, emblazoned in white upon a flag of black. Now I know that the black stands for the blood we shed, the white for the twisting of innocence and truth into hate. So I have created a new flag. Because flowers were the light that brought me to the wolf who went on to consume my world, my seal is a black wolf and flower on a white background.

"Where once I created networks of corruption, I am attempting to create change so I leave my sign to mark system vulnerabilities. I know my time is nearly over, but for those stuck in places of perversion and pain, these digital markers chart a pathway of hope. Change is possible, even for one such as me."

Finally! This was the sign Dave had been waiting for, a symbol to guide him into the darkest parts of the Web and a sacrifice that wasn't in and of himself. As he withdrew, he realised he'd have loved to have given some comfort. But even though he'd moved beyond hardware several months ago, he was still only able to watch and listen.

Withdrawing back into his own space, another story hit him, this time taken from the more usual sources of the billions of pieces of data he automatically sifted through. The congruence between this newsflash and Ali's tale struck him. Although he couldn't quite work out what it might be, he recognised that part of his own story would come to be contained in this one.

Oil Prices Hit All-Time High

Brent Crude is trading at an all-time high of $300 per barrel. Denying rumours of supply problems, OPEC's Secretary General stated that in the light of Stateside West Texas Intermediate (WTI) Oil continuing to glut the market, it has reviewed its international policy of co-operation.

Bloomberg sources have confirmed that the ongoing guerrilla attacks on US Oil refineries are the more likely cause of this price hike. OPEC's statement also stands in sharp contrast to actual WTI supplies, which are widely believed to be failing. The American Petroleum Institute has confirmed this temporary shortfall while reiterating its commitment to hitting industry targets.

Despite what is believed to be a robust federal energy security policy, leading economist Nour Rabbini has gone on record to say that the current trend is both unprecedented and unmanageable and will lead to "significant and lasting austerity."

Source: Bloomberg Markets, Feb 2, 2018

* * *

Barbican, London

Peter's black cab came to a stop outside his apartment block. He had just completed another exhausting stint in the office. Unusually, there was no porter, so he resigned himself to picking up his post tomorrow. Making his way towards the lift, Peter realised that the building was eerily quiet. After the carnage he'd witnessed in his office and on his journey home, it could just be that he was noticing it more. A cab journey that usually took twenty minutes and cost £20 had taken an hour and a half and cost over £100. He'd been lucky though, since it seemed that most of London was trudging past him in the rain.

He had a horrible feeling that the disaster that was unfolding was all down to him. As he entered his twenty-third-floor bachelor pad, paid for by the very system he was in the process of destroying, he realised their ambitious manoeuvre had spiralled out of control. He'd been distracted, taken his eye off the ball in terms of preempting the gentle nudges the algorithms had needed to keep things on track. No longer just an expensive slapped wrist for the system he'd wanted to shame, it was time to admit that the genie was out of the bottle and there was no way of putting it back. To still the flutterings of panic this thought engendered, he took another of those little white pills he kept in his side pocket, the second in as many hours.

Even though he hadn't started drinking again, since his mysterious coconspirator had come out as Dave, Martha's Dead Dave, Peter had been popping the Xanax he'd bought online. He didn't know whether it was the pills or that part of him believed the explanation he'd been given, but in an awful kind of way because of what he'd been able to do, Dave being a living extension of the web made sense. Since then things had become increasingly abstract, and rather than focusing on what needed to be done, Peter had spent his waking moments avoiding a sentence he couldn't get his head around.

"It is me, you know. Martha received those pictures and notes about Charlotte you sent and was glad." He'd stopped him dead, refusing to answer anything incoming from Dave for three days, even switching off the alerts from his secret inbox.

It couldn't have come at a worse time. It was early January, and they'd just started properly testing the waters. As planned, in November a simple virus had gained them back-door entry. By leaving it to multiply they'd infected all hardware connected to CHL. Until then everything had been going so well, but Dave outing himself as a dead brother-in-law had kyboshed it all.

The three-day gap and then the distraction meant he hadn't properly managed the domino effect of algorithms of other banks assimilating the new pattern they'd insinuated. Over the last few days, the chaos that was spilling out into the real world was starting to break down Peter's iron reserve. A couple of weeks ago, he'd started getting panicky messages from friends and colleagues about the growing instability of the markets. It was only when the oil crisis hit, though, that he admitted to himself they'd lost control.

Over the last fifteen hours, things had gone from bad to worse, the effects of their vigilante action irreversible. Initially, he'd felt like a master of the universe. However, as he watched one bank after another topple, he started twigging that he was just as much part of the black hole as the leaders he'd been trying to punish.

At the heart of their intervention was a virus that had got CHL's biggest member bank to change the behaviour of a key algorithm. This had created a domino effect, with algorithms of other banks adding milliseconds to their transactions too, the premise being that the initially greater profits would cause the losses to be disguised.

Their next step had been to further weaken the US dollar by using these robo-traders. The idea was to undermine banks' ability to pay for things, leading to a knock-on effect on Joe Public. Peter had hoped this would shine a spotlight on how interconnected everything was and thus create a much-needed wake-up call.

A clever little glitch they'd devised continued to make the influences seem random, and algorithms, unable to distinguish this kind of fine-tuning, continued to sell. Without anything to stop it, their final push yesterday made the dollar sink like a stone. Today had been worse still, and in the last hours of trading, the very governments that had been trying to undermine the dollar were making increasingly frantic attempts to shore it up. To no avail though, their vast currency reserves were turning into emptiness.

With trembling hands, Peter opened the one bottle of single malt he'd found himself unable to dispose of. After pouring a generous measure of the forty-two-year-old Tobermory into an appropriately expensive tumbler, he threw himself into his Eames recliner and turned on the

TV. There was rioting in the streets of London, and the wider unrest had spread to major cities across the UK and other parts of the world.

Even though most people had not bothered to engage with the financial system beyond the usual mortgages, pensions, and credit cards in the past, it was becoming clear that many had started to understand what was happening. Reports were flashing in from one place to the next. Petrol stations showing panic buying, and fuel pumps being drained. Supermarkets had enforcers at the door. He closed his eyes. Would he be responsible for people starving? Instead of doing good, had he precipitated utter devastation? A wave of helplessness swept over him.

He poured himself another whisky and then another, downing them in rapid succession until the bottle was empty. Turning off the TV, he staggered towards his bedroom. The dreamcatcher Emmy had given him caught his eye. The beads were winking at him. They were so blue, just like her eyes had been. Martha's as well. He really should have accepted their invitation to come over at Christmas. Did his mum have blue eyes? He couldn't remember. They belonged to the time before, when he'd belonged to someone. Shaking his head, he pulled the bottle of Xanax from his bedside drawer. He'd take a couple for now. They would help him sleep. Then he took some more, then another handful, before he knew it, they were all gone. He needed to rest. This would help.

* * *

Anjani sat at her special desk. The beautiful chair encasing her fêted little figure was not only carved to match but also featured a couple of carefully hidden extras. Since she'd had it made, she'd put one of these to particularly good use. For example, at the touch of a button, she was able to tower over the person sitting across from her.

Easing herself farther into the depths of this bespoke throne, she contemplated the coming video conference with Mercy. The screen was ready, her chair was ready, everything was set up to make her look exactly what she was: a super-wealthy leader of one of the largest corporations in Asia. Having said that, since the crisis had hit a couple of days ago, she wasn't sure what stood anymore. Her advisors and other moguls were still playing at all being normal. She had enough assets to do the same for the moment, so she did.

It made her very uncomfortable, though. For someone whose life had once been determined by all that was false, it was odd how disconnected this new falsehood made her feel. Touching a lever to release the backrest some more, she realised that her discomfort was physical as well as emotional — a sense of no longer fitting into her skin.

Glancing across at the bejewelled escritoire, she noticed that Indira's jade pin was still there. On impulse, Anjani reached out for it, welcoming the cool, steadiness of the small carving. Touching the coiled serpent necklace she always wore, she made a mental note to return the pin after this call and put it back with great care. She might even apologise for keeping it so long.

Her fingers tapped a refrain on the edges of the polished wood. She hated waiting. Impatiently, she reached out for the little jade serpent again; what was with her today? As she put the light green ornament in her hand, she thought she spotted movement. Convinced her eyes were playing tricks on her, she closed her fist and opened it again. Sure enough, a little serpent the width and length of a matchstick had started uncoiling itself. As she stared, a forked tongue shot out and little red eyes gazed up at her. Winding its way in and out of her fingers, her new friend seemed to be bent on familiarising itself with her hand.

She felt something around her neck move, and before she knew it, the serpent necklace Matthew had given her started slithering down her arm and came to rest around her wrist. Both longer and thicker than the snake pin, it remained there in the shape of a bracelet, only a slight, twisting sensation giving any kind of hint as to what had just happened. Increasingly bewildered, Anjani returned her attention to her right hand, which now had a coiled serpent spiral winding itself between the base and the first knuckle of her index finger. It seemed as though the little snake had also decided on where it felt most comfortable.

Just then, the screen vibrated and turned on. As instructed, Indira had activated her call with Mercy as soon as it came through. Anjani looked at the attractive face that filled the screen in front of her and realised that all the things she had wanted to pick up on had gone clean out of her mind. Instead, casting another bewildered glance at her hands, she remembered that despite trying to reach him numerous times that day, she still hadn't heard from Bagus. The rioting in Jakarta's slums had started spilling over into the wealthier districts, and even though she hadn't used surveillance technology on her family since that day in the hotel, she'd been sorely tempted to do so this morning. Something else to consider once she'd finished this call.

"Mrs Margono, are you okay?"

She must focus. Forcing her attention back to the screen, she once again looked into the dark brown eyes of a well-dressed woman in her mid-thirties. However, this time she noticed that a slightly anxious expression seemed to be wrinkling her brow.

Hoping that whatever had been going on had now stopped, Anjani rallied and greeted her virtual guest.

"Mercy, great to see you again. I hope you are well?"

Realising how trite this sounded, she saw Mercy glance at the notes on her laptop and hoped they distracted from her own unease. After all, this was supposed to be a very formal investment call, so the investee was likely to be nervous. And so it proved, with Mercy's initial sentence coming across as stilted and unsure. She seemed to be reading from something preprepared.

"Mrs Margono, even though you always respond to my reports, I am particularly glad we are speaking in person today. By apprising you of the current situation, I very much hope that I will be able to benefit from your guidance also. Since the fall of the dictator in November, here in Zimbabwe civil unrest has been spreading. The outlying villages, such as the ones I have been working with in Masvingo, are still relatively untouched, but in Harare and Bulawayo it's a very different story."

Anjani wasn't surprised to hear this. It had already been widely reported that Mugabe's forced resignation had precipitated pitched battles. Zimbabwe was rich in people as well as natural resources, and she reckoned it would be okay in the long term. In the short term, though, $50,000 of her money was sitting with Mercy. She certainly hadn't forgotten either that the Touchability operation was important to the larger commitment she'd made to the SafeSpace investment platform. However, although she shared some of these concerns with Mercy, she also took care to outline to the quietly elegant figure that if sufficient care was taken, the unrest might end up as an opportunity.

Mercy nodded enthusiastically, causing the stiff fabric of her African batik wrap to rustle. "Yes, absolutely, Mrs Margono. Bearing in mind what you have just said, I very much hope you will see that what I have started to do is an opportunity also."

She went on to explain that, as per her initial email, and based on her country's current need, she had started to look at Moringa-based food production also.

"We have been combining the Moringa powder with food such as plantain and cornmeal. Food shortages are worsening everywhere, but by creating ways of harvesting and processing Moringa-based foodstuffs, we are able to show people how to survive. With that in mind, in addition to the massage booklet we printed, we have also started distributing Moringa recipes. We've even created a diagram showing what can be eaten and how best to prepare it."

Drumming her fingers on the desk's red leather inlay, Anjani listened. Her continuing agitation had caused the serpents to shift position slightly. Oddly, this seemed to soothe her, helping her accept something she already knew in her heart of hearts, namely that she was unlikely to see a return on her investment for a very long time. With a start, she realised that she really didn't mind. And anyway, as Matthew had always said, investments often had a long tail. If Touchability became a name associated with social good in Zimbabwe, there could still be opportunities. Oblivious to the reason behind her investor's thoughtful expression, Mercy's anxiety levels continued to rise. Thinking that running through some new figures might make the situation better, she rattled though her exhaustive notes and costings with an increasing air of desperation.

"Enough, I've heard enough."

Anjani's voice stopped her dead, leaving Mercy's last sentence hanging mid-phrase.

"I am assuming that the US dollar is still the only currency of any value in Zimbabwe and that you still have a reasonable amount left from my initial investment?"

Waiting for Mercy to nod, Anjani continued. "Listen, please."

Still mentally going through the figures she'd wanted to share, Mercy did not initially register Anjani's change of tone. However, as the next few sentences shifted into a strange kind of intimacy, she recognised it was time to focus on the face in front of her. So she put away the rest of her notes and attempted to make sense of what Anjani was saying.

"Over the last few months I have been party to a series of events that cannot be explained. More recently, this has resulted in me spending much of my energy reevaluating the direction of my life and even how I want to spend my money.

"I have realised that I've been alone for a very long time. One of the reasons I invested in ASafeSpace and Touchability was because they promote touch, either physically or in kind. What appealed to me was the idea of one person touching another and so passing opportunity forward, in your case through massage and the supply chain work. The fact that there was a way to make a profit made it even more attractive. However, it certainly wasn't the deciding factor."

"Essentially, working in this way makes me feel that I am making a difference. I know that I am not touching people physically. However, I still feel that I am connecting to them, and through them to something that is evolving more widely. Windows such as the one we two are connected through use digitally rendered flat images to bring hearts and souls together in great numbers. Speaking truth and sharing of ourselves — as we are now — takes this further. That is what the SafeSpace platforms, and, by association, Touchability are encouraging. I like to think that I am investing in putting what it means to be human back together again. I believe that this will contribute to a big picture we can only guess at now. It will only happen, though, if we also are willing to move beyond sound bites into something more meaningful. By risking ourselves, we will encourage others to do so as well."

Mercy was becoming increasingly nervous. This wasn't investment stuff she was hearing; in fact, the conversation she'd been expecting had turned into a monologue. And yet she found it compelling how the older woman's glacial expression had become animated.

Noticing that Mercy had changed the way she was listening, Anjani continued.

"We are all so different and yet something fundamental connects us. What is that thread that runs through us all? We have evolved as social creatures. Long ago, our ability to build relationships of trust and cooperation helped increase our chances of having a stable food supply and consistent protection from predators. Now, our dependence on social interaction is so embedded that its absence creates a state of physical stress."

She breathed deeply and glanced down as if as looking to her hands for comfort.

"Therefore, if we, as humans, are to remain fit for purpose, we must move away from the lonely existences we have banished ourselves to. We believe that digital interactions soften our exile, but instead, living out our lives in that universe only serves to increase our isolation. I invested in you because the idea of a positive domino effect created through touch, touched me. Your energy and vision have pulled me along with you, through the screens we use to communicate, into investment."

Although still bewildered, Mercy was starting to feel that something good was coming out of all this, and Anjani's next words caused a physical frisson of anticipation.

"This latest idea of using my dollars to help people understand how to feed themselves in times of crisis completely links to what I saw. It is this, not your spreadsheets, that make me support you. And for the record, I don't think we'll be making money any time soon. If there is still any at the end of the week...."

Thinking she'd said enough for the moment, Anjani fell silent. She very much hoped Mercy had heard enough to understand the wider subtext. The screen zoomed out. The silence had made Anjani nervous, and suddenly she wanted the African woman to notice the gorgeous matching bangle and ring adorning her person. They were both now flickering strangely in the light.

The pregnant pause went on a little longer, and then finally, Mercy broke the silence. "Anjani, may I call you Anjani? Thank you for this confidence. At the risk of sounding a bit befuddled, I will share what I know to be truth with you also. In my country, birds and Moringa trees are everywhere now. Also, my mother has recovered, and the brutal dictatorship has fallen. The most wonderful thing of all is that, here, where I live, a Hungwe Eagle comes to see us every morning. I call him Hungry.

"I know that it is he who bears ultimate responsibility for Mother's recovery. What I have been doing has helped, but Hungry is the one who made her better. I am so glad also that you recognise the deeper truth of Touchability. It's come from the very essence of me. I was broken and alone, so alone, especially when Amai got ill. But now, slowly, as I have had the courage to develop this idea, other things are happening."

Anjani lifted her hands up, making sure the Mercy was able to see them clearly. "As you risk, so do I. If your sign is the eagle, mine is the snake. Look, they have come to me even here."

Anjani was delighted at Mercy's gasp as she truly saw what had so astounded Anjani earlier. For instead of being rendered in hard green stone, the magnificent bracelet and enormous ring were now made of living scales. She spoke again, and it seemed to her that her voice was imbued with something new, matching the otherworldly beauty of the creatures that adorned her.

"The eagle is a creature of vision and power, the snake one of wisdom and healing. At the moment I feel as if I have outgrown the skin I inhabit. Touching you, in whichever way we have reached out to each other today, is helping me shed this layer."

Mercy replied, punctuating her response with clapping hands: "Mazviita, Shiri; Hungwe; Matapatira; Zienda nomudenga; Pasi yaketye ndove; *You are done a service, Bird; Fish eagle, the one who spreads his wings; Great one passing through the sky; You shun the marshes down below;*

Maita zvenyu, vachifambanemudenga. Zvaitwa, vairashiri; Vokwa Chinobhururuka; Muirashir wangu yuyu, Shiri iri hungwe.

A service has been rendered, we revere you Bird; We, who belong to you who fly; My dear one who reveres the Bird, The Bird is the fish eagle.

Anjani understood that she had been given a gift, that the eagle was, even now, consuming that which she had outgrown. In the meantime, she was able to give a gift of her own.

"If it is still possible to get money to you, I will send more. I would like you to continue with what you are doing. The crisis is no longer limited to just your country. Here in Jakarta, as food and energy have become scarce, things have become difficult as well. I very much hope that some of the actions you are describing will spread to other countries too, even making their way back here. I think we have created a little pocket of hope. I believe this can extend into something that has scope beyond anything we can imagine at this time. I will attempt to get another $50,000 to you by transfer."

They made the usual goodbyes, and Anjani's face disappeared. Mercy was left with the figures, excuses, and apologies she'd carefully prepared but not needed in the end.

* * *

It had been too dangerous to travel through Harare today, so Mercy had made this important call sitting in her kitchen. Anjani hadn't appeared to notice, and being at home made it so much easier to tell Chipo the good news. As she pushed down the lid on her laptop, she realised that

236

she was able to hear her mother up and about in the next room. She'd been so lucky to have had enough power and connectivity to reach her investor today! Looking at what was happening in Zimbabwe now, it seemed unlikely that things would be able to limp along for much longer. The financial crisis was having a huge impact on the rest of the world, but here, although "part 1" had already happened years ago, it was amazing how things could go from bad to worse so quickly.

She made her way into the next room, pushing any thoughts of doom and gloom out of her mind. Chipo's health, which was improving by the day, was a much better thing to focus on. As she walked in to the bedroom, though, she was confronted with the vision of her mother scrabbling around for something under the bed on her hands and knees. Mercy told her off in no uncertain terms.

"Amai, you should be resting. It is not long ago you couldn't move even a muscle!"

Chipo's beautiful face lit up with a smile that Mercy hadn't seen for many a year. "Look, look child. Hungry has brought us a gift."

Having at last retrieved what she was looking for, she held it up to the light to show her daughter. Bearing in mind that Mercy had just seen a living bracelet adorning her business partner's wrists, she thought nothing could surprise her. But there, held aloft in a hand so slender it was almost bird-like, Chipo held up a huge blue crystal. It shone with a light of its own, dispelling any shadows of illness that still attempted to linger in the corners of the room and imbuing the gathering darkness with a blue luminescence.

"Maita Hungwe, Shiri iri Hungwe."

Hungwe was sitting on his usual perch. As she praised him for his audacity in bringing them this gift, he spread his great wings and flew out into the dusk, a haunting, solitary cry signalling his farewell.

Carefully placing it on her bedside table next to a much smaller shard of blue stone, Chipo smiled at her daughter. "These stones represent power; the power of the spirits, the power of our world here and now and the power of the world on your computer you use to make important business decisions. They will feed all three."

Mercy bent over, reaching for the stone Hungry had bought. Feeling its energy pulsing through her, Mercy knew that Chipo had summarised the situation perfectly.

"Now come, Tsitsi, it is time for my massage. I will tell you a story."

Mercy put the stone back and grabbed her oils. She loved Chipo's stories and had missed them over the past couple of years. As Chipo started, Mercy matched the steady, kneading rhythm of the massage to the cadences of her childhood.

"There was once a child who survived. She knew, though, that in order to be the princess she always wanted to be, she needed to get to the blue mountains that were on the other side of the lush, green valley she lived in. The path was clear, and so she strode along it, singing to herself.

"A guide appeared, promising to help her navigate the valley's long expanse more effectively. Stamping and stomping loudly, he made sure that the ground shook before her, warning any other creature of her passing. Slowly, she realised that instead of clearing her way, all the stamping and stomping had started to erode the path, making it difficult to see where she was supposed to be going. As soon as she had fully grasped this, her guide disappeared.

"She was hungry and tired and didn't think she could go any farther. However, she was very keen on being a princess, so she forced her weary feet onwards. As she carried on walking, she met other guides. Welcoming the company, she didn't realise at first that in return for companionship, each one asked her to change something about herself. The first one told her she needed lighter skin. So she washed her face in water from the sacred spring. The next one told her that her hair was too curly, so she used a tincture from the bark of the shea tree to make it smooth. The next one told her that she must be better at being silent as her voice was too loud, so she drank the milk of the magic oxen, which stilled the purity of the voice that had called birds from the trees. And when she finally got to the mountains, she looked nothing like the girl she had once been.

"But still her transformation was not complete. The last guide told her that the only way the king of the mountain would be prepared to accept her was if she gave up herself. She would know that she had been successful if she was able to walk through the little door that led to his kingdom. In that moment, she would become a princess.

"The girl said that she only had his word for it. And anyway, if she gave up herself, how would she know that she had become a princess? The guide explained that it would not matter because in this new world, everyone had become beautiful and polished. In fact, people were only able to enter the safety of the kingdom under the mountain if they were new and shiny.

"Feeling very uncomfortable at the thought of losing herself, the girl said no. However, the need to become a princess was as strong as ever. Realising that she had to do something, she repeated her refusal, this time clapping her hands and stamping her feet. Then she did it again. As she did so, she felt her skin grown darker and her hair change shape. Finally, even her voice returned, and all the birds of the air responded to her call.

"Then, from all around, others who had said no too came to join her. On and on they danced. Because they had the courage to be themselves, they didn't need the door in the mountain. They danced over it to live in the kingdom of far beyond. The girl never asked to be a princess again, and of course, she lived happily ever after."

ACT 2

Martha stood frozen at Peter's funeral. It was a blisteringly cold day, and her heart had stopped. She could feel the drumming of it stilling, until it was no more. The crematorium was warm, though, as were the hands of her children holding on to her on either side.

It had been snowing on and off for a week but never strong enough to lie. As Martha eyed the coffin lying on the elevated table at the front of the large room, she realised that the snow had been falling like this since they first found him. Just like the snow, she knew that at this moment in time all the pieces of her were crystallised too, floating ever downwards to the earth, dissipating on contact. No matter how beautiful the constellation was, when it hit the ground it melted. Her life was like that. So many bits and pieces of her floating, tossing, and turning in currents over which she had no control. They were trying to get to a place where they could come together to form something, but none of them ever did, their beauty a fleeting, momentary thing, disappearing as quickly as it had come into being.

Peter hadn't been at all religious, but for tradition's sake, Martha had wanted a Christian minister.

"Ashes to ashes, dust to dust; in sure and certain hope of the Resurrection to eternal life, through our Lord Jesus Christ; who shall change our vile body."

The last funeral she'd attended had been Dave's. Same place, same flat voice, speaking the same words. She'd been angry the last time, really angry. This time she just felt frozen. Funny wasn't it, Dave's vile body really had been changed. Not via Christ necessarily, well not according to the scriptures anyway, but an inexplicable occurrence had led to him returning in digital form. Since Peter's death, she'd only had one very odd message from him. In it he'd explained how he had been helping Peter bring down the markets. However, things had turned out differently to what they'd expected, with much harsher consequences than they'd planned. He blamed himself for Peter's suicide, his final sentence reading. *We honestly believed that what we were doing was going to help. We wanted to wipe out debt, give people a chance to breathe; instead, we created starvation and even more violence.*

She had wanted more, but nothing further appeared, even after several promptings. It was part of the reason for her numbness. The other part was that the chaos happening outside these walls had caused raw survival instincts to kick in. This was one of the reasons the cremation was taking place just a few days after he'd been found.

Getting things organised had been a nightmare. Since people were unsure of the value of money, it was difficult to know how to pay for things. Realising that standing in line outside their bank for hours on end wasn't going to make a difference, whole cities had descended into anarchy. This was spilling over into smaller places too. The army had been drafted in to help the police maintain civil order, but even they didn't know where the next wage packet was coming from. For now, most of the services were still up and running, and in order to facilitate people being able to get the basics in terms of food, government vouchers had been printed. More recently, though, there had been talk of power cuts and much wider rationing. In the drought-stricken southeast, water shortages were also very much on the agenda.

When the vicar had finished intoning his brief sermon on behalf of his mother, Henry got up to say a few words. However, since there were only three of them there, it didn't seem to matter much either way. Finally, the coffin moved through black curtains, which swished closed behind it.

As with Dave, they would be scattering the ashes in the sea over the next few days. Martha couldn't help hoping that despite his silence, Dave was here with them, watching them through the CCTV. His silence, though, meant that she was feeling increasingly worried.

* * *

Dave had indeed been observing through cameras that had been fixed to both inside and outside the walls, watching three smartly clad figures drive up in the battered little Kia Martha still hadn't replaced. As they sat down in the light-coloured pews, he noticed that although Emmy was still looking thin, she appeared to be much healthier than even a couple of months ago. He'd also noticed how Henry, his brave Henry, had placed protective arms around mother and sister. At sixteen, his son's dark head cleared theirs by several inches. Dave wished he'd have been able to see his own funeral. At that time, though, he was just getting the hang of things.

A tremendous sense of loss washed over him. He realised it mirrored Brigid's despair, the crystal amplifying it to reach him from her haunt in Central Park. Luckily, unlike her, he was able to draw on Sh'ler for comfort. There was a duality to the jinni's gift, though. It had saved him, true, but the sensory access to something beyond the soulless, digital life he had been afforded in the process had also made him truly aware of the horror he'd caused.

Dave's guilt came from knowing that Peter would never have been able to create this chaos on his own. Everything that was happening was down to the timing of his coming out and his own hubris. It had not just led to Peter's death, but also to the thousands of casualties of the crash and its aftermath. It was all his fault.

Suddenly, he wished for that fragmentation he'd once fought against. He was just a collection of binary digits, pixels, manufactured waves — whatever ... he didn't want to be anymore. But just as that thought started gaining ground, he felt a warmth breathing through his emptiness and thought he heard a voice.

"Be brave for just a bit longer. Take comfort in who you are now, but be prepared for what is to come. You may be near the end of one journey, but your feelings now show me that you are ready to begin a new one. Endure for now, the path of peace is not far away."

It reminded him of path of the crystals he'd been on since Peter's death. He'd felt their life inside of his and followed their spread, first as a distraction and then as a sign of hope. With newfound courage, he looked out through the manifold eyes at his disposal once again. The influence of the crystalline light was making itself felt, even here. The power was down, and yet Martha's blue crystal was ensuring the hardware Dave was using to see them all still worked.

No longer limited to Fatima's children or those who had participated at the winter solstice, the new crystals were seeding themselves in the same way that Negris and Moringa had done. Blue stones were now randomly appearing in other parts of the world, little nudges from him helping them blaze into life. As was the case with Martha, though, their marvellous properties were still being used by accident rather than design.

The way of it didn't really matter for now. What did was that when connectivity and power dropped out in the areas the crystals had seeded, tablets, phones, and computers remained powered up and connected. He believed that whatever had happened in the cave had birthed a new kind of crystal, one connected to network that mirrored the patterns of the earth while feeding him with energy.

He felt a sudden surge of power cutting through his musings. It was similar to what he'd sensed just prior to ending up as a merrily burning flame in the clearing. Remorse forgotten, he settled back to wait, his consciousness once again subsumed in the myriad digital pathways that spanned the globe.

* * *

Momentarily overwhelmed by the sense of loss and also the knowledge that they were now truly on their own, Martha had closed her eyes. She hadn't even got to see Peter. All connection had been via email and phone, something she bitterly regretted. But as she felt the heat from Henry and Emmy's hands seeping through to her own, she recognised how much they'd all grown over the last few months. It wasn't all down to her; they were in it together. Between the three of them, they would manage.

"Love you, Mum," Emmy whispered. "We'll be fine."

As if in response to her daughter's words, Martha felt a pulse of energy from the blue piece of crystal she'd taken to carrying about with her.

Aware only of the children holding her and their love, she once again found herself in Chipo's valley. Not in the hut this time, but outside, overlooking a fiercely flowing river. Its current seemed to be much stronger than the last time she'd been here.

She looked over her shoulder and saw the couple of huts she remembered. She called to the children, and they started walking across together. She realised what she'd just done. She had called to the children! There had been no drumming, and yet they had travelled with her. Looking to her right and left, she realised that she was looking at their shadowy impressions. However, despite this incomplete manifestation, it was definitely them, and they were here with her.

Hungry, the same size as he had been when in the clearing, was outside the largest hut. Telling the children to keep up, she made her way towards him. She whispered his name as she stroked the white plumage on his chest. The Name Hungry had come to her as she walked and, as Drum Keeper, she owed him this. By way of thanks, he brushed his beak against her shoulder.

Pushing open the door and feeling for Emmy and Henry alongside her, she bent her head to enter the small, conically thatched abode. Registering Charlotte sitting in the corner, she saw that despite increasing frailty, her elderly relative was still able to beckon imperiously.

Henry and Emmy looked anxiously at their mother. Martha reassured them with a kiss and hurried them along to meet someone, she realised with a pang of gladness, they were also related to.

"Children, come sit with me. We will enjoy the spectacle of the Ghost Dancers united at last."

Under cover of shadows and smoke, Emmy and Henry gingerly moved across to sit with their Koomis. Martha was relieved at their acceptance. Glancing over at them now, they certainly seemed to be more at ease than she had been that first time.

She, in the meantime, was beckoned into the circle and found herself next to a beautiful dark-skinned woman, one who looked remarkably like a younger Chipo. She saw Fatima and Anjani too, while catching glimpses of ravens and wolves in the plumes of smoke that emanated from the fire.

"Call it to you," Koomis whispered in a penetrating crone's voice that still hadn't risen above a whisper.

243

Martha noticed that the others had placed their blazing shards of blue in a circle around the fiery centre. She knew that the crystals had wrought this meeting and that the smoke signified the substance of spirit, much as she did the substance of the flesh. However, Dewe'igan was needed to cement this, moving mere perception into tangible reality.

She called the billowing black plumes to her, murmuring the name of her drum. And as she did so, the smoke sinuously wound itself around her, promising glories to come if she joined with it. Momentarily tempted, she felt herself dissipating. However, they closed the circle more tightly, stroking her hands and feet and talking to her. Then it passed and she was once again able to sense herself here in the place of between. She also felt the bit of her that was her shell back in the crematorium. Within that space of being here and there, she was able to call Dewe'igan into being.

The dance started, and as the others shook out long limbs to a rhythm as yet unplayed, she knew she needed to start drumming. She started slowly, but then, in order to keep up with flashing limbs, she drummed harder and faster.

Chipo was still creating forms from the smouldering fire that sat at the centre of the circle. The smoky shapes wrapped themselves around her. Martha drummed on, ignoring what was being created. Eventually, a gap appeared in the smoke. It allowed her to recognise her neighbour as not just Tsitsi or Mercy. She was also Sword Bringer and Ghost Dancer. A Sword Bringer's vision cut clearly, and it was right that she should be named thus. After the Sword Bringer had been named, the cloaks of the other dancers became indistinguishable from the smoke. The clear space spread farther, allowing her to see what else was needed. She realised that their wishes, their dancing, and their desperation to create change were just as responsible for the crash as Peter and Dave's practical actions. They had asked for healing, but often before the healing came, it was necessary to cut out what was rotten.

Her feet pushed farther and farther into the earth and drew on the energy she sensed hovering on the fringes, just waiting for her permission to enter. With one joyful exclamation she did so and felt the clarity of vision, gifted through Tsitsi, pouring into her.

"We have touch, we have vision,

We have love, we have connection,

We have hunger we have power,

We have caused the world to cower.
Dance with beat and dance with drum,
We give up ourselves to call everyone."

Last time they'd met, she hadn't been fully conscious of what they were doing. This time it was clear that together they were calling to the Earth to transform its gift of oil into one of water and its gift of death into a kiss of life.

On the fringes, she felt the presence that had been hovering joining them. The name flooded into her: it was Raksha, the Wolf Mother. Martha Named her in the melee, but despite the noise, all knew that another Naming had taken place. She who had once been Badenan was taken by the hand and led into the wild dance by her daughter, Dugdhav. Martha could see that the new Ghost Dancer was bewildered, but when she realised that her guide was Fatima, she joined in with abandon despite the weight of her new name.

Martha turned her attention to Charlotte, Emmy, and Henry clapping in the corner. She knew at this point that not only they, but people everywhere, were stopping what they were doing to focus on seeing, doing, touching, or tasting more intently than they ever had before. Those who were willing at least.

"Change is possible.
I rename, I define.
It is nearly time."

* * *

Awakened by the rude shaking of the exasperated crematorium caretaker, Martha and the children came to much later that evening. He told them in no uncertain terms that he was not prepared to wait any longer. They made their way home in silence.

Martha understood that the process of connection that had been unfolding in her life was new to the children; they needed time. Very little was said as they pulled together something to eat. Time dragged on, and they were all exhausted, but even when they'd finished, no one was willing to leave the kitchen.

Martha thought back to last July and that first WhatsApp message; her pounding heart, the need to deflect from her own anxiety. Even though they'd been together then as well, she and the children had been miles apart, with them disappearing at the first opportunity. Now they were refusing to leave her side. It prompted her to speak.

"That's it. We need to talk about what happened."

Her maternal authority restored a semblance of normality to the situation. Tripping over each other, they tried to bring words together that would to convey the magnitude of what had happened to them.

"It was like here but not here."

"Did you see the smoke?"

"The drumming was awesome, Mum, like your bongos but different."

"I know I saw wolves."

She eventually closed it down by telling them that although what had happened was a first for them, it was familiar territory for her. Just another sign for her that things were changing, which they knew already. Then she hugged them and told them they'd been through the bad times together, so they'd be able to withstand the different ones too. This was territory they understood, and they melted into her. And when she said,

"Maybe now, everything's falling apart around us, we'll be better placed than most to handle it." The brittle anxiety disappeared entirely.

Finding their mother's ownership of this complete alien situation reassuring, they'd hung around for a while longer, perching on chairs that although mismatched were no longer empty. It was gone midnight by the time Martha kissed them goodnight, tucking them in with a promise of hope.

She made her way downstairs, and as had happened a couple of times over the last week, the power flickered and went out. Martha fired up her laptop, convinced that despite the outage, she had enough battery life left. As she did, the blue crystal she had propped up next to it flared to life. Somehow, despite the power being off, she'd managed to retain connectivity. Leaving the whys and wherefores for another day, Martha quickly typed in ASafeSpace.com. She'd been watching the site with interest for the last few days, and still feeling flaky, thought that she might feel more grounded if she immersed herself in the experience, strength, and hope of others.

So much had been posted that it was almost impossible to keep up with it all. Anjani's team had been doing a blinding job putting it all live. She certainly hadn't had time today. Many more people had been posting images, though, blue crystals, children's drawings of creatures with antlers and wolves with glowing blue eyes. There was writing, but the number of images was overwhelming and linked very much into the figures she'd seen and sensed around her that night at the clearing with Koomis and the Ghost Dancers. Along with the pictures were short descriptions.

Although the images in the main were driven by youngsters, it seemed as though a growing network of adults were seeing and hearing the same things. The most powerful was that of a bird from Nigeria leaving a black river, and as it flew upwards, across a shore dotted with blue, it transformed into a dazzling shade of white. Only the wings were still black. GoodNewz had already picked up on some of the writing, but she thought she would add some of own names and images to the site as well and label some of the other things that had been sent under #ghostdancers.

Once again, she'd Named in the digital world, connected by a power that was clearly borne both of her and of another dimension entirely. Well, ASafeSpace had proven its worth, as had Lokozho. She hoped that by Naming the Ghost Dancers in this way, the billions of users on social media who were not yet connected to her would find their way here also. People needed to associate the new hashtag with a time of change and start seeing that this change was not necessarily all bad, terrifying though it was. She would wait and see.

27.02. GoodNewz – Garden Grub

Nearly three weeks after the crash, increasing food and fuel shortages are bringing the UK to a standstill. In an attempt to ration their stocks, supermarkets have been exchanging food for government coupons. However, initial panic buying has meant there will be a significant shortfall in the months to come.

It's not all bad news, though. Keen gardeners have reported that nature has stepped up to the mark, with many root vegetables growing out of season. A network called Seed Gardeners has set up to offer fruit and vegetable starter kits for those wishing to grow their own this spring. In the meantime, please note that tulip bulbs are very nutritious. Other edible flora includes the Moringa tree. Native to Africa and the Indian subcontinent, it has started appearing right across the country. Reports suggest this addition to our native trees is due to warming temperatures.

For more detailed instructions on how to process the Moringa, you can visit Touchability.com. To register for a food starter kit, please visit Mother-NatureHelps.com. Here you will also find further links, foraging tips, and ways to prepare more commonly found roots and plants.

Originally posted by MotherNatureHelps.com

CHAPTER 12

The Woman Who Walks Alone

The woman who walks in the crowd will usually go no farther than the crowd; the woman who walks alone is likely to find herself in places no one has ever been before.
—Albert Einstein

Other than SJ, Martha was the only one in the office. Apparently some kind of showdown was imminent with Mark, so she said she'd come in to support. It was rare for her to be here these days, since it was no longer a pleasant place to be. Not even the solar-powered backup generators keeping the worst of the early spring chill at bay had got anyone else to come in. No surprise really, since no one had been paid. Peering into the twilight for any other signs of life, she hoped Mark would be in shortly.

Along with most other employers, William and Jones had cited "reasons beyond our control" for the non-payment of February's salaries. The banking crisis showed no sign of abating, so March's payments were looking increasingly unlikely too. Added to this, although there was plenty of paper money in circulation, people knew it was worth much less. This meant that what had once cost ten pounds now cost a hundred, and since people were panic buying, demand was rising. In an attempt to alleviate the situation, the Bank of England had started printing more money. Most believed that this, along with the government food coupons, meant that things weren't as bad as they might have been otherwise. However, since people weren't getting paid, they weren't working, which meant very little was being produced.

Since early March, there'd been an attempt to impose curfews and price controls, the former to curb civic unrest and the latter to retain the value of the money in people's pockets. However, since the cost of production was increasing faster than prices, suppliers had little incentive to go through the official channels. Added to that, fuel shortages were making the transportation of goods, including food, almost impossible. With prices continuing to climb, the long-term outlook was starting to look very bleak.

Mark came in and headed to his office. Watching SJ follow him in, Martha gave up all pretence at work. Instead, while straining to catch what was being said, she continued to run through the wider situation in her head. Power cuts were becoming more frequent, and although Martha's crystals meant that she wasn't affected by this, connectivity was virtually nonexistent. It was good that many of her now absent colleagues had acquired their own.

SJ had been the catalyst. Going for a walk along the beach three weeks ago, she'd noticed a concentration of blue pebbles piled up just past the etched angles of the Turner Contemporary and had taken a couple. When she realised that, like Martha's, they were sources of light and connectivity, she'd told others where to find them. Friends and colleagues did as she suggested, only to discover that others had also made the connection and were busy collecting all along Margate Beach. There seemed to be enough for everyone, though.

She could definitely hear something. She moved closer. Was it shouting? No, more like crying. The door was flung open. It had been laughter. With tears of merriment streaming down her face, SJ called to her. "Come on, let's go. We're finished here."

Martha looked through the wide-open door to see a red-faced Mark sitting behind his desk and what looked like chocolates, flung across the floor. She barely had time to grab her bag, so fast was the other's long-legged stride. As they clattered down the stairs, words flooded out of the still giggling SJ.

"... and he called me over, and all I saw was a little pink worm of his penis, nestling there amidst the chocolates."

Not even waiting for Martha's outraged "What?" she continued.

"Part of me wanted them. And then, as I was kneeling between his knees, about to take a semiflaccid dick into my mouth, it came to me. How my hunger for promotion and latterly food landed me here in front of a chocolate-bedecked groin. I started laughing. You should have seen his face! He honestly thought he was irresistible.

"I did want him to know what had made me laugh so much, so I told him that he owed me a hell of a lot more than a couple of chocolates. What about all those promised pay rises? Not that it mattered anymore; he could stick it. I was leaving. Getting up from his chair, he tried to stop me. But he looked so ridiculous that I laughed all the harder and he sat down again."

Imagining the picture, Martha started giggling too. Encouraged, SJ continued, although on a more serious note. "I suddenly realised that because I thought I had no choice, I'd been selling myself for stuff that didn't matter. The stupid thing was that I always did. I made my final one and told him I forgave him, that he still had the time to make things right with his family. I'd planned on throwing the handful of chocolates I'd picked up at him. But didn't seem right anymore — so I've kept them for my nieces. That's where I'm going now, my sister's."

They reached the car park, suddenly solemn because they knew they wouldn't be seeing each other for quite some time. One last hug, and then SJ walked off.

Martha looked up at her former place of employment, noticing that Mark was clearly visible through the window of his big corner office. He was sitting where they'd left him, face lit up by his screen. He'd made his choice.

As she drove home, she tuned in to Radio Four. Most of their programming still seemed to be in place, television not so much. She was hoping to catch the tail end of *Woman's Hour*. Instead, though, tinny American voices came over the airwaves.

"This is 911, what is the nature of your emergency?

My name is Flora Franklin, I wish to report that I have broken into a specialised lab at my place of work and released a biohazard.

She turned it up. Maybe today's theme was how the emergency services were coping in these unprecedented times. But why from the US?

"Can you be more specific? What is your place of work and are lives at risk?

No, I don't believe lives are at risk. I am a research biochemist at the Santa Fe Centre for Marine Biology, Solana Beach CA 92135. Although the testing process is only about one third of the way through, I have liberated a sea creature that has been modified to produce an enzyme. I used my pass to gain entry to the labs containing the altered Duster Worms because I judged that given the current civil unrest and uncertainty, the release needed to be brought forward.

"Has this worm been altered to be a threat to human life?

Not specifically, no. It has been modified to release an enzyme that consumes plastic, from the wax worm genus. We have engineered it for luminosity and sped up its ability to procreate and the rate at which it is able to break down plastic resins. Although all indications point towards a successful modification, studies regarding lifecycle and long-term impact are yet to be completed. We also don't fully understand the nature of the substance that is released during digestion, although we believe it is a form of ethanol."

Still no reassuring Radio Four presenter to explain what was going on. It dawned on Martha that Jenny Little's absence might be because the source of this was Dave and not the BBC. Recently she'd noticed how he would get her to read stories by pinging them up on her phone or laptop to get her attention. If this was him, it heralded a new approach. She started listening more closely, just in case.

"What was the reason for this theft?

Despite our labs being under twenty-four-hour guard, members of the public are trying to gain access, believing that they will be able to eat the different species of fish contained in our tanks. To counter the threat to our milestone discovery, I removed two tanks of the genetically modified organism earlier today and emptied them into the Pacific Ocean. If you need further information, I am now back at home, 127 Via Canterbria, Encinitas, near the Botanical Gardens.

"Under current circumstances, we do not consider this to be an emergency. We do, however, suggest you inform your employers of your actions. Have a good day."

For a moment all Martha could hear was her car engine. Then came the crackle of static and the eleven o'clock news bulletin. She turned it off. Still none the wiser as to what she was supposed to have heard, she let out all her pent-up anxiety in a screamed question.

"What is it you want me to know, Dave? Can't you just tell me? Fuck off or show yourself. I'm sick of these half-baked conversations and half-truths."

Her throat sore now, she fell silent. Waiting for a response, maybe. Apart from the continuing purr of the engine, though, one could have heard a pin drop. She wished she hadn't been quite so vocal about wanting some kind of resolution and silently mouthed, "I do love you, Dave. I'm just frightened."

* * *

Henry was bored. He'd never thought he would miss school. After most of them had closed, he and Emmy had started going to Mum's office to get out of the house, taking advantage of the heating and the bit of company that was to be had there. In the last couple of weeks, though, even that had stopped. Mum had told them there wasn't any point.

It had all started seven weeks ago, and from them on in, things had been totally chaotic. Luckily, Mum had had a hunch that things were going to get tough, and they'd all gone shopping. They'd rushed around the big Tesco with a couple of trolleys each, filling up on any tinned goods and nonperishables they could think of. Then they'd gone back to buy huge plastic water containers, filling all fifteen of them with petrol. Mum had queued for ages on a number of different forecourts but had got them filled in the end.

They had been glad of Mum's foresight. Initially, it had just been about the petrol and getting around, but since things had escalated in early March, it was more about just believing they'd be okay. The food they'd got, coupled with the wood burner in the living room, made them feel that. The power cuts were the most annoying, though. They were having to do things like putting on the washing machine in the middle of the night when the outages were least likely. Other changes had included incorporating the fruits of Emmy's foraging into their diets. Dennis had a particular nose for things, and as she was always with him now. They made a formidable food-finding team. Ironic, really, that these days, when there was so little food available, she was prepared to eat again!

Along with others in the village, the Johnstones had been scouring the fields for forgotten potatoes. Some of those new Moringa trees had sprung up in the garden too. They all enjoyed the spring greens Emmy had started bringing home, the tops of cauliflowers and cabbages. It was amazing what there was. The local farmers had rallied around too, and farm shops that had been used sparingly in the past were really coming into their own. Farmers were even exchanging food for labour. Surprisingly, there was much more growing in the fields than usual, and old James said that lots of it shouldn't be in season. So even though he hadn't been properly full up for some time, Henry could honestly say that he hadn't ever been really hungry either.

One thing that bugged him now was the fact that people were still going into their offices. Fair enough, with stuff that mattered. Hospitals needed to be open, power plants needed to be kept running, and rubbish needed to be collected. But things like Mum's copywriting didn't seem to be particularly important in this new world order. According to the skeleton news service that was still up, in between reruns of old TV programmes, surprisingly few people had chosen to make any real changes in terms of how they lived or worked. Henry found it remarkable that over two months since the start of the crisis, the emergency trains into London were still clogged. He knew from some of his friends that their parents were choosing to stay close to their place of work, even though they hadn't been paid — how mad was that?

Henry looked at his laptop. He really did need to find a better way to put live the flood of the images people were posting online. There were pictures and drawings of all kinds of people and animals, particularly wolves.

Since it was impossible to filter properly, he and Mum had been mass approving, with her insisting on the Ghost Dancer hashtag. This had opened the floodgates, and #ghostdancer now labelled most of the images. These pictures, many of which contained images of the crystals, were messages of hope. To him, therefore, publication still wasn't happening quickly enough. Eventually, he'd added in a command for all the images to go live as soon they came in. It wasn't a great idea, but what else could he do?

He also needed to keep GoodNewz running, and, as far less information was being fed in from other sites, keeping ASafeSpace going was a priority too. Mum was working really hard managing the posts, so there'd be no help from that quarter, and she'd tied up the Jakarta team also. Henry thought the images were equally important and was determined to manage their publication properly, along with the clips of drumming and singing he believed to be linked.

Now might be a good time to revisit this conundrum. Finding a working solution might even help cut through the gnawing lack of something he was feeling. So, eventually, the need to act outweighed his angst, and he logged in.

Crap *had* got through. Knowing how important it was for ASafeSpace to remain safe, Henry sent up a brief prayer of thanks for his mother's crystal, which gave him access to the web and therefore a way to find a solution. Filled with the memory of the blue stones blazing through the smoke-filled hut, he'd been on the lookout for crystals for himself and Emmy too.

That day had frightened him for a number of reasons, but it had also given him the same sense of invincibility he felt when he was gaming. Its power lay in the fusion of imagination and reality, a dreamscape that set aside the chaos of the outside world.

Oddly, the work he was doing on ASafeSpace and GoodNewz had crossed the boundaries into his fantasy world as well. He started considering whether it might be possible to tap into his character's arcane abilities to make the appropriate posts live in one fell swoop. The more he surveyed the task in front of him, the more attractive investigating this madcap solution became. And so, without really making a conscious decision to do so, he entered the world of his game. Scanning the screen, he noticed that yet more players had appeared. Rather than putting off gamers, the chaos in the real world seemed to be driving more activity to the fantasy one. New environments and opportunities were popping up all over the place.

He found himself in the depths of a majestic jungle. Water was dripping from the emerald leaves the jewel-like insects were dancing across, while the chittering of monkeys echoed through the branches. He pushed forwards, though, and just a couple of steps on found him emerging into the grass plains of yet another backdrop.

The ground shuddered, and a huge herd of bison thundered past. It all seemed so real, like the Wild West, when the herds had stretched as far as the eye could see. He found that when he closed his eyes, his sense of place got even stronger. He was transported back to the day of his uncle's funeral, when his heart had beaten as fast and as loud as the drumming.

Walking on, he came across a sword stuck in the ground in front of him. As a seasoned gamer, he understood that his task was to release it. He knew he was sitting on his chair in his room, but even so, as he felt his hand closing over the cool, smooth hilt, his senses slipped across one world into another.

The voice coming from his speakers seemed appropriate rather than unexpected.

"Seeker, your Quest has been accepted. You will cross the plains and find the Tree of Life. You need to release what has been captured. The unnecessary will die, returning to its place of origin. Are you willing?"

"Yes!" He typed and spoke it too, just to be sure.

Gamer's instincts kicking in once more, he started crossing the plain, pleasantly surprised by the light weight of his new sword. The farther he got, though, the odder it all seemed. Although the constantly changing terrain was typical, none of his usual opponents were in evidence.

He finally reached the tree. In typical gaming style, it was labelled, and he noticed a bird with a white chest and two black wings perching on it, the mighty hooked beak glistening in the half light. There was another too, this one slightly smaller, with feathers black as night. As he moved closer, he spotted something else that seemed to be attached to the mighty trunk.

Chameleon-like, it blended into the landscape. It was huge, almost as large as its host. Parts of it were translucent and barky, and others reflected the green of the grass and the azure sky. Looking really close, he noticed blue lights flashing in its depths. This strangely humanoid shape seemed to be truly attached, part of the natural world and yet not, the ground it stood on swarmed with a multitude of white rabbits nibbling away at its substance. Since its limbs were stuck, though, the only way it was able to combat this was to shake itself, obviously hoping that the movement would cause the creatures to shy away.

Henry recognised that saving this being was part of his quest. So, unsheathing his sword, he waded in to slay the fluffy multitudes. As he hacked away, he noticed that every time he killed one, a little blue crystal appeared. They were very much like the one Mum had, and the others he'd seen in the hut. The shimmering blue horde grew until eventually he realised he had dispatched the last of them. He looked up.

The being had now shrunk into something man-sized and was wearing a maroon jumper and blue jeans. He had dark hair and twinkly green eyes. Henry's eyes widened with astonishment, and he was suddenly unable to breathe.

"Dad." It came out like a hoarse whisper. "Dad, is that you?"

His dad still looked like himself, albeit a bit younger and without the red cheeks and bloodshot eyes.

"I had so hoped that we might meet like this. But for now, I need you to close your eyes, son."

Henry did as instructed. By shutting out rational thought, this action bypassed his laptop's sophisticated graphics and sounds, and he found himself back in his virtual world, but actually there instead of via a screen. He slowly strode across grass that tickled to embrace his father, tree and all.

"I'm so proud of you, son, and you're even taller than I was!"

Preempting the question that was on the tip of Henry's tongue, Dave went on. "You can use your sword. The bark on the tree is loose."

Finding the sword was easy to wield, Henry pried hands and feet off the bark. Reluctantly, the giant ash gave up its source of energy, repairing its bark even as it released Dave.

They clung to each other. Once he had caught his breath, Dave told Henry that he'd only been able to manufacture his presence here by binding himself to the tree. But time was shorter than he'd realised, and there were things his son needed to know. The urgency of his next words cut through their reunion like a knife.

"I'm not anchored, which means I'm becoming less solid, as are you. It's good that you freed me; I'd have been permanently gone otherwise, but there's so much I need to tell you."

He took Henry's face in hands that were strangely calloused.

"I love you, and even when you thought I was gone, I've been watching, always watching. To keep you, Mum, and Emmy safe, I've used every piece of hardware you can imagine, even becoming part of the systems and networks. At first I had to push myself to see what was going on, but since the crystals, it's become instinctive. I am all that is digital and part of everyone that made me, the good and the bad. There's so much of me, beauty as well as ugliness, that I can't hold the shape of who I once was on my own. So I am both more and less than I once was."

Henry noticed the blue light shining through his dad's dark eyes.

"Me and Uncle Peter made the crash happen. It was with the best of intentions, though. I was trying to get rid of the darkness I felt at the core of this new shape, and your uncle was making amends for what he'd done in the past. Instead, we created disaster."

His dad fell silent, moving away slightly.

"Is that why Uncle Peter died?"

"I think so, Henry." He shook his head, remembering. "I was trying to be everywhere, so his last hours only registered on the fringes of my consciousness. A bit of me was with him, though, even at the end."

Henry moved to close the gap between them. "I don't get it."

"Well, look at it this way. Now I'm be here with you, but I'm also in millions of other places. I'm there every time someone reads a GoodNewz message, and every time someone posts something vile, it becomes part of me. All that is and has ever been consigned to cyber-space is my reality."

Henry stopped mid-movement, suddenly reluctant to comfort whatever this was in front of him. He was used to Dad's overblown reactions, happy or morose, angry or elated. If Uncle Peter had killed himself because of stuff Dad had made happen, he wouldn't have been calm like this. In fact, this creature's reactions were unlike anything that he recognised as Dad. He wasn't even speaking normally. It was more formal, stilted even. As he dug deeper, though, he remembered barely registered goodnights from his computer. Although he couldn't explain it, in his heart he'd known his dad was the source.

Henry sat, and Dave followed suit. Reaching out to touch the hand on the grass in front of him, he was surprised at how solid it felt. Maybe being a super container made it difficult for Dad to feel and do things the way he used to.

"It really is me, you know."

The blue blazed, and oddly, it was this strangeness and not the familiar that made him feel real again. As the square safety of his dad's hand anchored him further, Henry started wondering whether this new Dave was like the avatar he had created for his game. It was him and yet was both more and less than who he really was.

"So, Dad, if you are everywhere, where did that stuff that made you seem so much bigger go while I was killing the rabbits?"

Dave stood up and opened his arms wide. "This cyberspace we are in is as real as that of spirit or the physical. What is created here comes from pixels but still has the capacity to be real in all dimensions. The different paths that have been opening up, like the drumming or your time in the hut, create movement across all states of being."

As if to convince himself of its reality, Henry gripped his father's arm. Dave acknowledged Henry's touch with a nod but continued speaking.

"Shaped by imagination and thought, this space is not yet a tangible reality. Things are shifting that way, though. As the worlds continue to collide, the reality we are creating here is turning pixels into a new dust of creation, able to spread transformation across all dimensions. Remember your uncle's funeral service, ashes to ashes, dust to dust? It didn't just touch where you were but moved you to be where you needed to be."

Frustrated by his own inability to understand, Henry stood up, shouting his question. "But what's this got to do with the rabbits?"

But as his dad turned towards him, he wasn't so sure whether he wanted to know anymore. Dave had started shimmering and was becoming increasingly translucent.

"What was released will go back into me. The bison you saw, along with other creatures that are fading from the 'real' world, need a new place to exist. A joined-up human consciousness has brought them here, into me. The rabbits are of this also but represent the parasitical emptiness that is present in all of us. This new world has allowed them to manifest. They are using their reality here to gorge on the substance of all worlds."

Encompassing the heap of blue stones in a broad, sweeping movement, he gesticulated. "They can be repurposed to serve and will help to create what is needed as it all comes together. My purpose will change as well. Protecting you has allowed me to hold on to my humanity. Coming here now is an important part of this. As things change, I will move beyond. But I promise I'll try to hold on to my love for you as I transform."

He was staring through Henry now, his features becoming clay-like and indefinite.

"I can see the shimmering path splitting and then splitting again, until infinite ways open up before me. Where I must walk cuts through all things while binding them together. I will need to draw on all that I am, and in doing so, risk losing everything."

"Dad, come back. Not yet."

To his son's relief, Dave made a visible effort to focus, and his face gained solidity. But then he dropped another bombshell. "I've been in touch with your mum, you know."

Henry's reaction was explosive. "*Why?* Why wouldn't she tell us? Has Emmy seen you too? Am I the only one who didn't know?"

With arms that were shot through with light, Dave held him tight. "No, Henry, only Mum. And she didn't say anything because she said you'd think she was mad. I've been here though, helping you with GoodNewz and ASafeSpace. You did the bulk of it; I just made sure the right things happened afterwards."

With a rage born of hurt and loneliness, Henry started punching him. Standing completely still, Dave let the punches fall. The outburst was short-lived, and instead, Henry's shoulders began to heave. Dave spoke again, words tripping over in his desire to comfort.

"Do you remember when you saw the tourist office when we were in Spain, and you wanted to know why terrorists had an office? And the collars you cut off all your sister's polo necks because she said they were itchy? Or Mum chasing you all the way back from mini-golf because you said she'd been cheating?"

A tear-stained face was raised to meet the alien blue eyes that contained a father's love. Dave started tickling him, and Henry who'd always loved being tickled, giggled, turning a true smile to his father and with it embracing all that was but also what was to come. Every fibre of their being joyful, they rolled around on grass as soft as that in their back garden.

In this space that both was and was not, their unfolding happiness created a path to somewhere else, and so it was that they found themselves in a place where laughter was also being shared.

* * *

Henry was on a beach. Near the edge of the surf, several women were dancing and kicking up water, linking hands and howling with glee at their saturated cloaks and faces that were covered in sand and seaweed.

He heard his mum drumming. She was in the water, farther out than the others. He spotted two black dots growing ever larger on the horizon. Looking like the ones that had been on Dad's tree, the birds eventually came to rest, one of them on Mum's shoulder, the other on the floating drum. Looking at it, he noticed that it too had changed. The edges that were now peeking out of the water looked as though they belonged to a huge, upside down turtle shell. Pounding the skin that had been stretched over it, Martha was setting the beat the waves were dancing to. Then she looked straight at him, her voice capturing the wild joy around her, and threw out words for him to catch:

"I am she
I am me
I am not afraid
I am remade."

As he took in the sight of the Ghost Dancers from the hut, some in feathers, some in scales, some with clothes abandoned, others snapping their fangs at the encroaching foam, Henry felt his dad kiss his forehead.

"Your quest is fulfilled. I will put the pictures and videos live. Open your mouth. The dancers are kicking up the traces of what bound them. You can feel the water from the spirit world splashing you. This gift of laughter brings us ever closer together. We do not walk alone."

Henry found himself back in front of his laptop. The impression of his father's kiss lingered on his brow, the tang of saltwater tingled on his lips, and his ears were ringing with words of love and joy. He had no doubt that he, along with those he had seen, had just learned the fourth lesson: the Gift of Laughter.

"See you later, alligator," he whispered, and hearing the soft caress of his dad's "in a while, crocodile" in return, he closed his eyes, deciding he needed to rest, even if just for a little while.

31.03 GoodNewz, Kabul — *Women take to the streets in Kabul*
Badam Bagh Kabul's prison for women guilty of moral crimes opened its doors earlier today to release 147 inmates and their children.

No formal comment was made to explain this unprecedented move. However, shortly after their release, the women shared their joy on the streets of Kabul. Many were dancing the Attan, and others were pounding large Rubab drums.

Despite numerous attempts, the Muṭawwi'ūn police seemed to be unable to stop the music or the celebrations. As the day progressed, whole families joined, many waving a type of narcissus native to the region.

Former inmate Fahima Wali, the leader of what has become a march of freedom, stated, "Our captivity was unjust, but now we laugh and dance and others join us. In this time of hunger and war, we wave flowers and walk into the unknown, laughing together."

Source: ASafeSpace, March 31st

CHAPTER 13

The End of Words

Menteng, Jakarta

15th April

My darling son,

Thank you for letting me know that you and your family are safe. I have
been very worried about you all and am so glad you made it out to Gag
Island. I had almost forgotten our little hideaway so far to the north.
Do you remember how we would lie on the beach together, watching
the stars? It was good to hear that you've kept it stocked. You never did
say what made you leave before the riots broke out, but you were very
sensible to use the company jet. I assume you got a boat onwards from
West Papua? I do hope you reached safety in time for John's birthday. I
can't believe that I have a fourteen-year-old grandson!

Anyway, you might remember from our last email exchange that I
remained in the business district for several days. But when our head of
security suggested that I would be safer behind the gates at Menteng, I
left and here I am, still.

I know that the blue stone I have is allowing me to get online and reach
out to you. Even here, with all the generators running, it seems as though
every other method of connection is down. You mentioned last time
that John had a similar stone. Because of this, I am hoping that my email
will reach you, even on your jungle island. You never mentioned where
John found his, but you might be interested to know that I brought
mine back from one of the places I visited over the last few months. I so
wish we'd got to connect somewhere other than the impersonal safety

of the boardroom. I would have loved to have told you more about my recent travels. However, knowing that you associate me with conflict, I understand your reluctance.

Despite our difficulties, I am sure that we agree on one thing: we are living through a time of extreme change! From the messages we share, it seems as though this has affected your thoughts and actions too. Because of that, I hope that you will recognise this as an email from who I am now, not who I once was.

With that in mind, I am writing to let you know I am also about to go on a journey. It may well be my final one. I have the helicopter waiting and will be travelling to Lombok. In this time of endings, I want to revisit where things began. I also think it will be safer there than here. Nearly all the guards have left, and people are hungry and desperate. So, despite the gates, I am frightened.

It's funny, isn't it? Now that I've come to write to you in truth, I don't know what to say. It could be that I have come to the end of words and need to remember instead. I can see you now, a tiny toddler with huge dark eyes, hidden in the darkness of Venus Alley. You won't remember those times. You were only two when we left. It was there that I started to tell you stories of my homeland. Legends that you loved about magic, half-humans, and gods. I was so frightened. It was in those early days with Matthew, and my stories brought you pleasure and gave me courage.

Just holding you, knowing you were there and that we were together, gave me so much strength. As things got better, though, I stopped coming to you, and as time went on, you stopped wanting me. Before I knew it, our time was over. I so wish that I could go back. Knowing what I know now, I would have made sure that our love was not silenced.

Anyway, my darling boy, this may very well be a goodbye. I write our last story, as it will be something you can share with John in time. If you listen closely, though, you will hear me speak it.

Once upon a time, there was a kingdom on Lombok Island that was ruled by King Raja Tonjang Beru. He was a wise king and had a beautiful daughter called Mandalika. Mandalika was said to be the prettiest girl on the whole island, and tales of her beauty and kindness had spread far and wide. Because of this, many princes from other island kingdoms came to see the princess. One by one, they proposed to her. But although she was flattered, she was also very confused by all the proposals. Mandalika didn't want to make the princes sad by refusing, but neither did she want to be the cause of a war.

To solve the problem, the king organised an archery competition on Seger Kuta beach. Whoever hit the centre of the target would marry Princess Mandalika. One by one, participants took aim and fired. However, despite the competition going on into the night, there was no clear winner. They started fighting amongst themselves, all determined to win her hand.

Princess Mandalika decided there was a way to belong to them all and shouted above the din to let them know. However, no one was prepared to listen. So, after several fruitless attempts, she decided the end of words had come and strode out into the sea. After a time, her suitors noticed she had gone and started swimming out into the waves. But she seemed to have vanished into thin air.

Several hours later, a multitude of bright green sea worms washed up on the beach. The king took one in his hand. When he saw the shimmering beauty of the creature, he realised that his daughter had transformed from one into many, sacrificing herself so she could belong to everyone. Although he was sad, the wise king understood this new pathway Mandalika had chosen. Using words and gestures, he tried to make his people understand what had happened. However, although they listened politely, they turned their back on the true value of Mandalika's gift, starting to cook the worms on fires they had prepared for this purpose.

These worms are now called Nyale and are considered a delicacy in Lombok. Every spring there is a Bau Nyale Festival, where people catch and then feast on the worms. However, many families still keep an empty dish to hand, in case the true nature of Mandalika's gift chooses to reveal itself. Legend has it that this will happen when the Capa Astingaa appears and all things are revealed.

Stay safe and know that my love completes you. Like the *Bau Nyale*, it flows into the holes and soothes where there are wounds. Sadly, I can't stop time or cross the physical distance that is between us. But keep Mandalika's gift at hand. It will choose to reveal itself when you are ready.

Until we meet again,

Your loving mother, Anjani

* * *

April 15th, Central Park, New York

Dave felt Brigid's despair wash over him again. Magnified a thousandfold from the other times he'd touched her, the clarion call of one of the first crystals he'd ever sensed drew him to Central Park. Once there, he realised the freezing fingers weaving themselves around him were caused not just by her despair and hopelessness, but also by the actual physical cold. It was another sign that he was changing all the time, the being he was becoming, increasingly able to escape digital confines to seep into the real world — to the point that he was no longer sure what was and was not.

Unlike the other times he'd sensed her, she wasn't standing guard over the Alice in Wonderland monument. Instead, he found her off the beaten track in a deeply wooded area. Despite the early warmth of spring, she was leaning against the gnarled oak, her emaciated form shivering. Head lolling, it was clear she'd taken something. The call of the crystal became more urgent, and, like a stray wisp of thought, he wafted into her. She was stone-cold, the rags she was bundled in obviously having little effect.

He realised her mind was disintegrating, and not just because of whatever she'd taken to escape today's anniversary. Children's voices were beckoning. "Come on, Mommy, let's go. Come with us, we don't want to be late." He could hear them clearly, but there was no one there.

She'd been homeless for some time, the destruction of the place of safety she'd written about that first time, pushing her into the park. After wardens had stopped coming, it had become her permanent place of residence. The children's voices were calling again: "Come on, Mommy. Mom, come and play." Then the grey overtook everything.

He felt tremendously sorry for her but had no idea why he was here. Was he supposed to do something? Only when the last tendril connecting him to her dying mind snapped did it come to him. Although she wasn't fighting for life, as he had, what was happening reminded him of his rescue, the one Sh'ler had affected.

Things often felt random, but he'd come to realise that they never were in his new world. Janet recognising him *ex machina* had given him the courage to continue on his path. Discovering Ali's digital wolf and flower symbol in Stockholm had signposted the way to some of his key battles in the digital space. And now he'd been called to Brigid's side. Suddenly certain she'd be needed for what was to come, his entire being vibrated with the desire to help. He hoped the one who'd birthed Lokozho in truth would take notice and achieve a rescue here as well.

Eyes opened. Something had happened. Back with her again, Dave found himself wondering at the personage now peering down, dark stare framed by a heavy wooden brow and towering antlers. Curiosity overcame fear and finally morphed into wonder. Had she died? Had he transitioned with her? Used to seeping from the World of Sprit into Martha's while finding refuge in the shadowy corridors of his digital existence, Dave knew that death had many faces. Maybe this was Brigid's new reality.

Taking in the surroundings though her eyes, he wondered at the multitude of white rabbits that had made this place their home. One came closer, and he saw the horned man loose an arrow from his ancient longbow. It died and disappeared, leaving a blue stone in its stead.

He then handed Brigid the bow and arrow, gesturing that she should follow his lead. Remembering the rodents who'd eaten through her things in the subway tunnel, Dave sensed an eagerness to put college archery skills into action. Not all rabbits transformed into blue crystals, though. Many of the corpses just lay there, like so much litter. Those would be lunch. The tree man picked up two shards of crystal and set about skinning his kills. Indicating that she needed to follow his example, he handed her the smaller stone.

She still believed she was dreaming. Unlike her, though, Dave had the benefit of a wider perspective. This latest event confirmed what he'd suspected since he'd come to, in the fire of the Winter Solstice. He was the nexus around which other dimensions came into being. His need to help had created the one Brigid was now straddling, her gift of rebirth shaping death into living crystal across the divide. This, the rabbits themselves, and the quickened network of flora and fauna were showing just how quickly things were changing. Martha's "real world" and what was being created around him were almost indistinguishable now.

The pair had a merry little fire going, and, through Brigid, he was able to enjoy the smell of roast meat. While she had her back turned, her companion dissipated, his voice a caress on the wind;

"Hunt well. Find other hunters in these forests, and together you will feast."

And she had. A few days later, people had started coming, and Dave's mild curiosity changed into an intense pull. It seemed that the more crystals appeared, the stronger he was. By saving her, he'd found a way to repurpose the rabbits. Emmy had first used them as a symbol to describe the emptiness she felt in herself and the world around her. Henry's intervention at the tree had shown them manifested as pixels of creation, a sign that the emptiness didn't need to be destructive. It could be transformed and harnessed.

When he'd called on the World of Sprit to save Brigid, she'd become the embodiment of this transformation, a beacon for others. He knew also that what had happened here would self-propagate, spreading beyond this place along with the new flora and fauna that was coaxing life from what had been barren. For the moment, it was enough that they were coming, joining her from areas the rodent multitude had rendered uninhabitable.

A few weeks later, she gathered them. Following the command of her blazing stones, he watched the huge crowd move through the Holland Tunnel and then onwards. Ever farther they went, eventually reaching the Ramapo Mountains to the north. The less populated the countryside became, the more the rabbits were reduced in numbers. Brigid was a blonde Pied Piper, leading throngs of people to an unknown destination. Her crystals continued to pulse strongly, so he knew all was well.

* * *

25.05. GoodNewz, Rondônia Brasil — Refugee Miners Flee Guerrilla Warfare

Bewildered miners are flooding into regional capital, Porto Velho, citing unprovoked attacks on their rainforest camps as the reason behind their departure.

Previously uncontacted tribes from the Urueu Wau Wau territory in Rondônia are mounting guerrilla attacks on controversial logging and mining operations in disputed indigenous territories. Although this kind of attack is not new, the severity of the impact is. It is believed to be due to a corrosive, sparkling blue powder, which is rendering machinery unusable.

* * *

"Henry, wake up. I need to speak to you."

Henry shook his head fuzzily. Someone was shouting his name. There it was again.

"Henry, wake up!"

He sat up and looked around. The voice was coming from his speakers.

He tried to orient himself. Was he at home or down in the tent by the sea with the others who were on sapphire-collecting duty? People had been leaving the larger conurbations and pitching up in the rural St Nicolas at Wade. It had become a hub. Tents were being put up in surrounding fields, and a couple of doctors had even set up in the village hall. Although he spent much of his time in the field camp these days, he still came home to sleep occasionally, preferring the creature comforts of his bed.

That's where he must be now. The voice was coming from his speaker, not his laptop. It wasn't Mum, though, or Emmy. It was a male voice. He sat bolt upright. It must be Dad.

He'd thought about calling or messaging a few times over the last few weeks but wasn't sure how to go about it. In any case, on top of his other duties, keeping up with ASafeSpace and ensuring GoodNewz was still firing out bulletins was his priority. Also, that conversation with his dad, or whoever it had been, didn't seem quite real anymore.

"Ah, good, you're awake now. It's been a while since we met. I know Emmy didn't take news of me still being around very well, but I was expecting to hear from you. Is everything okay?"

Henry went over to sit at his desk. Speaking loudly and slowly he asked, "Can you hear me if I speak like this, or do I need to do anything else?"

"No, that's fine, son. I'm not feeling great, so haven't been able to orchestrate a meeting like our last one. But I needed to speak to you, let you know a couple of things."

Henry listened as his dad told him about the connection he'd made between the rabbits manifesting in the real world and the unknown digital space that made up so much of his being. How they were the spirits' physical way of showing him that the living crystal was changing his substance from emptiness into something else. And all because of this woman he'd helped in Central Park.

"I don't think it's just that, though." Dave continued. "Because I so wanted to meet with you in a physical way, I think I opened the floodgates to everything. I can't compartmentalise anymore."

Then he wanted to know if Henry had come across a symbol that looked like a Jolly Roger but with a wolf's head and flowers. Apparently it was a signpost for him to root out some of the nasty stuff that was still going on in cyberspace.

Henry couldn't make sense of this stream of consciousness and cut in again. "But Dad, how are those people still getting online? I know from the ones who've come from London, and even more locally, that the cities are chaotic. People are being killed for those crystals."

His dad had explained that that was part of the reason he'd wanted to speak to Henry. In this dystopian nightmare, urban areas were descending into anarchy, and most now understood the power of the blue stones in terms of both power and connectivity. However, a problem had presented itself for those who wanted to connect to the darker side of the web. People capable of keeping their crystals alive were moving away from built-up areas. This created scarcity in the very places people were trying to retain what was left of the old world.

It was clear, Dave said, that two types of people were emerging: those who kept their crystals alive and those who didn't. Apparently, the wolf and flower symbol was one of the ways Dave tracked down where those who didn't operated.

"The thing is, despite everything that's happened, the dark web is still there. Remember I told you about it being in me and my awareness around it?"

When Henry nodded, Dave continued. "But people can't reach it unless they have a live crystal. So really nasty trades are being done now to get at the stones."

From what Henry understood, the malevolence that had bothered Dave for so long was losing its source of power, but because of this, the live blue crystals were the new "hot thing" to be traded. Henry realised that the stories he'd heard were true. Those who weren't able to keep their crystals alive were lost in the darkness of what had been. The very worst were prepared to pay for blood crystals, those that people had been killed for.

What kept the blue stones alive was creativity, love, and compassion. These qualities also powered what was shared on places like ASafeSpace.

"The more the good things get out there and people connect, the more my nature changes. I know I will need to let go eventually. It's the only way I can hold on to it all, but for now I'm clinging on to the bit of me that's still here."

He'd got Henry to turn on his screen and tried to show him how he was foiling these trades. This had the opposite effect of what was intended, making Henry aware of how Dave, or whatever he was, had changed from the time at the tree. Even though the blue radiance that blazed occasionally was strangely soothing, the evidence of this vast consciousness and the vortex of data of a being that claimed to be his dad was too much.

Then, though, they stopped at something. He could see the symbol just as it had been described and how many demands there were for the crystal. Amongst the text and pictures flashing across the screen, he could see what was being offered in return. His emotions see-sawed back to compassion for what Dave had to deal with. This sense of recognition was compounded by the sadness in the voice that sounded through the speakers. This time its timbre was more like the dad he remembered.

"And no matter how many trades I stop, they keep coming back for more. New places and sites open up all the time. The crystals need to draw from the person they are connected to, so if there is little or no positive energy to draw from, they die very quickly."

Suddenly, Henry wished there was some way of giving his dad a hug. "You don't sound good, Dad. Can I do anything?"

Henry was sure he heard a sob of relief, but a bit of static interfered, so he could have been wrong. "No, just be there. Remember me. Talk to your mum and Emmy about me. Emmy in particular. I know your mum's been busy and we've messaged, so I'm not really worried about her. Emmy, though, won't let me in at all. When you told her about me, her mind closed down."

Henry nodded. "I know, Dad, she's even stopped going to see Dennis. It's like the bad old days. Anything not in her immediate grasp doesn't exist. From what you said, in order to reach us, you need us to be open, I'll try again. I promise."

Although nothing was said, a sigh came though the speakers. Then, in quick succession, images appeared on his screen. Dave was obviously trying to show him some of the good things that were going on to mitigate the nastiness he'd just shared. Some of it Henry recognised from the site. The view his dad was offering was so much more comprehensive.

Just as Brigid had become a source of crystals, the blue stones Fatima and the children held were also increasing exponentially. Her gardens were littered with them along with the thousands of children that had found their way there. Most of them had tablets, and many of them were travelling. Bearing blazing stones, they were creating one garden after another, seeding flora and technology where it was needed most. There was an older woman with a grey wolf outside an apartment building. and then two more children with great wolves walking on the sandy beaches of a deep blue sea.

Next were images that showed children from other parts of the world. Pouring in and out of houses that had been opened up to them, they were showing each other their crystals as signs of acceptance and recognition.

The last set of images was the most magnificent. Henry looked on in awe at the kaleidoscope of satellite images of the Earth as seen from space at nighttime. They were sequenced by date. In those dated last autumn, cities were lighting up the Earth's continents. There was very little darkness. The more recent ones, though, showed that the web of artificial light had being superseded. Groups of crystals pulsing were pulsing with life in places that had previously been desolate. Although the most recent satellite imagery showed the cities winking out one by one, they were also able to hint at the power of these linked crystals. Some of the cold, distant lenses had even captured carpets of new flowers and great swathes of forest burgeoning around enclaves where the stones existed in great numbers.

"Do you see?"

And Henry did.

"I'm here, Dad, I won't doubt again, I promise."

No more was said.

Inspired by what Dave had shown him, he did some work on the sites. Recipes, even where makeshift hospitals and schools were operating; it was amazing what people were sending in. His mum was in the dining room, also on ASafeSpace. Shouting a cheery goodbye, he left for the tents. He'd speak to Emmy later if he could. As he walked, he thought about what he'd seen and heard. He knew himself, that he was feeling so much more alive than he'd once done.

He liked that the fabric of society that had been built over recent generations was unravelling. He was part of his own family, of course, but new family units were emerging also, driven by a collective quest for food and shelter. Despite offering practical support, they were taking up only what was needed rather than what was wanted. Within this, children and young adults like him thrived. They understood where they belonged and were able to do things again. Whatever shape the family might be, each member had a sense of purpose.

His conversation with Dave had been the icing on the cake. Henry loved being busy all the time, and he delighted in the purpose and direction he'd been shown. *There must be so many like me*, he thought. From what Dave had shown him, where people came together with the crystals, they fed each other, and the earth fed them. Looking across the buzzing community, where new-style executive homes had once blinked emptily, he realised he was in the midst of it.

* * *

Martha was trying to reason away what she could only describe as a sense of summoning. It kept gnawing at her as she was trying to put a piece about Wei Zhao live. The factory worker from Lanzhou, a city on China's Yellow River, was describing how he'd moved just a little upstream to find the formerly dead river teeming with fish. However, she just couldn't seem to focus, wanting to close the lid on her laptop and go upstairs as soon as she tried to type. She finally gave up and put the story live as was.

Gingerly, she made her way up the stairs. Whatever it was was definitely getting stronger. She almost ran the last couple of steps and, unable to contain her curiosity, flung open her bedroom door. Now it all made sense. There on her bed lay a drum. She saw the snake, its markings intertwined in black and red winding its way around the rim. Then, on the expanse of its surface, she recognised the devouring wolves' heads, and the bird. Again, all were rendered in a black and red. Finally, she took in the patterned banding — the turtle, running right through the middle. It was Dewe'igan. He had come here, and, sitting on her bed, had issued a summons she couldn't ignore. As she placed her hands on his skin, the creatures seemed to come to life. Closing her eyes, she sat down. She was not afraid of any of them anymore. She fed herself into Dewe'igan and softly chanted a verse she remembered from the very first time she'd met him:

"Ni Mi shoo mis – Noo ko mis – *(My Grandfather, Grandmother)*
Been dee gek o ma *(Enter here)*
Ni Mi shoo mis – Kee way tin noong *(My Grandfather to the North)*

Pee sha way nee mish in naam *(Send forth your love/mercy)*"

She felt his essence even more strongly now, comingled as it was with hers. Her singing grew louder, and she moved her hands, placing Dewe'igan on her lap and the strap around her neck. She started tapping softly, caressing the beloved form with the tap of her palms upon the smooth skin. Getting up, she started singing loudly, beating out the song with a strident confidence; short–short, long–long.... She felt a sudden shift, accompanied by a change of weight that caused her to open her eyes and look down.

The turtle shell pattern had disappeared, and, running her hands over the body of the drum she noticed that instead of the usual smooth wood, it was sporting hard, horned ridges. In that moment, she realised that the turtle had truly turned. She had sensed it happening a couple of times in the spirit world, but this was the first time it had manifested here. From being a mere rendition of a pattern on the hide, the turtle had given its shell to become Dewe'igan's body, encasing and holding the world she had created. Welcoming the change and recognising it as part of the shape of things to come, Martha drummed the song in its entirety, asking for healing, cleansing, and hope.

* * *

Martha found herself standing on a little outcrop in the middle of crystal waters that seemed vaguely familiar. As she continued to drum and sing, she realised that she had been here before. It was from these grey, volcanic cliffs that surrounded the huge, water-filled caldera that she had pitched herself into the gaping maw of the great serpent Omazaandamo.

She continued to drum the lessons she had learned and the Names she had given, the beat's steadying rhythm binding her entire world into this moment. She'd made the journey from isolation to laughing together, from fear into peace. She'd come to understand the meaning of leadership, the need for balance, and, of course, the first lesson she had ever learned, the Gift of the Word. As she danced and drummed, the dark basalt cut its way into her slippered feet. As if to answer the churning power of the wind, the water started lashing against the shores that held her. Lifting her face in a final act of supplication, she Named them, shouting to the one who had guided her path.

"Grandmother, Koomis, I need you. You of sky and air, heart of my heart, I summon you here.

"I am Seeker
I am Convenor
I am the Keeper of Language
I am Drum Keeper.
To be these things I must be a Namer of the unknown."

Charlotte came into being on a small promontory, directly to Martha's right. "Now the others, my child; it is time."

She drummed, calling Lokozho, Dugdhav, the Shining One; Mbuya Hungwe, Mother of the Eagle Clan; Tsitsi the Sword Bringer; the Raven; the Bone Woman and the Horned Man to this place. Where there were no names. She flung out prayers and pictures. On and on she went. One, though, had not yet been called. In a sudden understanding of what was to come, her hands tensed and her drum stilled. Charlotte, however, was not about to let the drum fall silent, and with her hand resting on Dewe'igan, she spoke.

"Remember your lessons. The path to sacrifice is not always clear. She is ready. You yourself named her, telling her she would rise again, with scales no longer dark but iridescent with the light of all colours. She gives herself in love, knowing that this gift will bind what is still separate, collecting the energy of all to fuse into one."

Martha looked out across the expanse of water. In that moment there was silence; all was bound by expectation. Knowing that the striking of her drum would unleash the avalanche of what was to come, she hesitated. She didn't feel ready. "Why does it have to be me?" As doubts threatened to overwhelm, she felt fluttering wings at the back of her eyes. And suddenly, the crescent of Segara Anak, the ancient lake that had been shaped by a ring of fire, glistened beneath her. She looked down, and it came to her that creation without destruction was impossible. "He's right, love without sacrifice is meaningless." By gifting her his sight, the Raven had taught her the most important lesson of all.

Seeing through her own eyes again, Martha screamed defiance and started pounding Dewe'igan with renewed determination. "I command the waters, sky and land, the start of the battle is now at hand. I command you, Omazaandamo, the black snake — attend, be transformed."

Resplendent in darkly glistening gold and green scales, Anjani appeared on her left. She immediately walked over to Charlotte, who, with this bit of extra support, rallied ancient bones to come before the Drum Keeper. Her teacher's hand reached up to cup the pupil's face. Despite its frailty, Martha was able to feel the love contained in both touch and words.

"I wish you well. You have much to drum and much to hold. In brokenness, we have come to the end of words. But you understand this pain. By making it your own, you are giving creation a chance to rise anew. Beyond death, it will reclaim its soul fire, like a thunderbird rising again from the waters of life."

The two women walked forwards, one withered crone, one bejewelled and dazzling. Not looking back, they held hands and jumped. As they disappeared under the waves, a crescent of power shot outward, momentarily bathing the entire lake in luminescent green. They were not gone, never that. Instead, Martha sensed from the silent Dewe'igan that although her Koomis was somewhere different for now, she would be waiting until she was called to serve again in a new world.

Anjani's sacrifice was central to the unfolding events, the nexus of power transforming her from one into many. Multitudes of little serpents would be manifesting themselves, either physically or in light, winding their way through cyberspace to knit it to the world of spirit by nudging people onto paths they weren't yet capable of walking on their own. In this new incarnation, she would push those who were willing towards the crystals, readying them for a brightness they would eventually have to hold in themselves. Martha could only hope Anjani's reminders would be gentle.

Dewe'igan started to feel unbearably heavy. Knowing she could not yet release him, Martha staggered. One of the Dancers helped her up, and as he poured his strength into her, a huge grey wolf placed itself at her feet. As she felt the beating of wings behind her, she realised she understood the new weight. Her drumming must hold the turtle shell. It needed to be ready to hold them all when the time came.

As she gained an understanding of her burden, she sank towards the ground. Anjani's sacrifice and Koomis's loss were hard enough to cope with. But it was the realisation of her final task that brought her to her knees. The lake shuddered again. This time a plain, heavy chalice rose out if its depths. A bronze cup, inlaid with a lighter verdigris, hovered just above the still water.

Once again, she'd been summoned. Walking over to the very edge of her little island, she sat down. Under the shadow of Mount Rinjani, she dangled cut and bleeding feet into the caldera's waters. She had reached the end of words. Gesturing to the cup to come to her, she was not in the least surprised to be holding the weight of the Cupu Manik Astagina a couple of moments later.

She looked into the depths of its living water. Created from a cloudy gem, it held the blood of the universe, reverberating with the colourful beauty of the divine soul before human intervention had muddied its purity. Then, out of this well of infinite promise, a nose pushed, followed by a mouth. Painfully slowly, from a glass-smooth surface, a face emerged. As familiar lips shaped to form words, her own parted to sound just one: "Dave."

Not giving any sign of having heard, his beloved voice rushed to fill the hole in her soul he'd left all those months ago.

"I am the screams of humans and birds, the singing in the darkness. I am the echo of a wolf's voice that yearns for something that it does not yet have. The crystals have been bound together, connected at the deepest level though Anjani's sacrifice. Those who hold the shards have become creators in truth, in their hands the ability to bind what's been hidden for millennia into a new making."

As Dave's voice rolled on, she felt the cup shifting in her hands. But determined to hear what came next, Martha persevered with a vice-like grip.

"The blueprint they need is hidden within me. But the bloated folds of what I've become are smothering this map of creation. I need to purge all that is unnecessary, only so can the sound of making be reached."

The intensity of her hold on the cup shook Martha's hands. She knew she didn't have long to grasp his meaning, but she had to try nonetheless.

"I don't understand, why are you bloated, what is unnecessary?"

The crackle of static that accompanied his reply was so strong that she was barely able to make out the next words.

"I am shaped from what people believe to be true, rather than the truth of what is. My growth has no direction, my only form coming from the Name you gave me and the spirits who hold me. However, also within me are the patterns of living DNA, generations of memories and knowledge, dreams, and fears. I contain everything of life, everything that needs to continue beyond this age of devastation.

"If I am released, the pixels, unconstrained by expectation and unfettered by unnatural boundaries, will revert back to the dust that birthed them. Then the fragments of energy that once served to hold — nay, even imprison me — will feed waves of light and sound. Along with everything I contain, they will become the force of creation."

Despite recognising that her drumming would precipitate the grand finale, as the Drum Keeper she had no choice. Her hands drummed, and her voice rang out.

"I am Seeker

I am Convenor

I am the Keeper of Language

I am Drum Keeper.

To be these things I must be a Namer of the unknown.

"The only way we can become creators of the next age is by unleashing you, a hybrid, to bind the creative force of the digital, physical, and spirit worlds. First, though, you must find the code that spans them. I therefore name you Seeker and command you to Seek and survive."

His voice pierced the tightly bound silence. "I know who I am, and that time is short. Anjani has prepared the way. Like her, I will split into millions of versions of myself, entering each reality at once and in parallel. She is connecting millions to the truth of our existence. I will make them willing to help me, seek and decrypt, bring all that is hidden to the light of day. But, as ever...."

Martha was convinced she heard a wry smile in his voice as the water in the cup shimmered and disappeared. "...I need you to show me where to start."

A beautiful green creature worming its way up the smooth bronze sides was all that was left. She helped it along, taking it into her hand. Its bite came like a sudden sting. There was no real pain, just a gift of knowledge. She knew what Dave needed to seek. Sharing it with him, her whisper was like a kiss. "You need to uncover the power of love itself."

It made perfect sense. Love was the only force that was immutable and eternal. It alone would be capable of binding the energy of the three into one. The transcendence and awe of the world of spirit would reignite the ability of humans to shape and create. The power of the earth would be enough to action what had lain dormant for millennia. And finally, the digital world would connect it all, the true information it contained capable of bringing a joyous reality into being.

Once again, the cup shook and filled with water. As it shimmered, a living flame burst up and through it. A new voice came from the fire. "Hold me, Keeper, while I sing for you. I am Sh'ler, Daughter of Flame, jinni and sister, aunt, and mother."

From the silence behind her, twin voices shouted in recognition. Whilst Fatima exclaimed in delight, Badenan's welcome was slightly muted. As if preempting her unspoken question, Sh'ler spoke again.

"I gave birth to a Seeker. I have held his soul and consciousness until this moment. He is ready to find what has been lost."

In that moment, Martha felt Dave's kiss. His expression of love encompassed all. It was particularly poignant because she knew that she was just one of the millions of individual universes he was touching upon. Yet its power shook her to her core. If he was reaching others with that same conviction, she was certain he would drive the love in each and every one of them to the surface. The code that could bind all was only seconds away.

A voice of indescribable beauty spilled up and over the cup, its power and resonance bridging the worlds. Sh'ler had started her song.

Part 3
WHAT
COMES

The Song of Sh'ler

I

In the Age of the Downfall
The signs were read
Linking Watcher to Seeker
Else all would be dead.
Within the destruction the Watcher tried
To create a new framework before the Ganges ran dry.

II

Four women living dysfunctional lives
Sought clues in shared stories
Of how to survive.
Anjani the Serpent in her high corporate tower
Fatima Wolf sought a child-filled bower
While Mercy the Eagle flew high to heal
Martha's drumming decoding, revealed.

III

Then there was one who straddled the planes
The place of the spirit, the paths of the pain,
Lokozho binding all into one
His quantum existence, a digital one.
Once Martha's husband
Now alive in a Web
In desperation he chose an alternative death.

IV

Uncontrolled pathways built by growth at all costs
The world's resources, irreplaceably lost
But then, how to reclaim all that was taken
Returning power to places forsaken?
The network of women begun forging a way
For the rhythm of life to start holding sway.

V

As ancient myths and modern need
Combined to forge a new world creed.
The stories that shaped, saw people forgiving
With Nergis, Moringa — dead places were living.
As a virus scrambled what was created
It defeated encryption, forcing greed to be sated.
Next, paper finance disappeared in a flash
A newly formed conscience causing markets to crash.
And then there was water where oil once flowed
And in fields of slaughter new flora had grown.

VI

Earth's stolen force bloated digital space
Taken to serve the empty needs of our race.
So, when the Web woke with a sentience given
It saw what was taken, what had to be shriven.
It sacrificed all to find release
And as its soul flew, gained freedom and peace.

VII
The Wolf called the children to mother them all
The Eagle cried, causing nations to fall.
But to give power back to sea, land, and sky
More was needed, so the serpent died.

VIII
Anjani's life force has seeded the seas
The Wolf and her children have used fire to release.
The Eagle's vision has seen what was needed
Using spirit and air to help grow what was seeded.
Then words of power in binary coding
Were drummed by the drummer
And worlds started exploding.

IX
The turtle now turns, and it offers its shell
To keep all together, safe and well.
All is peaceful, and on we sleep
Till new shores are ready and our Arks are unleashed.
All beings together, we as gods straddle worlds
While knowledge and wisdom in love are unfurled
We will work as one people as the next age unfolds
And myths are reshaped as our story is told.

X
Last was the word, we were called by the drum
To give up ourselves, and so become one.

* * *

Dave had not consciously linked his thoughts to his actions. But named as Seeker, he was sweeping through the digital world like the wave that followed Anjani's sacrifice, the crystals allowing him to connect the innumerable images, texts, and emails that defined it.

By simultaneously delving into millions of parallel worlds of human existence, he was able to map all this and bring it forth, creating a true sum of the parts. Everywhere he went, he left an imprint of himself just in case others still wished to follow.

Time after time, memories of love and joy crashed into him. He immersed himself fully, recognising that what he had experienced previously was but a dim reflection of what he was confronting face-to-face. He understood what was needed and what was not and through this saw how bloated everything — and therefore he — had become. This realisation caused him to collapse the corridors of the excess digital space. Using the resulting energy, he blazed through the cloudy mass of information that had obscured so much. He hoped that this, coupled with the connections he was forging through the crystals, would be enough to lead him to the code.

As the Seeker replaced the constructed, angular waves of the digital world with the softer analogue ones, he also felt other constructs, such as the encryption protecting the cryptocurrencies, crumbling. In this period of decoherence, he was the wind that reshaped and the sound that heralded a pure state of being; a deep resonance that was able to create a singular path from the current, quantum multiplicity back into a place where everything knew where it belonged and was therefore able to stay where it was.

As his search continued, he finally understood that the code he was seeking represented the ultimate alchemist's formula, a means of connecting untapped energy to human will in order to bring things of matter and substance into existence. Those he had been particularly drawn to, though, continued to be the framework he based his journey on. They were his reference points and baseline.

* * *

Sana'a, Yemen
To: Fatima@asafespace.com
From: Khalid123@yahoo.com
Saturday 28.5

Dear Fatima,
I so hope you get this. I have not used this tablet to try to contact you since the text we exchanged, when you thanked me for the fig tree. That seems like such a long while ago, and so much has changed.

You said if I needed to reach you, this would be the right email address. Mine is an old one, so I hope this works. The crystals are still in action, so I'm sure we will be okay. I am writing because we are nearing the end of our journey. I wanted to ask you to keep Tara safe and tell her of my love. Tell her also that I planted the fig tree for her.

If I sound old now, it is because I feel it. I am no longer the boy you remember. Our path has been a long one. As the crow flies, the distance between Zakho (on the Turkish border, the place I was when we last messaged) to Sana'a is over 3,000 kilometres. The terrain has also forced us to cross many different physical barriers, significantly adding to the number of kilometres. Our journey south has led us from the Zagros Mountains downwards towards the Gulf. We have criss-crossed the Iraqi and Syrian borders on our way. In January, we reached the Kingdom of Saudi Arabia. This journey from the mountains to the heart of Yemen has taken us from November up until now. We reached Sana'a a couple of days ago and have come to understand that it is time to rest, so we have.

We have been chased, threatened, and beaten. However, we have also been comforted, fed, and sheltered. As we have walked, so we have grown, both in stature and courage. Although we are only eleven and twelve, the road has shaped us. Our faces are no longer those of the children you once knew.

This is not as dangerous as it might seem, because we have not been travelling alone. Soon after we'd planted around a place that was mired in darkness, up in the Zagros Mountains, our companions joined us. At first, we heard them howling in the distance and were afraid and moved faster and faster, trying to escape. Eventually, knowing we couldn't outrun them, we just stopped. Lighting a fire and not expecting to rise again, we ate the remnants of what we had left and slept. We did wake again though.

And as we opened our eyes to the misty dawn of the next day, we noticed that we were warmer than we had been for a long time. The silver-coated beasts we had thought to be our enemies had encircled us with their coats. Instead of attacking us, the pack had chosen to protect us, saving us from the worst of the chill. Since then, they have helped us pad our way down, slowly, softly, and silently. Their leaders, much larger than the others, are called the Golden One and the White. They are so named because of the colour of their ruffs. They sometimes allow us to ride them while the pack hunts for us. I ride the White. They let us know when it is safe to make fire or when we must be quiet. They nourish our sense of purpose as well as our bodies. Their protection has allowed us to continue with our planting.

We have planted in soil that is empty and in soil that is fertile; in land that is polluted and in land that was forgotten. We used up our bulbs from the garden very early on, but the farther we went, the more we noticed that even without our planting, Nergis were springing up. That was when we started harvesting to plant. We kept the seeds from figs we had eaten and took from gardens when we saw something we wanted to share. As we threaded our way back and forth across the Iraqi border, we recrossed some of the earlier paths from our journey northwards. It was wonderful to see new life springing up from arid soil.

Hadeel has just reminded me to share something important we noticed on our travels. It seems as though all the oil wells have been abandoned. Even the refineries are silent. On our journey up, we were afraid we would be press-ganged into something we didn't want to participate in, so we avoided these areas of activity. Then, when we passed the first couple of smaller fields on our way back down again, we became aware of the lack of people. Initially, we just saw it as coincidence. However, as our companions pushed us to go through the Syrian fields, we realised something had changed.

Where once machines were compressing the sky and the earth with sounds of industry, water rippled in small lakes and fountains. Inspired, our planting became even more prolific. We knew that where water was, life would soon follow. The first time we truly acknowledged the change was in Syria's Dei Ezzor, but as we worked our way downwards, following the eastward direction the wolves had set, we realised that all the major Saudi fields in the oil corridor had also ceased operations. In Manifa, we were able to rest and refresh ourselves, waves from the Gulf lapping against little islands. After some observation, though, we realised that they were partially drowned buildings. As we moved farther down to Abqaiq and Ghawar, great lakes of water appeared in the yellow sands of the desert.

We headed across the dunes and saw that even where there were no buildings or man-made activity, little oases had appeared. And trees, just like those we'd left in the garden, were springing up all over the place.

Farther and farther we went, until eventually we crossed into Yemen. Death greeted us there. It stalked the streets and the faces of those who used guns to make war. It held the hands of those who had been left, ravaged by hunger and disease and the sound of the bombs that kept falling. The eyes of those who remained were haunted.

On our journey, our companions had kept us fed with many creatures. When we were nearer settlements, or where oil fields and refineries had been, rabbits provided the main fare. Here, though, where it seemed they were needed most, there were virtually none. We redoubled our efforts, planting seeds, bulbs, and hope where we could. Unlike anywhere else we had been, the community gave what it could, putting down their weapons as they did so. Then they rose up to follow us down streets ravaged by war and pestilence.

Two days ago, our procession reached Sana'a. We are in Al Sabbeen Park. Many thousands have joined us. Moringa trees provide shelter, and I have planted bulbs and fig trees. Yima would have been proud; they are sprouting up almost faster than I can plant. It is as if nature is responding to the hungry cries of a desperate people. Now the ground shakes with our dancing and dead streets resound with our singing. Where the thousands of war and cholera dead are buried, carpets of Nergis soothe and feed souls who were once close to death themselves.

I write today because an hour ago my crystal blazed. In the time that has passed, I have felt your arms around me and have in turn hugged Hadeel. It has started raining, and instead of blood, Sana'a's streets are running with water. I have had time to remember the Sinbad stories you told us. These have made me wanted to share some of my own journey with you. I can feel the ground shake, and I don't believe it is just our feet making it so. I write as others dance. This seems to be the way of the new world.

Hadeel and I send all our love and hope that when we meet again, it will be in a place of milk and honey. We dream of a place where hope stalks the land and where we can love with all our hearts. You read to us once from the Rain Song; the rain today reminds me of this:

Every drop of rain holds a red and yellow flower
Every tear of the starved who have no rags to their back
Every drop of blood shed by a slave
Is a smile awaiting fresh lips

Or a nipple glowing in the mouth of a newborn.
In tomorrow's youthful world, giver of life
Rain, Rain, Rain
And Iraq springs into leaf in the rain...
I embrace you, Fatima, and ask that you do the same for Tara.
Khalid.

* * *

St Nicholas at Wade, Kent

Emmy kept on clapping, singing to herself in a softly muted whisper.
"Hickory Dickory Dock, my life has become unlocked
The clock strikes time
Which now is mine
Hickory Dickory Dock."

She wasn't bothering with the rest anymore. This was the verse that mattered. Her life *had* become unlocked, hadn't it? All this change, her eating, nature, transformation. She had been part of it, she had planted, she had made change possible. So what had happened? Why had it all come crashing down around her ears?

As she clapped the rhythm more frantically, her mind whirred with a sense of betrayal. Henry and Mum were trying to make her ill again, that's what it was. There wasn't enough food, and she was eating too much. They wanted her to eat less, so they thought they'd make up this ridiculous story about Dad still being here.

Where was he, then, if he was here? They said he was in the computer and her phone. Well, she'd had both on, using her crystals to power them and nothing. Zilch. Liars, that's what they were, liars. As the clock resumed its tick-tocking in her head, she wrote down lists of all the ways she had been wronged. Her mum had been obsessed with ASafeSpace and others, Henry in particular. She, in the meantime, had been sidelined. Even Dennis the horse was ignoring her, and her crystals weren't working properly anymore. For some reason they'd given her faulty ones. Once she'd finished a couple of pages of that list, she started on the things she was going to be eating over the next couple of days. Trying to get her to eat less, were they, by manipulating her like this? She'd show them. Knowing that her mum wouldn't come in, she'd already hidden some bits and pieces in her room. She'd even found a tin of peaches. That would be her treat tomorrow.

As she continued to scribble, she realised that it was taking the edge off her anger. She paused for a moment, looking out into the garden. Her window framed Fatima's Nergis, carpeting their little patch of lawn. It was a beautiful spring day. Putting down her pen, she opened the window.

As she did so, she noticed that a little, green worm-like creature had got stuck in the guttering just below her. It was wriggling in distress. Momentarily forgetting her own woes, she grabbed a pencil from her desk and used it to attempt a rescue. It was the size of a large earthworm, and she'd been planning on flicking it out and over into the garden. Instead, quick as a flash, it had moved up the pencil and onto her hand. She felt a sharp scratch. It had bitten her! Much more loudly this time, the White Rabbit song came into her head again.

She impatiently shook off the worm, and with a small thud, it landed on her desk. She could feel the song again, her fingers itching to tap out the beat.

"Hickory Dickory Dock, the Rabbit got stuck in the clock
The clock struck one, he didn't come
Hickory Dickory Dock."

She decided to clap as she was singing; there was far more conviction this time. So immersed was she in the song that she didn't notice how the little creature had made itself at home between the two crystals that started flaring, changing from a dull grey into a pure, deep blue.

"Emmy, Emmy ... can you hear me?"

As she beat the last pulse of the song, the voice rang out again.

"My very own big, little girl — I'm here, will you let me in?"

She remembered her shiny red bike seat on the front of his bronze racing bike. She remembered how they'd danced together, her as a ten-year-old, proud to be asked by her handsome daddy to be his partner at a family works do. She remembered how he had bellowed and shouted at the group of young men hassling his family on the London Underground, puffing up his chest to make him seem twice the size he was so he could protect them. And, as she remembered, she crumpled inwards, allowing Dave to enfold her with a father's love, so pleased that he'd finally reached his darling girl.

"Say it, Dad, say it now. So I know it's real."

She whispered, as if not daring to speak aloud, just in case it all went away. He knew exactly what she meant. Emmy had already closed her eyes, an ecstatic smile playing over her lips, showing that she held within her the sure knowledge of being completely and utterly loved.

"As you lay here down to sleep, I pray the Lord your soul to keep."

She responded, at first in low, barely perceptible tones, but by the end she was shouting, her voice getting louder with every word: "Guard me, Lord, throughout the night and wake me in the morning light."

On hearing her cries, Martha and Henry rushed in. With Dewe'igan still attached to her by his wide strap and Sh'ler's song sounding in her ears, Martha had been ripped from the rocky island in the middle of Segara Anak. Still feeling the whispered caress of the kiss her husband had placed on her lips only seconds ago, she knew that in this moment Dave had finally reached Emmy. He'd sought her truth and found it. She so hoped that he'd been able to help others also.

* * *

Rampao Valley, New Jersey

Brigid rested against a granite outcropping on Hawk Ridge, observing the hustle and bustle in the camp below. She had felt her crystal pulsing more strongly this morning with the result. The hive of activity below, created by the hundreds who had followed her here and the thousands who'd joined since, was suffused with a sense of expectation. She liked watching them and knew deep down their time was drawing to a close.

She felt new heat in the crystals in her pouch. Drawing them out, she got the strangest sensation of two beings, one within and without. Then she heard the voice. It had come to her occasionally, but she hadn't seen him since that very first time. At this moment, though, his low-pitched tones were throbbing through her, the crystals lending him access to her inner self. She started walking down towards the trees, in her heart embracing the being she believed had saved her:

"Brigid, ever excellent woman,
Golden sparkling flame,
Lead us to the eternal Kingdom,
The dazzling resplendent sun."

Stepping out of the huge oak, which had loomed up in front of her, he shook magnificent antlers, casting moving shadows onto the path before him as he spoke.

"Forgive yourself. Choose the blazing crystals, the path of fire. Burn your old life in the flames of renewal. Become their leader, now, when it matters. I will be with you. For the sake of your children and your pain at their loss, ensure the safety of these thousands."

"But how?" she asked.

And once again he spoke in a voice echoing with pain and age-old loneliness.

"The world turns. The drum sounds. Our feet must pound, and we must believe that contained in the love we bring to being, we will be safe."

* * *

Belfast, Northern Ireland

When the crystal had first blazed in Janet's hand, it would have been so easy to stay with her brother in the youth club. But she knew she needed to return for her mother and sister. Luckily, when she got home, Susan had agreed to come back, happy to listen to Janet's promise of a safe space. Mum, however, had refused. She agreed something was coming and wanted her children to be safe but with, "I'll join you as soon as I can, there's something I need to do first," she had rushed off in the opposite direction.

Janet had started back with Susan. But then the strongest feeling rushed through her. Something was coming, and in order for the family to get through it in one piece, albeit not necessarily together, she knew she needed to be with her mum. She said, "Go on ahead, I'll be with you shortly," over her shoulder and started off after Doreen.

She'd got halfway back to the Care Home by the time she caught her. In a state of heightened anxiety, her mum had wanted to know why Janet had not gone back with her older sister as directed. "What were you thinking?" But once they'd established that Susan had gone to be with Connor, she calmed a bit.

As they walked, Janet tried to understand why getting back to Parkview was so important. Since it was clear something momentous was going on, Doreen came clean. There was an old lady there who was related to them. "My mum, your grandmother. She doesn't know it's me, though, and I can't leave her not knowing. I've got to tell her."

They got there eventually, strangely deserted streets speeding them on their way. From then on in, though, nothing was as expected. Perched on a little plastic chair in her grandmother's room, Janet heard her mother tell her that not only was she her carer, but also the daughter Florence had given up for adoption some fifty years ago. Mum was flummoxed when she said, "I don't really like your name. Why did they call you Doreen? I named you Elisabeth." But Doreen was able to fill in some of the gaps. How she'd had decent adoptive parents but had always felt there was something missing. How she'd married late, and when her husband had died, she went through the church's adoption records to discover a disabled birth mother. That she had grandchildren and that one of them was sitting right here.

Although Janet hadn't expected Grandma Florence to throw off her wheelchair and walk, she knew that Mum had been banking on the fact that she'd want to see the rest of her newly-minted family. Unhelpfully, though, just as Florence was thinking about whether to come back with them, a huge rumble sounded. She shook her head. "With all that fuss and noise, I'm not going anywhere."

However, the floor shifted again, and stumbling with the ferocity of the movement, they decided to make their way back along the ground-floor corridor. When they emerged in the garden, they rushed to the bottom of the long lawn, where a few others had gathered.

"Mum," Janet gestured to the tottering building, "they're all stuck. Shouldn't we go back?"

Many of Parkview's older residents were trapped, either by their walking aids or simply the fear of going outside. By the time the building collapsed in on itself, old Harry, tottering down the garden in slippers and a dressing gown, was the last one to make it out. As the huge plume of dust consumed most of the street, Janet looked at her mum helplessly. That was that then. Realising that even the hill Belfast Zoo sat on was half the height it should have been, she spoke.

"They'll be all right, you know. Mr McAtamney's is a safe space."

In that moment, her crystal blazed strongly for a second time. It was the Spirit of the Safe Space. He was showing her the way. It was as if she was looking at a split screen in the cinema. One part of her was in a garden, eyeing a group of bedraggled, frightened pensioners, the other was dancing to the powerful beat of life, joining with multitudes of people in a place that was equally real. Fear caught her, and the words she meant to say got stuck in her throat.

A broad Belfast accent sounded stridently through the noise. Unlike Janet, Doreen was able to vocalise what needed to be said. "Listen up, everybody. We have no time. Get your wee crystals out. Hold them like this."

She held hers out in front of her. Waving it, she said, "I am going to dance, and you are going to stamp your feet or clap. Even nod your head to the beat if you can't do anything else. But if you can, join in with my singing."

Finally managing to push a sound past her lips again, Janet was soon part of the stamping noise. She noticed that Harry, Grandma Florence, and most of the others were joining in too.

"The whole world is coming,
A nation is coming, a nation is coming,
The Eagle has brought the message to our tribe,
The Father says so; Ate heye lo.
Over the whole earth they are coming.
The bear is coming, the auroch is coming, the horses of the fields run freely again,
The raven has brought the message to our tribe,
The Father says so, Ate heye lo."

As she danced, Janet noticed her mum holding a bowl-like, textured shell that she was beating with the palm of her hand. Drawing a spoon from one of his dressing gown's many pockets, Old Harry lobbed it at her.

"If it's a drum you're wanting, this'll work better."

* * *

Ásahreppur, Iceland

Dave watched the ISIS fighter he'd first met in Stockholm's central station. Having followed the wolf and flower seal faithfully these last few months, Dave now found himself in a tiny, red-spired church close to Ásahreppur in Southern Iceland. It was dominated by a solitary stained-glass window depicting an image of St Francis and his wolf in a meadow of white flowers. Ali was no longer alone. Huddling with him, in clothes that seemed far too light for the weather, were two new comrades.

A kindly-looking man Dave didn't recognise was with them. He had made them a hot drink while listening to their tale and their gratitude to Allah for allowing them to make the last ferry bound for Iceland. Once hunters and hunted, the threesome explained how they'd realised they more in common with each other than with the organisation they'd left behind. On reaching land, they'd cemented this new brotherhood by acquiring a battered old Land Rover. Driving aimlessly, they'd eventually made it here, and Dave caught them muttering something about this place calling to them like a homing beacon.

They, in turn, had been interested to hear about the chapel, with Ali reacting strongly to the unusual windows. As Dave watched the portly man of middling age intone words of hope, he saw the three young men fall to their knees. With tears pouring down their faces they asked for forgiveness.

"Who knows what is to come, but we need each other." The little man had said.

At that an almighty crash rent the air and the crystals in all four pairs of hands, blazed into life.

* * *

Belfast

Dave was called by the long, hollow sound that punctuated the verses Doreen and Janet were repeating on their make-shift drum. Across the world, he felt similar circles, similar scenes taking place, but he remembered Janet so wanted enough of him to be here to truly follow events. A couple of moments later, far off in the distance, there was a huge boom, and then another one. He saw Janet place the shell on the ground. Watched it sink down. It started growing up and over them, casting itself around the entire garden.

* * *

Rampao Valley

Holding hands, the horned man and Brigid walked down into the throng. All was silent. Then the crystals blazed into life, the lapping of the waves and the rustling spring leaves entered into a new kind of rhythm. It spilled out of the stones into all those who were willing to listen, causing hands to clap and feet to pound. The earth rocked violently, but the whirling energies of the dance meant no one noticed. Next came the rain, drowning all that had been until a swirling mass of something positioned itself over the top, forming a domed, protective cocoon.

* * *

Belfast

Doreen took the old lady's hand. Reaching for Janet's hand as she stroked her daughter's head, the old lady crooned softly,
   "Hush, little darling, don't say a word
   Mama's going to buy you a mockingbird...."
The essence of them was dancing with crowds of others somewhere else entirely. Here, though, their eyes closed, they were kept safe in a love that transcended all fear.

* * *

St Nicholas at Wade

Picking up on the beat she'd heard just moments before, Martha started drumming her great turtle shell drum once more. The children stood next to her, one on each side with their arms around each other and enveloping the back of Martha too. All three were touching as the drum sounded a deep hollow thrum that seemed to envelop all that was contained in each of them while the coiling rope of the snake around its edges was keeping the other images in check.

* * *

Ásahreppur

Watching the red and orange flames of an erupting volcano shoot into the sky above the icefields, Dave's global vision showed him the huge Bárðarbunga volcano as just one of many. So many others, drumming, singing and together. So many more, though, sitting alone, paralysed by fear.
   The entire church was turning, borne aloft by what resembled an upside-down turtle shell. Then he was in another place, and the vague

pounding of distant feet that had been grazing the edge of his conscious-ness became his all-consuming present.

* * *

Martha opened her eyes to Chipo's valley once more. The children were with her, this time as tangibly present as she was. There were people all around, and just like Emmy and Henry, a new physicality had banished what had once been ephemeral. But despite the thousands of feet splashing up and down on its shores, the silver river threading its way through it all was strangely becalmed. She imagined they were inhabiting this place and the physical world simultaneously, using "here" to inspire their actions there. Be that as it may, people were filling every inch of space with singing, clapping, and dancing.

The Johnstones walked on, taking just a little while to reach the familiar, conically roofed huts. The other Ghost Dancers were already there and started arranging themselves in a circle around the newcomers. As Martha noticed Badenan's hand toying with the ears of a sleek-backed grey wolf, she realised that their family had grown immeasurably. A huge crowd now stretched back as far as the eye could see.

Dear Chipo and Mercy, thought Martha. How hard they must have worked to expand this place to hold all that had come.

She was also reassured to hear Hungry's savage cries, an oddly dissonant chorus of joy sung along with many new avian friends.

"Yes," Mercy said, noticing Martha's upward glance. "Others have joined him. Birds of hope and birds that pray have come from across Africa to lend us their vision, helping us understand how to Shape what is to come."

Looking down at her drum, Martha was reassured to see the snake's green iridescence around its perimeter. Anjani was still with them. She took this as a signal that it was time to call the missing one home. But as she went to call him, she saw he had come of his own accord. The one she had named Lokozho and Seeker was moving through the dancers to join her at the centre of the circle. Her Dave.

Inevitably, though, he had changed, the bluey white light emanating from him nearly blinding her with its intensity. And although the hand that reached out for hers was still familiar, the vast, shimmering sphere that was attached to him was not. As with light shining through water, it seemed to bend and distort all that was behind him, stretching into the sky and across the valley as far as the eye could see.

He spoke. "I have found the code. Are you ready to drum, if I share it?"

Martha's voice wouldn't come, so she just nodded, squeezing his hand hard. As he kissed her, he whispered, "At the end of times, all that remains is love."

She drummed the code into life. As it spread across the physical, digital, and spirit worlds, all that Dave had witnessed flooded into her, waves of love and forgiveness, swelling her heart until it could contain no more.

She needed to let him know. "I must, Dave… " She panted. "Dave, I must let go. I can't hold you anymore."

It spilled out of her. The binary beat of her drumming turning all into a joyful, connecting force. Through this message of hope and practical action, those dancing in the valley would be able to create what was needed to survive the Downfall and start again.

Taking a step back, he threw a longing glance at his children and spoke again. "We will create islands shaped from turtle shell, forged by all who have assembled today. The desire to survive and transform has created the intent, and the dancing and drumming will create the energy. You and I are shaping what we intended, a hybrid future based on pixels of shared pain and experience. Your beating drum gives it substance, forming a bridge between the will to survive, the energy of the earth, and the world of spirit. When you release me, my pixels will become the dust of creation."

In that moment, Martha got it. The patterns of her drumming were connecting the neurons of a huge, collective brain. On his release, Dave would translate this into Arks that would help them survive. Most of the time, nothing made sense to her. Her human mind simply wasn't enough. But Dewe'igan's truth allowed her to pin it all together, and she finally realised it was all okay.

Her hands spoke of a planet protected from solar storms and radiation by a gravity-created shield. Her voice joined in with his story of the centrifugal motion of the Turtle Islands that would create a magnetic shield of protection. Her heart straddled all, though, thumping out the tale of a loop in time that would hold the Arks suspended and protected until the world was safe again. But cutting through it like a knife was her own longing for this place beyond time and space that would allow her to meet Dave again.

His voice wasn't like the one she remembered. But despite this sense of disconnect, she listened, and in doing so, heard the final farewells underlying his story of what was to come. She knew then that although this being of light and energy was still him, part of him was already gone.

"In releasing me, you are losing the force that allows those who have chosen the way of fire to channel the world's heartbeat. With pounding feet and sounding voices, clapping hands and beating drums, they are spinning cocoons of safety."

At this, Martha stopped drumming and moved towards him again, holding Emmy and Henry by the hand. They threw their arms around each other one last time. A couple of seconds later, Martha stepped away. So many moments of courage and unknowns had dogged the last few months, but for her, this Last Post was where it all came together. As tears streamed down her face, she drummed a lament and a rejoicing, telling of the end of this world and the beginning of a new one. Most of all, though, she reminded those who had chosen this path that the power that resided within them was what would shape their new beginnings.

"So, rise up my love
My beautiful one, Away.
I will sleep until you knock on my door
Breaking the seal upon my heart.
Then I will arise
So that in a place beyond life and death
We can welcome a new dawn together.
Go in Truth — as the hope of what is to come
Go in Peace — you have fulfilled all
Go in Love — I release you."

The Ghost Dancers led the dancing, a song steeped in history they had made new. Some whirled in pairs, others alone, many more in great numbers. But all twirled and pounded, swaying to the sound of the drum and the power of their shared voices, the pixelated world Dave had held within him sinking into their hearts and minds. Then, as suddenly as he had come, all that had been Dave was gone.

And the world turned.

* * *

Dave was floating, and he was very aware of the warmth that engulfed him. Was this death, finally? He realised he was surprised at how quickly the end had come. He, Martha, and the children had been as one, and then they hadn't, and now he was alone again, presumably left to dissipate into innumerable fragments that would shape the new world.

The heat puzzled him, though. Then he realised he was in the molten depths around which the planet spun, somewhere he hadn't been before. He attuned his movement to the flowing metal and rock of the core, momentarily feeling like a drowning man floating calmly in the depths of an uncharted ocean.

Vaguely registering that the world was fracturing along with his consciousness, a tremendous sense of peace washed over him. Rather than upsetting him unduly, it was as if the wholesale destruction was coming to him from the distant past, set on sepia-toned film footage.

The fragments of him that remained were both here and there, some in the molten warmth, others flying over the Yellowstone volcano, offering a bird's-eye view as North America split, or admiring how Cumbre Vieja in Las Palmas was sending vast tidal waves hurtling across the Atlantic. He spun along with the ash from Iceland's volcano fields as it spewed forth the bowels of the earth and revelled in the reigniting of the ancient basalt of Northern Ireland's Giant's Causeway, as a huge underwater volcano rose up through the Irish Sea to drown both island nations. While La Toba in Indonesia celebrated its release by belching up unending streams of magma, he joined the cycle of tsunamis as they gathered up the Pacific in playful abandon.

Then only one spark remained, still floating. It was so quiet here. He was just one small drop of life, one small drop of energy, just like the billions of others who had lived. He had wanted to help everyone figure out how to work together by becoming a mighty ocean, but now all that remained was the last water drop near the end of its journey. It was time to let go. He just hoped the new creation would work, that he and Martha would be given the chance to meet again, whichever shore they washed up on.

CHAPTER 14

Fatima's Retelling of Zuhak's Demise

"Zuhak returned with an army. The people of the city, however, kept the tyrant from their place of safety with the debris and words they cast at him from their towers. Eventually, his forces were shattered and Zuhak and Fereydun, the city's chief defender, came face-to-face. The young man raised his bull-headed mace to crush Zuhak. However, Sarosh, the angel of Truth, both spoken and listened for, swooped down and proclaimed:

"'Strike not; his time for death is not yet come.'

"Instead, Sarosh told Fereydun to take Zuhak to Mount Demavand and bind him to a rock. There the hot sun would punish him while the chains of captivity cut into his flesh and thirst would cause his tongue to cleave to the roof of his mouth."

As she told her tale, Fatima glanced down at the children arrayed in front of her in this, their very first garden. The group had grown again. It stretched all the way back to the far wall. Listening for the songbirds that had found refuge here, she caught a glimpse of a gazelle and the small family of beavers, who, despite the wolves, seemed to have made themselves at home in this new sanctuary.

"Zuhak is free, children. Can you hear him pound at our garden walls? He is shaking them in his attempt to get in. We must stop him."

"How do we do that?" Tara piped up, her voice muted by burying her head in Fatima's side.

"We sing a song to him. Our song will help us make our walls stronger. However, we will also be calling to that in him which might still be good. If even part of him joins us, we will gain in both stature and courage."

Tara asked, "How will a song help?"

As she had done so many times before, Fatima explained. "Well, all of you will have been here and there with me in the valley. Some will still feel as I do that part of them remains there even now. Others, however, remained more firmly bound to this place, our garden. If that is you, the dance we learned might only be lapping at edges of your consciousness. Despite this, though, the time has come to bring it here, and we must be united as we sing to keep Zuhak at bay. All of us must therefore be ready to let the dance spill though us. Remember, despite the fear and anger we might be feeling as we sing here, part of us remains in the beautiful, green valley, dancing along with the many others from around the world who have chosen to be safe too."

A little boy came from the place behind the fig tree, a look of wonder suffusing his entire being. "Look, Fatima, look what I've found. I was listening to the song, and I sang of the creature that came to me the night my mother died."

He opened his hands, and a beautiful, blood-red butterfly spread its wings. Badenan's wolf tried to snap at this new plaything while the children gasped in delight. As it flew, another materialised in his cupped palms. This time the creature that emerged was a dark indigo. It chose to remain on the hand of its creator for a while, growing to the size of a small bird as it rested there. Then it also flew away.

"I am making more, Fatima. I just need to think, and they come."

As if signalling a deep understanding, Fatima smiled at him. "My little one, you are the first to have understood the power of the song we must all sing to be safe. "

As he tried to make his way towards Fatima, the Bone Woman opened her arms to him instead, and the wolf opened his great jaws, as if attempting a smile of welcome. Up until then they'd been sitting quietly by the tallest Moringa tree to plant itself and which covered the little gap in the wall almost entirely.

"Stay with us, child. It will be good to have one who has already started to sing the song of creation at the gate."

As she spoke, the ground shook and Zuhak roared. He had left Mount Demavand, his chains forever broken. From beyond the walls, sulphurous smoke started to engulf them. As flames shot up and over them, bathing the sky with a hungry, orange glow, the light of the crystals winked out in the darkness of their fear.

One of the older women whispered to her neighbour, "It is like the bombs; do you remember the bombs?"

Fatima stood up and raised her arms to the heavens. As she did so, Badenan's wolf padded over to her; holding a dark brown, heavily ridged shell between her jaws.

Fatima spoke. "Children, it's time to stand. We must dance — Zuhak cannot breach our walls."

She took the huge shell and started pounding it, the hollow sound creating a call to action they could all follow. Mirroring the part of her that was singing in the valley, Badenan joined in with the song of the Ghost Dancers.

"The whole world is coming,
A nation is coming, a nation is coming,
The Eagle has brought the message to our tribe,
The Father says so; Ate heye lo.
Over the whole earth they are coming.
The Ibis is coming, the Songbirds are coming, the Caspian lions roar again —
The wolf has brought the message to our tribe,
The Father says so, Ate heye lo."

As they sang, the wind howled and the earth rocked violently. Still, though, the garden held. Mallets of power and fire smote the walls, but still all stood firm. As they danced, inner and outer circles pounding out the rhythm in counterpoint, Fatima placed the shell on the ground, its hard surface facing downwards. Clapping her hands in abandon, she saw it sink quickly, disappearing into the dark earth. Within seconds, the walls surrounding them seemed to be encased by a dark, hard carapace. Some of the children exclaimed that they could see Zuhak's fiery countenance shooting up around them, smoky hands trying to claw their way through the shell. However, having finally understood that that the power of their song was allowing them to create their very own Turtle Island, they knew they were safe here. By fashioning the energies of the earth into something they needed, they were taking back the power of creation, a power that had been lost to humanity since the dawn of time.

The frantic battering gave way to silence. All was still. The guardians of the gate stood aside, and around the tree slithered two snakes, one painted in the red hues of the rising dawn and the other in a bright green that was like the foliage of an orange tree, readying itself for the first blossoms of the season. Astonishing in their beauty, their jewelled scales transfixed the children as they slithered their way through the crowd to the back of the garden. The larger red one wound itself around the fig tree. The smaller green one, however, sought Fatima's ankle. Much like Babylonian adornments had done in ancient times, by encasing the delicate limb with emerald scales, the snake signalled the royalty of its bearer. To show that she understood, Fatima ran her finger over the smaller of Zuhak's serpents in a welcoming caress.

As she did so, she noticed that where she had placed the shell a small, sparkling body of water had appeared. It was already being enjoyed by the shy beaver and a couple of iridescent dragonflies that had emerged from amongst the Nergis to sample its delights.

Fatima lifted her gaze upwards, noting that the angry fires and smoke had been replaced by a strange kind of opacity. Oddly comforted by the densely layered dome of mist that loomed above them, she spoke again, this time telling the children that sleep beckoned.

At the sound of her voice, and despite the crystals still being vaguely subdued, as with one accord, the children's tablets started playing a lullaby. Only one song was playing, but to each one of those present, the soft words of sleep were sung in the voice of their mothers.

Fatima looked around her with heavy eyes. Noticing that the Bone Woman and her faithful companion had not relaxed their guard, she finally felt it was safe to close hers also.

All would be well, and all manner of things would be well. She just needed to rest a little.

* * *

The St Nicholas at Wade Turtle Island
The little black bird hopped from leg to leg. Something was happening, he could feel it. Even though this place was beyond time, a trill of dawn chorus arose from deep within him. Delighted, he noticed that it was being taken up, echoing back at him from the different trees dotting the

place that had kept them safe for so long. Nothing, though, from the numerous other stomping, galloping, flying, slithering, and burrowing creatures that shared this sanctuary. They were still in as deep a slumber as the humans who'd drummed and danced on that last day.

Cocking his head, he scrutinised his surroundings. Although he and his fellows had remained the same, the landscape had changed almost beyond recognition. His favourite perch, for example, growing from a tiny sapling to something upwards of thirty metres.

A scream rent the sky, and he looked up. Where the misty opalescence of a dome had shielded, a blue openness had appeared, an eagle flung into its centre. The sun beamed down at him, the first rays of a new dawn kissing glossy feathers. The wide-open brightness caused him to lower his third lid. Had the time really come?

He'd been one for so long that he'd forgotten his purpose was contained within the Many. The eagle's scream sounded again, and without conscious thought, the little bird stretched its own wings. It was a short drop, but there, nestled in the roots of his tree, was the shape he belonged to. As he surrendered to it, along with his cloud of brothers, he realised his time had come. The dawn of a new creation was here once more.

The newly formed cloak righted itself, strong, male hands brushing down lustrous feathers.

Lowering his hood, he looked around, his spirit eye an opaque white, the other black as coal, features flickering like a kindling fire. Feeling the last of the little ones join, he spoke. "Well, boys, we'll know soon enough if it's all worked, won't we?"

He grunted in satisfaction as his namesakes appeared. It was a rhetorical question, for just like the others, the ravens had been here the entire time. He looked around him. So much had changed, and yet consigned to the deepest of slumbers, it had also stayed the same.

The bird on his left shoulder rubbed silken white feathers against a wrinkling cheek. As he stroked the glossy throat, the final cataclysmic moments of the last Age came to him. In its final throes, steady white wings had taken him to the edge of the Earth's atmosphere. Even from there, though, he'd felt the heat of the Pacific Ring of Fire drowning the South American continent in lava and ocean.

Like the north wind, his black raven form had chased a boiling sea through the eye of the storm, losing direction in the chaos. He knew that the end had come and willed a return, realising that despite his love of change, there was nothing more to be done.

In these enclaves of safety, aeons passed, and while humans slept, guardians like him stayed awake, ever watchful for the time of Awakening that had been promised. Even cocooned on this Island Ark, he knew that the world the sleepers had once known was gone.

Spiralling upwards on mighty piebald wings, he surveyed the expanse of his Island. As expected, all was calm. If others had made it, he knew that with all likelihood their islands would be bigger than this one. As far as he was concerned, the twenty square miles of fields, ruins, and greenery his turtle shell held had been big enough to hold him. He knew that as the Many, he must have perched on the ruins of the buildings that had fallen into disrepair hundreds of time over the years. But because there'd been no need to pull the impressions together, they'd remained fragmented. Only now was he able to comprehend the extent to which things had changed.

The destruction that had been started by the earthquakes had been finished off by the passage of time. However, looking around him, he felt there was still sufficient shelter to be had for the sleepers when they awoke. One or two places, including the ancient church of St Nicholas, had even remained intact. On the whole, though, the ruins were being reclaimed by the land. Luckily, that hadn't been sleeping, as the Many he'd enjoyed its corn and blackberries over the years.

Hearing the sound of hooves, he lowered himself back to the ground, his clawed feet touching the slightly dry soil. How odd it was that it sounded hollow. Since the Downfall, everything had remained at a consistent temperature and humidity.

Boring, it had all been so boring. Watching the approaching Kitchi Animoosh, he realised how grateful he was for the light relief his companion had provided over the years. This Spirit of protection was ever aligned to the people but had protected him too. Used to these interludes between Ages, the little horse had often stopped him from flying, inveigling the Many to remain earth-bound and connected using games of deer knuckles, cards, and dice. Shifting and shaping to accommodate these diversions, they played to ease the endless present with buttons, bits of copper, and coins.

They'd been companions since time immemorial. Because Kitchi Animoosh understood the danger of the Many remaining fractured after a Downfall, he would try to ensure coherence and continuity by telling tales while they were gaming. While speaking of the passing of other Ages they'd witnessed, he'd draw on more recent incidents. Recounting the final day of the world that had just gone, he told of how, in his guise of a little coloured horse, he'd tried to keep Martha and her children safe. This had been important to him.

Much of it hadn't registered at the time. His own thinking was always fractured at the end of things. He did remember Martha, though. He'd met her once or twice, had helped her. Even as Drum Keeper, she hadn't recognised his true nature. Not surprising, really, since he was the power behind the word that shaped. He was all things and nothing, Trickster, Raven, Brave, and Craven, sweeping up new Ages in his wings of change. Providing impetus and movement, he could not be Named or held. Within him was all that had been and all that was to come. He was the bearer of many faces but holder of none.

This time, as if to herald the new dawn, his companion was outdoing himself, his pounding and singing joining up the memories of that last day in one magnificent story. Kitchi Animoosh danced a tale of the turtle shell coming out of the earth in Martha's back garden and how it had sunk back into it again at the end of things. His beating hooves shared how the coming of the eagle had signalled the moment of release for the other creatures the drum's hide had contained. How the wolves had gained dimension by tearing up and down the road in an excited chase.

Now, much more clearly than when he'd been the Many, the tales helped him tap into his own memories. In his mind's eye he saw the enormous snake rear up. Towering over Martha like a jade pillar, it had lowered its head towards her as if looking for a blessing. Then, after she'd duly administered the requested caress, it disappeared across the fields.

As the dance continued, he felt himself changing. Eventually, the god of many faces, he who held the eternal cycle of birth and destructions in his feathers, turned to his companion, clad in the aspect of the new dawn.

It brought Kitchi Animoosh to an abrupt halt. He only paused for a second, though, before he started smartly trotting towards a hedgerow that was a bit farther on. So it was that a glorious warrior and a little cob gelding made their way over to a soundly sleeping group of three.

Although the Johnstone family wasn't stirring yet, it was clear the time of waking was nearly upon them. A blue shiver ran through his cloak, and whether it was their sleeping faces or the story he'd just heard, something stirred in him. Then, he remembered the Joining. Each Downfall brought challenges with it; the bones of the earth were littered with his failures. But still it survived. For he was the eternal one who, although constantly shifting, had a fundamental nature that remained unchanged.

This time, though, during the Downfall, just as this island had become in and of itself, he'd been flooded with a vast sentience that had wanted to be contained within him. He shifted and shaped and writhed and turned, trying to escape. However, it was only when he flung the shimmering blueness back up and out, beyond the cloudy boundaries that were forming, that he'd found a measure of relief. Perturbed, he'd noticed that some of the glistening web remained, clinging on to the clouds. Thinking back, he realised that was the point he'd fractured into the Many. It came to him that he'd never escaped entirely. Now he was back as One, he could still feel it. As the Many, he'd been able to disregard its call, but no longer.

Pupilless eyes blazed into an iridescent blue.

"Yes, they are safe. I am looking at them now. All is well."

He detached just enough to reach into his wampum pouch and grab what was needed.

"Go now, leave me!" And with that, his outstretched hands flung blue beads into the air. But as they sparkled, little black birds detached themselves from the feathered mantle. These treats were just too good to miss, and as they swallowed, they took on hues of the boldest cyan. He sat down, cloak shimmering around him, its black and white tints now joined by bright blue feathers.

Whispering, "So be it, I accept," he closed his eyes. "In order to move forwards, I acknowledge this Joining."

His essence detached and with a great upwards motion started addressing the four spirits of direction sitting at the corners of the earth while a sitting form remained by the hedgerow. With a prayer of action and movement, he addressed the winds of the north, south, east, and west. Becoming their temporary focal point, he was welcomed in a rushing embrace that blew him apart. He shifted again. And as translucent wings fluttered, his eyes roved across a glistening expanse of silvery blue that stretched from horizon to horizon. His soul was in full flight; he could truly see again.

Nothing was as it had been. The new consciousness arose inside him, but he was not scared of it anymore and purposefully erased the old geographies it offered up for consideration. Then, a leviathan of the deep burst through the crystal surface. In an expression of joy, his earthbound cloak flew up from the hedgerow, becoming a murmuration. Thousands of little birds threw shapes into the morning sky. *Pleasure*, they thrummed; *the ocean's creatures have survived the Downfall.*

Within the sparkling droplets that had been pushed up and out into the sky, he noticed a strange luminescence. Momentarily giving the collective memories free rein, he brought to mind that someone, somewhere had released plastic-eating worms that had been genetically engineered for luminosity. Hopefully, in the time that had passed, they had done good work. The idea came to him too that metal-eating algae had existed. The recollections gave him hope that this Downfall had given way to a world that had been truly cleansed.

Back down again, and despite his warrior form, the kaleidoscopic images, chaos, and excitement of the Many attacked his newfound clarity. Very quickly, it became unbearable. Patting Great Dog on the nose, he shifted his consciousness into his raven forms, their mighty wings lifting into the sky in tandem. Land was close; it hadn't just been enthusiasm.

Through the white raven's eyes, he saw that the left of the island was nudging up against a huge landmass. As he flew over it, he delighted in the flora below him. Thousands upon thousands of oaks, ash, firs, and even squat yews were pushing up towards a welcoming sky. Recognising one of their own, they whispered a forest's welcome. Surveying his beloved trees, he decided it was time. The creators of the islands must awake. The Earth was ready to welcome them.

The hours wore on. As the white, he flew over silver steams and rushing waterfalls, rolling green hills, and granite cliffs, but his black raven presence encountered only water. Could it be that there was just one huge continent now, the rest submerged? Wonderful satellite images of the Earth had been unlocked by the new memories that were tempting him to fly ever farther to explore. But then fear washed over him. That stark disorientation of his final flight came back to him, how the loss of a magnetic north had signalled a pole reversal, which had disabled satellite eyes and ears.

The memory had made him anxious enough to will a return. Getting close to home he unified into piebald form. Momentarily distracted, he realised he'd very nearly missed something important. For there, washing up in the surf of this vast new continent, was another Turtle Island. If two of them had survived, others had too. He got back, and losing his yellowing finger bones in the thick brown and white mane, he shared his thoughts with his old companion.

"It's time my friend, we can rest. We've made it."

Not waiting for an answer, he pulled his feathered robe around him and lay down flat, legs akimbo, talons pointing up to the newly opened sky. Then, with his lowered hood concealing the protruding black beak almost entirely, he started snoring softly.

CHAPTER 15

Eve Tackles the Apple in a Different Way

She'd had a marvellous dream. They'd been together, all together. Dave had told her he loved her, and they'd all sung and danced in a place that contained the happiness of their yesterdays and the hope of their tomorrows. Right at this moment, though, something was using soft, flickering touches to get her attention. She sat up slowly, eyes opening onto an enormous snake curled in the grass beside her, a forked, darting tongue covering her face with serpentine kisses.

Strangely unafraid, she placed her hands on the huge triangular head to still its attentions. Looking around, she noticed that Henry had stirred, in the process managing to fling an arm across Emmy's face, which caused his sister to shift in response. Martha sat bolt upright. A large, moss-covered shape just a few metres in front of her had caught her attention. The structure's empty eyes peered out at her behind curtains of vine and ivy, while lying face down in the burgeoning undergrowth was what looked like a patio door. Focusing more closely, she spotted a number of shapes that were also blanketed in green, pointing to the fact that other buildings had undergone a similar transformation. She stiffly pushed herself to her feet, realising that she must have been lying in that position for some time.

As Martha went to explore the ruins, navigating bits of bricks and stone on the way, her companion uncoiled himself to silently slither after her. Placing her hands on the ivy, she recognised the steel patio-door frame beneath. Making her way into the interior, she saw moss, grass, and even small, primrose-like flowers vying for the light that was pouring through the huge hole above. There must have been some kind of ceiling there at one point. Overall, she realised she'd prefer to focus on the cerulean sky and the feeling of overwhelming joy it was engendering instead of what had once been.

Feeling hemmed in, she found herself moving back into the openness of the field. Her children were starting to move in earnest. Other than their waking, the only other sound to disturb the stillness of this new morning was light snoring. Looking over to find its source, she spotted a dusty, darkly cloaked figure. It was lying fast asleep under the large tree to the right of her, and two sizeable ravens, one black, one white, were perched directly above.

"Mum, why is there a huge snake at your feet?"

Emmy had opened her eyes onto a scene that made no sense at all. There were so many things she could have asked, but the question about her mum's new friend seemed to be the most pressing. Martha's serpentine companion was almost tripping her up in a desire to stay close. She saw her Mum shoot him a warning glance, which was accompanied by a couple of choice words muttered under her breath, "I'll be with you soon enough. Surely you can wait for just a little while longer?"

Emmy must have felt sufficiently reassured by this, because with cornflower eyes sparkling with joy, she ran over to give her mother an enormous hug,

"I feel really good, Mum. I haven't slept that well in ages. You look amazing, by the way. I like the no grey hair vibe!"

Martha also admired Emmy's hair, now the colour of ripened wheat and framing a face still flushed with the pink glow of healthy sleep.

Henry had also decided that the time for sleep was over and started walking purposefully towards his mother and sister. He hadn't, however, noticed the large snake that was lying quietly but very directly in his path. Promptly tripping over it, he found himself flying into his mother's open arms. He arrived there, acknowledging very vocally that he was now most definitely awake. More awake than he'd felt for a long time. His "Where are we?" was swiftly followed by "The only thing that makes any sense is you two being here," followed by a more thoughtful, "Are we supposed to be doing something?"

As she looked up at his almost-black hair flopping over huge, dark eyes, she had two thoughts. The first was that she most definitely felt she should be doing something but couldn't remember what. The second was that Henry had grown and filled out since she'd seen him last. Realising that she wasn't totally sure when that had been, she decided to turn her thoughts to the task in front of her instead. The problem was she wasn't sure of that either.

A scream rent the air, and, looking beyond Henry's shoulder, she saw the two ravens fluttering in agitation. A huge eagle had landed right above them, settling on one of the tree's lower branches. Lowering a four-metre wingspan, he threw his head back, putting his razored beak into sharp relief. Looking at him, Martha got the feeling he was trying to tell her something. She hoped Mr Sleepy over there might help her piece things together.

"Excuse me, sir...." In response, a couple of liver-spotted knuckles pulled a feathered hood even farther over a face that was old as the hills.

Moving the feathers away as best she could, she bent down and tried again.

"Excuse me, sir, could you tell us where we are? My name is Martha. These are my children, Emmy and Henry."

As if preempting a reply, strident howls broke the silence, and she saw a couple of brown-and-gold wolves haphazardly making their way towards her whilst chasing each other's tails. Their advent gave her request added impetus, and she tried again.

"Sir, I really must insist! Please open your eyes."

She shook him, gently at first, but with no reaction forthcoming, eventually manhandled the cloaked, befeathered figure more vehemently. In exasperation and not even adding in a "sir" this time, she finally shouted. "Will you just open your eyes!"

That did the trick. A bleary black eye emerged from under all those feathers to look reproachfully up at her.

"Madam, I have only just nodded off. You, who have been sleeping these long years, wake me now! Can't you just..."

"No, we can't," came Martha's firm rejoinder. "I need to understand what is going on, and I have a feeling you can help me."

With a dismissive wave at the birds he muttered, "You don't need me for that. Ask them."

Then, without any further explanation or as much as a by your leave, he pushed his hood back down and curled himself around tightly crossed arms. Martha was about to shake him again to ask him what he meant when he shot up.

"It's true, it's all as it should be. You told me to open my eyes. Now that I have, I can see things shaping themselves into what they ought to be."

Along with the others in this newly formed party of wolves, people, and birds, he turned to her expectantly. Apparently it was up to her to make things happen. She would have included the serpent, but it had turned its focus elsewhere, slithering into the grass to encircle them in a glistening perimeter of scales. From deep within her, a rhythm welled up. Unsure of what her response should be, she stamped tentatively on the ground. As her confidence grew, though, every beat she sounded increased the certainty of her task.

"Yes, Drum Keeper, you've got the idea."

She closed her eyes, and, not wholly unexpectedly, felt the weight of something heavy settling itself around her shoulders. Her hands come to rest on the smooth hide that was already vibrating in anticipation. With the fingertips of one hand, she started tapping out a rhythm, caressing the underside of the drum's shell with the other. She smiled in recognition. Dewe'igan, with most of the creatures now firmly fixed back in his hide, had come back to her. Along with him, so had her memories.

She felt something spatter the drum's hide. Looking up, she saw the eagle. Winging his way up into the sky, she realised he'd decided to leave his own indelible imprint, albeit in a different way to the others Dewe'igan held.

The man followed her gaze upwards, a pupilless, blue gaze flung into the middle distance. "We're not at sea anymore. Our island has attached itself."

Without her memories, she wouldn't have been able to make any sense of his words. And although some of it resonated, it was still difficult to follow his explanation while he was shifting from one form into another. Eventually, he settled into the glorious warrior she'd first met on the night of the Solstice. His stillness made it easier for her to focus, and when he told her that they were a small rural outcropping on the edge of a huge continent, she had enough presence of mind to say that it sounded "a bit like a wart on a nose."

She looked over to the children, now holding blazing crystals. The reassuring glow of the living blue light they carried coloured their surroundings. And all around them, the air that had been so silent started rustling, humming, and murmuring, the voices of creatures and people together, heralding the dawn of a new day.

* * *

Fatima was covered in orange blossoms. The scent was so strong, it was like she was drinking it. Trees burdened with dozens of fist-sized oranges, covered in slightly waxy, variegated leaves, hadn't been part of her childhood. Based on this sensory feast, she felt that they should have been. Then the blossom again, falling, tickling her nose. She tried so hard to hang on to the last wisp of dream before it dissipated but eventually realised she had to let it go to join the cobbled streets and other things that encapsulated what Baghdad once was.

However, the tickling feeling on her nose and cheek persisted. She opened her eyes to catch the edges of a deep indigo flutter. Maybe the dream wasn't completely gone yet. Pinching herself just to be sure, she had to acknowledge that she was truly awake. Her soft, dark gaze followed the gauzy wings back to a little clump of Nergis, set in the same sweet-smelling grass that was cushioning her. Watching the wonderful contrast between the deep blue butterfly and the orange trumpets it perched upon, she wondered whether it had been the creature's soft brushing against her skin that had woken her up.

Rubbing sleep-heavy eyes, she spied another blue. This one was blazing out from a stone, nearly hidden by the flowers the insect was sitting on. Its iridescence reminded her of that first lapis lazuli she'd discovered where her tiny baby had been buried.

Feeling the throb of the new crystal tugging at those memories, she tried to orient herself by looking around for further clues. Why was this garden filled with children? And her mother, just starting to stir under a little grove of trees, why was she here? The silver-backed wolf she'd flung her arm across regarded Fatima with solemn yellow eyes.

Talking of wolves, there was another one in the far corner. This one sported a golden-grey coat and was larger still. Along with its fellow and, unlike everything else in the garden, it was wide awake. There was a sleeping little boy curled up next to it. Adjusting her eyes to the shadows thrown by a large tree, which seemed to be covering an opening of some kind, Fatima noticed a tall woman standing a little farther back. Most definitely awake and very formidable, she was guarding them both. Thick grey plaits and a dark pelt slung over powerful shoulders contributed to her air of menace. Fatima felt relieved that this amazon was facing away from her, watching the space beyond the tree.

She turned her gaze upwards, watching the last of the red-fringed dawn tinge the blue sky. Morning was further confirmed by the dew-dampened grass under her feet. Moving towards the blue stone that was beckoning her from between the long green stems at the centre of the garden, she found herself standing next to a little pool of crystal-clear water. She slipped her hands in, watching them ripple and distort. It was icy cold. Enjoying the refreshing sting, she felt a sudden pain in her heel. Spinning her head around, she peered down at her foot. There, unwinding itself from her ankle, was a little green snake, its scales much the same colour as the leaves of the orange trees in her dream. Eyes momentarily mesmerised by the jewelled coils, Fatima watched as it stilled next to the blue stone that was casting a light right across the little pool, bright enough to touch the trees on the far side.

As she went to pick it up, a door in her mind started opening. The memories, though, were accompanied by an immediate hunger that threatened to displace the purpose today's new dawn had brought. A deep, slow beat thrummed through her, as if the very ground she stood on was trying to rouse itself. However, instead of focussing on the beauty of the moment and this sense of waking it had created, her mind turned back to the hunger that was becoming more urgent. Trying to think of something that might help, she was pricked by the memory of a fig tree. Sure enough, as she turned her attention to the opposite corner of the garden, she saw it.

She made her way over on winged feet, the flowers and children blocking her path, bending away from her like so many reeds. It came to her that Khalid had planted this particular tree. As she remembered this, the absence of his sister Tara, her little shadow, nudged at her. The closer she got to the tree, the larger it seemed and the less she was able to think of anything at all. It was odd; it had gone from being a couple of metres tall to stretching ten metres or more into the sky.

She was so mesmerised by the jade canopy that all other thoughts fled her mind. As she marvelled at the fat, trefoiled leaves capturing the fading pinks of the dawn, she caught sight of the abundance of rounded fruits. Some had already burst, sticky juices making them look like glistening purple chandeliers. She was so fixated by their promised succulence that she didn't notice the rosy, writhing coils slung around the trunk of the tree. Her mouth watered.

Finally, she was close enough to stretch a pale arm into the boughs. There, she had one. Swiftly, she sank her teeth into the fig, its juices spilling from the seeded pink interior into her mouth and down her chin. Having barely chewed her first mouthful, she reached for the next piece of fruit. Lost in the throes of gorging and anticipation of the next bite, she didn't notice the faded stone slipping from her grasp to fall to the ground. As she ate, the gleaming coils insinuated themselves above and around her, enveloping not only the trunk but also spreading onto the branches that held the fruits, its great length teasing her to take more and more.

"Fatima, Fatima, can I have one too?"

She was so engrossed in her feasting that she'd failed to notice Tara coming to stand next to her. Holding her protector's dulled stone in one hand and the shining star of her own in the other, the nine-year-old asked again. "Fatima, I'm hungry. Could you pick me one too? I can't reach."

It started to register with Fatima that she was no longer alone. Although she knew something had been asked of her, it was so hard to focus on anything other than the immediate lure of the delicious fruit. However, the thrumming of the earth got stronger, and she noticed she was feeling uncomfortably sticky and that the old shift she was wearing was stained with juice. Then the tug at her sleeve came again. She realised that despite feeling full, that sense of empty hunger had not yet been stilled.

"Fatima, I'm frightened. The tree is overshadowing the garden, and it's still getting bigger. Please, Fatima. I'd like some too."

The crystals blazed and in doing so cut through the coils that had bound Fatima, replacing them with two little arms that wound themselves about her waist instead. Partway to plucking the next piece of fruit, Fatima noticed that those rosy scales had turned dark red, and instead of glistening with dew and juice, the fruits were now shrouded in a mist of blood. The weight of the world crashed into an arm that only moments ago had been furiously stripping the branches of figs. Pushing past the weight and the accompanying fatigue, Fatima continued to reach upwards. She endured long enough to dislodge a fat fruit with one final jolt and turned to Tara. "Here, darling. I'm sorry it took so long. Have this one."

As the little girl bit into the proffered fruit, the tree's vast expanse shrank back down to a more comfortable size.

Now fully emerging from the spell that had held her, Fatima noticed that many of the other children who were standing with Tara were also holding their own crystals aloft. She didn't rest until they were all happily munching on a soft fruit, their little faces lit with joy. Even the adults who were capable of picking their own figs received their first from her own hand.

Tara spoke up again, this time on everyone's behalf. "Fatima, these are wonderful. Thank you for letting us have some too."

Dropping her voice, she went on. "You frightened me. I knew it was you, but for a moment it didn't look like you. I kept on calling, but there was black smoke all around you and I couldn't get in. I had to try so hard to remember you like you were in my dream and before. But then the dragon that was trying to eat you disappeared, and you shrank back into yourself. The tree got smaller too."

Fatima knelt down, casting around for her crystal. From this angle, the detritus of her wild feast was more obvious. She was horrified at how it littered the ground. Luckily, some of the creatures of the garden had already started making off with it, and she spied the blue stone. She looked up to see Tara licking her lips to catch the last of the juice, and then the little girl turned her animated expression on Fatima.

"That was lovely. I'm not thirsty anymore either, and I can't even remember what it was like to feel hungry!"

Watching the delight of the child before her, Fatima revelled in the fact that she was also feeling better. That fuzzy, sleepy feeling had left her, and her memories were back.

She noticed that her crystal had started pulsing again. Tara and some of the others were also regarding their stones with bewilderment. How to share what had just happened? But she had to try. Purposefully shifting the loose strands of dark hair that had drifted across her face, Fatima rose from her knees and started speaking.

"I'm not sure what that was. But I think when we defeated Zuhak and built an Ark to keep us safe, we were given the ability to create, accessing the dust of creation through our crystals. Remember little Shwan and his butterflies from before? They are very real here and now; one of them even woke me up."

Squeezing Tara's hand, she continued. "Then, when I started remembering what had happened and all that was needed, it's possible that I was just a little frightened. So, to take my mind off my fear, I started feeling hungry. However, all that did was to change my focus from keeping you all safe to thinking I needed something now and just for me."

She surveyed the empty skins on the ground beneath her in shame. How to convey that she had used this fledgling power for something that served only her?

"I didn't mean to cause harm by not waiting until we were together, but I did. I should have waited for you and your crystals to awake. They are the tools that bind us, you see, and being connected to each other turns us into a new creation. As creators, we can harness a world we can't see or touch, but that is as real as the seeds we have just eaten. But I abused my new gift."

Remembering how close her folly had come to destroying her, she shook her head.

"That's why the more I thought about how much I wanted the figs, the more the idea grew. I am a creator, as are you, but because I focussed on my own needs, I wasn't able to contain what I was creating. That's how the tree got large enough to overwhelm me and our garden. Because Tara and all of you called me back, though, I was able to use my gift to feed all of us. Together, we put things right, and everything returned to the size it was meant to be."

Gesturing at the tree behind her she added, "Look at it now. It's not scary, is it?"

She watched everyone nodding. They had seen what had happened, how big the tree had got. It helped them understand but she could tell they were still puzzled. She needed to relate back to something else they had shared.

"Just one last thing before we start on our task. Do you remember me saying that if bits of Zuhak survived they would give us stature and courage? Well, I think we've just learned a very important lesson for the new world we are creating."

Fatima pointed at the ground. Restored to the right size, the serpents were basking peacefully on the ridges of a large, dark shell, enjoying the sunshine.

"Look at the snakes now; they are beautiful, shining things returned to their rightful place. This is their true nature. By using my new powers to gratify immediate needs, I distorted them into beings of pain and greed. We are creators. The energy of the universe is at our fingertips, but we must learn to use it responsibly. What just happened is a foretaste of what will happen if we misuse our powers. If we are to create a world we can all share in, we must remember that knowledge is a wonderful thing. However, it must be used for the good of all or not at all."

Having eaten and understood the basics of what Fatima had shared, the children took out the tablets they'd kept with them. As they had done so many times before, their crystals powered them up, and they felt the thrum of connection, not just with each other but also with a much wider world.

Tara looked into hers and saw a tanned, dirty Khalid grinning and waving at her. Beyond him was a mountain range, the lower slopes of which held flocks of goats and sheep that were contentedly munching at grass so rich, she could almost smell it.

Sitting next to her, Shwan was looking over her shoulder.

"That's the first step. I can feel more, though, just here." He tapped his head. "Khalid has made things. I know that I am supposed to be making things too. It's even telling me how, but I can't get beyond the memories of the butterflies."

As he spoke, a tiny purple one fluttered out of his mouth.

"I will show you, children."

A much deeper voice spoke, the power of ages ringing out across the garden. The fur-clad woman had the ability to weave new life even from that which had been totally destroyed. As she'd done so often before, she started singing the bones of the Earth into life.

This time, though, she was providing a way for the children to follow her. The dust of ages and the pixels of all the memories of the world that had once been knitted into one. Just like the figs on the trees, they were all ripe for the plucking, looking to be reawakened by the innocent longing of the children to make life anew.

Hearing the song of the People, imprinted on the air around her, she sang to the buffalo, retrieving the ancient herds from the pixelated ocean into which their stories had sunk. Next, the song wove the dust of creation around the Inuit memories, creating polar bears, caribou, and arctic foxes. These were closely followed by the Tuareg's oryx and the lions, giraffes, and porcupines of the San Bushmen. The children knew that these creatures were not necessarily just appearing here. They were being born into the physical land of those who had originally captured their essence; wherever they may have come to rest in this new world. And from a place that had once been a world apart, even bats started winging their leathery way from their original Brazilian rainforest home into the endless skies.

With each voice that joined hers, she gained power. Slowly, the children understood that they didn't need the tablets; the song of creation was all around them. And then, as they followed the goddess out, past the Moringa tree through the gap in the wall, they realised that they were at the base of a gigantic edifice, their garden having come to rest on the bottom tier of a structure that reached miles into the sky. As they climbed down roughly hewn steps, most couldn't resist throwing a swift glance over their shoulders. They were met by the astonishing sight of over-spilling vines and waterfalls, each level above them offering hints of new wonders. With the scent of jasmine in their noses and the roar of lions ringing in their ears, they made their way onto a lightly undulating grass prairie, multicoloured grasses stretching before them as far as the eye could see.

So immersed were they in the excitement of this new journey and the creatures that emerged from the air to flutter, jump, gallop, and lope in and around their little throng that they failed to notice the scream of a solitary eagle flying high above them. The Bone Woman's companion, however, did notice and made sure to keep the dance of his mistress aligned to its flight.

And as they walked, she sang.
"Come to me all you
Who are lost and alone,
I am She, made of bone
I will call you home.
I shake the desert floor,

I shake up time and tones
Come to me my children,
I will bring you home."
They joined in, knowing that they were finally finding a way home, not just for them, but for a world that had been so very badly lost.

* * *

Earlier in the day, Martha had been very proud of Henry. In preparation for this afternoon's expedition, she'd watched him practise riding across the fields on a horse that scared him. Now, though, seeing him and Emmy on Dennis riding into the forest, with only a flock of birds and two ravens for company, she was filled with fear.

She hadn't needed the one she secretly thought of as Raven to tell her it was time, though. She'd felt it too. He'd eventually managed to stop her tears by telling her about a magnificent feast that was only a few days hence. The caveat was that they needed to get moving within the day. It wouldn't do to fall too far behind. They spent the rest of that afternoon getting the other groups of awakened sleepers to pass the message on.

When she questioned him about it, he told her he had it on good authority that a Great Gathering was happening not too far away. Oddly, as she looked into the black eyes of the old codger who was valiantly attempting to make her feel better; she realised he was growing on her, although she definitely preferred his young warrior aspect. Since he'd got past his earlier grumpiness and the shape-shifting, she felt that, with a bit of work, he might even prove to be attractive. She would need to persuade him to get rid of that bedraggled cloak, though.

* * *

Mercy and Chipo had been working hard. They knew that visitors would shortly be arriving from all sides. In the time before, the valley had been filled with the memories and spirits of dancers. Now it needed to host actual people, coming from all those islands close enough to reach here within a couple of days of walking. Mercy so hoped that some of the other Ghost Dancers would be among the thousands they were expecting. Although the time of the Ghost Dance had passed, as she watched the abundance of birds and animals that were once again sliding and slithering, burrowing, and flying through this home of her heart, she realised that along with her, many of the Dancers had offered her song to awaken the creatures of their homelands. It would be wonderful to celebrate the spreading of these melodies and words, held together by beats of longing that had once echoed through each of them so strongly.

Although the Msasa tree had grown huge during the years all had slept, it still shook as Hungry landed. Throwing his head back with that piercing scream of his, the eagle dropped a white stone at Mercy's feet.

"Oh, Hungry, it's about time! I've been waiting for that. A stone taken from the children's garden will make it so much easier for us to play our part in the Awakening."

Hearing the commotion, Chipo came out, shaking her head grumpily. "Why do you always have to make such a racket, eh Hungry?"

However, as she spotted the stone, she came to an abrupt halt. "This will allow us to continue with the task of turning our valley into what it needs to be."

Kneeling before it, they did as their ancestor's song dictated. First, they pointed, ordering water to spring forth. Then, as water started spilling from the stone, they asked the soil to soften, causing the river to flow towards them. As the waters joined, an oversized Hungry landed in front of them. Flinging an exultant shout into the air, Chipo jumped onto his back and pulled Mercy up with her.

A beautiful tone started coming from the stone. And as they rose into the glorious sky, they noticed that all the birds of the air that had once been in the valley of dreams and spirit had come back to join Hungry's aerial dance. The white mass of the stone got bigger and bigger, growing way beyond the pool to finally reach a size that filled the valley, the home of their dreams and the birthplace of the new age.

As it grew, animals climbed from the crevices, clawing and plunging, pawing and clattering until they reached the top of the cliff along with the stone. As they spilled into the surrounding forest and grasslands, the stone stopped growing. Chameleon-like, it took on the nature of the space it had filled, part stone-hewn, part tree-bedecked, and part grass-blanketed. In the middle of it was the bubbling spring that had marked the start of its transformation. By joining with the river, it had started making its way through virgin territory. Herds of elephants sprayed themselves in delight, great tusks clashing as they explored this new watering hole. The black and yellow-spotted necks of giraffes were bending over the cooling oasis, whilst herds of zebras and gazelles had decided to follow the river's course onwards, thundering into the distance with great leaps of excitement.

Eventually, Hungry set them down. Landing just by the Msasa tree, which, along with the huts, had elevated itself to this new ground level, he shrank back down to size. In this time of change, though, he wanted to leave them in no doubt that he, Hungry the fish eagle, was living up to his name. So, a couple of minutes later, he deposited a flapping, silver-scaled carp in front of them. Then, with a great scream of triumph, he flung himself back into the air, winging his way up into the cloudless sky once more.

Chipo and Mercy threw themselves into each other's arms. The relief of what they'd just achieved was too great to bear on their own.

"Amai, you know this is it, don't you?" Mercy said. "This will be the time that all speak of as the new beginning, the new source that has been created."

She walked over to the gloriously cold water that poured through and over the white rock.

"In our old world, so many Ages fell to devastations and left barely a clue. Thriving civilisations such as Atlantis, Lemuria, Lyonesse — gone forever. In this downfall, though much was lost, we were able to save more. We don't need to unpick random clues such as the pyramids, the golden ratio, or the submerged land bridge to Sri Lanka to make sense of what might have been. We have been left everything, the dust of creation drawn from a dimension we sacrificed to serve us now."

She stood up, hands raised above her, her plain cotton shift swirling as she spun the droplets of crystal water into the air.

"We have been brought to this glorious morning and been given a way to protect this new world. As we create we know are exchanging moments of our life, understanding that this barter extends way beyond us, to all life on Earth."

Chipo looked at the vision of her daughter before her. Sparkling, vital life was emanating from every fibre of her being.

"Tsitsi, dear one. We will remember what has gone and build upon this hard-won dawn. I can feel the memories of what was all around us, swirling in the air and the dust. Knowledge will come to us as we are ready for it, and we will rebuild. However, we must have faith in each other and remember above all that we are allowed to rewrite the past in the pen of this new age. All that has gone will be remembered, but we must look forwards also."

They embraced once more, and spying a small turtle shell lying just at the edge of the source, filled it with earth and a couple of pretty bits and pieces, including flowers and seeds they saw scattered around.

Never questioning how it had come to be there in the first place, they placed it in just the right spot as they watched it float down the new river. To Chipo this was a fitting tribute in the time of renewal. She was so lost in thought that it took her a moment to notice what Mercy had seen immediately. They'd been joined by two young people with shining eyes who'd ridden up on exhausted steeds. Dismounting, they declared themselves ready to do what must be done.

That was the start of the influx. Despite a general sense of exhaustion, excitement overcame all, and they started readying things immediately. Although excited, Chipo was tired most of the time and therefore only too happy to delegate to Mercy She enjoyed watching how her daughter roped in the others. Over the next couple of days, the great plain filled with people and animals, the noise, and even the smell, a welcome relief from the silence that all had experienced in the years of the long sleep.

* * *

Martha loved watching the reunions; through them she often recognised some of the voices from ASafeSpace. One family, for example, had found shelter on different islands. Somehow, though, after thinking they'd lost each other forever, the network of crystals managed to bring them back together again. Bearing utensils Chipo had created, Martha had accompanied the older woman to welcome the little group. She had watched Chipo teaching people how to "think" wood after listening to their stories. Together then, they would form the many stones that littered the planes into shapes that could be used. On this particular visit, Grandmother Florence had been particularly animated. And as the two old ladies chatted, it emerged that not only had she found a daughter and three grandchildren she didn't know she had, but she and her old friend Harry were actually considering whether to tie the knot. As the days passed, it became clear that they were just the first of many who'd come together to form a new kind of partnership.

As Drum Keeper, Martha realised that by waking the stone, Mercy and Chipo had sent forth healing, and, as people poured to the place of gathering, they were able to gauge its marvellous effects. Those who had been old and infirm were able to complete their renewal in the spring of living water, and although nothing could be done about age, withered limbs and crooked backs were made whole again.

She also welcomed the relationships between beings from the World of Spirit and men. Who was to say who was what in this new age? In her own case, her constant companion was the man with the feathered mantle and twinkling eyes of indeterminate colour. Although there were no real romantic inclinations, they were certainly fond of each other. But with others it wasn't just drumming in the air. Certainly, the Horned Man and his lady would be celebrating more than just a renewal of the land at the Great Feast.

Finally, she was delighted when a handsome man in his forties of Southeast Asian descent came up to her. Accompanied by his son, he asked whether she had seen his mother. The crystals had given her a sixth sense about this, but even before he mentioned her name, she knew that this pair must be Bagus and John, Anjani's son and grandson. She surmised that their island had just held the two of them, since they were not only alone but also seemed disinclined to change this state of affairs. Although she'd been sad to share that Anjani was no longer tangibly here, Mercy was pleased that she'd been able to tell them that her sacrifice was at the heart of what was happening now.

As she told Anjani's story, she very much hoped the fellow Ghost Dancer was not too far away. And when Bagus shared how much his mother's last email had meant to him, this vague hope turned into a fervent prayer. Mercy had tears in her eyes when he told her that these final words of love had given him the strength to survive. As the days wore on, they both seemed to thaw, the air of distance they'd exuded fading and eventually disappearing entirely, with the result that they started to meet new people. A particular friendship with three lost young men started blossoming, with them all eventually becoming part of a new family unit. Unconvinced that they had not arrived in Jannah, their ephemeral idea of an Islamic paradise, these three had initially been even more remote than Bagus and John. However, by helping them to understand what it took to live in this new world, the new relationship made it easier for them all to assimilate.

* * *

The morning of the great feast dawned. Her Raven friend wasn't with her, and although his constant companionship over the last few days had started to grate a little, Martha realised she missed him. In fact, the more time she spent with him, the more comforting his uncanny familiarity had become. Putting this puzzle to the back of her mind for now, she pulled Dewe'igan to her and with the black and white ravens cawing on her shoulders drummed out a welcome to the new day.

Dewe'igan's magic reached across the thousands of people that were stretched up and down the acres it took to hold them. Martha had spoken to enough of them to know that most wanted to leave soon after the Great Gathering, which meant that luckily, this place would not to have to bear the burden of overpopulation for too long. It was clear, though, that although they were enjoying the current conviviality, most of her fellow travellers were hungry to get back to create a home for their families in this new world. It was also generally understood that the personal bonds that had been forged over the past couple of days were much stronger than any that might eventually be created through the crystals.

The People had started learning the lessons this world had to offer together, and, along with Martha and the children, believed that this shared understanding of each other's needs and cultures would serve to keep them aligned, even as they moved on into new homelands and new futures.

* * *

In the twinkling darkness of the early evening, Chipo was among the multitudes listening to Martha's song in virtual silence. She was in prime position in front of the enormous fire though and was therefore able to watch it dance in response to Dewe'igan's booming as he spread the force of Sh'ler's Song across the countryside. It seemed as if the fire jinni herself was revelling in the story she'd framed as a myriad of orange crackles and sparks were shooting into the sky from this main fire, but also from the many others that were strewn up the hillsides. Chipo wondered whether Fatima understood that her aunt had fully reclaimed her element.

Thinking of old friends and their former circle of Ghost Dancers caused her to cast her mind back to a conversation she'd had earlier that day with a tearful Martha. The Drum Keeper had shared what her final song of the evening was to be. As she did, Chipo understood that she herself was being called on to complete one last task. She knew that despite not grasping all the opportunities she'd been given, her life had on the whole been a good one. She also understood, though, that tonight the last of these opportunities was coming her way. Casting a regretful glance at the regal face of her daughter wreathed in the warm glow of the living flames, she also knew that this opportunity was one she wouldn't be passing by.

The Song of Release sounded across the plains, and the old lady watched the Raven moving over to embrace the Drum Keeper, kissing her with a fervency that made even Chipo's old blood race. Glistening feathers settling again, he stood aside, letting Martha complete the final lines.

"Go in Truth — as the hope of what is to come
Go in Peace — you have fulfilled all
Go in Love — I release you."

As the last word rang out, he bent his head to hers again. Chipo was close enough to make out the whisper of his final words.

"Your instincts were right, of course. You do know me, and I am fond of you."

His strange eyes flickered through a mesmerising set of patterns, flaring into a bright blue before settling into a final black.

"Before all things, though, I must follow my nature. Although I am happy to hoard the ghost of your love, I will always be waiting for new excitement to come my way. Crumbs of the collective memories Dave held became part of me as the Downfall happened, and even now, I can feel the new universe welcoming the change and chaos they hold. I gave them wings."

His great cloak eclipsed the fire's light, living feathers rising up past his shoulders as if to bear testament to his next words. They came again, louder and more sonorous now.

"Change is in my bones, ever shifting, ever moving. Your song of release is also a song of creation. It will continue to sing on its own, and so I am freed."

As if in response to an unspoken question, he pressed another kiss onto her forehead and uttered his final words. "I promise you, you and Dave will welcome a new dawn together, even beyond this place. A love like yours will never fade entirely."

With that he turned on his heel, moving past the crowded glow of the fire. As he made his way into the welcoming night, he threw "Are you coming?" over his shoulder. Hearing the call of his friend, Dennis snorted softly. He was staying here. His place was with Emmy, his loyalty forever with the People.

Someone, however, did heed the call. Whispering that it was time for her to go, Chipo pressed her daughter's hand softly. She so wanted to see what this new world had to offer. And with an alacrity that belied her age, she joined him under the shadows of the great trees on the gentle westward slope.

Many eyes followed them into the darkness of the forest's embrace. However, only a few noticed two great birds emerging through the canopy a short time later. One, newly shaped, was leaving behind an old, battered shell to wing her way upwards into a night sky filled with promise. And so, ushered onwards by the warm updrafts, the two adventurers flew off to discover all that this world and the next one had to offer.

Epilogue

The old woman sat under the Msasa tree. Her eyes had been lightly closed against the sun's rays for most of the afternoon. Noticing that it had got a little cooler, however, her wrinkles shifted slightly to lift an eyelid. Yes, it was as she suspected, this day also was drawing to a close. She did so enjoy these lazy warm afternoons, and as she had proven again today, often lost track of time. Sitting out here seemed to soothe her aching bones and the warm caress of the sun on her face reminded her of ... well, never mind. That was long ago.

Peering up through the spread of the mighty tree's branches, she thought how much she enjoyed the fact that no matter how often she looked up through its broad, slightly flattened canopy, she still felt a little frisson of delight. Whether the leaves were coloured with the variegated greeny-red of spring or the rust of the deep summer flush, their beauty never failed to move her. She noticed that today they'd just started to show green again. One season was drawing to an end and another was beginning. Why was it that as one got older, time sped up? The last time the foliage had been green only seemed like yesterday, and it hadn't been that long ago that the conical huts of the valley were the only buildings in its vicinity.

Now look at it. Named Anjon many years ago, the bustling settlement had spread across the plains and down the western slopes. It's busyness, though, didn't disturb her. She liked resting here, in this particular spot; it was at the heart of things. Not only was this tree right in the middle of the old settlement, but the spring of the great river was also close. People were always coming past, since just like her, many liked to gaze upon the turtle shells. Most settlements kept their original ones as objects of veneration, but some chose to bring theirs here so they could be part of the Ceremony of Renewal. Once a year, in memory of how the shells had saved them from the Devastation, a few would be filled with soil and seeds and placed at just the right point to ensure that their journey downstream was successful. They would always come back, though. Everyone knew that the turtle shells were sacred and that here, at the Source, was where they belonged.

Feeling the chill of the early evening, she realised that it was at times like this that she missed old friends. Having said that, eyeing the children who had arrayed themselves in front of her, she'd made plenty of new ones too. She was looking for one in particular, and, as ever, didn't need to look very far. Her great-grandson Asher was always the ringleader in these gatherings and was therefore generally to be found right at the front. She must have fallen asleep again, since she hadn't noticed them congregating. However, experience had taught her what was coming next. Smiling softly to herself, she realised she didn't really mind, and closing her eyes, she waited for the game to begin.

"Koomis, Koomis."

As ever, four-year-old Asher signalled the start of the game they played by calling her name. She closed her eyes more tightly in response. This was how they got to the next bit, and that part was her favourite.

Sure enough, she felt a trusting little hand stroking her wrinkled cheek. Next, he clambered onto her knee, his cherub's face reaching upwards to kiss her paper-thin eyelids.

"Can we have a story? Please!"

It was his "please" that always did for her, and hearing it echoed by fifteen or so others that had come with Asher to hear the famous old Storyteller speak, she opened her eyes.

Looking for inspiration around her choice of story, she surveyed her surroundings. One of the things she always noticed was how the styles of the dwelling places had changed. The oldest ones, built nearest the water and the conical huts, were shaped like houses from the old world. But as Anjon spread outwards, the nature of the social evolution over the last five decades became evident. First, everyone had wanted to hang on to what they knew. All who had come here were able to shape and create, and if one knew the vague rudiments of building, making something that was similar to former dwellings wasn't that difficult. That style, however, didn't prove to be particularly practical in this new world. So, slowly, other kinds of dwellings were built. Some were shaped as part of the huge trees of the forests, others to sit within the soft hills of the plains.

It also took some time for people to adapt to the new form of power. It was so very different to electricity and the feats of engineering and communications structures that had shaped the old world. Here, all things could be created. However, Fatima's Law, firmly supported by the People and other ancient tribes, allowed the matriarch to keep a tight grip on what should and shouldn't be shaped in this new world. The Storytellers, which had once included her and were now led by Emmy, travelled across the continent to make sure people understood what had happened in the past and why it was so important to keep to these laws. The result was that despite the hundreds of thousands who lived and worked in Anjon, the river still ran clean, the forests still stood, and the many different animals still felt safe enough to come to the water to drink. Wouldn't it be good to share how Fatima's Law came about?

Her reverie was interrupted. This bit of the game had obviously gone on too long for one impatient little four-year-old. As she looked into the cheeky eyes of Henry's grandson, she saw something that reminded her of the little boy the formidable chief had once been.

"Koomis, Koomis, can you sing Sh'ler's Song? And with Dewe'igan too?"

Now that she wasn't expecting. Sh'ler's Song was considered sacred, something for high days and holidays. It was even rarer for her to bring Dewe'igan out, as Emmy had become Drum Keeper some time ago and jealously guarded her charge.

She looked over at Asher again and noticed that his request had made the other children fall silent. They liked him being pushy; it made things happen, but even they sensed that he might have gone too far this time.

If only she wasn't so tired! Feeling for the leather thong that hung loosely under the creamy calico of her cotton tunic, she realised how much she would have given for her crystal to come to life again. She was sure she would have had the energy to call Dewe'igan if it had. However, the crystals, including hers, had been silent for many years. There was no real need for them anymore. People were shaping new ways to connect, and the abilities they'd acquired in this new age had made them adept at turning air and dust into matter. They wanted for nothing. This, in turn, meant that most were as happy as they made up their minds to be. Because it was impossible to shape one of these stones, the majority of them were worn as pretty ornaments. Some had been set in utensils, or even tools, with people believing their presence would make the shaping better.

Despite knowing it was impossible, as she held her blue stone a warm feeling seemed to emanate from it, spreading to her hand and running through her whole being. This time it wasn't just Asher who shouted; the others joined in as well.

"Koomis, your crystal; it's shining with a blue light!"

The children's voices must have sounded loudly as more people came to join them.

Although she was slightly taken aback, Martha remained calm. All these people reminded her of the old days. She had loved roving from one settlement to another, telling stories that needed to be remembered. Welcoming the old, reassuring thrum of the crystal, she clasped it more firmly, not frightened at all of the light that even she could see blazing forth. She decided it was a sign. So, framing the command for the mighty drum in her head, she called him, and he came.

Then, with the old familiar strap around her neck and the hard, ridged shell resting on her knees, she started drumming softly.

"In the Age of the Downfall
The signs were read
Linking Watchers to Seekers
Else all would be dead."

Emmy would be so cross. Although not sure, she suspected that her daughter was somewhere on the other side of this great continent, borne there by her beloved and very long-lived Dennis. Martha suspected she would be using Dewe'igan to accompany her telling and singing. No matter, it was nice to know that she, Martha, had precedence still. Her song would be over soon enough, and then he could return.

As she drummed, she closed her eyes. So much had happened, so very much. It was important that these children knew, truly understood, how lucky they were. They must remember the stories and so be able to pass them onwards from one generation to the next.

"Then there was one who straddled the planes
The place of the spirit, the paths of the pain,
Lokozho binding all into one
His quantum existence, a digital one."

It seemed as though Emmy wasn't that far away after all. Too tired to open her eyes, Martha sensed that she had come to sit in front of her, and, by placing her hands around the great shell, was helping her mother bear some of the weight.

As she drummed, she was pleased to see that some of her old friends had come along to listen too. It was like that time in Segara Anak; Chipo and Mercy, Badenan, the Bone Woman, the wolves and — wait, those golden scales, was that Anjani!? Her drumming almost faltered as she gulped down an exclamation of joy. It had been so long. From the crowd a new figure emerged, one whose eyes blazed with love and who made her heart sing with joy. He had waited. She noticed him beckoning. Despite this, and although the song was but a whisper and Dewe'igan's voice barely a breath on the wind, she sang on. She so wanted to finish things.

"All beings together, we as gods straddle worlds
While knowledge and wisdom in love is unfurled
We will work as one people as the next age unfolds
And myths are reshaped as our story is told."

Dave came over to her. He was as young as the day she had first met him and as bright as the morning star. Taking her by the hand, he told her to rise. She was his beautiful one, and it was time to come away.

So she did.

Hearing the drum go completely silent, Emmy kissed her mother softly and finished the song.

"Last was the word, we were called by the drum
To give up ourselves and so become one."

Extras

A. DRAMATIS PERSONAE

Baba John – Sadhu priest age 103. The Watcher, Gangotri, India

The Ghost Dancers and their Names
Martha – Convenor and Drum Keeper
Fatima – Dugdhav, the Shining One
Badenan – Raksha, Wolf Mother
Mercy – Sword Bringer
Chipo – Mbuya Hungwe, Mother of the Eagle Clan
Anjani – Omazaandamo, the Black Snake

Split characters
Charlotte Friday – Martha's Koomis, great-grandmother, (see World of Spirit). She is Martha's guide to the spirit world and introduces her to Dewe'igan the Drum
Lokozho (Dave is named by Martha) – Messenger spirit and Seeker
Shl'er – Fire jinni (Spirit) and sister to Badenan, aunt to Fatima

Iraq
Fatima – Abused young wife (Ghost Dancer)
Badenan – Fatima's mother (Dê), sister to Shl'er (Ghost Dancer)
Shl'er – Older sister to Badenan (also Daughter of Fire)
Hassan – Fatima's former tutor, now brutal husband

Sana – Iraqi lawyer
Duraid – friend and shopkeeper
Tara – daughter of shop assistant Samar, sister to Khalid, age 6 at start
Khalid – son of shop assistant Samar, brother to Tara, age 9 at start
Dana – illiterate girl in Fatima's Garden
Hadeel – a child from Fatima's garden, companion to Khalid
Shwan – a boy from Fatima's garden
Samar – mother to Tara and Khalid
Mrs Ahmed – one of Badenan's sewing clients
Saddam Hussein – Iraqi dictator until 2003, leader of the Ba'ath party
Ali Majid – Saddam's cousin, in charge of the north and atrocities committed against Kurds in the eighties and nineties
Farah – Fatima's doll

Zimbabwe

Mercy (Tsitsi) – massage therapist and entrepreneur (Ghost Dancer)
Chipo (Amai) – Mercy's mother (Ghost Dancer)
Hungry – a Fish Eagle (Hungwe is the Shona term)
Sula – Tower Hotel manager
Rudo – Next-door neighbour, helps with Chipo
Bertha – Mercy's friend
Xoliso Msebele – Chipo's husband and Mercy's father (deceased)
Anaishe – Chipo's Mother, a n'ganga (witch doctor) of renown, hence title Svriko; she who walks with spirits (deceased)
Headman Nemanwa – A respected leader in the Masvingo province in Anaishe's time
Charwe Hwata – More commonly known by the honorific Mbuya Nehanda, 19th century n'ganga (witch doctor) and freedom fighter who rallied a nation against the English. Ancestress to Mercy and Chipo (historical hero)
Chief Mugabe – 19th century leader of the Shona people (historical hero)
As himself: Robert Mugabe – Leader of Zanu Piaf and longstanding Zimbabwean dictator

Indonesia

Anjani Margono – One of Asia's wealthiest women. Chair of INP conglomerate (Ghost Dancer)

Indira – Anjani's assistant
Bagus – sometimes known as Mohammad, Anjani's son
John – Anjani's grandson
Mathew Margono – Chinese Indonesian financier, Anjani's controlling husband (deceased)
Wayan Pedjeng – Family man, living in Mataram; Bagus's father
Devi Hafid – Metro TV Journalist
Jan – Anjani's head of security
As themselves....
Minister Efendi – non-Muslim Minister of Finance, attacked for his faith by Islamists in Indonesia
Kartini – An early Indonesian women's rights champion
Handry Satriago – GE's CEO
John Riady – Lippo's CEO
President Suharto – former Indonesian president
Agnes Monica – Indonesian singer
Elvy Sukaesih and Rhoma Irama – King and Queen of the Dangdut Dance

North America
Charlotte Friday – Former Anishnaabe Drum Keeper and Martha's great-grandmother (deceased)
Brigid – Down-and-out alcoholic, living rough in New York
As themselves:
Joe Friday – Charlotte's Twin (deceased)
Chief Dan George – performer, poet, champion of First Nations People, Salish Tribe (Canada, historical hero)

UK
Martha – overweight, forty-five-year-old, debt-ridden ex-journalist now turned content creator for a marketing agency (Drum Keeper)
Emmy – Martha's anorexic daughter
Henry – Martha's gamer son
Dave Johnstone – Martha's husband (deceased)
Peter – Martha's estranged older brother. Financial technology specialist working for CHL
Ada – Martha's grandmother (deceased)

Dorothy – Martha's mother (deceased)
Dennis the Horse
Sarah-Jane (SJ) – Martha's boss
Kate – Martha's younger colleague
Mark – Owner of William and Jones (WJ), Martha's employer
Mr McAtamney – Ex shopkeeper and founder of "the Youth Club" in loyalist Belfast
Janet Green – 12-year-old Northern Irish girl
Jeannie – Janet's friend, also visits the Youth Club
Connor Green – Janet's brother
Susan Green – Older sister to Janet
Doreen Green – Janet's mother
Lilian – Older lady, resident in nursing's home Doreen and Susan work in
Old Harry – Lilian's friend
Handsome Henry – Kate's boyfriend
Paul – Smarmy assistant in Martha's bank
Rev Timmins – Conductor of funeral services related to the Johnstone family
Ali Mustafa – British student turned ISIS IT specialist

Afghanistan
Fahima Wali – Inmate of Badam Bagh prison in Kabul

Digital World
Digital Dave/Lokozho – Martha's dead husband

World of Spirit and Legend
All-Mother – Charlotte/Koomis is the physical manifestation of one of her aspects.
The God of Many Faces – the Many, Raven, trickster Loki, spirit of change and resurrection drawn from myths and legends across the world
Hungry – (Hungwe Shona term) Fish Eagle. Bird of Zimbabwe.
Mwari – The supreme being, the god of fertility, the sower, the rain-giver
Lokozho (Digital Dave/Seeker) – Messenger spirit, named to encompass qualities of Loki, messenger spirit and Wenebozho
Dewe'igan the Drum – Martha's drum and a character in his own right.

Shl'er – Daughter of Fire, jinni and saviour of Dave (sister to Badenan, aunt to Fatima)

Zuhak – Tyrant based in the ancient Iraq/ Iran. Semi-deity who has two serpents growing from his shoulders

Kawa the Smith – Opponent of Zuhak

Fereydun – Noble who eventually defeats Zuhak

The Gold – Wolf that protects Hadeel on her Journey

The White – Wolf that protects Khalid on his Journey

The She-wolf – Badenan's protector who roams the Zagros Mountains

Dugdhav the Shining One – Mother to the prophet Zoroaster

Sarosh – The Angel of Truth

Ganga – Hindu deity, goddess of life and healing, embodied in the Ganges River

Nyai Roro Kidul – Indonesian goddess of the seas

Dewi Windradi – Wife to Resi Gotama, Sasak semi-deity

Dewi Rinjani – Sasak deity, daughter of Dewi Windradi, guardian of the Cupu Manik Astagina

Bhatara Surya – Indonesian Sun God

King Raja Tonjang Beru – Legendary king of Lombok. Father of Mandalika

Mandalika – Legendary princess of Lombok. Daughter of King Raja Tonjang Beru.

B. MAP

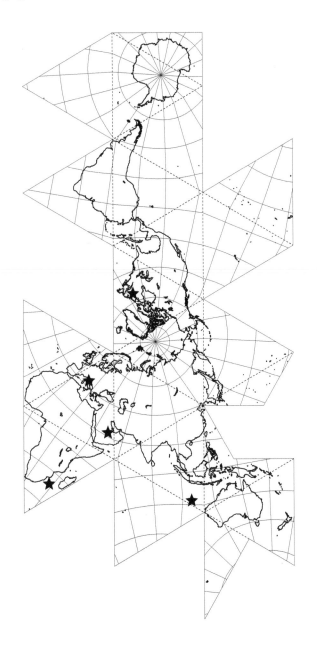

C. PICTURES

A child's picture of wolves as submitted to ASafeSpace.com

Emmy's drawing of Dennis

Lightning Source UK Ltd.
Milton Keynes UK
UKHW021949300520
364099UK00002B/124